THE ISLAND OF MALDONA

By the same author:

MEMOIRS OF A CORNISH GOVERNESS
THE GOVERNESS AT ST AGATHA'S
THE HOUSE OF MALDONA

THE ISLAND OF MALDONA

Yolanda Celbridge

This book is a work of fiction.
In real life, make sure you practise safe sex.

First published in 1996 by
Nexus
332 Ladbroke Grove
London W10 5AH

Copyright © Yolanda Celbridge 1996

Typeset by TW Typesetting, Plymouth, Devon
Printed and bound by
BPC Paperbacks Ltd, Aylesbury, Bucks

ISBN 0 352 33028 7

Contents

Prologue   1

1. Mistress and Slave   9
2. 'Lariat's'   24
3. Whipping Girl   37
4. Ocean of Delights   53
5. The Dungeon   67
6. Sarah's Awakening   82
7. Grecian   97
8. Mermaid   107
9. The Templar Castle   123
10. The Labyrinth   136
11. The Rules of Maldona   149
12. Aphrodite   162
13. A Goddess Whipped   171
14. The Secret Garden   182
15. The Noble Beating   196
16. Circe   210
17. The Dungeon Again   221
18. False Maldona   238
19. Duel Underwater   250
20. The Black Mountain   263
21. Anthesteria   273

Prologue

AELFRICIUS MALDONAE SERVUS ANNO DOMINI MCCCXLVIII SCRIPSIT. AELFRIC, SLAVE OF MALDONA, IN THE YEAR OF THE GREAT PLAGUE, AD 1348.

I, who have never before left Northumberland, have seen terrible things since my Mistress Jana took me from that unhappy place, where they wanted to burn her for her True Wisdom, on false accusation of plague-bringing. How long we have wandered strange seas among creatures of the darkest dreams, in our hope of finding Spain and the castle which is to be Maldona.

The winds and the Great Plague, scourge of all the world, took us to the Grecian seas, far from the shore of Andalusia. It is here that I sit, in my narrow cell, to pen my chronicle, being the only slave who has schooling. I think it fit to begin my account of our journey before we leave this place.

Outside my window lies the blue Aegean Sea, where the spirits of ancient gods live: my mistress seems to think that the fates or, as she curiously insists, coincidence, brought us to found Maldona in this island whose castle awaited us. Above us stands the mountain, a strange black cone such as we have none of in our old England, or, I warrant, anywhere else. I think of it as Mount Olympus, the abode of the gods, but I fear that the gods there are no friends to man. For there are no Greeks on this island, no one but the small band of knights, refugees and Templars like ourselves, who escaped from the Holy Land with, so my mistress thinks, the treasures of our Order.

It is they who, over a dozen years, have built this castle, for wherever Templars go, they must build, even if no threat is near! In wine, the superior, a melancholy man with a well-pocked face and frame much bent by torments at the hands of the Saracens, admitted that neither Turk nor Saracen nor even Barbary corsair dared approach the island, because of the gods of the cursed mountain.

The small band of Templars are hard of body, but lonely in spirit, and have kept themselves by fishing, growing vines and olives, and making unleavened bread with the crops they can pull from the soil. It was no difficult task for my mistress to use her magic and make these lonely knights her slaves, for her rank of Parfaite of the Order of Maldona is higher than any male's: the knights hold in awe the Order of Maldona, the only Templar foundation of women, who are the higher creatures. Judicious use of whip and smile – they are well used to one, and quite astonished by the other – has made them the most docile of slaves. Nevertheless we know that they possess secrets which even under the four-thonged flagrum they are unwilling to share with their mistress, and Mistress Jana is too wise to hurry their tongues.

Fragments of wisdom slip, sometimes, and are stored behind those diamond eyes of hers. We are in sympathy, for long association in war and peace with the Saracen has made these men almost more Arab than Christian, and so it is with our small band of adepts in distant England. The cruel destruction of our Templars by the kings of France and England, and the Pope of Rome, owes much to their hatred of the Eastern wisdom that years of fighting in the kingdoms of Tyre and Acre have imparted to our knights; as well as to covetousness of the vast treasures our Order has amassed: secrets of the mind as well as earthly gold.

Andalusia is our ultimate destination, for there, under the rule of the Moors, the wisdom of African, European and Arab is fused under a sun of truth. The superior says that the gods here are not of the sun or stars, but of the fishy sea. My Mistress Jana explains that all gods may serve the purposes of Maldona.

And, stripped for their work in the fields, the slave

knights all show the tattoo of the rose, the symbol of Maldona's Order! Sometimes the tattoo adorns their breast or shoulder, sometimes their manly places. My mistress knows these truths, because she is the only woman on our island, and it is her custom to take a whipped man to her bed, as reward for his fortitude under the lash. If I show signs of jealousy, she whips me too, and grievous as is her lash on my naked body, I bear her marks with pride, as do all who serve her, for she is womanly perfection. She has borne children, and had them stolen from her by our ignorant persecutors, yet her body, grace and fortitude are those of a young maiden.

A subterfuge, in the confusion of that dreadful plague year, enabled us to escape from Alnswick, where some secret adepts remained true to my mistress and Maldona, and cunning effigies of us were whipped and burnt in our place. At the dead of night, we journeyed north to Berwick, there to take ship in a frail barque, bound for Santander in Spain. We intended to travel across Castile to Andalusia and the safety of Moorish Spain, where the Amir of Ubrique has his realm.

I am no seadog, but survived our journey, praise Maldona, praise the Almighty Demiurge! Our craft was manned by adepts, slaves of my mistress, who themselves were strangers to the sea and her ways. How great a goddess is the ocean! We skirted the east coast of England, and passed Dover into the Channel, where plague ships, cast adrift in the stormy ocean, flew the black flag of death. How I shuddered as those wretches, sometimes yards from our hull, pleaded for rescue! But my mistress is harsh as the sea.

Then, we passed Brittany and went south through the Sea of Biscay, towards Spain, and in that bay I thought we should surely die, for the storms were from the very bowels of Hades, and all except my mistress were sick, so that the plague itself would have seemed a release. At times I thought we should sink in the swell, and two men were lost in the sea, but we did not turn back to seek them, my mistress saying that they had returned to the sea whence all life cometh.

3

At length we had calmer waters, off the country of the Basques, and saw that the ports of Bayonne and St John flew a black flag, so we could not land there. We followed the coast to Saint Sebastian, and the plague followed us there too, until I thought we must carry it with us. At Santander the black flag flew also, and as we entered the harbour, the duke's men loosed arrows at us, to drive us away. This perturbed us all, except my mistress, whose resolve to reach Andalusia became fiercer. She explained to me one night as she bade me lie with her (for such is my mistress's pleasure), that under the sun of the south land the rose of Maldona would flower eternally, like the rosy skin of flogged virgins, and her ardour gave me new strength.

At Corunna, it was the same, and at Porto and Lisboa and Cadiz, all closed to us. Our solace was that we had abundant water, and fish from the sea, so had no hunger, save for landfall. My mistress said we should pass through the straits which divide the Pillars of Hercules, and come to the southern coast that way. The crew then took fright, and said that the place was cursed, that the mountain of Ceuta and the rock known as Gebel-al-Tari were the abode of demons, or sirens. My mistress took anger, and said there was no siren stronger than she, and the demons were her slaves, but one of the adepts, a strong fellow we called Decius, made as if to mutiny. Then my mistress ordered him to fight her, if he was a man.

It was as we entered the straits, with Europa on one side and Africa on the other, and truly we felt that we were between heaven and hell in that strange place as Decius and my mistress stripped themselves naked to our eyes and began to wrestle on the ship's deck. I wanted to help, but she forbade it, and truly she needed no help, for she crushed Decius, despite his manly size, and made him suffer grievously with pummellings to his eyes and throat, and grasping the orbs of his manhood, which she attacked most fiercely until he lay groaning and helpless, clutching his privities in agony as her strong hands throttled him. It was then that Decius submitted to Maldona's greatness, and his punishment was a scourging, then banishment.

He was lashed naked to the mast and then my mistress scourged him with twined rose branches, and wondrous was the squealing and shaking of the traitor as his back and arse were marked in punishment. After that, we hove to in a desert inlet of Africa, and he was cast into the water to swim ashore. My mistress said that if he survived, he would undoubtedly be enslaved by the corsairs of the Barbary Coast who infested these parts, and we were eager to make for the friendly shores of Spain, where we knew the Templars secretly held sway. But as we tacked towards Gebel-al-Tari, and had the rock almost in our grasp, a fearful storm blew, and sent us spinning far from land, our instruments washed away, and giving us no means of knowing where we were except the moon, sun and stars, and our mistress said bravely that we had no need of more.

After the storm had abated we drifted for 40 days and 40 nights, past shoals of strange fishes and lands of cruel rocks and mountains, and were beset by monsters of the deep who were the creatures of nightmare. I myself saw dragons twenty feet in height, and all golden and gleaming, with scales and horns and hooves, and breathing fire, but when I told my mistress she whipped me most severely for my phantasms, to put them out of me, with full 30 strokes of a pickled rod on my bared nates, which hurt me almost beyond endurance, though I did not cry out, for my honour as her loving slave.

And after my beating, as was her custom, she took me to her quarters and bared her breasts and cunnus to me and took my manhood in her mouth until he stood hard, then made me pleasure her in her wet woman's place, and also in ano, which is a sweet sin. It is often her practice to ensure that a male slave delivers his seed in ano, and I know this, for she likes to be watched at her couplings, as she likes, also, to take the whip on her bare back or arse before the eyes of men.

She did this after the storm had abated, in thanks for our deliverance. I gave the punishment, 'a sacrifice' she called it, lashing her to the mast as Decius had been lashed, full naked, and striping her nine and forty times with the scourge of roses, which she took with but a shiver of her fine arse, but no sound of protest save a whistling in her throat which I knew was a sound of rejoicing in her strength. Her fortitude under my cruel lash gave heart to the adepts and resolved them in their duty to our Order.

It seemed we were driven to the east, and my mistress said it was a sign that we must travel far before turning again to our destination in Spain. Alas, I do not know what it was, but some madness of travel, some weariness of the soul, took hold of us all, men being weaker vessels than women, and we began to see monstrous things, often at night, when the crew would be fearful and stand watch only in groups of three, for luck and safety. I myself saw dragons, but my mistress told me I was light-headed from the sun which blistered our English heads, used only to the blessed cool of our north country. How we longed to be home at that time, at once becalmed, then tossed by unseen wind spirits, in that unknown sea! It was so, that we longed even for the approach of corsairs, who would enslave us, but at least we would be amongst men again. My mistress scorned such talk, and said that no man could enslave her, the Mistress of Maldona, that was to arise wondrous and cruel in the scorched land of Spain . . .

In those 40 days and nights we became gaunt and fierce, as animals, not men. I alone kept some vestige of manhood, for I lay each night with my mistress.

It was about this time that she resolved to take a second scourging, to propitiate the gods of the antique sea in which we drifted, and this was to be fiercer than the last, 'a perfect beating' as she named it. Every man of the crew was to flog her sweet naked body in turn (sweet, because though she was beautifully cruel to her slave, nevertheless I love her with my soul, ever since I joined Maldona in far England, and to love with all one's soul is blasphemy to the feeble-minded who are frightened of beauty and truth).

She took the terrible whipping with joy, though I could not count the strokes that laced her trembling back and thighs, and she was pure and naked for her beating, save for a mask of bird feathers: for the teaching of Maldona is

6

that the soul is a bird, imprisoned in the flesh's cage, and that when the naked flesh endures the sweet torment of the lash, the spirit is sent by the ecstasy of pain to fly free and serene. As she was tied to the mast to make her sacrifice, my mistress smiled and said that in submission is the only freedom: in the bearing of pain, and the discomfort of the sweetest and most sinful pleasure, that is, the penetration of the most tender part, where pain and ecstasy are conjoined. The rose is the symbol of Maldona, for her flower is the perfect beauty, the whorl of a woman's cunnus, which must be approached along the thorny stem of bodily chastisement.

After she had taken her strokes, and hung panting in her bonds, she begged us to take her body and use her for her humiliation, and we obeyed, slave and adept alike, knowing that in our mistress's submission lay her true dominion. We took her, two men, or even three, at a time, sparing no hole of her body, nor did she ask to be spared. And when we were sated with our dark sacrifice, a dove flew over us as though in magic, and in the distant blue, we sighted the island. We threw ourselves at her feet and cried, 'Adore Maldona!'

I must add that Mistress Jana of Maldona has by now taken the tattoo on her body. She prised the secret: it is done by a witch, a woman who lives on an island not far, but our mistress will not say more. From here we see the tips of many islands, and sometimes boats from them, but none dares approach us, though they must know we are here. As well as the curse of the mountain, we have swords and spears aplenty, and a stout barbican to our castle, and the Templar name is feared. The knights, slaves now, were fearful that Jana wished to go to the island alone, and I think their brains were fuddled by nightmares.

They said that the woman was a sorceress, who would enslave our mistress, that she had only one eye in the centre of her head, that she was a mermaid who lived at the bottom of the sea, that she had three breasts of which one was a second head, or a dozen other phantasms. Nevertheless, Mistress Jana sailed alone, returning after a day and a night, and as she descended from her vessel, we saw that she was naked, and abased ourselves before her beauty. She said that she would now go naked amongst us, for her tattoos were her robe.

Truly she is a wondrous sight. Her bare body glows with the likenesses of fish, dragons and flowers, of sun and moon and stars, swords and daggers, symbols and figures that we know not. Above all, on front and back she carries two red rosebushes, the shafts growing from her cunnus, which she has shaved bare, and from the valley of her croup, so that her breasts and shoulders are a tumult of blood-red rose petals. As well as that, she has a rose tattooed on her mons veneris, and also on her bare gluteus, so that her rosebushes seem to grow from their own flowers. Thus is Maldona eternal, growing from and feeding on herself.

I have asked her for a tattoo, but it is henceforth forbidden, as it is forbidden to leave our island. Instead, she garlands us with flowers and ropes of seashells, and paints our eyes, lips and breasts with bright dyes of red or purple: we wear Grecian costumes, as though we are women, and this pleases her. I suspect that the knight slaves sometimes make themselves as women, for they have been alone here long enough, but my mistress pays these sins no heed, saying that nature understands all, and is merciful. And, truth to tell, her passion for my body, and her attention with whip or scourge to my bared fesses, become more lustful when she bedecks me as her girl-slave. I too take pleasure in being treated thus, though I cannot explain such a thing. Jana says that fish have many strange colours as they swim in the waters of love.

She has learned something from the witch, or mermaid, for she is pensive, and has the adepts always at work on our ship, to make her ready to sail: as though she expects to depart from here at any moment, or once she has found the secret of the Templars' concealed treasure. But I am forbidden to speak of such things on pain of a naked whipping. Adore Maldona!

1

Mistress and Slave

Jana Ardenne, idly stroking the polished leather of her four-thonged whip, looked out on the river as she waited for her slave, Cassie, to serve her breakfast. It was a bright autumn day, the rays of the golden sun slanting across Chelsea Bridge, and Jana thought mischievously that the leaves on the trees in Battersea Park were as vivid as a well-thrashed bottom. Perhaps she would invite Cassie to take a stroll in the park later on, because, although Cassie was one of Jana's two slaves, she was also her most favoured lover. Jana yawned and stretched, relishing the little touch of her black silk peignoir against her nipples.

Casually, she undid the belt of her peignoir and let it hang open as she walked to the full-length wall mirror opposite her bed to admire herself. She gazed with approval at her bared 21-year-old's body, knowing herself to be at the peak of beauty and physical strength, and unashamedly loving herself for it. As she said to Cassie, if you cannot love yourself, you cannot love anyone else. She saw the honey-blonde tresses tantalisingly strewn over full, soft breasts, perched high on their foundation of hard muscle; muscle won by many months of pitiless self-punishment in the gymnasium and the wrestling arena.

She watched, entranced, as the sight of her naked self brought her broad nipples to a tingling hardness, so that they stood like little apricots in the middle of her wide pink areolae. Her free hand stroked her taut, flat belly, the deep cleft of her belly button, and strayed down to her swelling mons, shaved as naked and smooth as the skin of a baby. She breathed deeply as her fingers touched the protruding

9

fleshy lips of her sex, and she debated whether to touch herself there, on the nympha, a clit which, even when not caressed, stood prominently outside the bright sex-petals.

Jana flexed her thighs, and watched the slabbed muscles tremble, and gave a little sigh of satisfaction. Her own beauty never failed to enchant her, and she could feel a tremor of desire in her belly as she brushed the handle of her whip just once over her nympha, making her tingle and swell just a little. But no, there would be time later; breakfast would be here at any moment. Without refastening her peignoir, she went back to her window.

A passer-by far below in Cheyne Walk glanced up, and, seeing Jana's bared golden breasts, stared with open mouth, which Jana thought somewhat vulgar. Grinning maliciously, she began to knead her breasts in a way as vulgar as the man's stare, and raised her whip, making motions of flogging, while putting on a leer of invitation. As he scuttled away in embarrassment, she thought with amusement of the story he would undoubtedly tell in the pub later, of a strange penthouse flat in respectable Cheyne Walk, where unmentionable pleasures seemed to be offered. Jana laughed out loud.

Yes, a walk in the park would be nice, and then luncheon somewhere – in the King's Road perhaps – followed by a nap in the afternoon, with Cassie by her side on the black silk sheets of her wide bed. All in all, a leisurely day, before the party that evening – a very special party, at Caspar and Netta's house in Lennox Gardens. Jana stroked the shining thongs of her whip, and looked forward to a lazy Chelsea Saturday.

Cassandra entered the room with a tray of coffee, croissants, butter and confiture, and bowed to her mistress. It pleased Jana to be served her meals by a proper maid, and for such duties Cassie wore a very tight black corset of shiny satin, trimmed with écru lace, and a starched white bonnet under which her long raven hair was neatly bound in a bun. Apart from that, all she wore were mesh stockings, a garter belt and straps, and a pair of high red stilettos, on which she balanced with expert poise. Her slender, pert brown breasts were naked above the corset, as were her bottom and mons, whose swelling, shaven ripeness gleamed in the slanting morning sun. Jana looked at her slave's arse globes, and the tender pink petals that peeped so proudly from the folds of her sex, and felt a tremor of excitement, even though only an hour ago, Cassie had been beside her, naked, in bed. Jana smiled as Cassie gravely placed the tray on the coffee table, then knelt before her, her lovely olive bottom stretched high, and kissed Jana's bare toes. Jana looked down at Cassie's bared breasts, forced high and full by the tight corselage, and felt a little tickle in her sex. Her slave's jutting brown nipples were hard, and Jana knew that the act of abasing herself before her mistress always excited her.

'I laced my corset as tightly as I could, Mistress,' said Cassie shyly. 'Are you pleased with your slave?'

'You know I am, Cassie,' whispered Jana, allowing her fingers to stroke the smooth, taut skin of Cassie's bared bottom. 'Why, you're lovely. And your bum is all goose pimples. Am I tickling you too much?'

'Mistress, you must touch your slave whenever you please, and tickle me with . . . with . . . what pleases you.'

'With this, you mean?' asked Jana softly, and gently stroked the tips of her whip thongs across Cassie's buttocks, making her shiver and draw a sharp breath. With her other hand, she removed Cassie's starched cap and drew out the pins from her hair, allowing the lustrous black tresses to cascade over the slave's shoulders. Then she began to stroke her, winding the strands of silky hair between her fingers.

'You know, Mistress,' said Cassie in a trembling voice. 'You know very well, and you are teasing me. The touch of your whip is as beautiful to me as the touch of your hand.'

Jana swallowed hard, and could not help feeling the seep of warm moisture between her thighs. She sat down to her breakfast tray and as she did so, raised her whip, and with a deft flick of her wrist, brought the four thongs down with a hard crack across Cassie's naked buttocks. Cassie gave a

11

little cry of surprised delight, and Jana saw her buttocks flinch prettily, as a faint flush from her whip stroke appeared across the olive skin.

'Get up, slave, and serve me,' she said. Cassie obeyed, trembling, and poured coffee and slapped butter and confiture on to the hot croissants. Jana liked her food dripping with butter, and Cassie made sure that the sweet rolls were soaked in it, so that her mistress was unable to prevent rivulets of hot golden butter and sweet confiture coursing alarmingly down her chin, and threatening to stain her precious silk peignoir.

She shrugged off the peignoir, which billowed to her waist, exposing her bare breasts and shoulders, and she saw that Cassie could not take her eyes from her. Silently, Cassie knelt beside Jana, her eyes still fixed on the proudly erect nipples atop her mistress's creamy breast-skin, which, as Jana ate with gusto, soon became streaked with rivulets of melted confiture and butter. Smiling, Jana took a croissant and pressed the golden bread, whole, to Cassie's lips.

'You haven't eaten yet, I suppose,' she said.

'I must not precede my mistress,' replied Cassie.

'Eat, Cassie. No – don't raise your hand. I like to feed you, like a pet pussy cat.' And Cassie sucked and chewed on the wet bread until she swallowed it. Her lips glistened with butter.

'Thank you, Mistress,' she said, blushing. 'I am glad to be your pet.'

Jana finished her cup of coffee, and stretched herself, raising her breasts so that the butter and confiture dripped down on to her belly. 'Pussy cats like to lick, don't they?' she said, yawning as she stretched. 'So lick your mistress, pussy cat. Start ... down there, and lick upwards. Clean me, my little kitten.'

Still on her knees, Cassie leaned over Jana's body, her head level with Jana's breasts, then lowered herself until her tongue touched the little pool of butter which had formed in Jana's belly button. Eagerly, the tip of her tongue darted over the soft cavity, until she had taken all the butter from it.

'Oh, that tickles,' said Jana, giggling. Cassie followed her belly, licking every inch until the smooth skin was covered by a smooth sheen of butter. Then Cassie paused, and, sighing, placed her tongue on the underside of Jana's breast.

She began to lick the drops from her, and at each lick, she softly kissed her mistress's bare breast-skin. When she reached the stiffened nipples, her licking and kissing grew more tender and more insistent, and little mews, like a cat's, came from the back of her throat. Jana's full teats were licked clean, but Cassie, her eyes shut and breath hard, continued to kiss the erect nipples, sending shivers of pleasure down Jana's spine. She felt her sex become wet with the pleasure she received from her slave's tongue, and put her hand on Cassie's black hair, stroking her as she kissed and gently chewed Jana's nipples.

'Oh!' she exclaimed, 'That hurt!' as Cassie's teeth exerted a sudden hard pressure. 'Don't stop, don't –'

At Cassie's love-bite, she felt a hot spurt of love-oil wash her quim, and, with a little moan, she pressed Cassie's head down from her breast, across her belly, until the slave's lips were on Jana's prepuce, just above the swollen pink flesh of her stiffening clitoris. Cassie needed no instructions but swiftly changed her position, and, still kneeling, buried her face between Jana's thighs.

Jana clutched Cassie's hair tightly, and writhed gently with her pelvis, matching the darting strokes of Cassie's tongue as it flicked over Jana's engorged nympha. Then she lifted her legs, bending them sharply, leaving the peignoir a tousled heap loose around her buttocks, and clasping Cassie's neck with her muscled bare calves. She pressed Cassie's head against her quim in a tight grip, and Cassie whimpered and moaned as she sucked the swollen lips of Jana's now soaking cunt as her tongue flicked mercilessly on the stiff, engorged nympha. And now it was Jana's turn to moan, little mewing noises punctuated with gasps of joy.

Still holding Cassie's face to her quim with one leg, she abruptly disengaged the other and lowered it until her toes were resting on Cassie's shaven mound. Cassie, squatting now, parted her thighs as wide as she could, while still loving Jana's wet sex, and Jana began to rub her slave's own wet cunt with the tips of her toes.

She ran her toes up and down the swollen petals, and Cassie's hips began to gyrate gently as she rubbed her mistress's bare foot between her soft inner thighs, which were slippery with her own love-juice. Then, suddenly, Jana thrust her toes, all of them, inside Cassie's slit, and began to move gently in and out of the soft oily opening.

Cassie whimpered. 'Oh, yes, fuck me, please, Mistress! Fuck me!'

Jana continued for several moments, then removed her toes from Cassie's cunt, only to fasten them on to the slave's stiff nympha, which was standing proudly clear of her enfolding lips. With her prehensile toes, she was able to grasp the swollen clit and squeeze it rhythmically, making Cassie shudder and squirm in tormented pleasure. Jana felt Cassie's love-juice gush hot and oily over the sole of her foot, as her own juices cascaded over Cassie's probing lips and tongue, and Jana knew that as she shivered and writhed in her own pleasure, she was not long from reaching a climax which would be all the more beautiful because neither woman could easily move and dissipate the hot stabs of honeyed beauty.

Jana felt herself shudder: she cried to Cassie that she was going to come, now, Cassie, now, any second, oh! oh!, and as Cassie heard her mistress cry out in orgasmic delight, she howled deep in her throat, and the two women, mistress and slave, their cunts flowing with love, twisted in spasms of melting ecstasy.

As they sat still, gulping their breath and caressing, a noise was heard from the door of the next room. It opened, to reveal a tall, heavily muscled young man, his hair trimmed in a harsh crew cut, barefoot and wearing jeans and a pink T-shirt.

'Cassandra! Mistress!' he cried. 'I'm sorry if I –'

Jana smiled, helping Cassie to her feet. 'You mustn't be sorry, Henry,' she said. 'A slave, having no rights, has no right to be sorry.'

14

'Of course, Mistress.' And Henry knelt to kiss Jana's feet, as Cassie had done.

'Now clear away my breakfast things, and run a bath for Cassie and me. Then we shall see about a walk in the park, for it's such a fine day. Unless you have work to do.'

'Well, Mistress, yes. The office ... I have to be on the net with Tokyo and New York. It's rather a complicated deal, and I can't delegate it to anyone else. Rather multi-million, you see. You'll excuse me?'

'I'm glad,' said Jana. 'You can go, slave, as soon as you've carried out your tasks. Which include washing the dishes.'

Henry nodded solemnly. 'Thank you, Mistress, thank you,' he said, bowing, and proceeded with his duties. Jana heard the sound of water running. She began absent-mindedly to stroke Cassie's hair again.

'You'd like a walk in the park, Cassie?' she said.

'Your pleasure is mine, Mistress. Yes, I should like that.'

'Then luncheon, maybe at that new place in the King's Road. It's got some sort of cowboy name, I think.'

'Lariat's, Mistress.'

'It sounds like one of those American places, surf and turf, you know, lobsters and crabs and prime ribs. They give you lots to eat, and I'm hungry as a horse these days. All this exercise, and' – she gave Cassie a swift kiss full on the lips '– love makes you hungry too, doesn't it?'

Cassie smiled, her beautiful enigmatic smile that always made Jana tingle as she thought of Cassie's exotic ancestry, a cocktail of the Mediterranean, generations of mysterious sloe-eyed beauty, which made Jana, the blonde Northumberland viking, quite envious.

She took Cassie by her hand and led her to the bathroom, where Henry turned off the gold taps of the large marble bathtub and gestured to the steaming water, foaming with scented unguents. As though oblivious to her slave's presence, Jana slipped off her peignoir, and, without looking at Henry, held out her arm theatrically to let it fall. Henry darted forward and caught it before it hit the turquoise-tiled floor.

Naked, Jana unlaced Cassie's corset, and stroked the deep red imprints the stays had left on her olive back and belly, then knelt before her slave and slowly unfastened her garter belt and straps. Cassie lifted first one leg, then the other, to allow her mistress to roll down her stockings, and finally slipped out of her garter belt. All the garments were thrown casually aside, to be retrieved by Henry, who smiled as he pressed them to his lips and nose, and breathed deeply.

Jana turned to look at him, impassive. 'You may go now, Henry. Do not linger over our soiled underthings, boy, or you'll be late for your office. Go and dress appropriately, and I'll inspect you before you go.'

When Henry had departed, the two women climbed into their bath, and, their arms around each other's shoulders, lay back to explode in mischievous, girlish giggles.

'He's such a lamb, isn't he, Cassie?' said Jana. 'Such a willing slave. I think he deserves to join us in bed one of these nights. And he hasn't earned a thrashing for a while. It's only fair to let him commit some tiny mistake, so that I – so that we – can lace that juicy bottom of his.'

Cassie nodded eagerly. 'Mmm,' she said, blushing. 'I love to see a man squirm. Especially sweet Henry.' And the women kissed.

Then Jana disengaged from Cassie's embrace, and slid to the other end of the bath, propping her head against the scalloped marble headrest. She put her feet on Cassie's belly, and stretched her arms in the air, with a sigh of contentment.

'You may soap my feet, slave,' she said with a giggle. 'I think that pot of blue stuff, with the Parisian name.' Cassie picked up a jar from the array of creams and soaps and lotions which stood by the bath like a row of sentries, and began to rub the fluid between Jana's toes, making her shrill with ticklish laughter.

'They all have Parisian names, Mistress,' said Cassie gravely, working up past Jana's ankles, up to her hard calves and swelling thigh muscles, as Jana grinned with feline pleasure.

'Oh, Cassie, it's Saturday. I don't feel like being called Mistress, except by Henry, of course. I feel like being called Jana. For heaven's sake, we're friends.'

'OK, Jana,' said Cassie with a smile, 'but I prefer to call you Mistress; you know that. It's fitting. You wrestled me for my title, and you beat me.' Her hands reached Jana's mons and began to soap her there gently, allowing her fingers to play inside the fleshy petals where her tongue had so recently given pleasure.

'Mmm,' sighed Jana, 'that's lovely. But don't frot me again, Cassie, or I won't have any energy for our walk. Anyway, I only beat you because you cheated.'

'Cheated!'

'You let me beat you, cheeky. Oh, yes, that's gorgeous. But no diddling.' Cassie's hands were tenderly soaping Jana's breasts, kneading her nipples mischievously and watching them stand and swell.

'If I let you beat me, Jana, it is because I wanted to be your slave – the slave of the Mistress of Maldona. It is more beautiful to be a slave than a mistress.' But Cassie's mouth opened in alarm as she saw Jana suddenly clutch her brow, and close her eyes as her forehead wrinkled in a frown of fear. 'Jana, what is it? Did I hurt you?'

'No, no . . .' said Jana faintly.

'When I said Maldona, you . . . you sort of seized up. What's wrong? You are Mistress of Maldona, you know, even though you have gone outside. Your house is safe, we know that from Caspar and Netta's frequent embassies. Is it that you miss the House of Maldona? It would be simple to arrange a visit. I'd love it.'

'No,' said Jana, gasping for breath. 'Of course I miss our house, Cassie, as must you. But we shall return, you, Henry and I, when the time is right and our work outside is done. But this is not the time. It is just that for the last few nights, I've been having this strange dream, a nightmare almost, and I've been trying not to think about it. Yet I must. I am being instructed by the spirit of Maldona, by my own ambition, to do something, to build something of which I'm not sure I am capable.'

'Oh, Jana, the Mistress of the House of Maldona is capable of anything.'

'I'm not sure . . . Oh, Cassie, I'm a little frightened.'

Now it was Cassie who moved beside Jana, and stroked her hair, kissing her forehead. 'Tell me, then, Jana sweet,' she whispered.

Jana breathed deeply. 'I dream that I am swimming in the sea, all alone. It is night, and the sea glistens silver in the moonlight. I seem to be dressed in a sort of business suit, with a handbag and smart shoes and everything. What am I doing in the sea, miles from anywhere? Perhaps I am the survivor of a shipwreck. There is an island far ahead, and I am trying to reach her safety.

'Something is following me, I cannot see it, but I can hear the threshing of the sea as it swims behind me, closing on me. But the faster I try to swim, the more my body is tangled in seaweed, monstrous great algae in tormented shapes that look like human limbs, with horrible black parodies of flowers that look like grinning, grotesque human faces. I fight and fight, but I cannot escape the seaweed's embrace. Then I somehow slip out of my suit and throw away everything, and it all sinks with a horrible gurgle to the bottom of the sea, taking the strangling seaweed with it, and the seaweed seems to shriek out in pain.

'I'm left naked and can swim now, slippery as an eel, and I reach the island, leaving the sea monster behind. But it's still coming . . . it gets a bit hazy then, but to escape the monster, I find myself climbing this mountain, the only mountain to be seen. I climb and climb, and I see in the distance a dim shadow emerge from the water. I knot a thong of lianas from an overhanging tree branch, to use as a weapon, a whip to keep away the monster.

'But as fast as I climb, I see it coming after me, up the slope, which gets steeper and steeper. I climb until I reach the clouds, and then I am in the middle of this awful cold mist, and then I break through, and I'm sitting on top of the mountain, just a little plateau the size of a room. All around me is this sea of clouds, all white and swelling, like . . . breasts and bottoms, as though all the virgins of the

18

House of Maldona are arrayed in their lovely nakedness for me! Ripe young bodies, firm and smooth, as though you could walk on them. The mist laps at my feet.

'Suddenly, the monster bursts through the cloud and is in front of me. It is a woman, naked as I am, but with long seaweed for hair, covering her face. On her breasts she has scallop shells, around her waist strings of oysters, open, with shiny white pearls gleaming, and for a mink she has a huge pink sea anemone, its tentacles waving and dancing at me. She reaches out for me, but I begin to beat her with my liana whip, very hard, and she whimpers but does not try to flee.

'I whip her as hard as I can, on the breasts, on the belly, on her sex, and making her twirl around, I lash her bum and her back, striping her and striping her as she moans with a horrid mournful sound like a ship's siren. She falls to her knees, and I go on flogging her on her bare white bottom, really viciously. I want to flay her, to destroy her, for daring to trouble me.

'And suddenly she turns round and sweeps the seaweed from her face, and, oh, Cassie, it's my face! Pale and white as though I'd been drowned and floating in the sea. Then I throw away my whip and run away over the white hillocks of those lovely naked bodies, forgetting that they are clouds, and I am falling towards the sea, miles below, where I can see the reflection of the moon, which is where I am heading. After an age of screaming, I fall into the bright moon . . . and then I wake up, all sweating.'

'Oh, Jana,' said Cassie, kissing her, 'what can it all mean?'

Jana stood up and, reaching for her towel, climbed out of the bath. 'I don't know, Cassie,' she said uncertainly. 'I've been trying to forget it. I didn't want to worry you and Henry. You'd think there was something wrong.' She laughed nervously. 'I just feel, ever so strongly, that there is this island, somewhere, waiting for me, and that I must go to it, and find that mountain. Oh, oh, you'll think I'm silly, but isn't there such a thing as destiny, Cassie? Please tell me there is.'

'It was destiny that brought you and me to the House of Maldona, Jana,' said Cassie softly. 'The destiny that made us want to submit, bare our bodies to pain and beauty and love.'

Tenderly, she wrapped her mistress in a fluffy white bathrobe and, knotting a long towel over her breasts, put her arm round Jana's shoulders and led her to the living room, where she made her sit on her white leather sofa. Jana felt herself trembling, despite the perspiration that beaded her skin, pink from the hot bath.

'Cassie, bring me my cigarettes,' she said hoarsely. 'I haven't had one for days, but I need one now.'

Noiselessly, Cassie obeyed, opening a drawer and extracting a half-full pack of Gauloises and a gold Dunhill lighter. She lit a cigarette, and placed it between Jana's lips. Jana took a deep drag, inhaled the smoke, and kept it inside her for almost ten seconds before closing her eyes and exhaling rapidly.

'That's better, Cassie,' she said, quickly inhaling again and burning the cigarette halfway down, 'thank you.'

'Jana, you're trembling so,' said Cassie. 'Shall I get you a brandy?'

'No, but thanks. I'm all right.' Jana stubbed out her cigarette and lit another. Cassie sat down beside her on the sofa and stroked her damp forehead.

'Jana, you're not all right,' she said, putting her arm round Jana's shoulder and cradling her, rocking back and forth in a gentle swaying rhythm. 'I'll get you that brandy. I insist.'

Jana nodded.

When Cassie came back with her glass of brandy, Jana took a generous sip, then put it down on the glass coffee table.

'I don't know what came over me, or what's happening with these dreams, Cassie. Somehow, I'm frightened. I feel . . . that I'm not myself.'

'It is unladylike for the Mistress of Maldona to be frightened,' said Cassie, a twinkle in her eye now. 'And I know what is necessary to make you feel whole and loved.'

Jana felt the brandy warm her and her trembling subside, and grinned ruefully. She looked into Cassie's eyes.

'I suppose, then, that I have committed an imperfection,' she said softly.

Cassie nodded, and brought the glass to her mistress's lips. Jana swallowed, and stood up, her head bowed. Saying nothing, Cassie led her to their bedroom and laid Jana face down on the coverlet, burying her face in a pillow. Then she lifted the hem of Jana's bathrobe and pulled it up over her head, exposing her pink bare nates. Jana moaned softly.

'Yes, Cassie, do it. Do it to me. An imperfection . . . for Maldona to feel fear.'

'A lady's beating, Jana, is in order,' said Cassie, taking the four-thonged whip that Jana had caressed not long before. 'A full seven on your bare bum, that should knock the fear out of you.' And without warning, she raised the quirt high and brought it savagely down on Jana's naked buttocks. Jana felt the fire streak her exposed flesh, and gasped.

'Oh, yes, Cassie, my sweet slave,' she moaned, 'but harder, much harder, please, please.'

A second stroke landed, and a third, and Jana felt her arse begin to squirm and clench in anticipation of the awful, sweet pain that coursed through her, setting her body on fire and filling her with savage joy. As Cassie whipped her with fierce tenderness, Jana knew that all her fears were nothing; there was nothing in the universe except her own body and the stinging fire on her bare croup. She panted as the four thongs streaked across her arse globes, now writhing and jerking uncontrollably at the sweet kiss of the whip.

Jana continued to squirm and flinch even after Cassie had gasped that the lady's beating was over, and her throat welled with little sobs of pleasure. Cassie removed the covering from her head, and bent to kiss her hair and nuzzle the back of her neck. Then she moved her lips to kiss the tender globes which bore the vivid marks of her whipping; she kissed her mistress there, making her coo with joy, and licked the reddened bare skin until Jana laughed out loud, squirmed round and sat up.

'How wonderful, Cassie!' she cried. 'Oh, you're so sweet and right, and you know me so well! I must look at myself.' She went to the mirror and twisted round, stroking her whipped bottom with sighs of admiration. 'How well you do it,' she purred dreamily. 'You should be Mistress of Maldona, not I.'

'You forget that I was – until you wrestled me to submission. But, Jana, I have to say that I've been dreaming too. I've dreamt of . . . of being in the arena, under the sun, with all of Maldona watching, and being tied to the frame, and taking a noble beating – yes, that hard – with a stroke from all the adepts and parfaites, and never making a sound, even as the cane laces my bare back and my bum and my thighs, too. And at each stroke I am happier and happier. I think I am longing to go back to our House, Jana, if only for a short while.'

Jana opened her wardrobe and, without replying, inspected her clothes to see what she would wear for the walk she had planned. She frowned, deep in thought, and when she had selected her outfit, she turned to Cassie, and her eyes glowed with an intensity that made Cassie tremble. Jana felt her heart swell with determination, and a dawning knowledge of what she had to do. She put her hand to Cassie's cheek.

'Yes, we must go to Maldona,' she said slowly, 'but not the Maldona we come from: the new Maldona, Cassie, Maldona reborn.'

Jana quickly dressed in a red silk blouse, tight enough to need no bra, and left with enough buttons undone to prove the fact to any scrutineer, of which she was sure there would be no shortage. Then, a black leather mini, under which she wore no panties but a garter belt and suspenders holding up sheer red silk stockings. The ensemble was completed by black high-heeled boots which covered her legs like gloves, halfway up her thigh. When Cassie had laced these for her, she declared herself ready.

22

'We'll go for our walk, then straight on to Lariat's for lunch,' she said. 'That's why I'm putting my togs on.' She looped a gold chain-belt round the waist of her mini, and a heavy gold chain around her neck, its shiny links brushing the tops of her breasts almost down to her nipples. 'Phone for a table, Cassie, please. Twelve-thirty, I think, and then get kitted out yourself.'

'Won't you be cold?' asked Cassie.

'Not with my sable over me,' said Jana.

It was then that Henry knocked on the open door of the bedroom. He stood in the doorway, briefcase in hand, resplendent in blue pinstripe.

'Ready for inspection, Mistress,' he said shyly.

'Good, Henry. Well, let's see.'

Henry put down his briefcase, unhooked his red braces, and lowered his trousers. Jana saw that instead of boxer shorts, his cock and balls were encased in a dark leather chastity belt, buckled tightly, with a little hole at the end through which the tip of his penis peeped. Jana smiled.

'Very good, Henry,' she said. And all of a sudden, she went to him, put her arms around his back, and kissed him full on the lips. 'Go now, and good luck.'

'It hurts, Mistress. My restrainer, I mean. I fastened it as tight as I could, as you said, but ... well, it's awfully tight.'

'As I said, Henry ... good.'

Cassie grinned hugely. 'The poor boy,' she said. 'Jana, why do you torment him so?'

'Because he's my slave, Cassie, and a slave-boy must always be aware of the fact. As he sits in his office making his millions, he must never forget that I, the Mistress of Maldona, am his ruler.' She reached under Cassie's towel, and clamped her hand on Cassie's naked quim, squeezing it hard until Cassie gasped. 'And neither, my sweet slave, must you.'

2

'Lariat's'

Jana and Cassie strolled for a couple of hours in the bird-sweet acres of Battersea Park, holding hands and smiling at each other like new lovers. Old fellows with their dogs and their shabby brown raincoats and cloth caps, with rolled up cigarettes dangling wetly from thin lips, gave envious or just curious looks, with the wistfulness of desire that old age could not dim. The women smiled politely, and Jana wondered if there was a special mail-order store specialising in the correct kit for old men in parks.

'Do you think, when I get old, I'll not want to . . . do it?' said Jana suddenly.

Cassie abruptly put her arms around her and embraced her. 'Don't say that,' she whispered. 'You shall never get old. Even if you did, I should still be yours.'

They found a bare board café and had a cup of coffee among bus drivers and men in black leather jackets, all of them ogling Jana unashamedly and trying to peek beneath her white sable, which she had deliberately left undone, hunching low over the sloped table so that her cleavage was heartbreakingly visible. Cassie, as befitted a slave, was more modestly dressed in a grey raincoat over a blue cashmere sweater and white silk blouse, with pearl silk stockings, and sensible black slingbacks. Her only daring features were a pair of heavy silver globe earrings, and a thick, studded silver slave choker.

Both women grinned, relishing their teasing of the staring men, and when they finished their coffee and got up to go, Jana whispered loudly, 'Wow, I couldn't have stayed sitting down much longer. My bum's really on fire! You really know how to spank, don't you, darling?'

And when they regained the pavement, they looked back, waved cheekily at the open-mouthed café, and walked off shaking with uncontrolled laughter.

They made their way over Battersea Bridge, which gave Jana a thrill as it swayed alarmingly in the breeze. 'Soldiers must break step when crossing bridge,' she read from the notice. 'Do you think we'll make it?'

Arm in arm, they marched in military step, giggling, and made for Oakley Street. Back in Chelsea, they attracted no attention, whatsoever. Jana looked at her watch, and saw twelve noon. So they ambled along the King's Road, window shopping, until they came to Lariat's, about a hundred metres west of Sloane Square. It was a diner, American style, with glass doors and panorama windows, so that the beau-monde of Chelsea could see and be seen, and the inevitable Budweiser neon. A redundant fan lazily spun over a polished plank floor. There was a modest crowd at the bar, and only half the tables were occupied. Jana pushed open the swing door and they entered. It was cool and dark, with only the window tables lit by the high sun, in whose rays eddies of dust floated serenely. Just like in the Western movies, Jana thought.

The decor was aggressively kitsch-Western. When Jana's eyes had adjusted to the cool shadows, she saw row after row of aged photographs: cowboys, rodeos, stagecoaches and stern men with huge moustaches and equally huge pistols. There were lithographs of famous bank robberies, famous train robberies, and the expected wanted posters for Jesse James and Billy the Kid. Oddly, Jana saw that the tables were covered in paper tablecloths, in the French style.

But, more than the predictable artwork, what caught her eye was an impressive array of cowboy equipment hanging from the ceiling. There were lariats, of course, and ornate saddles, six-guns, Remington rifles, branding irons, and Jana saw, unconsciously licking her lips, whips of every kind, from short horse crops to fierce braided bull-whips. She looked up, fascinated by the thongs and loops and tassles of the cordwainer's art, regretting that those shining, vicious coils were too high to reach up and stroke. Cassie, too, was entranced.

Their pleasant reverie was broken by a cool American voice.

'Hi, I'm Gloria, can I help you?' said a smiling cowgirl, snowy blonde, with a stetson hat and a sort of cheerleader's outfit comprising a suede mini, calf-length boots and a Native American, fringed waistcoat, left open to bare a generous expanse of tan breast-skin, and cut off to reveal a lovely dimpled belly button. Her legs were smooth and bare, and she was obviously wearing nothing under the tight suede jacket. Jana wondered if she had anything on under the brief skirt. Most interesting was the equipment dangling from her trim waist: she wore a cowboy belt, complete with shiny cartridges and (presumably a replica) a Colt .45. On one side of her belt was coiled a rope lariat, and on the other a leather horsewhip. Cassie told her they had booked.

'Yeah,' said Gloria, consulting her pad. 'Let me see . . .' But Jana had already installed herself at a window table, throwing her sable with a flourish over the chair beside her, and tossing back her hair with a roguish smile. Cassie followed, and sat down opposite.

A few moments later, Gloria brought menus resembling, and nearly as large as, saloon doors.

'Would you ladies care to –' she began.

'Dry martinis, two, doubles, one twist, one olive,' said Jana, without looking up from her menu.

'Yeah, sure,' said Gloria uncertainly, sensing a subtle put-down of her waitress's dominion. But she brought the drinks speedily, her gunbelt jangling as she walked. Jana ordered them both the steak and lobster platter, and a bottle of Nuits St Georges.

'Time for a treat,' she said. 'We can go home and have a nap to shape up for the party.' Gloria's eyes flickered at the word 'party', and Cassie smiled.

'It will be nice to see Netta and Caspar again,' she said. 'They've been away how long? Must be a couple of months. Making nice, naughty films, I suppose.'

26

'Yes,' said Jana, munching a nacho with a fiery Mexican dip from the complimentary snack bowl. 'We're going to have a little show at the party tonight. Caspar is really a very good director. Maldona is very lucky that he hasn't been snatched up by Hollywood. Although his material might not be considered too strong for mass audiences in a few years, the way things are going.'

'Jana,' said Cassie gravely, 'you know that the essence of Maldona is not mass appeal. Maldona is select, secret, and works in silence.'

Gloria swirled gracefully to their table, with two brimming platters of steaming meats.

'There y'all are,' she said. 'I'll be right back with the wine and salads and stuff.'

Soon, they were sitting before a feast of which an earlier Jana might only have eaten a quarter. But constant exercise and training of her strong girl-muscles, the regime of Maldona, had given her an appetite as healthy as her superbly muscled body. Both women began to eat, the butter from the chunks of lobster mingling with the juices from the blood-red steak to glaze their lips. They sipped wine, gazing at each other.

'Thing is,' said Jana, 'that the ethos of Maldona is more and more visible. As we make converts submit to our rules, we see subtle changes taking place. Discipline used to be a naughty word, something people giggled over in the tabloid press – you know, prurient stories about flogging headmasters, cabinet ministers visiting discreet houses in Jermyn Street, and so on. Those who chose to submit, or to rule, had to do so in secret, relishing the knowledge that it was "kinky" or some nonsense. They liked being an exclusive minority. But now that is changing.

'Look at some of these films from Hollywood, and even the old Westerns from way back. How many times do you see the most frightful whippings, of women as often as men? And now, in your leather-jacket swagger movies, it seems the most natural thing for a girl to be tanned on her bare bum by the latest karate hunk. It is accepted as normal. Go to any party, and if a man chats you up, ask him if he would like to spank, or even cane you, and his eyes will light up.

'Look in the shop windows: teenage girls wear teetering high heels and lace-up boots, and corsets and things, that even ten years ago you wouldn't have seen outside Shepherd Market, or in a fetishwear catalogue. And any phone box in central London is positively wallpapered with cards of girls offering correctional services, both giving and receiving. But, Cassie, furtive and shabby pleasures, that is not the way of Maldona! The way of Maldona is naked, loving and glorious, the acceptance of discipline and the sweetness of pain for the beauty of a woman's soul! And that is Maldona's work: to teach that discipline is love and beauty, and a woman's true freedom.'

'Very prettily put, Jana,' said Cassie, with a twinkling eye. She crunched a lobster tail and chewed the pink shell, sucking all its juice. 'But, you sweet girl, don't you admit the principle of pleasure in punishment?'

Jana grinned, mopping up the last of her meat juices with her French bread. 'You mean, did I like feeling your quirt on my bare bum this morning?' she said, not very quietly. 'You know the answer's yes. And you know that when I strap you and Henry to the frame, and take a good willow to your naked arses, I get all wet as I make you squirm. That is the whole point of chastisement: submission to the cleansing pain of the lash is pleasure in itself.' The two women leaned forward and clinked glasses.

'Adore Maldona,' said Cassie, her lips only a tongue's breadth from Jana's lips.

Gloria shimmered to their table and asked brightly if they had enjoyed their meal.

'Adore Maldona,' said Jana, and suddenly her lips met Cassie's in a powerful, sucking kiss that lasted a full minute. When the women disengaged, not caring that all eyes were either glued to them or staring at the ceiling, Jana saw that Gloria was still standing beside her, rather close for a waitress, and that her breasts were trembling as she breathed low and hoarse.

'Yes,' said Jana sweetly, looking Gloria in the eyes, 'the meal was fine.'

Gloria swallowed. 'Would you like anything else?' she said, almost in a sigh.

'Espresso with a twist, twice,' said Jana, still looking deeply into Gloria's eyes and pleased at the slight flush that darkened the woman's tan. 'And I'm sure we would like something else.'

Gloria looked at her for a long moment, not smiling, and then, slowly, the glimmer of a grin appeared on her full red lips and the tip of her tongue peeped out to lick them. Abruptly, she spun on her heel and sauntered back to the kitchen. Jana said nothing, but looked at Cassie with pursed lips, mock serious, and slowly raised an eyebrow. Cassie's lips trembled, and then spread into a broad grin.

'Our cowgirl seemed interested when I mentioned the party,' said Jana slowly. 'Maybe she hasn't been in this country long. Maybe she's lonely, and it would be fitting and ladylike to invite her to one.'

'Caspar and Netta's,' said Cassie. 'Why not? She looks . . . strong. Big bones, good arm muscles, tall – it's all that beef the Americans eat. Don't tell me you'd like to bring her to our rules.'

Jana shrugged. 'Maldona sees beauty everywhere,' she said, as Gloria arrived with their coffees.

Gloria leant over the table to put down the silver tray, deliberately giving Jana a full view of her breasts. She was indeed naked under her leather shirt, and her breasts hung like two ripe round pears, topped with pink cupolas which stood with surprising prominence. It was the briefest of glimpses, but when Gloria stood up, her face wore a little smile of satisfaction. Jana nodded, and smiled back.

'I'm very pleased,' she said softly.

'We serve the very best coffee,' said Gloria.

'I didn't mean the coffee, Gloria. I mean the attentive service. I expect you earn a lot in tips.'

'Some.'

Jana looked round the room. The crowd was thinning, as couples left in their frou-frou of Chelsea glitz and single men looked at their watches and remembered football matches. 'Would you like to sit down?' she asked sweetly.

'It looks as if there's a lull, and I'm sure you Americans aren't as stuffy about protocol as we English.' She removed her sable from the chair beside her, and Gloria, after a moment's hesitation, sat down.

'I guess it's all right,' she said, 'just for a minute. My shift's nearly over anyway.' She perched awkwardly on the chair, to indicate to her boss that she was just being briefly courteous.

'I'm intrigued by this place,' said Jana, lighting a Gauloise and blowing a stream of fragrant blue smoke over Gloria's shoulder. 'All those lariats, and saddles, and things, and those whips! They look quite ferocious.' She touched the whip that lay coiled at Gloria's belt, and stroked it, looking into Gloria's lustrous brown eyes. 'And this one. It must be heavy to carry. But such an . . . exciting gimmick for a diner.'

'It's not so heavy,' said Gloria, returning Jana's gaze. 'Not to carry. It sure would feel heavy if you got it across your back, though.'

'Would it, indeed? I wonder where you are from in the States, Gloria? Cowboy country, perhaps?'

'The best there is. Sante Fe, New Mexico. And I'm a real live cowgirl, brought up on the ranch. Y'all know New Mexico?'

'Gloria, I do know it – at least I've been to Taos, to see where D. H. Lawrence is buried, and you don't have to keep up that y'all stuff.'

Gloria blushed. 'Well, I was brought up on a ranch,' she said, 'and these things I'm wearing are all mine. But I guess I should admit I've just graduated *summa cum laude* in archaeology from UCLA. I'm taking a year off, you know, to travel and stuff, before I start for my doctorate.'

'What's the "and stuff"?' asked Jana quietly.

'Why, see places, meet people. I may find a dig to join, when I've got some money together from this job. Maybe the Aegean, Greece, Turkey, you know? I've been on three digs there already. I just love the Mediterranean; it seems to free the spirit somehow.'

'You sound quite a fascinating person, Gloria. Tell you what, after your shift's over, what, in about half an hour, why not come round to our flat for tea? We live in Cheyne Walk, by the river. I'm Jana and this is my –' she stopped herself saying 'slave'; that would come later '– my ... friend, Cassie.'

'You both live there?' asked Gloria, slyly.

'Sure,' said Jana easily. 'We share with another guy. He's a financier. I don't know when he's getting home, because he has business all day.'

'Cheyne Walk! You must have famous neighbours.'

'No, Gloria, my neighbours have famous neighbours.'

'Oh ... yeah, I see,' said Gloria. Jana scribbled her address on a corner of the paper tablecloth, tore it off, and handed it to her.

'Come round in half an hour or so,' she said. 'Penthouse flat. And you may have overheard, there's a little party on tonight, in Lennox Gardens. If you're free, you'd be welcome. Although, well, our friends might not be your sort of people.'

'Everybody is my sort of people. I never miss a party, and I'd love to come. My place is just off the Cromwell Road, so it's not too far. England is such a cosy little place.'

'Good,' said Jana, picking up the bill which Gloria had discreetly placed under her coffee cup, and indicating to Cassie that she should settle it. 'See you shortly, then, Gloria. Archaeology and the Wild West! How fascinating! I'm just dying to ask you all sorts of questions.' Jana deliberately put a tone of girlish enthusiasm into her voice, but looking at Gloria all the time with Gloria returning her penetrating stare. She knows, she knows, Jana thought.

'Yeah, I'll bet you are,' said Gloria softly.

'That sounds a bit cheeky, coming from a mere waitress,' said Jana, 'so I don't think you deserve a tip. Cassie, give her the exact change and no more.' She grinned at the momentarily nonplussed Gloria. 'I didn't say you wouldn't get a tip, Gloria, but when you come round, we'll work out what it should be. By the way, don't change out of your costume. I like you the way you are.'

* * *

Cassie answered the doorbell, and opened to a flushed and panting Gloria, wearing a belted grey raincoat which made her cowboy boots seem incongruous.

'Wow!' she said. 'No elevator! No wonder you look so fit, Jana.'

'Rather old-fashioned, here in England, but I suppose you like it that way. Here, give me your coat, and Cassie will make us some tea. Have you a preference? China, Assam?'

Gloria shrugged. Jana moved to her side, and helped her off with the heavy designer coat, allowing her hair to brush delicately against the American girl's, and breathing in a musky scent that was mingled enticingly with the odours of men and woman, food and wine, as though in smelling the girl, Jana inhaled an entire company, a world. The dutiful hostess, she made a great ceremony of hanging up the coat as Gloria's eyes roamed around the apartment, taking in the leather chairs, the stacked bookcase, the thick carpet and Persian rugs, the ornate gilt fireplace, and the mirrors on walls and ceiling.

'Very roomy,' she said. 'Mirrors . . .'

'You approve?' asked Jana, motioning her to sit on the sofa under the bookcase and joining her there.

'It's great. And so many books. Morocco, leather, does that mean you're a collector?'

'No, I like beautiful things, and I actually read them,' replied Jana, lighting a Gauloise. 'Collectors are so obsessive, so anal. You don't smoke, I take it?'

'Sure I do,' said Gloria. 'I mean, occasionally.'

Deliberately, Jana took a cigarette from the pack, put it in her own lips and lit it, then passed it to Gloria, who smiled as she accepted it. Jana laughed.

'What's funny?' said Gloria suspiciously.

'Oh, nothing. It's just the first time I've had a real live cowgirl who has a degree in archaeology sitting on my sofa. I'm pleased you came.' She touched the horsewhip that lay on the white leather beside Gloria. 'You look quite super,' she added softly. 'I'd love to try your things on.'

Before Gloria could answer, Cassie glided in with a silver tray of tea things and a dish of *petits fours*. She poured cups of tea, and stood, hands behind her back, as Gloria and Jana drank.

'You're not joining us?' asked Gloria.

'No,' said Cassie, 'it's not my –' but Jana motioned her to be silent.

'Cassie has things to do,' she said curtly, and Cassie inclined her head and left them.

'She's your good friend?' asked Gloria, raising her eyebrows.

'A very old friend,' replied Jana. 'And much more.'

Gloria's eyes roamed Jana's bookshelf, greedily relishing the shiny leather spines.

'How lovely,' she said. 'I wish I could have such books. You have such eclectic tastes.' Her gaze rested on a white morocco binding which Jana had deliberately placed at eye level, among a shelf of brown. Gloria reached for it curiously. 'That one looks as though it should be on the top shelf,' she said, opening it. 'Why, it's in Latin. *De Artibus Castigationis.* Wow, this is something.' She gaped at the frontispiece, which showed a naked woman strapped to a whipping frame, being flogged by a woman who was naked also, but wearing a strange bird-mask and a harness of shiny metal that seemed to connect to fans of plumage that emerged from between her bare thighs to cover her belly and buttocks.

'It's a translation, actually,' said Jana. '*The Arts of Chastisement* by the Parfaite Cecilia of Ubrique – that's a place in Andalusia. It was translated and published in Amsterdam, and if you look, you'll see why. A little raunchy for the England of that time, or perhaps any time.'

Gloria leafed through the pages and whistled, but her leafing grew slower as she lingered over the illustrations with wide-eyed interest that, Jana saw to her satisfaction, was much more than mere interest. Gloria began to shift her buttocks, as though the soft sofa were uncomfortable.

'I keep it within arm's reach, because I like to look at it,' said Jana after a pause. 'It's quite a curiosity, isn't it? All those pictures and descriptions of men and women being . . . chastised.'

'How cruel people can be,' murmured Gloria, putting

33

the book aside as though too much curiosity would be in-delicate.

Jana laughed. 'But a curiosity,' she said, 'that's all. And now I'm curious about these cowgirl skills of yours. *Calamity Jane*, *Annie Get Your Gun*, and all that – I like to see them as proto-feminists. Can you really use that lariat?'

Now it was Gloria's turn to laugh. 'Of course. You want to see? It's a sixteen-footer, but I guess there's plenty of space in this room.'

She stood up and unclipped the rope from her belt. The lariat was heavy and oiled, and about an inch thick, Jana guessed. Gloria uncoiled it and let the looped tip dangle on the floor.

'What should I lasso?' she said. 'There aren't any horses hidden in the closet, are there?'

'Not horses,' said Jana. 'Try that table.' She indicated a small Georgian occasional table by her window. She watched, fascinated, as Gloria told her to stand back and lifted the lariat. From the corner of the room Jana looked as Gloria lifted her arm and made the rope blur in a whist-ling dance, until suddenly there was a crack and the end of the loop of the lariat was stretched tight around the little table. Gloria pulled gently and the table slid bumpily across the carpet towards her. She turned round and grinned.

'Very impressive,' said Jana.

'It's easy. You try.' The table was replaced, and Jana tried to imitate Gloria, but her throw fell short. Gloria po-sitioned herself behind Jana and took her arm, and Jana felt the girl's body against her back, and her breasts press-ing gently against her shoulder-blades. She failed again on her second try, but on the third she managed it, and clap-ped her hands.

'Now you're a cowgirl!' cried Gloria excitedly, and gave Jana the briefest of hugs. They repeated the trial until Jana could do it slickly and unaided. Both women were giggling now, their eyes bright with amusement.

'It's a pity I haven't any steers in my closet,' said Jana. 'I mean, it has to be much more interesting to lasso a live animal.'

34

Their eyes met. 'Sure is,' said Gloria quietly. 'Would you like me to be your steer, Jana?'

'You're a big girl,' answered Jana. 'Yes, I would.'

'I've been lassoed before,' said Gloria, swallowing. 'As a game, you know. It's kind of fun.'

'And who did the lassoing?'

Gloria blushed. 'Oh . . . boyfriends; you know.'

'Well, now you can be lassoed by a girl. Wouldn't you like that?' Gloria's face was very close, and Jana felt her hot, quick breath. She licked her lips. Still holding the lariat, which she let trail after her like a snake, she went to the window and closed the drapes. Gloria looked on calmly, and without any question. 'OK, Gloria, step out of your gunbelt, and go over to the table. Push it out of the way.'

Looking at Jana all the time, the tall girl unfastened her belt and let it drop to the floor, then moved gracefully to the window alcove. Jana flexed the rope, sending a ripple through it, then reeled it in and held the wide loop over her head.

'What a lovely outfit you have,' she said. 'And this rope is so oily and dirty. Take your shirt off, Gloria. I don't want to spoil it.'

'I'm not wearing a bra,' said the American, brushing a blonde ringlet nervously from her forehead. But her voice held more promise than protest.

'Neither am I,' said Jana. 'You think I'm shocked by a woman's bare breasts? Take your shirt off, Gloria –' her voice was harsher now '– and put your hands over your face, in case I make a wrong throw.'

Slowly, with trembling fingers, Gloria unbuttoned her shirt and revealed the full magnificence of her naked, swelling breasts. Jana felt a moist excitement in her sex as she looked at the nipples, round as little pink plums, and saw them shiver and stiffen under her very gaze. Gloria breathed nervously, looking at Jana like a rabbit caught in headlights, and covered her face so that her breasts were hidden by her forearms.

'You're very pretty, Gloria,' said Jana softly, and without another word, she whirled the lariat over her head and sent it spinning towards Gloria. The wide noose dropped neatly around her torso, not even touching her head, and came to rest on her broad hips, where Jana pulled it tight. Gloria took her hands away from her face and grinned.

'Wow, that was good,' she said. 'I'm tied tight, aren't I? What it must feel like to be an animal.'

Jana began to pull gently on the rope, tugging the half-naked woman towards her across the room.

'We are all animals, Gloria,' she said, and as she drew her captive towards her, she began to unbutton the few buttons that secured her own blouse, letting the garment hang open and baring her breasts to Gloria's gaze. Gloria stared, mesmerised, and said nothing as she came closer. When Gloria was standing, roped, before her, Jana deftly slid out of her blouse and the two women faced each other, naked to the waist.

'I want to feel your breasts against mine when I kiss you,' whispered Jana.

Gloria closed her eyes and nodded, yes. Then Jana felt her strong arms clasping her naked back, and she held Gloria against her as their bare breasts pressed and their lips met in a hard kiss. Gloria moaned faintly, and her mouth opened. A wet, darting tongue flicked against Jana's lips, and Jana opened her mouth to receive it against her own in a kiss that glowed with tenderness. Jana pursed her lips and sucked Gloria's darting tongue, and, panting and smiling, they parted.

'Oh . . .' said Gloria. 'Oh, that's nice, Jana. I've never – I mean only once, like that, with a woman . . .'

'But it is nice, isn't it?' said Jana, nuzzling Gloria's neck with her nose and lips. 'Can't girls give each other a softer, gentler, pleasure than boys? Don't worry, Cassie and I aren't dykes, as you Americans rather inelegantly put it. We belong to a sister-hood which . . . I mean, we see beauty and love in everything.'

'Kiss me again,' pleaded Gloria, but Jana broke away and lifted her lariat.

'First, I'll show you my house,' she said, 'or at least the private part of it. Now go and fetch your gunbelt.'

Gloria was allowed loose rope to do so, and then, with a jerk, Jana tightened the lariat and led her gently towards the bedroom.

36

3

Whipping Girl

'More mirrors!' exclaimed Gloria excitedly. 'So you watch yourselves when you do it? What a turn-on.' She looked round and saw Jana's rack of instruments of chastisement – whips and tawses and canes – as innocently displayed as an array of umbrellas in a cloakroom. Gloria drew breath sharply. 'And what are those?'

'You can see what they are, Gloria,' said Jana quietly, 'and what they are for. Are you frightened? Do you want to go? We are just playing, you and I, but if you don't want girls' play, why, I won't kiss you again, and you may leave.'

Gloria smiled impishly. 'Oh, I want to play all right,' she sighed. 'This is fun. And kissing you is fun, too. You have such lovely lips, and ... and lovely breasts. Such big nipples.'

Jana took Gloria's hand and placed it across her breasts so that she could feel the stiffening in the tips of her nipples. Then she took the nipple of Gloria's right breast between her finger and thumb, and began to rub it softly, and Gloria shut her eyes again and gasped.

'God, you're making me all wet,' she said faintly. Jana dropped the lariat and began to massage her other breast with the palm of her hand, feeling the cupola harden as she caressed it in slow, circular movements. 'Don't stop,' moaned Gloria.

'Don't tell me you weren't turned on by my punishment book,' said Jana. 'I saw your eyes.'

Gloria sighed, but said nothing, and Jana pinched her nipples harder, so that she moaned, then nodded in agreement.

37

'Say it, Gloria,' whispered Jana. 'Say you liked seeing those bare women flogged, and the men's bums writhing under a woman's lash. Say it.'

'Yes . . .' gasped Gloria. 'Oh, don't stop. Kiss me again, sweet Jana. Yes, I loved it. I felt all wet in my pussy just thinking about it. Is that what you want to do to me? Is that why you brought me here? Well, do what you want, I can take it. I've been whipped on the bare many a time. Just kiss me, and –'

'And what?'

'Do it to me down there. Kiss me, lick me with your lips and tongue, Oh God, fist me, everything. I was lying before, I've been with women more than once. Sometimes it's so much better than having a cock fucking you; all tender and gentle, and so sweet to smell her perfume and taste her juices as she tastes mine. Oh please, Jana.'

Abruptly, Jana released Gloria's breasts, and stood back. She flicked the rope, and nodded towards the bed.

'Skirt and boots off first,' she said.

Trembling, Gloria obeyed, and Jana gasped with surprise and felt a glow of wetness in her sex as she saw the magnificence of Gloria's mink; a lush forest of soft blonde curls that seemed to cover her like a carpet of scented golden buttercups.

'On the bed, face down and bum in the air,' she said crisply.

Gloria obeyed, kneeling on the crimson silk coverlet and spreading her thighs so that Jana could see her swollen pink cunt-petals protruding through the hanging mass of hair. Jana put her hand on the engorged sex and found her soaking wet.

'So you lied,' she said softly, loosening Gloria's whip from the gunbelt. 'You know that a girl who lies must be thrashed.'

Gloria's face, washed with desire, suddenly broke into a radiant smile. She pushed her bare bum higher in the air, and to Jana's surprise placed her fingers on her sex and began to rub herself. 'God, yes, Jana, do it. I didn't dare ask . . . I thought it would be too good to be true.' Jana lifted the whip, a good four feet of braided whipcord, and slashed the air. The whip whistled. 'Yes, yes,' moaned Gloria as she continued her frantic masturbation. 'Lace me with your whip, Jana. Make my rump all red, go on, go on.'

At that, Jana lashed the whip across Gloria's naked croup, and was gratified at the effect it had. Gloria jumped and squealed, and her fingers rubbed the clit that was hidden by the forest of curls at her pubis. A second stroke, and she cried louder; a third, and her voice screamed in her strange ecstasy, then subsided to an insistent, growling moan deep in her throat.

As Jana lashed her, scarcely counting the strokes, Gloria's body writhed like that of a woman possessed. At each stroke, her taut, muscled buttocks clenched and squirmed, and she trembled uncontrollably as Jana's pitiless lash reddened the naked croup until it was as red as the bedspread. Jana shuddered as she felt the wetness flow from her naked quim, hot and oily on her soft inner thighs. Sweat glistened on her face and breasts as she raised the whip in a furious rhythm, almost angry at the pleasure the flogged woman was taking from her. She lost count of the strokes she had laid on those squirming, crimson globes, as her victim, or exploiter, pleasured herself with eager fingers, her own thighs gleaming with oily moisture.

At last Jana could not restrain the fluttering in her belly, and threw aside the whip to join Gloria on the bed. She bent down to embrace the woman's arse, covering her reddened flesh with tender kisses, then swivelled herself under Gloria's raised loins to meet her sex-petals with her own mouth.

She felt Gloria's fingers, and bit them gently, then took them inside her own mouth and sucked them while rubbing the woman's engorged clit with her nose and lips.

Gloria moaned and Jana released her fingers, then extended her tongue to touch the stiff nympha, standing well outside the protective cunt-folds. She tongued Gloria mercilessly as the American woman cried loud in anguished pleasure.

39

Jana still wore her mini-skirt, but her quim was naked beneath. She moved in a sliding, sensuous motion so that she lay flat on the bed with her quim below Gloria's mouth, and, clasping Gloria's full buttocks, drew the woman's sex down to her lips. Her tongue probed and kissed Gloria's distended petals, and Jana gasped as her mini was pushed up over her belly button and she felt Gloria's flicking tongue penetrate her soaking slit.

Gloria's hands pressed Jana's buttocks to her as she gamahuched her, and Jana moaned deep in her throat as she felt the love-juice flow over her lips and face. She felt Gloria's body shudder as she spread the buttocks wide and, vigorously tonguing the throbbing clit, tickled Gloria's anus bud with her thumb. Gloria responded, thrusting a finger right inside Jana's tender anus, and as they loved each other with tongues and lips and probing fingers, first Gloria and then, after a few seconds, Jana, shivered and whimpered and cried out hoarsely in their spasms of ecstasy.

They lay on the bed, soaked in sweat and motionless except for the heaving of their breasts, until Gloria broke the silence.

'That was something else,' she said in a weak voice. 'God, Jana, I knew I wanted you as soon as you took off that fur coat in the restaurant, but I didn't know it was going to be like this.' She shifted and lay beside Jana so that her head was propped on her elbow, her flushed, joyous face gazing with love into Jana's mask of serenity. Gloria lowered her head to kiss Jana firmly on the lips, and Jana smiled. Gloria began to nibble at Jana's face, kissing her eyes and playing with her hair. 'I bet you have lots of friends,' she said. 'Girlfriends and boyfriends too. Do you always pick them up in restaurants and places like that? I guess I'm just another conquest.' She sighed.

Jana smiled fixedly, and said nothing, content to be adored. But she reached down and placed her palm on Gloria's luxuriant mink, stroking her gently, which made Gloria sigh louder.

There was a light knock on the door.

'Mistress?' came Cassie's voice. Jana saw Gloria's eyebrows lift in a silent question.

'Come in, Cassie,' called Jana. 'Gloria and I were just chatting.' The door opened and Cassie entered, only to grin broadly at the sight of the two naked embracing women.

'How lovely,' she murmured. 'Mistress, it's Henry on the phone. He says he will have to work quite late, and may he have permission to meet us at the party.'

'Yes.'

'He also wants to know if he may loosen his chastity belt, as it is so uncomfortable.'

'No.'

'Yes, Mistress.'

'Oh, Cassie, I suggest you bring a bottle of champagne and three glasses, and then we shall all have a little nap, and Gloria is going to tell us all about Greek archaeology. She won't need to go back to Cromwell Road; we can fit her out in some of my kit.' Cassie bowed, and withdrew. 'You see, Gloria, when I said that Cassie was my friend and more, what I meant was that she is my slave and I her mistress. Henry, too, is my slave.'

'Will there be other mistresses and slaves at the party tonight?' asked Gloria.

'Of course.'

'I wonder what it's like to be a slave,' said Gloria. 'To be . . . to be your slave. To be beaten all the time on the bare.' And she shivered deliciously.

'Maybe you'll find out,' said Jana, pulling Gloria's head to her breast. 'Have you been a slave before?'

Gloria shivered again. 'Once, I had a lovely man. I was up in the Cascade Mountains in Washington State, digging for artefacts of the Salish Indians, and I met this guy . . . a real, old-fashioned mountain man, 25 but with the wisdom of Geronimo. And strong! One day I actually watched him wrestle a bear! It was only a cub, a grizzly, but still as big as a man. It had been stealing chickens and pigs and such, and was causing mayhem. So he caught the beast in the act, and instead of shooting it, he wrestled it to the

41

ground and hogtied it, so that he could put it in his pick-up truck and drive it 30 miles away, then release it. I was so excited watching him wrestle that animal, and then watching him tie it, that on impulse, that night in bed, I asked him if he would tie me up so that I could feel what the animal felt. He did, and, boy, did he know his knots! I was well and truly hogtied, nude, couldn't move a muscle, with my ankles and wrists bound in front of me, and, you know, I found myself getting all wet down there at the thought of being so helpless for him, and my bare ass sticking out from my ropes and all, and had the crazy idea that I'd like him . . . like him to spank me. And I said to him, why not give me a thrashing on the bare. He started to slap me with his hand, but I said after a while that it wasn't enough, so he took off his belt, a big thick studded thing, and whipped me properly. And when he stripped and came inside me, still bound, I came almost at once. That became our loving game, all the time I was in the Cascades, but then I had to go back to UCLA, and I've lost touch with him. He was such a sweet man.' And she sighed again. 'And ever since then, if I have a friend, whether it's a man or a woman, I show them my lariat and my whip, and . . .' She giggled. 'What luck to find Lariat's!'

'Well, it's a long way from Washington to the Greek Islands, and it's the Greek Islands I really want to hear about,' said Jana, snuggling with her new lover. Clinking glasses could be heard as Cassie approached. 'So we'll all have a glass of wine, and you'll tell us all about them, won't you, Gloria?'

'Gladly, Mistress,' whispered Gloria.

'You will be just perfect at Netta and Caspar's', said Jana as she finished off her supper. It was nearly eight o'clock, and the three women were ready to set off to the party in Lennox Gardens. 'Their parties tend towards the fancy dress, and you'll probably find, I hope to your satisfaction, that there's an Ancient Greek, or Mediterranean, flavour to the proceedings. Perhaps you could go as Atalante the Wrestler, or perhaps an Amazon princess, or even a

42

hetaira, a courtesan. You have the fine strong bones and the sturdy frame with ripe breasts and bum, and good muscle tone. I'm sure I have some kit that will suit you.'

'Proceedings?' said Gloria, fresh from her shower and wrapped in one of Jana's bathrobes. 'You make it sound like a horse trial. With me as the horse.'

'Think of it more as a game,' said Jana. She pushed her plate away, and drained her wine glass. 'Time to get ready. What we'll do, to add spice, is not to let each other know what we're wearing. You go first, Gloria: go to my closet, and pick out whatever you want, then put your coat on over it, so that we will all surprise each other. Remember, the more outrageous the better.'

Gloria rose, her face flushed with girlish excitement at the prospect of dressing up.

Jana made the taxi stop at the end of Lennox Gardens, leaving a couple of minutes' walk for her and her companions to reach the house of Netta and Caspar. Gloria opened her mouth to question this caution, but then smiled, nodded, and said, 'Mmm.' Jana smiled back, a smile of complicity.

'You catch on quick,' she said. 'Netta and Caspar are very dear, very intimate friends, as you'll see, and very valuable to –' she was about to say 'The House of Maldona' but checked herself '– well, to us.'

The large terrace house was brightly lit, and sounds of party-going murmured behind heavy drapes. Jana paused on the steps before ringing the bell.

'Gloria,' she said, 'I think I know something about you, even in such a short time. But I don't know you well. I know what you like, but you must be aware that there are ... degrees. Some of the things you'll see here tonight might strike you as a little unusual. But whatever you feel, please know that no one will force you to do anything you don't want. In fact, any suggestion has to come from you, and I shan't think you rude if you decide to up and leave at any time.'

'I never back out of a party,' said Gloria, smiling. Jana

rang the bell, and moments later, a spyhole released a chink of light. Then there was the sound of bolts, and the door opened to reveal a tall woman, mid-thirties, with cropped silver hair, who welcomed them with a wide smile of her lips, which were shiny with a delicate mauve lipstick.

She wore a sheer dress of very thin black latex, belted tightly at her narrow waist; a deep cleavage that left most of her large, well-tanned breasts deliciously bare, with the taut nipples outlined clearly against their black rubber sheath. She threw up her hands in genuine delight at Jana's arrival, but instead of greeting her with an effusive kiss on the cheek, in the manner of party hostesses, she at once knelt and kissed the tips of Jana's red calfskin boots. Netta carried at her waist a supple willow cane, and when she rose from delicately kissing Jana's feet, she unfastened it and handed it reverently to Jana, who accepted it with a gracious smile.

'Welcome, Mistress, and welcome also to your slave Cassandra,' said Netta with a curious shyness. 'My house is your house, and my rod is yours, and my body is yours to chastise. You bring a new slave?'

'Netta, I present Gloria. She is a friend, not a slave. But ... she knows.' Gloria put out her hand and shook Netta's, and this time Netta did proffer a brief kiss to Gloria's cheek.

'You are a friend of Maldona,' she said, 'and so my friend also. The party is upstairs. We've been waiting for you, Jana, quite eagerly of course. How can things start without our mistress herself? But where is the slave Aelfric?'

'We call him Henry here in London,' said Jana. 'It is simpler. Well, he is doing some money business, and he said he would come directly here afterwards.'

Netta nodded, and led her guests first to her 'apodyterium' or changing-room – really, a large cloakroom off the marble-tiled hallway – where the women doffed their coats. First, Cassie hung up her raincoat and revealed herself to be wearing a light slave's tunic, white in the Grecian style, with bare arms, a silver belt and a short,

44

swirling pleated skirt of feathery silk. She wore silver globe earrings, and round her neck her silver choker, connected now by a thin chain to her waistband, from which two similar chains snaked down her bare legs to twin slave bracelets on her ankles. She blushed a little as Jana clapped her hands in appreciation of her costume's demure simplicity.

Gloria disrobed, and under her coat she was wearing, to Jana's delight, one of her own more daring outfits. It was a one-piece garment of black leather, arranged in thick straps like a soldier's webbing, which criss-crossed her upper body. The straps covered her breasts and pubis, but only just, so that on either side of the strap which bit tightly between her thighs and looped up through the cleft of her buttocks, a luxuriant tuft of golden pubic curls peeped, as though trapped there by the merciless leather. The webbing gleamed with silver studs and buckles, like the matching high-heeled thigh boots which came up almost to her sex, revealing only a delicious sliver of tan thigh-skin. The choker at her neck was of black leather too, with a red ruby set in a silver clasp at her throat. She had artfully coiled her horsewhip into the straps of her leather, and it dangled with menacing grace at her side as she moved.

'You've chosen well, Gloria,' said Jana, licking her lips and undoing her sable coat. Now it was the turn of Cassie and Gloria to smile in delight. For Jana wore nothing less, and nothing more, than the parfaite's harness of Maldona.

'What is that?' cried Gloria. 'It's . . . it's gorgeous! I want one! I'm sure I've seen it before.'

'No!' replied Cassie quickly. 'Don't say such things! Only the Mistress may wear the parfaite's harness. To think otherwise is imperfection.'

Gloria gave her a curious look, but said nothing.

Jana wore a harness of filigree golden chains which dazzled even in the soft turquoise light of the apodyterium. The chains criss-crossed her body like a glittering gossamer web, leaving breasts and rouged nipples and the swelling naked mound of her pubis, entirely bare. The heavy folds of her sex-petals hung red between her coquettishly parted thighs, glistening with sultry menace, and the red nympha, her hard clit, stood proudly like a little naked penis under the fleshy prepuce. It was evident that Jana had applied generous rouge to her sex and nympha as well as to her nipples, which were stiff with the excitement of her naked exposure. Curving from her lady's place, and standing ramrod straight over her belly and the small of her back, stood two poles, like folded fans, which seemed to emerge from her sex and anus.

'I know where I've seen that,' said Gloria. 'In that book – the book of punishments.'

'And this,' said Jana softly, and with a certain smugness, 'is the very same garment that was in the picture. It is the flogging harness of the Parfaite Cecilia of Ubrique, in Spain, the author of the book. She was an adept of a secret Order of women, many centuries ago, an English Order founded mysteriously –' Jana was careful not to give away too many secrets at this stage '– with her mission to instil into her charges a love of obedience and discipline, both mental and physical. The Parfaite is, I mean was, the highest rank of adept, and responsible for administering the most severe physical chastisement.'

'With that?' asked Gloria innocently, pointing to the white four-thonged whip which hung from the golden loop around Jana's waist.

'With that,' said Jana, nodding, 'but I'm not ready yet for my entrance to our party. Just watch.' She grinned mischievously, and squeezed her sphincter muscle hard, feeling the electric pleasure in her anus and sex as they touched the triggers of her peacock fans. Gloria gasped in delight as the twin poles sprang into rainbows of light, the feathers radiant with beauty and colour, so that Jana was now modest, her sex and buttocks fully screened by the shimmering fans.

'It's so beautiful!' cried Gloria. 'How clever!'

'I think we are ready to ascend,' said Jana, opening the door of the apodyterium. Netta waited outside.

'Jana, this Order of women in Spain,' said Gloria, her eyes narrowed slyly, 'was it called Maldona? I seem to have heard this name.'

'Why, yes,' said Jana, 'it was called Maldona.'

'An Order dedicated to chastisement; to discipline by whip on naked woman-flesh?'

'To the achievement of moral and physical beauty,' Jana replied softly, 'through the cleansing power of pain, whether at the whipping post or in the gymnasium, where the muscles, through harsh training, are pushed to the utmost limits of endurance.'

Gloria nodded. 'No wonder you have such a beautiful hard body,' she said admiringly. 'Strong, yet tender and soft too. You say Maldona was. I want to know if Maldona is. Does Maldona still exist?'

Jana took a deep breath, feeling Cassie's eyes upon her. 'Yes,' she said.

'Here?'

'Yes. Maldona is everywhere.'

'And you are the Mistress of Maldona?'

Jana nodded.

Suddenly, Gloria knelt in obeisance and kissed the tips of Jana's boots. 'Let me submit to you, Mistress,' she murmured. 'It is what I have been seeking, and never dared admit, to myself or others.' Jana looked down at the prostrate woman, her broad back gleaming with sweat under the leather straps which already seemed to bind her in slavery. Gloria had indeed chosen her costume thoughtfully. She gently stroked Gloria's hair.

'It's early, Gloria,' she said. 'There is a lot you don't know.'

'Then teach me, please? I know enough to want to submit to you, to feel my body chastised with your whip, Jana, sweet Mistress, and my mind freed.'

'You are a sympathetic woman,' said Jana, motioning that she should rise, 'but I am not yet your mistress. The first thing to know is that you do not submit to me, you submit to the rules of Maldona. Now let's go upstairs, and see if we can't change your mind.'

The house Caspar and Netta occupied in Lennox Gardens was actually two houses knocked into one, so that it had the aspect of a mansion, or nobleman's town house.

Jana was reminded of the museum in Burlington Gardens, where she liked to go and see the Mayan skull carved from a single block of unknown volcanic crystal, whose eyes seemed to follow you round the room. Here, there was a winding marble staircase, with balustrades and chandeliers, and the walls hung with paintings whose subjects gave a clue to the delights that awaited in the large salon above. Caspar, the cineaste, had assembled a collection that from afar seemed as impressive a collection of old masters as any room in the National Gallery.

Surely, there hung the frothy confections of Fragonard or Boucher, their laughing girls on a swing; the austere portraits of Jan van Eyck, the friendly Dutch landscapes of Ruysdael, the Impressionist swirls of Monet or Renoir. There seemed to be every century, every school, represented in this collection. Slowly, they went up the staircase, through a throng of drinking, talking guests who had spilled over from the salon. They were dressed in bizarre and gorgeous costumes of leather, rubber, silk and silver, or combinations of all, and all bowed at Jana's passage, with murmurs of respect.

Followed by Cassie and Netta, Jana paused to let Gloria study the paintings as they ascended. And soon, with a yelp of amused delight, Gloria realised that these paintings were not by the old masters, but were clever pastiches. Here indeed was a girl high on a rococo swing, her skirts billowing; but instead of lace underthings, the spectator had a full view of a naked quim, the details of lips and nympha painted in loving pink detail. There, a sober Florentine prince or banker of the fourteenth century with his dutiful wife: but she is not standing meekly beside him but standing exultantly over him, holding a scourge, as the worthy, stretched naked on a rack, receives a vividly coloured lacing on his bare buttocks. Beside him, his bags of gold thalers lie spilled, gnawed open by rats, in mute ironic comment on his agony.

A stately Dutch interior, in the manner of Vermeer, shows a housewife, soberly coiffed in a white bonnet with a plain brown bodice, reading a letter in her parlour. But her skirts are up, her buttocks and sex are exposed, and two men are pleasuring her, one in her quim and the other in her anus, showing every sign of ecstasy as she unconcernedly reads.

A Gainsborough here? A noble lord stands proudly with his gun and his dog, overlooking his demesne. But in the copse of trees behind him, his wife is laughing as, skirts up in the air to reveal a naked arse, she is pleasured by a grinning naked farm-boy, who is beating her reddened bare nates with a yew rod as he fucks her.

An English romantic idyll, with farmers binding the hay into stacks. And in the centre, no haystack, but a woman bound, naked but for her tight corsets of rope, chain and thong. The smiling rustics await their turn to take her between the plump naked buttocks.

Aphrodite rising from the waves. Botticelli? No, this Aphrodite squats obscenely on her scallop shell, her distended cunt-lips and clit plainly, grossly, visible, and in each hand she holds the swollen cock of a satyr, directing them to her sex and anus.

'It's fabulous,' breathed Gloria. 'So good. I'm all wet just looking at these things, and smelling the wonderful perfume, the aura of beauty and pain that pervades this house. Jana, Mistress, please take me!'

Jana smiled, and said nothing. At the top of a staircase, before the gilt salon doors, was a little doll's house. Jana directed Gloria to look inside.

'It's a *trompe-l'œil*,' she said. 'In the National Gallery, there's a miniature house made by the Dutchman van Rysselbergh. You look in, and see a complete interior in 3D. This one is a bit different.'

First, she looked herself, and saw a dungeon, where females were chained, tied, nude or encased in rubber or leather catsuits, hooded and masked and gagged in order to be whipped, merely spanked, or birched. The centre of the tableau was a woman, naked but for a parfaite's harness, and a curious mask of bird's plumage, who wielded a four-thonged white whip to the scarred back of a chained virgin.

Gloria belt down and peered through the spyhole. 'It's fabulous,' she whispered. 'So cruel, and so beautiful. Who is the harnessed woman in the centre?'

'It's me,' said Jana.

At that moment the gilt doors of the salon opened, and a short, heavily muscled man, his garlanded head entirely shaven, and wearing an androgynous Grecian tunic and sandals, knelt before Jana.

'Welcome, Mistress,' he said, kissing her feet.

'Thank you, Caspar,' said Jana. 'Your manners are impeccable. You may rise, and our spectacle may begin.'

There was an instant hush as Jana and her party entered the salon. All bowed, some of the women even turning to make a backward bow and raising their skirts, if they wore them, baring themselves to show they desired to be caressed with Jana's whip. Jana walked slowly round the room, nodding at faces she recognised and deigning only to flick the bared bottoms of her supplicants with the tips of her whip thongs, the lightest of teases which nevertheless brought sighs of joy from those who had been touched.

At the far end of the salon stood a lavish buffet, and for a moment, Jana fancied herself in her beloved Spain, or Greece, on the Mediterranean seashore. Silver dishes were piled high with crustaceans, oysters, eel, caviar and olives, and there were several glinting bottles of wine. Jana positioned herself beside the table, and without speaking or looking around, she held out her hand, into which Caspar at once put a glass of champagne. Introductions were made and Caspar began to explain, with small modesty, that his profession was film director, specialising in the erotic, the outré, and, as he insisted, the morally uplifting. Above the table, a garish mural depicted a multitude of naked orgiasts in a classical setting, entwined in twos, threes and fours, or grimacing in savage pleasure as men and women alike enjoyed the beauty of whipped and squirming bare skin.

'You make ... triple X movies?' asked Gloria. 'You know, that's always been a fantasy of mine. I daresay a lot of girls have the same one, to be a high-class whore in a fuck movie. Just imagine, all those studs, doing it to you in a never-never land of pleasure, where there are no comebacks, no responsibilities. Every girl's dream. Mine, anyway.' She looked at the giant screen which covered the far wall of the salon. 'Are we going to see some of yours?' Caspar looked at Jana, who nodded.

He wrinkled his nose. 'Gloria dear,' he said, 'I am a cineaste, I do not make fuck films, as you call them. Under the brilliant southern sun, in the castle –' he looked again at Jana for guidance, his eyebrows raised as though to ask how much the newcomer had been told '– in the castle which is Maldona, under the brilliant sun of the southern land, I record the beauty of our Order and her rules, her torments and her ecstasies, for the benefit of those who would join us, and the instruction of generations to come. Although our aim is that future generations will need no instruction, for they will know the rules of Maldona.'

To the surprise of all, Jana's nostrils flared in anger, and she hissed at Caspar, 'Slave, you forget yourself. You have committed a grievous imperfection. A punishable imperfection.'

'How, Mistress?' said Caspar in astonishment, yet with a glint in his eye at the prospect of receiving her chastisement.

'And now a question! That, too, is against the rules. In Maldona, we do not question. Remember that, Gloria. We state what we want, and what we feel in our hearts. Questions imply an incompleteness, and incompleteness is imperfection. Now, Caspar, it is up to you to identify your imperfection.'

'Mistress,' said Caspar carefully, 'perhaps –'

Cassie interrupted, her eyes bright with anger. 'Maldona's rules, like Maldona herself, must remain hidden, as they have been hidden for centuries. It is only in the dark that Maldona can do good. If our rosebush is exposed to the bright light of inquisition by the unknowing, she will wither and die. We proceed by stealth and caution: a nod, a glance, a kiss between adepts may speak volumes. Some truths, in short, are meant to be secret.'

51

Jana nodded, satisfied.

The hubbub of conversation and laughter had recommenced, to the accompaniment of a soft, insistent drumbeat. Gloria's eyes circled the room, and Jana saw wonder at the outlandish and decadent costumes of the guests, most of which outdid Gloria's now timid-looking leather restraints. There was a flavour of the Greco-Roman, with many women wearing little but the *zona*, the Greek thong, around pubis and arse, and the *apodesmos* around the breasts, with bracelets around ankles, necks and forearms. Some wore flowing robes of translucent blue or red silk, under which they were nude. Garish paints – blacks, turquoise, even white – adorned lips, eyelids, breasts and occasionally a fully exposed shaven pubis, making the woman's body a pretty kaleidoscope of colour.

The men favoured Grecian tunics like Caspar's, or intricate constructions of leather like the one Gloria was wearing, and heavily decorated with shining silver chains and buckles. Many carried short canes or whips at their belts. Jana was obliged to raise her voice.

'I had hoped to see that girl, Sarah Pennington,' she said. 'I have rather a soft spot for her, because she was the first woman I ever caned, even though she tricked me into caning her, the sweet little slut.'

'Tricked you?' said Gloria, puzzled.

Jana turned. 'Ah, a question, Gloria. But you know the rules. Punishment is in order, and I'm feeling stern tonight. But I'll answer your question.'

'I believe Sarah will be joining us,' said Netta.

'She pretended to steal a candle from my gift stall at the Portobello Market,' said Jana absent-mindedly, 'and got me to cane her instead of calling the police.' She smiled. 'What a lovely, clever bitch she is. She took it on the bare bum, and loved every moment. In fact, I'm getting just a little excited at the thought of lacing her again. How she wriggled as my cane stroked her! You say she'll be here, Netta? I'll wait.'

'You shall see her in my film,' said Caspar proudly.

'She quite excels herself.' Jana licked her lips. 'Show the film now, Caspar.'

4

Ocean of Delights

To everyone's surprise, the screen filled with the giant image, in grainy black and white, of a huge turtle, or terrapin, flapping lazily under the sea, probing through garlands of weed and shoals of glinting fish. There was no soundtrack, and all that could be heard was the insistent beat of the unseen drum – as though leading to some unguessable climax – and the rustling of the garments as the already aroused guests positioned themselves for caresses to the expected accompaniment of a lush, full colour erotic masterpiece.

'It is a film about turtles,' said Caspar cryptically. 'Dolphins, too, and all sea things.'

'I expected a film about Maldona,' said Jana in surprise. 'You have just visited the finishing school, haven't you, Caspar? Your report was quite glowing. About the maintenance of strict discipline, I mean.' And she was amazed to feel herself blush.

'Yes, and I made a small detour,' he replied. 'To the Aegean, actually, the Turkish coast just north of the crusaders' citadel of Bodrum, now sadly spoiled by tourism. However, I took a party of my young Rosebush ladies, from the finishing school, to a deserted area which abounds in friendly, or not so friendly, wildlife. Some of it quite human . . . It was instructive for them. This is indeed a film about Maldona, for are we not all naked fishes swimming in her bountiful sea?'

'Rosebush?' said Gloria uncertainly.

'Caspar owns the Rosebush School, in Knightsbridge,' said Jana. 'It is very expensive, and the young women are

53

rather ... special, as you will see if Sarah Pennington deigns to grace us with her presence. I am surprised Henry is not here.'

'I think,' said Caspar loftily, 'my work is entering a surrealist phase.'

On the flickering screen, another shape swam into view, towards the floundering giant turtle. It was a woman, nude except for a pair of white panties which clung to her, transparent in the water, so that the pumping muscles of her buttocks could be seen clearly as she swam with strong, sure movements. Her blonde hair floated after her in a stream, like the trailing seaweed which caressed her young, elfin body. Briefly, she turned her face to the camera, though seeming not to notice it. Jana gasped with delight, and slid her arm around Gloria's waist.

'Sarah!' she cried. 'How sweet.'

'That is Sarah Pennington,' said Gloria thoughtfully. 'She's very pretty, Mistress. And such a big bum ...' She giggled.

Deftly, Sarah Pennington straddled the turtle, and with little tickling pats to its scaly neck, guided it up and away from its clump of rock and seaweed. She rode the beast expertly and gently, like a horsewoman. There was scattered applause at her artful mastery of the sea beast, and more applause when the camera zoomed for a close-up of her silk-sheathed buttocks: clearly visible through the wet translucent silk was a network of crimson whip marks, so vivid as to be newly dealt.

The camera, unseen or not, followed Sarah as she rode the turtle, and Jana wondered at the young woman's ability to hold her breath. She must have been underwater for two minutes at least, she thought, and felt a pang of envy, which quickly changed to determination that she too, Mistress of Maldona, should – must – acquire such power of endurance.

The turtle moved upward now, into clearer light; Sarah was riding it to the surface. The camera followed as the strange pair broke water and emerged into a startling blue sky, where Sarah gulped air. Jana shuddered, her arm tightening around Gloria's waist.

There, in the near distance, loomed a barren red rock island, over which towered a mountain, evidently a dead, or dormant, volcano. And it was the mountain in Jana's nightmare.

'Mistress?' said Gloria uncertainly. 'Are you OK?'

'Yes, yes, it's just that . . . it's so beautiful. Oh, Gloria, how I long to go there, to that sea and that island.'

There, she thought, I've said it. I must go there. Something, or someone, is driving me. She looked at Caspar, but no emotion was visible under his saturnine, impassive features. Surely he could not know? Coincidence, she told herself, that was all. Gloria peered closer to the screen.

'I know a lot of those Aegean islands,' she said, 'but I don't recognise that one.'

'Caspar said it was close to the Turkish coast,' said Jana.

'Well, that would explain it.'

'What is she going to do now, I wonder?' said Cassie. 'I wish she'd take those panties off and let us have a closer look at that nicely laced bum.'

As if on cue, Sarah tapped her steed's glistening shell, and the turtle abruptly dived again. The camera followed her back under the water, but not into the deep, so that the play of light dappling through the water made Sarah seem like a sea creature. Shoals of bright fish eddied around her in lazy motion, caressing her tight, smooth breasts and flat belly like a lover.

And now two more figures appeared, swimming strongly towards Sarah on her turtle shell. Both were women, the same age as their prey – Jana could not help thinking of the scene as hunting – and both were nude, with, she noted, lush pubic minks to match their dark russet hair. Their heavy breasts bobbed gently in the water as they swam, as though swimming with a life of their own, the woman's body no more than a congregation of parts – feet, buttocks, arms – all spinning and writhing in a rhythm of their own, yet clinging miraculously to form the sweetest of creations, a woman's whole body. Jana began to stroke the top of Gloria's buttocks, very softly, marvelling at her joy that she too possessed a form of such loveliness.

'It is not only men who can appreciate and love a woman's form,' she whispered in Gloria's ear, as the two newcomers swam in a delicate, mocking dance around Sarah on turtleback. 'We women can love ourselves, Gloria, for we can know ourselves in a way that men cannot, the poor creatures –'

'Kate and Melanie,' said Caspar, rolling his tongue lasciviously round the syllables. 'Mischievous creatures, yet full of beauty and potential, which are the same thing.'

' "The truest beauty is the beauty that is about to flower",' said Gloria suddenly. Then, 'I forget who said that.'

Caspar laughed. 'Very pretty,' he replied. 'Probably dear Oscar Wilde. He said most of the pretty things.'

'They are twins,' said Gloria, staring at the image of Kate and Melanie, who joined Sarah Pennington on her turtleback and embraced her. Gloria shivered. 'There is something spooky about twins. They have strange powers.'

'All women have strange powers,' said Caspar smugly. 'That is why men must master them . . . or obey them. One or the other.'

'Sometimes,' siad Jana, 'obedience, utter submission, is the true mastery.'

The images on the screen began to jar and change abruptly, flickering from the underwater embrace of the three women to seemingly disparate images: a flower, a tattooed breast, a mountain, naked females wrestling, an albatross, a cloud, a man and woman fucking, and, for split seconds in among these flashing images, a long shot of the island, shimmering in the heat haze, with its dark volcanic growth towering over the blue sea in which the women swam.

Each time the image of that mountain flashed on to the screen, Jana's heart leapt. Her throat was dry, and she drank her champagne faster than was decorous.

'I want to go there,' she whispered, clutching Gloria tightly by the waist. 'I must go there. I must, but I don't know why –'

She was about to tell Gloria about her dream but muffled her tongue with a gulp of wine. She looked round at the darkened room, which trembled to the sound of the drumbeat. She gasped at the image of a mermaid, a naked woman who was half fish below her belly, and above, covered in golden scales. Seaborne, she approached the turtle at a distance, then grinned and swam away, towards the island, her hair streaming behind her like weed, encrusted with glittering shells and anemones.

The cameras followed her, focusing on her powerful strokes, the swell of her heavy breasts and rippling golden muscles, and the sensuous writhing of her fishy tail, until, in close-up, it was revealed that the nude woman was no true mermaid: the appearance of her legs and buttocks was the result of an intricate rainbow of tattoos. As if delighted by her subterfuge, she flipped over on her back, submerged herself, and, underwater, beamed at the camera, before opening her thighs to reveal a naked sex glittering with golden scales like gorgeous skin-tight panties.

The camera zoomed closer and closer as the mermaid, still grinning, opened the petals of her sex to reveal that she was tattooed inside as well: the normally pink cunt-flesh was a shimmering pattern of gold, like the rest of her upper body. Her thighs, calves and ripe powerful buttocks were splendid with whorls and little figures and tableaux, in lush contrast to her golden torso, and Jana craned to see the details, but the camera tantalised, swooping and diving through the soft crevices of the woman's body, without lingering on any of her bright portraiture. Jana saw, or thought she saw, livid whip marks on the woman's buttocks: a tattoo of chastisement which would never fade, and she felt her belly flutter at the audacity of the conceit.

'The art of the film is the true art of our century,' said Caspar softly. 'Fleeting, disjointed, inexplicable, and touching subliminally the primal id, the darkness in our dream-minds. It is said that Surrealism is the child of the age of cinema, but it's really the other way round. Yes, I think I am surrealist in thought and deed.' He laughed harshly. 'Perhaps you, Mistress Jana, are the same. Maldona, after all, is the first surreal creation, all those centuries ago: order in chaos, and chaos in order . . .'

The guests, reclining on cushions like Roman orgiasts of old, began to caress each other as they gazed at the tantalising kaleidoscope, subliminally aware that the clever juxtaposition of images – the savagely erotic with the seemingly pastoral – was not random, but was building to a climax. The beauty of the images of fish, flowers, stars and birds made more breathtaking the graphic illustrations of perverse pleasure which punctuated them. Nude wrestling between two women was no languorous affair but a deadly contest of kicking, twisting and gouging according to the ancient Greek rules of Pankration, which – and Jana felt herself increasingly excited – were the rules of Maldona. The frequent images of couples fucking were cruel rather than tender, glimpsed sometimes in coarse close-up of the genitals alone with tantalising brevity: men fucked women in mouth and anus as well as in their founts, the cameraman, presumably Caspar, dwelling with gloating precision on the thrusting of a monstrous penis into the puckered tight anus bud of the squirming female. In some shots a woman was pleasuring two or even three men at once, with every orifice and willing, frantic hands in lustful play. One pair even fucked under the water, writhing like sea-serpents in a savage embrace, their nude bodies caressed by fish.

The birds were now not peaceable albatrosses, but falcons, eagles and hawks, swooping like dead weights out of the sky to tear their fishy prey out of the water, or else savaging a smaller, helpless bird in mid-air after a plummeting fall of dizzying beauty. Against dark velvet night, glittering owls savaged the mammals of the field.

A heavily muscled man stood naked but for a horned goat's mask, his penis erect and rouged, and flogged the bare body of a trussed and gagged woman with a switch. After her flogging, she took the branches and kissed them, pressing them hard to her bare breasts and rubbing against her well-stiffened brown nipples.

The images grew harsher and more sombre, but always cut back to the laughing trio on their turtle, a picture of innocence and joy. Kate and Melanie pulled Sarah's panties from her, with much wriggling and grimacing, and let them float deliciously away up to the surface, like the petal of some giant sea flower. Sarah pretended to mind, but did not; she parted her thighs and rested her legs on the thighs of her friendly tormentors, pulling her sex-petals open to reveal the glistening pink flesh inside as she grinned at the camera. Now, Kate and Melanie did the same, stretching open their cunt-petals and gently masturbating each other's nymphae as they rubbed Sarah's glistening slit. Jana's eyes widened, and she heard a sigh from the embracing guests, as they saw, in close focus, that each girl was tattooed on her shaven pubis. The screen filled with three open founts, the lips heavy and swollen, being rubbed by delicate fingers, but not obscuring the rose-flowers which were tattooed around the sex-petals that seemed to wave like fronds in the swirling seawater. The tattoos were done so artfully that the cunt-lips seemed indeed to be petals – bright red whorls around the central hole, the rosebud herself. Like the mermaid, the three young women had the soft flesh inside their sex delicately etched with the tiniest of pink petals, glistening with oily juice as though the roses were freshly, and permanently, watered. The three women, kissing each other on the lips and breasts, applied themselves to slow, stroking caresses of each other's roses, closing their eyes in real or feigned ecstasy at the joy of their masturbation. Their mouths were closed tight, and Jana thought they must soon break to take air from the surface. She saw their breasts heave prettily as they struggled to contain both pleasure and breath.

And she saw too that in Caspar's room or, as she thought of it, his theatre, the guests began to do the same; skirts and tunics were loosened or raised, and there was the soft sliding of leather straps being undone. Jana had no doubt that the darkened scene was being filmed, by infrared, but nevertheless she found her own hand slipping from Gloria's waist to her unresisting sex-petals, which she caressed, running her fingertips against the oily moisture and feeling her own cunt growing wet too, longing for Gloria's fingers to touch her there and rub her stiffening nympha. She was dimly aware that nearby, Cassie's head was clenched between Caspar's thighs under his raised tunic, and Cassie made little bobbing motions as her lips caressed the man's penis. Caspar stroked Cassie's hair and made little cooing noises as she tongued him. Jana felt happy that Cassie had found pleasure, and she hoped it was equal to her own.

She gave a little gasp of joy and turned to kiss Gloria's open lips when Gloria, breathing hard, closed her eyes and placed her hand between Jana's moist thighs.

Abruptly, the filmed scene changed to a man and woman fucking, now shown in close-up. The man was African, his skin ebony, and the woman a soft alabaster. Their faces were unseen – all that could be seen was the maddened pumping of the man's buttocks and the writhing of the pinioned woman beneath him as he fucked her without tenderness, with the brutal concise movements of an animal rutting. They seemed to be in the open air, but the shallow depth of field hinted only vaguely at a beach, rocks, a glinting blue sea; and the woman lay on a dark lustrous bed of sea flowers.

As the man fucked her, she bucked to his rhythm with increasing desperation, as though begging him to bring her to a climax, and Jana could see her fingers rubbing her nympha as she writhed, her body oily with mingled sweat and love fluid that seeped in a shiny stream from her wide, filled cunt, making the thick dark trunk of the penis glisten as it served her.

Gloria's fingers were inside Jana's own cunt now, and Jana had to stop herself from moaning with delight, her act of self-restraint adding to the secret pleasure she gained from her slave's caress. The world had narrowed to the shining screen, and the trembling body of Gloria beside her, as though everyone else in the room had melted into darkness. And she embraced Gloria fully, drawing their bodies together as her hand probed the sweet wet secret of Gloria's swollen cunt-petals. Gloria moaned softly in her throat, and shook as Jana touched her stiff clitoris.

Suddenly, the black man withdrew from his lover's embrace, leaving her gasping and wriggling much, Jana thought, like a fish beached. The woman's face was still obscured, but Jana was mesmerised by the sight that greeted her as the man took his cock from the woman's open cunt: he was a giant, the phallus standing stiff as a tree and at least fourteen or fifteen inches. And the dark shaft, with its gleaming brown glans wet with the woman's juices, stood up at an angle parallel to the man's belly, so that his navel was covered by that throbbing brown acorn. Jana shivered in excitement, her sex soaking, at the strange beauty of such a proud, defiant erection.

The woman, her face out of focus, gazed at him in longing and fury at her abandonment, and increased the fervour of her masturbation. Now, the African's face was clearly seen, his white teeth grinning cruelly against ebony skin, a dark prince taunting his white slave, and suddenly Jana felt a longing to be totally in the power of a sadistic master, who fucked her, tormenting her, with such a massive phallus; the symbol of male beauty and power and cruelty. She knew from Gloria's trembling that she felt the same.

'God,' breathed Gloria, 'we can love each other as women, but isn't there something deep in us, Mistress, that longs for the boot, the whip, the dungeon, that longs to submit to a magnificent male brute . . . isn't there? Oh, say yes.'

'Yes, Gloria,' moaned Jana. 'Oh yes. But look –'

Now the black man, penis still standing hard, extended his foot and lazily, as though the woman was nothing more than an animal, kicked her buttocks to flip her over on to her belly. There was an instrument of punishment in his hand now, and the camera lingered on it: a transparent membrane, the gut of a shark or whale it seemed, and tightly filled with sharp oyster shells. He lifted the strange quirt, and brought it down on the woman's naked buttocks, making her jump in a convulsion of shock and pain. From the rear, they saw her jaws leap open, and though there was no sound to Caspar's cruel film, Jana could hear her scream.

Gloria's fingers worked faster and faster on Jana's swollen, tingling nympha as the dark man continued to flog the helpless woman, slapping the quirt of sharp shells with massive force on her squirming bare buttocks. Now the flogging scene was punctuated with images of the three women masturbating with increasing force and tenderness, and with ever more ominous stills of the looming volcanic hill on the island close by.

Sarah, Kate and Melanie kicked their steed gently away, and the turtle paddled serenely off, leaving the three suspended in mid-water in a writhing dance of naked love, hands stroking and caressing each other's trembling wet cunts with tender ferocity, and their faces twisted with the welling of ecstasy. Delicious eddies of gleaming love-oil floated from their naked cunts like sea creatures emerging from their beds.

The quirt of seashells continued its merciless descent on the naked wet buttocks of the squirming woman, mottling her skin with a mosaic of deep crimson. Jana knew that she was not long from a climax under the pressure of Gloria's expert, tender fingertips, and she could feel that Gloria too was on her plateau. Jana took a very deep breath and Gloria did the same, then their lips and tongues met, not breathing, their breasts shaking as they both shuddered in silent orgasm, their cunts flowing with the soft hot oil of their ecstasy. Her lungs bursting as she held her breath, Jana imagined herself under the water with Gloria, no, with Sarah, Kate and Melanie too, all entwined like petals, and the force of her orgasm seemed like a hot flood, pent up to be suddenly released, an ocean of joy in her tingling wet cunt.

On the screen, the three girls threshed the water as they too writhed in silent spasms, and bubbles of air rushed up from their opened, gasping mouths before they too sped to the surface, hands still clasping each other's cunts, like a tangled bouquet of flowers. Jana opened her eyes, and detaching her lips from Gloria's, gulped air.

She felt the tremors of her orgasm still fluttering through her belly, and her breath was hoarse and panting against Gloria's neck, drinking the scent of her hair and skin. All around, caressing shapes moved softly, moaning the gentle laments of ecstasy.

The film was at its own climax. The man threw down his heavy quirt and now straddled the flogged woman's buttocks, stretching them harshly apart and lifting her to reveal the soaking wet gash of her swollen sex. He plunged hard into her with one swift, brutal thrust that made her arch her back and buck as that single stroke of the massive dark cock brought her trembling, whipped body to an orgasm of mesmerising power. The man's own silent scream of release seemed to Jana almost irrelevant as she watched the woman shudder in a seemingly endless spasm of agonised pleasure.

Now the camera focused the whole scene. The lovers lay on a beach, beside an azure sea. The woman's face was bared clearly for the first time, streaming with tears, tongue thrust out and her lips quivering. It was Netta, Caspar's wife. And above the lovers loomed the dark volcanic mountain of Jana's dreamed island.

'The human body is an unlovely artefact,' drawled Caspar, a haze of fragrant Turkish smoke floating from his lips. 'That is why we adorn ourselves, to become for a moment, something other. Look around.'

Caspar and Jana reclined on cushions, arms lazily around Cassie and Gloria, who, smiling, fed them grapes and titbits of the sea, whose shells Caspar spat with gusto on his Ottoman carpet. The room was still in smoky half-light, and they surveyed a sea of nude or half-garbed bodies, stroking and caressing as the image of the island surveyed them, frozen on to the screen. Some couples caressed each other with whips or canes, the harsh cracks of the lash riding over the drumbeat.

'These people are only play-acting,' said Jana with sudden vehemence. 'Look – mistresses and slaves, as they would like to be. But in the morning they'll all be dressed in suits, sitting behind desks. It is a game, nothing more. It is decadent.'

Caspar laughed. 'What better game than decadence,

sweet Mistress?' he purred. 'I am your slave – Netta too, and are we not happy thus?' Jana slapped his face, without altering his wide smile. 'Thank you, Mistress,' said Caspar, his eyes twinkling. 'Was it my film that has inspired you?'

'It was my – but yes, it was your film, Caspar.'

'Only a slap for punishment, Mistress?' said Caspar with an impish smile. 'You haven't forgotten my earlier impudence, surely. You promised chastisement.'

'And you shall have it, Caspar. Real chastisement.'

'Thank you, Mistress,' he said softly. 'Netta too? She has earned it, surely, for her impudence with the African gentleman. I mean, to give herself without your knowledge or permission, that is surely against the rules.'

Now it was Jana's turn to laugh. 'That is a nit-picking interpretation,' she answered. 'You know very well that as my adept, you bear my authority when out of my presence, so she acted within the rules. Even as she is acting now, and I mean acting. Look at her, the slut.'

Jana's voice and expression were amused as she observed Netta, her skirt raised, receiving an enthusiastic bare-bottom spanking from a man naked but for a studded leather cock harness and a black executioner's hood. Her wriggles and shrieks, while pleasing to Jana's ear, did not seem commensurate with the severity of this playful punishment, though her naked bum was well reddened by the hard slaps.

'That is what I mean,' said Jana after a while. 'Look at your wife, Caspar, with her executioner; he's not a real executioner, she is not really on any scaffold. It is a play. And these others, pretty tableaux no doubt, and the crack of the quirt and tawse is sweet music to us all –' Gloria giggled nervously, while Cassie smiled and pursed her lips in a kiss to her mistress '– but these lovely bare arses squirming as they take their crimson are not the flesh of slaves, any more than the arms that flog them are those of real masters or mistresses. A slave works, suffers and dies, and his lash is no matter of pleasure. The ancient Greeks, prudent as well as philosophical, disposed of rebellious slaves by simply flogging them to death: a pretty example to the others, and avoiding the clutter of our English disembowelment. Slavery is, in a phrase, for real.' A moue crossed Caspar's lips, but Gloria and Cassie nodded sagely.

'I want to make these people know what slavery is,' said Jana fiercely. 'They dress as Greeks and Romans of old, but I shall take the chosen of them where we shall create the world they play at, to the place of my dream . . .' She stopped, realising she had let slip her secret, known only to Cassie. Gloria and Caspar raised their eyebrows, and Jana felt herself tremble. 'It is the island of your film, Caspar,' she said, feeling a strange desperation in her breast. 'The Greek island . . . of the black mountain. I had to climb that mountain, to fight a monster, and, oh, how could you have known?'

'I am your Dungeon Master, and Master of Arts,' said Caspar. 'I must divine your noble intentions, or perhaps coincidence played her part? We of Maldona must not doubt the power of coincidence.'

Jana nodded. 'We shall go there, and take our island,' she said. 'Only those worthy may accompany me: Cassandra my slave, and Henry – Aelfric, by his name of Maldona, and where is he at this late hour?' Jana permitted herself a scowl of discontent.

'Myself and Netta, Mistress?' said Caspar, a trifle too eagerly, Jana thought, pursing her lips.

'Yes,' she continued, to his evident relief, 'I shall have use for you, Dungeon Master. You shall select the candidates for our expedition, for me to make the final choice.'

'Sarah Pennington should come, Mistress,' said Caspar, 'and the twins Kate and Melanie. With your approval,' he added hastily.

'There will be tests,' said Jana, rising, but I am going to leave now. This idea preoccupies me; I shall administer no chastisement tonight. The next chastisement shall be a true one.'

As she rose, the drumbeat stopped, and guests paused in mid-caress, bowing their heads, and murmuring, 'Adore Maldona.'

'Gloria, Cassie, come,' said Jana curtly. 'We have not

time to await my slave Henry, nor young Sarah, wherever they may be. Gloria, you may sleep with us tonight, and I deem that you too shall be of my expedition.' Gloria's face clouded. 'That is,' added Jana, 'if you wish to be a true slave of Maldona.'

'The timing, Mistress,' said Gloria awkwardly. 'I'm expected for a dig, for a month at least, and I am supposed to leave next week: but, beautiful fate, it is there, Mistress –' she clutched Jana's breast-fan '– in the Aegean! One of the islands. I may come to you, later, if you permit, to this dark place you are taken with.'

'Yes, I permit,' said Jana faintly. 'Taken with? I wish it were only that.' Then, aloud, for all to hear: 'Slave, we do not take Maldona, Maldona takes us.'

Caspar and Netta, whose spanking had been completed to her evident satisfaction, accompanied Jana down to the front door.

'You can wipe that smile, Netta,' Jana blurted in a sudden rush of anger. 'What you've done here is nothing but a game, a travesty of the rules of Maldona. You too, Caspar – I think that here in what you call your dungeon, you are going soft. Decadent is the right word, and when we build the second Maldona, build her from bare rock with the sweat of our backs, and every muscle screaming for a respite from the pain of my lash, then you shall know what true punishment is.'

Caspar and Netta bowed low.

'Mistress,' said Caspar, 'there is the question of my – of our – punishment for my impudence this night.'

Jana smiled with icy cruelty. 'Of course you shall be punished,' she said, nodding to allow each lithe body to kneel, then lick and kiss the tips of her boots. 'And flogged tighter than you ever imagined, my sweet adepts. But not until I can do so as Mistress of the new Maldona.'

66

5

The Dungeon

'We'll walk,' said Jana curtly, as they left the house in Lennox Gardens. 'It isn't far, and I want some air.'

'You're angry, Mistress,' said Cassie. 'Is it because Henry and Sarah didn't come as promised?'

They turned right into Milner Street and Jana began to walk briskly towards the King's Road and the river, not looking at the others, who scurried respectfully to match her pace. Jana, her face stony, did not answer for a while.

'Have we – have I – done anything to displease you?' asked Gloria. 'Didn't you enjoy yourself at the party? I thought it was quite thrilling, especially that strange film. It was quite a turn-on. So bizarre –'

'I'm not angry,' retorted Jana. There was a silence as the three women walked on through the cool Chelsea night, their costumes as much at home in the austere white elegance of the streets as peacocks on a lawn.

'I think you are,' insisted Cassie, smiling. 'The film troubled you, didn't it? It was so like your dream.' She shivered, although it was not cold. 'Do you think Caspar is taunting you?'

'It's coincidence,' snapped Jana. 'How can proud Caspar know my dreams? Unless . . . unless you told him.'

'Not me,' said Cassie, hurt. 'You know that.'

'Well, I suppose I am angry,' said Jana at length. 'It's just that everything annoyed me in little ways, and they add up. Henry not arriving, the insolent! And the rudeness of Sarah, not being there for me!'

She bit her lip, not wishing her slaves, or herself, to feel how hurt she was at sweet Sarah's absence, at her

... betrayal. Jana remembered the smooth firmness of Sarah's bare bottom laced by her cane on that morning when Jana's sex had first moistened at beating a naked girl – her initiation to the rules of Maldona. She scarcely dared admit that in a strange way, the sly, elfin beauty had taken Jana's virginity.

And something in her heart still quickened as she thought of that tender initiation, and the girl who had seduced her. She wanted to love Sarah for that sliver of power she still held over her heart, but to punish her at the same time, to see her bottom smart under a hard cane, even though she knew that whatever pain made Sarah dance, Jana would always be –

'Beholden to her,' she said suddenly, out loud. 'That's the word, damn it.'

Cassie and Gloria, eyes wide, glanced at each other in silence.

'It's early,' objected Gloria. 'Maybe Henry is there now. We could return.'

Jana shook her head. 'We are not going back,' she said curtly. 'Not, I think, for a very long time. I shall miss London; how beautiful she is! Look around. All the lights and colours, a story behind every window, every curtain. The mystery of the city. My city ...' Her voice broke off. 'But I think I don't belong her anymore. And that makes me sad.'

We belong in the sun, Mistress,' said Cassie softly. 'In the cruel, naked southlands. You know it, as your ancestor Jana Ardenne knew it centuries ago.'

They continued their walk in silence, until they came to Cheyne Walk, and Jana led them to the riverside, where she leaned over and gazed at the still glinting water. They stood, Cassie and Gloria frowning in uncertain expectation, until, at length, Jana spoke.

'They say there are fish in the Thames in London again,' she said dreamily. 'The water is clean now. Sometimes I wonder what it must be like to be a fish, to swim so pure and free, in sweet silvery nakedness, every one alike. No cares, no rank, no striving.'

'Without striving, Mistress, there is no life,' said Cassie. 'Are you that unhappy?'

Jana turned on her fiercely. 'How dare you speak to your mistress like that!' she snapped. 'I . . . oh, Cassie, I'm not unhappy, not exactly, but there is something missing. I don't know what. It is that dream, it was telling me something.'

'You know already,' answered Cassie. 'It is telling you to leave London once more, and go in search of your island, and rule a new Maldona.'

'I am Mistress of Maldona!' said Jana with desperation in her voice.

'Jana,' said Cassie, putting her hand on Jana's neck, 'your pleasure is in striving, in conquering. To be the Mistress is not enough for you. You must always aim higher; to stay still shall never bring you contentment. It is not enough for my mistress to *be*, you must *become*, you must constantly recreate yourself as Mistress of Maldona. That is why we'll go to the Greek island, and find your paradise on the sea. Think of it: in Spain, the life of Maldona comes from the merciless sun which browns our bodies; the sea, there, is our sweat as we labour and writhe under the lash. But life is the ocean, and our spirits are islands in that ocean. So we must go, as soon as possible. Here in London you are enslaved by your very freedom. You have rank without power, except the power you have over Henry and myself, and now Gloria. Caspar and Netta choose to obey you, but they will obey whoever holds the title Maldona.'

'Not you?' said Jana bitterly.

'You know better, Jana,' said Cassie softly. 'My loyalty is to you alone.' She grinned ruefully. 'I suppose that is against the rules, and deserves punishment.'

Jana grinned too, and kissed her lips. 'It does,' she said. 'A very hard punishment, sweet Cassie. It will bring me joy to see that bum of yours glow for me, for to tell the truth, I am slightly annoyed at being deserted by Henry and Sarah.'

'The lights are on in your place, Mistress,' said Gloria drily. 'Should we see if there is anybody in?'

'And I bet your parfaite's harness is itching like crazy,' said Cassie slyly. 'Wouldn't you like me to take her off and rub some cream where she chafes?'

'You bitch,' said Jana with a slow smile. 'Yes, you're right, actually. Oh, Cassie, my love, you're always right.' And she kissed Cassie again on the lips.

'I'll always be your bitch, Jana,' said Cassie. 'Let's go up. I'll serve you champagne, if you like, in a nice bath, and then we – the three of us – can plan our journey, and talk.'

'You mean chat,' said Gloria impishly, and all three grinned, their eyes bright.

'You're right,' said Jana, as they crossed the road and approached her house. 'It's just that when you are in the middle of things, as I am now in London, it is hard to see them clearly. Looking back or looking forward is maybe the only satisfaction. It's like a whipping: the lovely trembling as you wait for the cane to stroke your bare fesses, and the stinging reminder of the lash's kiss afterwards, are the true pleasure. The stroke itself is a brief moment, whose treasure is expectation or remembrance.'

'Does that mean, Mistress,' said Gloria gently, 'that you would like something to treasure? Now?'

Her fingertips gently touched Jana's buttocks, and Jana shivered and smiled, drawing her breath as she felt her heart beat with excitement and her sex moisten at the thought of a whipping. She knew she needed to feel her bottom smart under a hard, loving cane.

'Mmm, yes,' said Jana, opening her front door and licking her lips in the darkness of her hallway.

The hallway was unlit, but a chink of light shone from the very top of the house. Cassie reached for the light switch, but Jana put her hand out to stop her, and shook her head, a shadowy smile gleaming on her lips. She tapped the intercom; it had been turned off.

'Let's surprise them,' she whispered, and on silent feet the three women padded up the carpeted stairway. 'This used to be two flats,' murmured Jana in Gloria's ear, 'but the lady who owned the downstairs retired to Worthing,

70

and I bought it, and knocked through. I haven't really put the downstairs to much use, except for ... a few innovations.'

'Worthing,' said Gloria sagely. 'I see.'

They came to a landing, where Gloria wrinkled her nose at the acrid scent of scorched wood.

'I had a sauna put in, of course,' said Jana.

'Of course.'

'And a few other things. Do you like saunas?'

'Why, yes, I love them.'

Jana nodded approvingly. 'And I'm sure you'll love my other things.'

Cassie giggled, and Jana put her finger on her lips. In silence, they continued to the top apartment.

At the door to Jana's flat, they paused. A beam of flickering light shone beneath the door, and there were voices from the closed room. Breathing quietly, the women listened to soft laughter and the clink of glasses. The voices belonged to a man and a woman.

'Any guesses?' whispered Jana. 'I'm sure you like a bet, Gloria, all Americans do. Six to four on it's –'

She thrust open the door and stepped quietly into the vestibule. Beyond them, half-visible through the sitting room doorway, were the voices' owners.

'– Henry and Sarah!' cried Jana, striding briskly into the sitting room, her face a beaming smile of genuine pleasure. 'What a nice surprise!'

Henry started, dropping his champagne glass, but Sarah did not move, as though the interruption was quite normal and even expected. She sat beside Henry on the leather sofa – the one, Jana remembered with sudden longing, on which she had first caned Sarah's bared buttocks – and Henry was making a clumsy attempt to withdraw his hand from beneath her skirt.

'You're not really dressed for the party,' said Jana, as Cassie and Gloria followed her into the room. 'Or are you?'

'Mistress,' said Henry, wearing his business suit, crumpled now, and his face crimson with embarrassment, 'I was

71

just going to get changed – I didn't realise how late it was. We met by the purest chance, you –'

Jana waved him into silence. 'And you, Sarah? To get back to Rosebush and change, then get to Lennox Gardens – why, you've scarcely started on my champagne – you'd never have got there before dawn, would you?' She stood above Sarah, and looked down at her with searching eyes. 'Or were you proposing to borrow one of my costumes? You know you are welcome. What fun, eh?'

Sarah smiled coolly and sipped her champagne. 'Oh, I'm ready for the party, Mistress,' she answered. 'But if you've left, I suppose there is little point in going. Please do have a glass of champagne with us.' And she tapped Henry's knee, nodding towards the kitchen. More crimson than ever, Henry rose awkwardly, unable to hide the massive erection which bulged against his pinstripe.

Sarah wore the uniform of Rosebush School: a short skirt of pleated grey wool, rumpled and pulled well up over her white silk stockings, with no move on Sarah's part to adjust it for modesty under Jana's gaze; white cotton blouse, tight against her pert, conical breasts, its hem pulled from her waistband to droop idly over her skirt; and the silk school tie, a red rosebush entwined with thorns, on a green background, knotted loosely round her neck. Her blonde hair streamed long and dishevelled, caressing the outline of her taut nipples, which not even the sheerest of brassières obscured. Lazily, Sarah scooped a few straying strands of hair up over her forehead, and smiled almost benignly at Jana.

'Not much of a costume for Lennox Gardens,' said Jana drily. 'I was expecting something more exotic. And aren't you too old to be a simple schoolgirl? You've already entered finishing school.'

'Exotic is for you, Miss,' said Sarah demurely, fluttering her eyelashes. 'I am proud to be a simple virgin of Maldona, to wear her uniform even here in London. And I think that my costume would seem quite exotic at Lennox Gardens, amongst all those lovely bizarre things, don't you? But please sit.'

72

Jana sat down beside Sarah, and motioned Cassie and Gloria to seat themselves on cushions. She breathed in the fresh, almost marine scent of the girl – Jana still thought of her as the elfin schoolgirl she had chastised on that very sofa – and felt a sudden urge to put her arms round her and kiss the wide, innocent lips.

'Nice of you to invite me,' she said, trying to be sarcastic. 'It's my house, Sarah, and –'

She swallowed, feeling a sudden electricity in her sex as Sarah put her hand on her thigh.

'You must think me awfully naughty for seducing your slave,' she murmured. 'How can I apologise?'

'Oh, you'll apologise, Sarah,' said Jana sweetly, 'but it'll be my game, not yours.'

Sarah's smile faltered for an instant.

'Mistress, it was my fault,' said Henry, returning from the kitchen with three glasses. All except Sarah stared at his crotch, and saw with impish but regretful smiles that he had subdued his erect penis. 'I met Sarah, yes, by chance, in the street actually, and as we were both going to the party, I thought –'

'Be silent, slave,' snapped Jana, 'and await my orders. Don't compound your offence with foolish lies. You have fucked Sarah before, and taken her whipping on my orders, so it is quite normal, if imperfect, that you should both get the idea to fuck unbidden.' Henry blushed, and busied himself pouring champagne. Jana sipped, and grinned brightly at her guests. 'Well,' she said, 'we may have our own party. It's not late, and I'm sure Sarah has lots to tell us, about her Greek trip, I mean. Caspar's film was most . . . attractive.'

Jana thrilled to see that for a brief moment, Sarah was nonplussed, before her smile slyly returned to its trusting serenity. Yet as the excitement of her power over the young woman made her tremble, so too she felt a fluttering in her belly and a seep of moist desire caress her fount. The shafts which thrust into her sex and anus now seemed like hot arrows of pleasure, their darts focused on the person of Sarah Pennington.

'Oh,' said Sarah, feigning nonchalance, 'you have seen Caspar's film.'

'You didn't expect that?' pressed Jana, now placing her own hand on top of Sarah's and squeezing her. 'Well, we saw you and the twins – Melanie and Kate? – and your most interesting adventures. And we saw your naked fount, Sarah, but so far away! How nice it would be to see her close up. Your sweet little tattoo. May we, please?'

She grasped the hem of Sarah's skirt and ruffled it, then slid it up an inch over her stockings. Sarah looked at Jana full in the eyes but said nothing, her grin flickering in mocking invitation.

Trembling, Jana pulled the skirt up over Sarah's thighs, to the tops of her stockings with their silver garter clips, up over the creamy golden skin and the white garter straps of delicate écru lace, to the sky-blue panties which clutched firmly over the swelling of her mons, and whose shining silk was dark and moist over her sex-petals, clearly outlined under the tight thin fabric. Jana smiled, and let her fingers rest on the wet panties, and was pleased that Sarah shuddered almost imperceptibly.

'You are wet, Sarah,' she said. 'So excited – your fount is streaming with juice.'

Sarah took a deep breath. 'You excite me, Miss,' she said faintly.

'Henry, I think, was busy here before I arrived,' answered Jana crisply. She began to stroke the swollen lips of Sarah's sex under the wet, oily silk, and was rewarded with a little moan in Sarah's throat, which became a strangled little yelp as Jana brushed her stiff young nympha standing between the ripe folds. She put her fingers between the white garter strap, and into the waistband of Sarah's panties, pulling them down over the swell of her mons. Jana smiled as she saw the smooth, shaven beauty of the girl's sex.

'Last time I saw your fount,' she said slowly, 'you weren't shaven, but had your mink cut in a lovely little butterfly. But now you're shaved – although you know well virgins of Maldona may not shave, and not even prefects are allowed to, until they achieve the rank of adept. I suppose, though, that your shaven sex lets us appreciate your rose's beauty.'

Abruptly, she pulled Sarah's panties all the way down across her thighs, and was obliged to pull hard at the wet seam which stuck obstinately to the fleshy moist folds of Sarah's quim. The other women craned to look, but Henry knelt, abashed, and turned away. They gasped at the sight. Sarah's mons and sex-lips shone with a dazzling swirl of rose petals, whose whorls disappeared inside the tender pink recess of the slit. Awed, Jana touched the girl's naked sex, and stroked her with reverence.

Sarah's smile had turned to a grin of triumph. 'Nice, isn't it?' she said, and Jana knew her unspoken challenge dared her jealousy.

'Very interesting,' said Jana, caressing the crimson wet fount with a strong, impersonal rhythm – as though stroking a cat's neck – and making Sarah's bottom wriggle. 'And very lovely. But we must see all of you.'

She unhooked Sarah's skirt, revealing the smooth bare thighs, then unfastened the clips of her garter belt, and gently tugged the panties down to her ankles and over the buttons of her ankle boots. Sarah's sex was naked, and she coquettishly spread her thighs, placing her hand over Jana's on her bare quim. Jana felt the pressure as Sarah used her palm to rub her naked clitoris, and felt moisture hot on the skin of her own thighs.

But suddenly Jana withdrew her hand from the throbbing nympha, as Sarah made a moue, and then with her fingers grasped each of the sex-lips and pulled them hard apart. She gasped as she saw that the tattoo extended deep into Sarah's slit, the moist pink walls decorated with intricate flowering whorls.

'So beautiful!' she gasped. 'Oh, Sarah sweet, how it must have hurt!'

'Yes,' said Sarah simply, 'it hurt, but there is no beauty without pain. I am forbidden to say more, but you may look!'

She leapt up and assumed a crouch, her naked bottom

high in the air and her buttocks spread so that the bud of her anus was clearly visible. There, too, the rose twined; stems, leaves and petals which turned her whole sex and anus into a tender flower. Jana thought she had never seen anything so beautiful. But her expression was cold with anger that Sarah could think herself entitled to keep secrets from her, and insolently say so in front of others. Forbidden? By whom?

'Who gave permission for the tattoo?' she said, her voice trembling, angry at herself for being enchanted by the girl's beauty.

'Why, Caspar,' said Sarah.

'He had no right!' cried Cassie.

'Caspar, in loco Maldonae, had the mistress's authority,' retorted Sarah.

'What's done is done,' said Jana with a cold stare. 'And beauty justifies all imperfection.' She saw Cassie and Henry widen their eyes at this heresy.

Sarah smiled and righted herself on the sofa, making no move, however, to replace her skirt, and sat unconcernedly with her thighs and shaven, tattooed sex naked to the company. She picked up her glass and sipped, then held it to Henry for a refill, her eyes on Jana. Nervously, Henry obliged.

'Imperfection justified, however,' said Jana sweetly, 'is not imperfection unpunished. There is also the matter of your intrusion into my house, Sarah. Now I don't know which is greater – my desire to hear the story of your adventures in Greece, or my desire to punish you.'

'I shall be punished, Mistress?' asked Sarah with a sly, innocent smile.

'Assuredly,' said Jana. And at that, Sarah's smile grew as wide and dazzling as a sunflower.

'Why don't I tell you while I take punishment, then, Mistress?' she said. 'With your permission.'

'Agreed,' said Jana, rising to her feet. 'We shall go downstairs, and it will give me an opportunity to show you around the lovely new things in my house. You guessed as much, didn't you? You look so happy at the thought of baring your bum for a lacing.'

'I obey you, Mistress,' said Sarah coyly.

'Then you'll find yourself telling me more than you intended. No one forbids except I, Maldona. Now pick up your skirt and panties, girl.'

And, roughly, she took Sarah's arm and led her to the bedroom.

'Take everything off, Sarah,' said Jana. She had left the bedroom door open so that the others could see. Trembling, Sarah obeyed, slowly unbuttoning her blouse and undoing the lace garter belt, then rolling her silk stockings down her thighs. Jana was pleased to see Sarah's uncertainty: her captive had imagined another, softer game. When Sarah was naked, she ordered her to crouch on all fours and take the tip of her boot in her mouth, placing the other hard on her neck. With Sarah in this position of obeisance, Jana summoned Henry and ordered him to be naked for her. His face clouded, he stripped, and without bidding, assumed the same position as Sarah, before Jana's feet.

'Both doggy fashion,' said Jana cruelly. 'Now, Henry, let me see you as a real dog. Your nose between Sarah's fesses, if you please.' And, sighing in shame, her slave knelt behind Sarah and pressed his nose and lips to the cleft of her cheeks, and at Jana's command, breathed deeply of her naked anus bud.

'Better,' said Jana. 'But you're neither man nor dog, my slave, unless I see that cock rise. Stand for me while I disrobe.'

As Jana removed her parfaite's harness, thrilling at the slow, satisfying sound of the twin tongues leaving her sex and anus, she saw Henry's prick tremble and become stiff, a magnificent pole hanging in lonely pride beneath the taut belly muscles. She suddenly wanted him, there, in the holes so recently empty, but knew that she must play her game to its conclusion. What secrets was Sarah forbidden to tell her?

'How lovely and stiff your cock is, Henry!' she said as she stripped. 'You may look at me, slave. Don't you want to put him inside me? Don't your balls long to spurt their cream into your mistress's cunt?'

'You torment me, Mistress, you know I do,' stammered Henry, his voice muffled by Sarah's bare arse-globes.

'Well, you'll have to make do with your little friend's nice bum, and that gaping cunt your fingers have made so sloppy wet. Does she smell nice? Breathe deep, my dog. She won't smell so nice when you are both sweating in my dungeon.' She felt Sarah's lips tighten on her bootcap. Abruptly, she pushed the girl's mouth away and unlaced her boots, and kicked them off.

When Jana herself was nude, she picked up all of Sarah's clothes and grinning fiercely, dressed herself. The virgin was smaller than she was, and her school uniform was a tight fit, especially the blouse, which imprisoned Jana's swelling breasts like a corset. She took her time rolling up the sheer stockings, a size too small, and the panties and garter belt. The tight panties hugged her naked mons deliciously, and she felt the cold wetness that had seeped from Sarah's fount against the now engorged lips of her own moist sex.

'Watch me fasten my garter straps, Sarah,' she ordered in a languid voice. Sarah raised her head to see her mistress re-embodied as herself, a cruel grin playing on her parted lips. 'Won't it be sweet to be punished by yourself, Sarah?' she said mockingly. 'But I haven't put on your tie: I'm keeping that for you and your lover.'

She bent down and deftly knotted the necktie around Henry's tight balls, making him grimace, then ordered Sarah to open her mouth and take the other end between her teeth. She did so, shivering, and with a kick to her naked rump Jana drove the pair on all fours back into the sitting room. Cassie and Gloria grinned at the spectacle; Cassie went to open the door of the apartment, and the three women followed the kneeling pair as Sarah led Henry by his tethered balls, clumsily crawling down the stairs to the first floor.

'You're hurting me!' cried Sarah. Jana did not answer as she slid her key into the lock of the leather-padded door beside the sauna. She had Sarah's arm twisted high behind her back, forcing her to remain kneeling. The door swung noiselessly open, releasing a powerful scent of rubber, pine and leather.

'My God!' exclaimed Gloria. 'It's beautiful! A dungeon! Here, in your own house, Mistress.'

'Go in, all of you,' ordered Jana curtly, and delivered a kick to the soft rose between Sarah's quivering bare thighs, making her squirm.

'Ow!' she cried. 'Oh, Mistress, I didn't mean –'

Jana kicked her again, and this time she was silent as the heavy door thudded shut behind them.

'This used to be a bedroom,' said Jana. 'I think you all agree it has changed for the better.'

She flicked a switch and the chamber was bathed in soft blue light, which gleamed from the smooth black leather that entirely covered the walls and ceiling, burnished so that the room's occupants looked at themselves multiplied in dark mirrors. The window had been filled, and the room was soundproofed to a cloying, intimate hush, in which Jana's voice sounded without echo.

'Rise, slaves,' she said to Henry and Sarah. Sarah released the leash which bound the man's balls, and the two rose unsteadily to their feet, keeping their heads bowed. 'You may inspect my dungeon, Sarah,' she added. 'I hope it is to your taste.'

Jana could not repress a grin of satisfaction as she followed Sarah's eyes around the chamber's fixtures, and saw the real apprehension in her eyes.

'Not quite what you had in mind, miss?' she taunted her captive. 'You'd imagined a nice bare-bum caning, over a cosy sofa, perhaps, and all tears and kisses afterwards. But after all, you have made the finishing school. Why so shocked?'

'This is more than I ever dreamed of in finishing school, Mistress.'

'And don't you like it? If you can't take punishment, you know the rules – you are free to walk.'

'I'll take punishment, Mistress,' said Sarah quickly,

almost nervously, as though the love of Maldona might be withdrawn from her.

Jana licked her lips. 'Then you know punishment is total, and unquestioned.'

'Yes . . . Oh, please, yes. I am naked for you, Mistress. Punish my body until I am worthy of your love.'

Sarah's words made Jana's heart jump, even as she briefly thought that perhaps this was another of Sarah's manipulative games; that she had already known what awaited her in the dungeon, and longed for it.

The leather walls were hung with a variety of shining metal instruments: pincers and branding irons, handcuffs, leg irons, gags and cruel masks, harnesses of wire, rubber and leather, a brass cache-sexe studded with sharp nails on the inside, thongs of steel with studded plugs for anus and fount, gags and clamps to secure breasts, balls, and all the most tender parts of the body in any combination of restraint and pain.

There were racks of whips and canes, all polished, and a pot bunched with long-stemmed roses, freshly cut and standing in water, their thorns gleaming spiky in the blue light, and their petals an eerie purple. In one corner stood an oaken pillory; opposite, a life-size human figure in cast iron. There were flogging horses, crossbars and whipping grilles, and the centre of the room was occupied by a steel frame of rods, pulleys and wheels, from which menacing rubber thongs dangled.

'I have my eighteenth-century forefather, Elias Ardenne, the slavemaster, to thank for most of my collection,' said Jana with pride. 'I've assembled a family collection; that, dear slaves, is how the Ardennes made their money – by slaving and the manufacture of the equipment of slavery. There is such beauty in these cruel things, isn't there? Look at the smooth lines of the brass knuckles, the crispness of the branding iron, the flower-like loveliness of the cat-o'-nine-tails. My dungeon is the poetry of submission, the nobility of torment.'

Jana's sex was wet with the desire to make Sarah's flesh squirm; her belly was tingling and her nympha stiffening in the tight, sweet prison of Sarah's wet panties. Her throat was dry as she gave her orders: hushed, her slaves moved to obey. Cassie and Gloria smiled with fierce joy but she saw that Henry's lip was trembling as he followed his instructions, and his eyes would not meet Sarah's. The rush of moisture in Jana's sex was quite irresistible as she watched her victim delicately strapped and prepared for her chastisement.

'Oh . . . oh . . .' mewed Sarah faintly as her nude body was twisted and bound. 'Please . . .'

'My, this uniform is tight, Sarah,' said Jana mockingly. 'I don't see why you should have the pleasure of nudity when I have to suffer thus.'

6

Sarah's Awakening

Sarah's eyes were wide with apprehension and her mouth hung open as she gazed at Jana's mocking smile. Her long blonde tresses fell awkwardly over her face, but she was powerless to brush them aside. Jana stood akimbo, surveying her captive, taunting Sarah by rippling the muscles of her arms and breast under the tight school blouse. She relished the strength and power that flowed in her, as though her biceps and breasts and thighs would burst their skimpy garments.

'My, Sarah,' she said, 'I think you've neglected to train – you're getting flabby!'

She knew this would hurt, especially as it was the opposite of the truth; Sarah was lithe and powerful, and the constraints in which her body now panted accentuated her hard ripeness.

She hung suspended prettily in mid-air, bobbing helplessly like a cocoon or larva of some giant tropical insect. Her lips hung slack and wide and a thin trickle of saliva moistened the corner of her mouth as she gasped for breath in her tight corset.

This was a corset of black rubber, laced across her belly with leather thongs, leaving her breasts free and forced into a harsh swelling by the pressure of the imprisoning garment. There were slits at its side which pinioned her upper arms, the forearms being locked around her knees, and the wrists fastened in handcuffs. Sarah's legs were folded on to her torso, the knees squashed against her belly and the calves high in the air, where ankle bracelets secured them to a taut chain which suspended her from the ceiling.

As a result, her body swayed upside down, her only purchase being the ceiling chain on her ankles. Her long blonde hair hung to the floor beneath her head, and her naked buttocks and sex were stretched helpless to the gaze of her captors.

'I expect you are wondering what form your punishment is to take,' said Jana. Sarah moaned and nodded, making her body rock on her solitary chain. 'Well, you'll get punishment, of course, but I want more from you than punishment,' said Jana idly. 'I think it would be fun to know more about you, miss.'

She went to the vase of roses and selected a long stem, then placed it delicately against the lips of Sarah's sex. Sarah started as she felt the light brush of the stem against her sex-petals. Jana laid it across her belly, so that the flower tickled her lips and the lower stem rested in the crevice of her sex. Then, gently, she put the rose flower inside Sarah's mouth.

'To be flogged is one thing,' she said. 'To be scourged by a sharp rose branch is another, and, Sarah –' she bent down and placed her lips on Sarah's cheek '– to be flogged on the naked quim is very special. I wonder if you can stand it. Or should I release you and let you go? You are quite free.'

There was a choked sob from Sarah. 'I . . . I can stand it, Miss,' she whispered, her voice muffled by the rose petals that filled her mouth. 'Oh, please be gentle with me.'

Jana laughed cruelly. 'Can this be Sarah I hear?' she said. 'Sarah, whose bare bum will smile under the harshest caning? I wonder if she will smile as the rose stems lash her, and land on those sweet fat sex-lips of her fount?'

Jana inclined and nibbled Sarah softly, first on one swollen sex-lip, then on the other, finally pressing her own open mouth full on the young woman's quim. Two pairs of moist lips met in a sucking kiss, and Jana thrilled as she felt the electric prickle of the thorns on her own tongue.

Sarah's fount was glistening and oily wet, and Jana licked some of the seeping love-juice before transferring her lips to Sarah's own. As she kissed her slave, she felt the caress of the rosebud against her mouth, and the wetness flow in her own sex, mingling with the moisture that had already anointed Sarah's soaking panties.

'You taste sweet, slave,' murmured Jana, then abruptly stood. 'But it would be too uncomfortable for you to be flogged upside down. That is a degradation fit for mere men. We must right you.'

Cassie, Gloria, and Henry stood back – Jana noted with satisfaction that Henry was fully erect at the sight of Sarah naked and trussed – as Jana manoeuvred two thinner chains from the ceiling, with clips on the ends, which she attached to the stiff plums of Sarah's nipples, making her shake and give a little mew of discomfort. She tightened the ceiling chain so that the pink soft nipples and golden breast-flesh were stretched taut and straining. Sarah was still upside down: the chain pulled at her breasts without taking her body's weight.

Next, Jana repeated this operation with two more chains, whose clips were slightly smaller. These she attached to the very lips of Sarah's sex, pinching her so that she squealed, and spreading the tattooed cunt-lips so that her gleaming moist slit was fully exposed. As Jana proceeded to tighten that chain, Sarah's full, fleshy lips were drawn upwards, enfolding the rose stem in a cruel caress. But still, Sarah's weight was carried only by her heavy ankle chain. Jana stepped back and smiled in pleasure at her work.

She bent down and cupped Sarah's neck in her palm, and with one muscled arm, lifted the woman up to a horizontal position.

'I expect you are more comfortable now,' she said.

'Yes, Mistress,' said Sarah. 'Will I be chastised now? Is this how you want to take me, on my naked bum and ... and my thighs, and my cunt, too?' She gulped.

Jana nodded. 'Your nice bonds, Sarah, and the rose stems you hold in your fount, mean that when I whip you, the slightest movement will cause you the most awful discomfort, won't it? We've trimmed the thorns, so that they are blunted, but still quite severe. So you will have to keep very still indeed, and the effort of keeping still as I lace your naked bum will be a delicious part of your punishment. But I can't stay holding you like this if I'm going to chastise you properly, Sarah,' she added, in a businesslike tone. She looked ominously at Henry, and drew a deep breath of satisfaction as she saw the naked man fully stiff, his penis standing above his naked shaven balls like a proud sapling. Now she addressed Cassie and Gloria.

'You may touch the man,' she said. 'Tell me if his balls are full of sperm for our rite.'

Flushed, Gloria touched Henry's straining balls with her fingers, then Cassie's hand joined her there, stroking and caressing the soft shaven skin, and letting their fingers stray up the trembling hard shaft until each woman had a fingertip on the swollen crimson helmet of the man's cock. Henry breathed heavily, shut his eyes for a moment, and sighed.

'Is this my punishment, Mistress?' he asked in a quavering voice. 'To stroke me and never let my balls release their spunk; to keep me in torment?'

With a curt gesture, Jana ordered her women to cease their caress.

'No,' she said. 'Punishment means a hard striping, my sweet man-slave, but you shall also serve the woman.'

Trembling, Henry was escorted to stand over Sarah's tethered body, his naked manhood poised over her head like a warclub. Smiling, Jana bent down and scooped Sarah's long blonde hair into her hand, then harshly lifted her by the hair, which pulled the weight of her body up; her face and lips were now directly under Henry's naked balls, and Sarah's nose twitched as she smelt his man-scent. Her body trembled almost imperceptibly as she breathed deeply, and Jana knew it was a shiver of desire.

Deftly, she parted the long tresses into two ropes and knotted them tightly round the shaft of Henry's straining stiff cock, so that when she let go, the weight of Sarah's body was taken by the man. Henry gasped, shuddered, but righted himself, the muscles of his belly and back pleasingly taut as he took the strain of holding Sarah by his cock.

Then, swiftly, Cassie and Gloria fastened the man's wrists into handcuffs, suspended by ceiling chains, which Jana tightened until Henry was stretched on tiptoe, arms wide and buttocks spread for a flogging.

'You must stay stiff for us, Henry, as you take your flogging,' said Jana, 'otherwise Sarah will suffer quite dreadfully. Look . . .'

And quickly she tightened the chains holding Sarah by her nipples and sex-petals, so that the chains were once again taut: but now, if Henry's support softened, her body would tumble back and her breasts and cunt-petals would take her full weight in a sudden rush of pain. Sarah knew this, and shivered, and as Jana looked at her full pink quim, she was not surprised to see Sarah's love-oil flow thickly in the new, terrifying excitement of her plight.

Jana completed her work by tying Sarah's hair above the shaft of the man's stiff cock into a bow that cascaded over his prick and balls like a horse's mane.

Sarah's lips almost touched the taut ball-sac, as she whispered through her mouthful of rose petals, 'Shall I be flogged now, Mistress? Please, please. Can't you see my fount is wet to feel your lash? All over me, on my naked thighs and croup, on my fount herself if you desire. Please, Mistress.'

Jana unhooked a pair of small trimming shears from the wall behind her and snapped them open and shut.

'Not yet, Sarah,' she said. 'You're not ready for punishment yet, and I have all sorts of questions to ask you.'

Gently, she pressed the shears against Henry's bare cock, and he gasped in horror. Jana smiled, and with a clack of her shears, snipped off a tuft of Sarah's hair. Sarah started in surprise, and moaned as her movement pulled the clips on her nipples and quim. Henry's naked balls were within a fraction of an inch from Jana's shining blades, and he shuddered. Yet even as he moaned, his cock seemed to grow harder. Jana held the cold blade against his balls and rubbed them gently, then stroked the shaft of his naked penis with the cold steel, before tapping the slit of his peehole. As Henry's breath became feverish, Jana grinned and took the blade away, to lay it on Sarah's breast.

'Sarah, we love you and – and we want to know you,' said Jana softly. 'Tell us who you are, tell the truth, when you are helpless and knowing that you have nothing to lose. The most excruciating pain awaits you whether you lie or not, and thus you may offer yourself the blissful pleasure of telling the truth. First you must tell us everything about your trip to Greece, the things that someone forbade you to tell – under what pain, I wonder? It cannot be worse than the pain you are shortly to receive. Imagine! A whipping of rose branches on your soft naked cunt!' She snipped another inch of Sarah's hair. 'When you are properly coiffed, you may tell everything. And I mean everything . . .'

Jana reached forward and put her fingers inside Sarah's mouth, and took hold of the rose flower which nestled inside. Her fingers rested a moment on Sarah's moist tongue, and she felt her slave lick her fingertips and close her mouth round her. Jana felt her skin tingle with love as she felt Sarah's warm wet mouth and lips caress her fingers, and sighed as she looked at the soft curves of the girl's body, the perfect breasts and buttocks, so firm and gentle, yet so beautifully contorted by their harsh bonds.

She breathed deeply, smelling the sweat which glistened on Sarah's body, and realising that her powerful girl-scent was not the scent of fear, but of overwhelming desire, a desire which matched the tumult of Jana's own longing. Her quim flowed with moisture, and she ached to press her petals to the glistening oily cunt-petals of her helpless slave.

She snapped off the head of the rose, and withdrew her trembling fingers, then swiftly lifted her skirt – Sarah's skirt, still sweet with her perfume – and pulled out the waistband of the panties, then opened the swollen lips of her cunt and pushed the rose, wet from Sarah's mouth, inside her as deep as she could.

Sarah's body trembled as she hung, bathed in the blue light of the dungeon, and Jana looked at her smooth thighs, the buttocks tight and trussed, and wanted to kiss every inch of her bare skin. She thought that in the beauty of her helplessness, Sarah was the loveliest creature on earth.

'Now –' said Jana.

Suddenly Sarah interrupted her, moaning convulsively and then began to speak in a low, soft monotone, as though from far away.

'Mistress,' she said. 'My Mistress, hear me, please.'

Jana knelt, her shoulder touching Henry's quivering thigh, and motioned Cassie and Gloria to kneel also. They obeyed, eyes riveted on the tethered girl, and smiling wide in awe. It was as though the place was imbued with the sanctity of an ancient oracle, where the darkness and mingled perfumes of sweat and womanhood conspired to summon numinous truths from the naked sacrifice who trembled in her bonds. Cruelly, the naked priestesses surveyed the tamed body of the godlike man-slave, straining in his fetters, his eyes filled with the foreknowledge of his own punishment.

Jana knew all at once that this was no playful chastisement: that her chamber of punishment was revealed as a temple and that she had conjured a presence that must be heard, through the medium of Sarah Pennington's body, and obeyed.

'I hear, Sarah,' said Jana gently, holding her blade against Sarah's naked breast. For a moment, looking at Sarah's body, blonde hair and elfin face, she thought she was looking at a younger, more slender version of her own self. Sarah breathed sharply, almost sobbing, and Jana felt an electricity surge in her breasts; she knew, somehow, that Sarah felt the same, that she was going to take her punishment not for herself, but for her mistress, as she was now going to speak for her, to say what Jana dared not confess . . .

Jana knew that Sarah, in total, helpless submission, was manipulating her, just as she had once expertly provoked her into giving a bare-bottom caning as punishment for an impudent, unconcealed theft. Once again, Sarah, submissive, controlled her captor. And everyone in Jana's dungeon knew it.

Panting heavily, Jana raised her blade and sliced through a lock of Sarah's hair. The lock fell on Henry's bare toes, but he made no reflex to kick it off. Sarah moaned, as though her body had been stabbed.

'Spank me, oh spank me hard, my bum's all bare under my panties. Pull my panties down and spank me on my bare bum, please, I'll do anything if you'll make me all sweet and hot and red. Yes, my panties off, the silk sliding down my thighs, how cool the air is on my fesses. Please warm them for me, tickle me hard, oh yes, *yes*! That was so good, and – yes! God, do it harder, oh, oh, again, again, see how I'm wriggling. You are so strong, your hand so dry and hard, like a lovely polished club, spanking my bare bottom, see how they squirm for your strong hand –'

'Sarah!' cried Jana. 'What is this? Who is spanking you?'

'She's regressing,' said Gloria urgently. 'She's in some kind of hypnosis. Let her go through with it, Mistress. It's healthy – she'll say things you would never hear otherwise. But continue your treatment, go on cutting that beautiful hair. It must have something to do with her regression; a remembered sacrifice.'

Jana lifted her blade and snapped it, so that a thick tuft of Sarah's hair fell, causing the captive to moan, as though the cutting of the tress wounded her physically. Then her moan became quicker, and her body shook with little gasps and sighs. Her voice was now urgent with remembered desire, remembered dreams.

'Such lovely hair,' she whispered, 'so soft and long, like a girl's, like mine.'

'Whose hair?' demanded Jana. 'A boy's?'

'Such a beautiful young man, and I had to hurt him. How I hated to hurt him, and how I longed to be hurt in his place. And how I hated him for making me want it!'

Jana snipped another lock of Sarah's hair, with cruel suddenness, and Sarah gasped. Her mouth opened wide and her lips brushed Henry's tight balls, making him wince. Jana smiled, her eyes hooded and nostrils flared in cruel desire. Only a few strands of blonde hair held Sarah's head up, tethered to the shaft of Henry's cock. Her mouth, unconsciously, lapped at the man's balls, while her teeth stroked the taut wrinkled skin, as though searching to hold herself there. Gloria's eyes met Jana's and her mouth opened wide in astonishment. Jana nodded.

'Yes,' she said, glancing up at Henry. 'With her hair no longer supporting her, dear Sarah shall have to find another hold. What better than –' she nodded at Henry's balls. 'You'll take pleasure, won't you, slave? To support the sweet head of your friend while I flog her? Her pretty teeth biting you in that soft place, holding herself by your manhood. True dependency Aelfric, my love –'

'I obey you, Mistress,' said Henry, his voice cracking. The clash of the blades echoed in the chamber as Jana severed another strand of Sarah's mane.

'Ooo . . .' moaned Sarah. 'It was by the water, the soft cool water that caressed me as I swam, naked like a fish, lovely under the sun's rays, floating and diving, and the water swirling on my belly, my thighs, my breasts, as though I were a sweet mermaid. Then I drifted close to the shore, and swam under the branches of a willow tree. They stroked my bottom, gently yet sharp and stinging with a little prickle. My bare bum, all wet and glistening in the sun, and I felt the willow stroke me there. I felt an electric shock, as though someone had touched my nympha, my sweet little acorn. I had never felt such a thing before.

'I swam back under the willow branch and let her caress my bum again and again, and now my fingers were caressing me too, my clitty, my hard little nympha, glowing and shivering and all electric as I flooded with lovely warmth. My fount was all oily and wet, my juices floating away in the soft water, and I thrust my bum up against the branches, longing for them to stroke me harder . . . to whip me, ever so gently. And then the breeze, as though by magic, stirred them, and I felt them dance to me, the softest of lacings on my naked skin but enough to make me shiver and cry out.

'I came! Oh God, it was the most delicious feeling I had ever had. I seemed to explode with pleasure as that sweet willow caressed my bare bum, moved by the soft wind to whip me so gently, as water-flowers lapped against my breasts, and fish, little golden darting fish, swam round me as though worshipping my beauty, as though I were one of them. I had never before felt the ecstasy of being bare in the sun and the water, and a gentle tree whipping me with her leafy strokes of soft love, beating me in adoration of my beauty.

'I opened my eyes and saw they were not my only worshippers. Behind the tree I saw two bright eyes.

'I imagined a faun, a foal or deer, that joined in the chorus of silent worship in that glade, but no, it was a two-legged beast. A man. All I saw were the eyes, staring, fixing me with a fiery gaze, but I knew it was a man, his eyes full of power and glowing with a desire that I had never seen before. It was pure, naked desire, naked as my own body, without knowledge or conscience of me except that I was a woman, I was a female helpless in water, and suddenly I was afraid. Dazed by the sun, I imagined some fierce satyr, all hairy and bellowing, half-man, half beast, with . . . with a great cock that would thrust and split me with its lustful strength . . . I was confused; mesmerised by those flaming eyes.

'He stepped out from his covering, and I gasped, for he was no satyr but a boy, naked like me, his white body smooth and hairless, but for a lovely mane of golden hair that swam round his brow, and a forest of glistening golden curls there, between his legs. And he was erect as I imagined a satyr. Full and proud he stood amongst those curls, a cock so hard and pink and shiny-tipped that I had never felt such terror nor such desire. He was quite unashamed, and smiled to me, to my heart and my womb, with his beautiful white teeth.

' "I swim here, Miss," he said simply. "But you've beaten me to it. And see what you've done to me." He grinned, making no attempt to hide his stiffness, but rather the reverse, laughing in pride at his rampant cock. And I blushed; I felt myself blush all over! He had seen me, seen me caress myself and writhe to the strokes of the willow branch on my naked bum!

' "I can do magic, you know," he said, almost casually. And then there was a strange thing: he touched the tip of his cock, the shiny crimson helmet, and made his cock jump and twitch, as though he had loosed some beast from its cage, and from his forest of curls, a butterfly flew up! It was golden like his hair, like my own, with pretty blue stripes. I watched as the butterfly fluttered towards me – I couldn't breathe because he was so beautiful – then landed on my bare wet breast, and stayed there, fluttering his wings to nuzzle at me. And I felt myself getting all wet in my fount again!

' "My butterfly is thirsty," he said, stepping closer to the river bank. "He needs to drink from your breast, Miss." I felt the wings of the butterfly beat against my nipples, felt them stiffen, and I thought the young man very beautiful, as though he were the butterfly lapping at my breast. He slipped into the water, and floated to my side, and I made no move to resist as he put his hand on my breast and scooped up his butterfly. Then he released the little creature, and it fluttered up into the branches of the willow tree, where it settled on a twig, as though watching us.

' "We have no need of him now," said the young man, and kissed my breast, his tongue flickering against my stiff nipple. I could not resist, I felt so beautiful, as though all the loveliness of that sunny glade and the soft water and the bright butterfly were flowing through the trembling bare nipple of my breast. I was all gooseflesh! And my fount was flowing like the water that lapped my body.

'It was like a dream; he took me, his stiff cock finding my open fount surely and deftly, and entering me under the water, which rippled and sucked at our bodies as he fucked me so gently yet so hard, swimming into me and against me as though I were a waving anemone and he a fish, kissing my lips now as he fucked and bathed his strength in my woman's oils. He made a little sigh, his hands clutching my fesses, as he worshipped me with his seed, and I convulsed; his hand stroked my nympha and I came with him, suddenly imagining, wishing, that his soft hand were a willow rod caressing my bare bottom with whipstrokes! I sighed as I came for him, my breath harsh, and he grinned, and made a little purr of satisfaction, as his head sank to my shoulder.

'I was breathing hard; I had never experienced orgasm with a man's body before. My boyfriends seemed feeble creatures indeed now. The young man whispered in my ear that my fount was a rose, and he would worship her. He carried me from the water, and laid me on the grass, and then placed his head between my thighs, and I felt his hair kiss my belly as his lips kissed my petals. He licked me and purred, until I became all wet again, and then he turned round and lay on top of me, his hardness next to my lips.

'I was helpless with new desire, and took his penis into my mouth, sucking her like a soft jewel, while I felt his tongue lap my clitoris, my stiff little tingling nympha. We tongued and caressed each other thus for an age, until I felt his seed bathe my lips and tongue, and come hot into my throat; my own belly shook and I glowed and tingled, as I climaxed once more, and so sweetly. It was then that he became stern and begged me for forgiveness.

' "Forgiveness?" I said in surprise. "It was lovely – so strange. You sweet man, why must I forgive you?"

' "For taking you against your will, Miss," he said, all solemn, and I laughed.

' "Against my will! Why, that's silly!"

' "No," he said, "and you must punish me – *then* forgive me, if you will. I have drunk of your sea, the liquid of your womb, and have spilled my seed in the temple of your mouth." He sounded like a priest!

' "You are so serious, you love," I said, kissing him.

' "Yes – and you shall make me squirm for it, Miss."

'I must have looked puzzled, though excited too, for I think I guessed what he meant. He laughed now, with a lovely deep voice that seemed almost too manly for that sweet boy's body – although how could that big cock, still trembling and half-stiff, so thrilling to see, let me think anything different? He said softly that at school he had been used to punishment, and had come to realise it was a necessary part of pleasure, and, a strange thing, of worship. It was awfully thrilling to understand that this wild, beautiful man worshipped me, worshipped my womanhood!

'He told me to snap some willow branches – light, springy ones, about five or six – and, shivering, I obeyed his order! All was so quiet except for the cracking of the branches as I broke them, and each snap made my spine tingle with joy, for I knew what was going to happen, what he would make me do, and that I should gain the strangest, most wicked pleasure from it. I was going to thrash a man; thrash him with rods on his naked buttocks! The thought had me wet, trembling, and I felt a sudden surge of rage at him for having used me for his pleasure – I was conveniently forgetting my own – and now to use me further, for this new wicked delight. I was annoyed at him, and at myself for allowing such excitement to invade me, that now I truly wanted to hurt him!

'He saw the fire in my eyes, and smiled softly. He *knew*! I held my willow branches and he pressed them into a quirt, his hands on mine. Then, as I stood, flexing my cane, he picked daisies and buttercups from the grass and braided them swiftly into a little crown, which he placed with solemn reverence on my hair. I felt so beautiful and full of a strange power, and nodded to him, without speaking, that he should position himself for his punishment. He knelt on all fours, his head in the grass, his lips nestling in flowers, and his smooth bare bum-cheeks thrust up so pale and tight to receive my lashes. The muscles of his back and bum rippled beautifully as he crouched, abased, before me.

'I raised my quirt of willow branches and stroked him with it, not hard but timidly, and he made a little sigh. I was surprised at the vivid red that flamed so fast and prettily on his naked flesh, like a new flower I had grown. My next stroke was harder, and made him flinch, so I could see it hurt. And then I lifted my arm high, my body dancing with fire and pleasure, and delivered a blow that I was sure would make him yell! He did not: instead his whole bare body trembled – relief? pleasure? – and he made a low moan deep in his throat. My quim was so very wet. It was fabulous!

94

'I was now truly inflamed with my desire to chastise him – for being so bold, so importunate, so beautiful! I felt he had no right to be beautiful, to infuse my pure body with his beauty, and with the longings he had awoken in me . . . although I knew it was the caress of the willow on my bare bum in the water which had started the awakening of me. As I flogged his naked buttocks, I thought that perhaps he was the spirit of the willow come to life; except that the willow was supposed to be flogging *me*! The wickedness of this thought made me lash him as hard and cruelly as I could, as though to drive a demon from myself. But the harder I flogged, the softer and sweeter were his moans of pleasure, the more thrilling the squirm of his crimson bum, and the wetter I felt in my quim!

'I must have given him at least a dozen cruel strokes and his bum was a livid crimson blossom when I laid the quirt aside, and, panting and trembling, touched the soft flogged skin of his red buttocks. I told him it was over, and that he had learned his lesson. How silly I felt. But he did not rise: instead, with tears on his cheeks – tears of thankful joy – he turned and kissed my feet, licking my toes!

' "You are sublime, Miss," he whispered. "I am well thrashed – for you see a thrashing must be given by a woman. For a wicked male to submit to the avenging power of his goddess is the highest pleasure, the noblest service. In chastising the soft globes of my body, Miss, you grasp my soul and love her . . ."

'I couldn't think of anything to say – what I longed for was too strange, even now. I longed for the man to take me, and make me submit to the lash in my turn. It was as though the rite were incomplete. But after kissing my feet, he rose, and kissed the rod that had beaten him, and then, his face flushed and dreamy with tranquil wisdom, that filled me with envy, he turned to go. I yearned to feel that wisdom, that beauty which suffused his punished naked body! He did not look at me again: his head was bowed. I expected him to fetch his clothing, but then saw he had none.

' "You came here . . . nude?" I gasped, and he nodded

shyly, yes. "You . . . you will come again?" I said, and then he looked up wickedly and grinned, before turning and slipping back into the leafy forest whence he had come. I called to him and said wait, and rushed after him, but he had gone, his only trace the whisper of the branches at his passage. I was in turmoil; desire, sadness, rage and bitterness filled me. Men! I thought, they only want to use a woman, and how I wished to be used by that sweet man, whose name I had not even learned in the enchantment of our loving, used and whipped and loved until I was his veritable slave!

'Trembling with fury and desire, I took up my willow quirt and spread myself in his crouching position, my bum high and my thighs wide. Then, lifting my left arm as high as it would go, I . . . I began to flog my own naked buttocks, as hard as I could, flinching and shuddering at the pain of the rods on my bare skin, yet fiercely relishing the dreadful hot smarting. I lost count of the number of strokes I gave myself, but it most have been well more than a dozen; I lashed my bare bum, making her squirm till I thought she would burst with hot pain! And it was only when my arm tired that I ceased my beating, and sank to the grass, sobbing.

'After an age, I rose and swam once more, letting the cool water lap my inflamed skin; now my body glowed with a delicious warmth that was pain and yet beauty too. I lay floating on my belly, holding my breath with my head under the water, as though I were a water flower like the lilies which caressed me. And drifting like that, my fingers passed to my nympha and, a flower filled with love and longing, I masturbated to a climax, silent but for the rippling of the water as she worshipped my bare flower's body. I was no longer angry at my body, just full of longing and envy – longing to feel the pleasure *he* had taken by my punishment. And knowing that I too must know the joy of a beating from loving hands.'

7

Grecian

'You shall certainly have that, my dear Sarah,' said Jana softly as she snipped the last strand of Sarah's locks. Henry groaned, half in pleasure and half in pain, as Sarah supported her full weight from her mouth, her teeth biting on his naked balls, his massive cock fully stiff as the balls were held by the woman's teeth.

'Oh God,' he moaned. 'Oh, that hurts so much and is such sweet pain.'

'You mean "Oh goddess", Aelfric, for that is what we women are, goddesses. And now you shall be chastised, as a goddess must be chastised, Sarah,' said Jana calmly. 'Afterwards you shall tell me the secrets of Greece.'

'Please hurry, Mistress,' pleaded Henry, the slave Aelfric. 'It is lovely to have a woman's mouth on my balls, lovelier to have your mouth though – Oh! That hurt!' At his words, the suspended Sarah bit him gently. 'But this is a new torment for me.'

'It is supposed to be, slave,' said Jana as she flexed her cane. 'And it shall be a torment for poor Sarah as well. Her bare bum will sting now as no bum has ever stung before.'

Sarah smiled slyly, and her bare buttocks clenched in anticipation of the caning she craved and knew was going to get.

Jana felt her sex moisten as she raised her cane in the eerie light of her dungeon. The blue light made the hanging Sarah seem like a sea goddess, and the trussed Aelfric a sea god.

The first hard stroke of the cane on her bare bottom made Sarah gasp as her teeth tightened on Aelfric's balls, and Henry, the slave Aelfric, gave a little squeal of pleasure or pain.

Jana deliberately delivered the next stroke to the same place on Sarah's buttocks, the cane cracking on her bare flesh in the electric silence, and the woman's naked bottom jumped as though possessed by a devil. The slave Aelfric groaned.

'Please, Mistress,' he said faintly, 'I beg you to make this rapid.'

Jana smiled as she lifted her cane for the third stroke. 'Oh no, Aelfric,' she said, 'it won't be rapid. A proper punishment is never rapid. She is slow – a punishment is feminine, you know, always she – and we goddesses have the privilege of taking our time, for time belongs to goddesses, not to mere men.' She raised her cane and striped Sarah's bottom with another stroke, and Sarah made an 'mmmm' of pleasure. 'Yes, Sarah, you like it, don't you?' purred Jana, 'and I think all my friends like it too, seeing your bottom squirm like that. A good flogging will get more of your secrets from you, won't it?'

Jana noticed that Gloria had her hand deep in her fount and was pleasuring herself. She smiled as she thought, I have another slave who will do my bidding. I shall take her to the Island of Maldona.

Another savage stroke was delivered from Jana's cane to Sarah's bare bottom, making her quite crimson. Sarah wriggled like a hooked fish but moaned in pleasure as her teeth tightened on Aelfric's balls. Aelfric's penis, despite or perhaps because of his pain, was fully erect to its height of ten or so inches.

Jana tapped her slave's bulb thoughtfully, leaving Sarah to wince from her caning. Then, suddenly, she put her lips to Aelfric's bulb and licked him so that now he was moaning in ecstasy rather than in pain – though Sarah still had her teeth on his balls.

'Mistress,' he said, 'you are so kind.'

'A mistress,' said Jana, 'is never kind, slave. As you will find when we arrive at the Island of Maldona.'

Jana lifted her cane and delivered another cruel but kind

stroke to the naked bottom of Sarah Pennington, then turned around and lashed the slave Aelfric on his bottom.

'Oh, Mistress,' he sighed. She took her cane in both hands now, lifted her arms high, and brought the cane down on his buttocks with all the strength of her muscled arms. Her slave cried softly and began to sob.

'More, slave?' said Jana.

Aelfric sobbed again. 'Please, Mistress,' he whispered. 'Yes . . . beat me, Mistress. Make my bottom crimson with your love.'

'I will accede to that, slave,' said Jana tenderly, as she lifted her cane. 'I have many slaves – Caspar and Netta for example. And in Maldona I shall have many more. I warn you it shall be your task to select suitable slaves to rebuild the new Maldona on the island in the Aegean which I have selected, and where Sarah shall attend me.'

Sarah squirmed in agony and pleasure as another hard cut was casually delivered by Jana to her already reddened bottom.

'Mmmm!' murmured Sarah unexpectedly, from deep in her throat, as she hung on to the male slave's balls. She quivered in the spasm of her climax as Jana delivered a full ten strokes to her naked bottom. And at that the man cried out and creamy seed spurted in a jet from Aelfric's hard penis.

When the beating was over, Jana signalled that she could be released and the slave Aelfric sighed in relief. But then Jana commanded that Gloria should take her place. And this time it would be Sarah Pennington who should administer the beating.

Gloria suspended herself naked, with her loving teeth on Aelfric's balls and her thighs bent up so that her bottom was well bared for a lacing.

Jana, ignoring Aelfric's protests and tears, bent down and kissed Gloria's wet sex – obviously wet because she knew she would receive a royal naked lacing from young Sarah. Jana let her lips linger on Gloria's stiff nympha, and licked her until she could glory in the taste of the American woman's salty juices.

Gloria smiled and sighed in the pleasure of being tasted, as her teeth held Aelfric's balls, now accustomed to this new hardship. And Jana's lips stayed on Gloria's cunt for a long time, her tongue bringing her to orgasm as Sarah, her own bare bottom smarting, impatiently waited to deliver a punishment such as she had just joyously received.

Jana's mischievous tongue on the American's nympha brought Gloria to a violent orgasm, which had Aelfric the slave moaning at the pressure of her teeth on his balls. But as a slave must do, he stayed silent when Jana began the real flogging of his bare nates, with a four-thonged whip of metal-braided leather.

At the same time, Sarah was caning Gloria with a six-foot willow. Ten vicious strokes, and Gloria took every one without a murmur, save for sighs of pleasure and relief. It was very obvious that each stroke caused her to relax, and Jana wondered what guilt Gloria needed to be delivered from. Sarah Pennington, the submissive, manipulative beauty, seemed to take her role as domina quite seriously now, for she caned Gloria's exposed bottom with all the vigour of a headmistress. And Gloria, her teeth anchored to the slave's balls, moaned in ecstasy.

Occasionally, one of Sarah's strokes took her right across the exposed wet lips of her fount, possibly even on the nympha herself, and this made tears come to Gloria's eyes, but the only sound she made was to mew, and Jana could not know if it was a mew of protest or of welcome. She guessed that the mew was of welcome. For Sarah's strokes were harsh but careful, and her bright eyes could see what others wished.

As she flogged, she spoke in a dreamy voice. 'There is a sorceress on one of the islands,' said Sarah. 'Caspar and Netta knew of her but not where she lived. She makes the sacred tattoos on a woman's sex. But the twins Kate and Melanie swam and swam, sometimes riding on turtles' backs – I honestly thought they were mermaids! – and they found the island where the tattooing witch lives. She lives alone and calls herself Circe, and women must swim to her if they wish the sacred tattoo. I mean on the petals of the sex. Well, not just women, there is a sacred tattoo for men as well. On the cock and on the balls . . . I suppose that having the balls tattooed by a witch must be quite painful for a man. Perhaps not. Who can know? Kate and Melanie, the twins, told me this. They were quite curious to see. But there was no man there with Circe. It seems that the tattoo, when applied to a man's balls, makes him into a god, as it makes a woman into a goddess. Circe had a whole list of gods that her tattoos on a man's balls could make him, but I didn't know all the names. I think Apollo was one. But she was very quiet and very insistent that her work achieved her effect.'

Sarah paused in her work.

'Oh, please don't stop,' said Gloria. 'Please, sweet Sarah, don't stop. With every stroke from your cane I know you love me. I think it is the only way a woman can know she's loved. Is that crazy for me to say? The cut of a cane . . . on the bare, why it is maybe the truest expression of love, and love is what a woman needs most, whether from a man or another woman.'

'Love is what a man wants too, Mistress,' moaned the slave Aelfric as he felt the cane on his body.

'I beat you with love, my sweet slave Aelfric,' said Jana softly, 'but some of us are meant to give love by showing power.'

'You, Mistress?'

'Yes, my slave. That is why you are my slave, isn't it?'

'Yes Mistress, oh yes, don't stop.'

As Jana flogged Aelfric's bare back – the shoulders this time, not the naked bottom – she understood that most people need chastisement for physical pleasure, the intense sensation of the caning, but some need it to assuage some guilt, some crime . . .

Jana redoubled the force of her strokes on Aelfric's bottom. His balls were held in Gloria's teeth as she herself was caned by the crimsoned Sarah. Jana wondered, why does Aelfric – Henry in this world – need to be punished? Then she thought, because he has guilt from making so much money in the City of London.

Jana finished his beating and he sighed with pleasure and tears as she released him from his bonds.

He knelt and kissed Jana's feet, taking the toes of each foot into her mouth, and thanked her for his beating, at the same time as Gloria thanked Sarah for hers by a kiss on her creamy, smooth brown bottom and then between her legs, on her wet slit.

'Mistress, please let us go soon, together, to this Greek place.'

'Yes,' said Jana. 'I think Caspar has selected suitable slaves for me. We shall fly to Athens tomorrow, then take a ship to the island which shall be Maldona. But first there is a matter to take care of.'

'What matter, Mistress?' said Gloria hesitantly.

'I think I know,' said Cassie, as Jana the Goddess Maldona silently bent over and touched her toes to receive a dozen of Cassie's fiercest strokes on her bare. And then a dozen of Cassie's most tender kisses where her rod had striped her mistress.

'Well,' said Jana, her face and naked bottom both flushed with love, serenity and the pleasure of her beating. 'I think it's time to go to our Greek island.'

As the plane soared over the sparkling sea towards Athens, Jana inspected her group. Caspar has chosen well, she thought. There were the twins, Kate and Melanie, a complicitous pair who Jana suspected liked secrets. Jana smiled, thinking that as Mistress of Maldona there were to be no secrets from her, and she licked her lips at the vision of the twins squirming as a pickled olive branch caned them on the bare . . .

She squeezed hands with Gloria and Cassie.

Caspar had selected a German member for the group, named Thorsten. He was very tall, well over six feet, and his muscles bulged under his tanned skin, for he was a builder by trade, which was why Jana was delighted to have him. There would be much work rebuilding the old Templar castle into the new Castle of Maldona. Thorsten lived in London and was part of Netta's scene.

102

The group was small, but Jana knew that as the knowledge of the secret island of Maldona spread around the scene, there would be no shortage of eager young acolytes.

The flight attendants obviously realised that there was something different and exclusive about this group, and left them alone, especially when Jana said, loudly and mischievously, 'The worship of the female bottom is the highest worship a man can give. And man is born to worship woman. The thing is,' Jana said, rather casually, 'that all men are submissives, but all females are too, except for the chosen few of us who are mistresses. A woman's bottom is twin moons, Selene, to be kissed and worshipped by a male tongue, a male penis.'

Kate and Melanie turned around with mischievous interest, and Thorsten pursed his lips in pleasure.

Jana continued. 'When a woman takes a man in her anus, takes his sperm in that dark place, there is a particular pleasure and it is the pleasure of being worshipped for the round full beauty of our female bottoms. That is why we like to spank and be spanked, on the bare bottom. For, to a woman, the bottom is the symbol of life as a man's balls are to him. You see, my faithful, life imitates herself – a man's tiny balls are reflected in the globes of a woman's bottom. But his huge stiff cock is reflected in our small but powerful nymphae.'

Kate and Melanie giggled. Each was wearing a short skirt, one lemon, one pink, and a simple cotton blouse in the same colour, and as Jana continued, each parted her thighs, lifted her skirt – neither wore panties – and put softly caressing fingers to work on the rainbows of their founts. They began to rub their nymphae, their stiffening pink clits, quite openly, and soon assumed blissful smiles.

On boarding the flight from London they had been wearing lime-green tights, but as they approached their destination and the temperature started rising, they had no need of them and had simply taken them off, giggling. Thorsten had looked hungry, so Melanie had taken the two pairs of tights and handed them to him. He had sighed in ecstasy as he pressed the twins' soiled tights to his face.

Jana was delighted when this great German bear, breathing the essence of the now bare-legged and masturbating twins, could not restrain himself from opening his jeans and revealing a massively stiff penis, a good twelve inches in length, around which he decorously wrapped the tights that Kate and Melanie had bestowed upon him. Jana gasped – she had never seen such a beautiful thing before. Such a strong shaft, such a lovely crimson bulb –

Restraining herself, Jana continued, rather sternly. 'A man's buttocks are made to be taut, ready to be flogged by his mistress, in punishment for his insolence in possessing something denied to goddesses – in particular, Aelfric, your rather many-inched cock. How long is it? A good ten? I suspect so. I think when we have built the new Maldona you will get a lash on your bare bum for every inch of that impudent stallion.'

Suddenly an air hostess appeared, a blonde almost as tall as Thorsten himself, and, Jana instantly estimated, with a good 44 inches of breast-flesh that her height enabled her to carry with superb firmness.

'Would anyone like –' she began, then gasped in smiling astonishment.

'Thank you, Mistress,' said the slave Aelfric, and to the obvious astonishment of the air hostess, bent to kiss Jana's leather boot.

Then, to her further astonishment, the solid German, his naked massive cock fully erect, bent to kiss the other boot.

'Oh God!' said the air hostess. Then, looking at the worshipped Jana, 'Or should I say Goddess?'

And suddenly, to Jana's delight and astonishment, there in the back of the flying machine, the stewardess knelt and took Thorsten's massive penis right to the back of her throat and sucked until she had delivered full sperm. The stewardess's face was quite red with pleasure, and so was Thorsten's.

Jana figured that they had an hour to go until they reached Athens, and they seemed to be quite secluded at the back of the compartment, so she asked the stewardess what her name was.

'Sandra,' the woman said sheepishly, still looking at Thorsten's prick which, although she had milked every drop of sperm from it, was still standing to its full height, with Thorsten grinning like the evil but useful bear Jana knew he was.

Jana looked down, and saw blue sea and green islands, which seemed to be smiling up at them. She now saw that the air stewardess had her skirt up, her pink panties down over her thighs, her cunt-lips open and was preparing to be penetrated by Thorsten's huge erect cock! Smiling, Jana decided to play a little game, yet a serious one, to show who was the true goddess up there in the sky, high above the sea.

She fetched one of her canes from her airflight bag – a very soft but springy rattan. She watched as Sandra, skirt up and panties down, sitting astride Thorsten, orgasmed and drew his sperm at the same time. Jana thought the smiles on both their faces were beatific at the beauty of the moment of orgasm.

'Right, you two,' she rapped. 'This is a respectable airline and bad behaviour must be punished. You'll both bend over and take six of the best, on the bare.'

Both Sandra and Thorsten had wide eyes. Jana told Gloria that she was to attend to Thorsten while she, Jana, attended to the woman.

Sandra knelt for her punishment. When she lifted her short blue stewardess's skirt Jana pulled her knickers back down her golden legs, then placed her tongue on Sandra's tenderest part, her nympha. Nestling between the swollen lips of her beautifully wet cunt, she kissed her.

Sandra moaned in joy as Jana's lips caressed her cunt, which was covered by the briefest mink of soft downy hairs, then as she felt Jana's finger penetrate her anus very slowly and tenderly, she cried out in joy, her cries suddenly muffled as the aircraft's engine began to howl in preparation for the descent to Athens.

'Please don't stop,' said Sandra, her voice faint.

'I won't stop,' said Jana. Her finger was deep in Sandra's anus now, the tall blonde woman moaning in pleasure.

Jana's thumb was on Sandra's nympha and by the dual pressure of forefinger in anus and thumb on nympha she brought her to a thorough climax. And as her bottom was writhing in orgasm, Jana lifted her cane and delivered six strokes to Sandra's bared bottom in cruelly rapid succession, then the same to the giant Thorsten's own bared nates.

'Oh thank you, Mistress,' said the air hostess Sandra, rubbing her flushed croup as the plane prepared to land. 'But I love a bare hand spanking too. May I have a spanking from you, sometime soon, on the bare . . . please?'

'You'll get it,' said Jana, 'once you join us, and become a slave of Maldona – the island castle that is to be the home of our Order of slaves and mistresses.'

'I will join you there, Mistress,' said Sandra. 'At once. And I suppose I must expect more than a spanking.'

'Yes indeed, dear Sandra,' said Jana with a smile. 'Now go and fasten your seatbelt like a good slave.'

106

8

Mermaid

At the Athens airport, in sweltering heat, a tall, young man with a perfectly combed head of shiny black hair and wearing a crisp yachting uniform greeted them with a white-toothed smile. He bowed, and Jana acknowledged his bow with what she hoped was regal hauteur.

'Madame Jana?' he purred.

'Yes. I take it you are Chris.'

'Correct, Captain Christopher Christophorides at your service, Madame. Mistress Netta in London has given me full instructions. Tomorrow I am to take you to –' he looked round nervously '– to your destination.'

'And tonight?' asked Jana.

'You will be tired from your journey, and I have booked you all suites at the Grande Bretagne on Omonia Square. It is the best hotel in Athens, opposite the parliament building. You will be able to see the guard – they are most picturesque, but very dignified at the same time.'

'Are they the ones who wear those lovely pleated white skirts and white tights?' asked Gloria innocently. The twins giggled.

'Why, yes,' said Chris. 'It is traditional Greek martial costume.'

'I love men wearing frilly white skirts,' said the air hostess Sandra. 'And tights, and maybe one of my blouses, and some of my lipstick, not forgetting a nice pink frilly petticoat.' Her eyes twinkled and she touched Chris's hand for a moment, and the tall young Greek blushed, as though she had touched some secret chord in his heart.

'Well, this way, please,' he said, and led them to a

Mercedes stretch limousine, parked in a no-parking zone in front of the terminal, which had ample room for them all to squeeze into the back seats, except for Jana, who rode in front.

'The car belongs to Monsieur Caspar and Madame Netta,' said Chris proudly, as he pulled out of the airport and on to the shabby road into Athens. There was dust everywhere, shimmering heat, and noxious exhaust fumes. Jana felt her eyes water.

'Yes,' said Cassie, 'Athens disappoints at first. It is a choked Mediterranean city, like Beirut or Marseille. Athens is best seen at night.'

'The Acropolis by night is wonderful,' said Chris. 'I suggest you ladies and gentlemen rest for a while and then we shall walk out in the cool of the night to have dinner in the Plaka – it is where the restaurants and nightclubs are. And above the Plaka, the Acropolis, the illuminated Parthenon.'

'I know the Plaka,' said Sandra airily. 'I am an air hostess, remember? And I know the places to go.'

'Then,' said Jana, 'you and Chris can be our joint tour guides. But tell me, Chris, where do you stay?'

'Oh, I have a little apartment on Delphi Street, in the port of Piraeus,' he said. 'It is near my ship.'

'That is quite sweet,' said Jana, 'but to spare you the tiring drive back to Piraeus, I suggest you share one of our suites. Thorsten will not mind, will you, Thorsten?'

Thorsten bowed in obedience.

Chris stopped the car in front of the Grande Bretagne, which occupied the entire western side of Omonia Square. Opposite, the parliament building sported its promised complement of skirted men in tights marching solemnly. The twins smiled, and Sandra simply licked her lips. Flunkies in braided black and gold uniforms rushed to take their baggage, and Chris consigned his car keys to a garage boy.

They walked into the huge air-conditioned lobby. The heat outside was almost painful, and the light, hazed by traffic fumes, was blinding and white.

'This is the grandest hotel in Athens, Mistress Jana,' said Chris proudly. 'It was used as German staff headquarters – regrettably – during the Second World War. But it shows the Germans have good taste,' he added hastily, looking at Thorsten. 'I am sure you will be well pleased, Mistress Jana. The restaurant is first class, and the bar has the driest martini in Europe. If you need any assistance in finding your way around, please do not hesitate –'

He was interrupted by a tall man in the most splendid gold braid they had ever seen, who rushed from the receptionist's desk and, placing his palms together as though in prayer, bowed to Jana, who acknowledged his bow with a nod and a faint smile.

'Why Madame Ardenne!' he cried. 'How wonderful to see you again! Why do you not visit us more often? Your suite is prepared just as you like it!'

He kissed her outstretched fingers with a feather's touch.

'Thank you, Stavros,' she said. 'It's nice to see you again, too.'

Sandra burst out laughing and touched Chris's fingers, and he blushed again.

Jana arranged a rendezvous in the bar at 8.30, since the life of Athens does not begin until late, when the air is cool and the dust and traffic fumes of the sweltering day have cleared. Everyone arrived promptly, and Jana smiled in approval at the splendour of their costume. Clothing was light, but simple pastel frocks were artfully adorned with jewels, scarves, and earrings – Cassie had a penchant for huge hoops dangling from her pierced lobes. Jana herself wore a mini-skirt of pleated white silk, very like those worn by the soldiers at the parliament steps, and a matching silk top which left her arms and brown midriff bare, the soft cavern of her navel like an eye in the middle of her flat belly. Her feet were adorned with Grecian sandals whose intricate straps came up to the bottom of her bare, muscled calves.

Chris was every inch the Greek macho, with a white blouse, billowing like a woman's, open almost to the waist, and his chest jangling with medallions. His trim buttocks were encased in ironed, skin-tight designer jeans. He sat beside Sandra, who was radiant and the most feminine of all, in a flouncy orange mid-length layered dress which seemed as though she wore a rainbow of frilly petticoats. Her arms were bare and, Jana noted with approval, well muscled.

After glasses of milky ouzo – Thorsten sniffing the aniseed and changing his order hastily to beer – they went out towards the Plaka, where they found an open-air restaurant with a view of the illuminated Parthenon atop the Acropolis. The restaurant was full and they had to wait a long time for their meal, so that many bottles of passable white wine were consumed; Jana advised against the retsina obligatory to tourists, since the pine resin was only added to make bad wine digestible.

Every table was occupied by glistening, excited faces. Only one table, to the side, was occupied by a single person: a woman in dark glasses, her hair swept back in a demure bun, and wearing a shapeless dress with long sleeves and high neck, whose shapelessness was nevertheless redeemed by the brilliant marine azure of the fabric. She picked at her food and Jana decided she was simply a lonely woman, a strange thing in a city where it is almost impossible to be lonely.

Jana began to explain what they would find on the Island of Maldona: the old Templar castle and, what she hoped to find, the treasure buried within.

Gloria sighed. 'What a pity I can't come with you at once,' she said. 'But I promise I shall finish with my dig as soon as possible, and join you.'

The food came and they ate hungrily. It was the standard Greek fare of moussaka, roast lamb and salad with white feta cheese and black olives. When they had finished their muddy Greek coffee, the moon was full and high, shining down on the Parthenon.

'It's beautiful,' breathed Sandra.

'Let's go to a nightclub,' said Sarah Pennington.

Jana nodded her assent and Sandra led them down an alley to a smoky cellar where couples in various states of dress and undress danced. Jana was not impressed.

'Most nightclubs are the same, really,' she said, sipping brandy. 'We are going where there is no falsehood, my slaves.'

The only members of the company to take the floor were Chris and Sandra, Chris writhing and gyrating in what, he assured them with a sly smile, was an ancient dance from the islands in honour of the goddess of love, Aphrodite.

The music paused, and in the gloom, Melanie said, 'Mistress, isn't it funny to see a big mountain of rock in the middle of the city? It is as though the past has erupted from the centre of the earth.'

'Why don't we climb up?' said Thorsten suddenly. 'Mistress?'

Jana nodded her assent, and soon they were scrambling in moonlight up the rocky slope towards the bright temple.

'Actually, it is not the original Parthenon,' said Chris, showing off to Sandra. 'That was blown up in 1687 when a Turkish arsenal of gunpowder exploded during the Venetian siege of Athens.'

'This one is just as nice,' said Sandra, pressing his hand.

Panting, they reached the top of the mountain, and stood entranced and silent, looking at the lights of the vast city twinkling like so many stars in the pale moonlit night.

'Well,' said Jana, 'we must make an early start tomorrow, so we shall return to the Grande Bretagne for a nightcap, then to bed.' She looked round. 'Where are Chris and Sandra?'

'I bet they're fucking,' said Sarah Pennington simply.

'Slave!' snapped Jana. 'I shall not tolerate vulgarity! You have earned yourself a caning!' She smiled as she saw Sarah's satisfied grin, and could feel nothing but love for the girl and the full bottom whose naked flesh her cane had caressed so many times.

'Now, Mistress?' whispered Sarah hopefully, her eyes pleading.

Jana grinned. 'I have no cane, slave,' she said. 'But . . . perhaps a bare-bum spanking would suffice.'

'Very well, Mistress,' said Sarah humbly, bowing her head.

111

'Better still, a slippering.'

'Oh, yes, Mistress. I must atone for my vulgarity.'

'Where *are* Chris and Sandra?' said Jana impatiently. 'Well, as we await their return from whatever murky pleasures they have been taking, I suppose we can pass the time with your punishment, Sarah.'

Sarah's white teeth sparkled in the moonlight as she grinned. The minx, thought Jana with a smile, she has tricked me again. Just like the first time she provoked me to punish her.

'Sarah,' she said thoughtfully, 'I rather think you must run the gauntlet. All of you, those wearing sandals, remove one – Thorsten, you your belt – and form a line, standing at the ready.'

'The gauntlet, Mistress?' said Sarah, in a voice that trembled slightly.

'Yes. You shall run – no walk, for these rocks can be sharp, and I don't want you to fall and hurt yourself – and as you pass, each of my slaves shall lace you on the bare bum with one stroke of shoe or belt. And when you have completed one pass, you shall turn around and repeat it, and so on until I give the word to stop.'

'Oh,' said Sarah uncertainly.

'You are wearing panties?'

'Yes, Mistress.'

Sarah wore a tunic of bright blue silk, pleated like her mistress's, with a belt to pinch the waist.

'Remove them and hand them to me.'

Sarah did so, and Jana resisted the urge to press the panties to her lips. These were also of blue silk, but adorned with little shiny starfish, which Jana found adorable.

'Now lift your skirt and knot it up above your navel with your belt. Yes, that's right. Go to that rock there –' she pointed to a boulder about twelve metres away '– and start your walk when I give the order. Slave Cassandra, hand me your other sandal, please. It is not fitting that Maldona should be barefoot.'

Cassie did so, and Jana flexed the supple yet firm leather sole and smacked it against a rock, where its harsh crack resounded over the silence of the mountain and the murmur of traffic below. She signalled that Sarah should begin to walk her gauntlet.

Sarah began to walk slowly, picking her way along the rocky path, and it was Cassie, grinning wickedly, whose muscled arm, toughened by the regime of Maldona, delivered the first stroke to the full bare bottom gleaming under the pale light of Selene, the moon goddess. Sarah gasped at the force of the blow, then gasped again as Thorsten laced her with the buckle end of his belt. Henry also struck with the buckle end.

Jana watched, entranced, as Sarah's tattooed fount approached her, the rose petals seeming to quiver and flow like ocean waves as her thighs and buttocks shook at each blow. The beating took place in total silence, and after the fourth vicious slap to her bare croup, Sarah made no more sound but kept her lips closed tightly. The only sound apart from the crack of leather on her naked buttocks was the breath that came harsh and deep from her young breast.

When she reached Jana, her eyes glistened with salt tears.

'Had enough, Sarah?' whispered Jana, so that the others should not hear. Sarah shook her head – no, not enough. She turned and presented her naked fesses to her mistress, who raised her arm high and delivered a fierce blow to Sarah's already crimson buttocks, making them clench and quiver. Such was the force of Jana's stroke that Sarah shook and gasped anew. She began the second walk of her gauntlet, her buttocks shuddering and deepening in red now, as her body shook in silent torment. Jana saw her body and the moon above, and her now short blonde hair adorning the orb of her head. Above, the silver moon, she thought, below, the gold of the sun, the gold of the corn, and below that, the red fire that is within the earth. Sarah is complete.

The beating continued relentlessly, until Sarah had walked her gauntlet a full ten times, and once more Jana whispered, 'Enough, Sarah?' and once more Sarah, tears streaming down her cheeks, shook her head.

113

'I say the gauntlet is complete,' said Jana in a loud voice, and clasped Sarah to her breast, covering her lips with kisses. Then she signalled to Sarah that she should turn and lift each leg one at a time, so that her mistress could replace the panties.

Jana knelt, and before fitting the panties snugly, she kissed Sarah's raw, reddened bottom as though kissing a lover's lips. And then the entire company of Maldona rushed to embrace the girl, smiling through her tears. Thorsten scooped her up and placed her on his shoulders, and began to parade her round and round the mountain top, to the cheers and applause of the others. Jana turned away as she wiped a tear from her own eye.

'How wonderful,' whispered Gloria, at Jana's side. 'Just like the ceremonies in the old days, when the priestesses of the goddess Athene were flogged on the bare back in this very place if they made any mistake in the recitation of a prayer; or the mysteries of Eleusis, in the shrine of the goddess Demeter, where her virgins were ceremonially flogged in order that their pain, the pain of woman as the earth, should wring crops from the earth every spring. It was a great honour to be so flogged for the great goddess Demeter.'

At that moment, the bright orange dress of Sandra and Chris's white blouse shone from behind a rocky outcrop.

'Well, finally!' said Jana acidly. 'We shall go back to the hotel, now. Chris, I hope you and Sandra have been absorbing the culture of this sacred temple of the goddess Athene.'

She looked more closely at the approaching pair, and saw that it was not Chris at all, but Sandra, with Chris's white blouse tight against her breasts. And in the flouncy orange dress, Chris smiled shyly with rouged lips.

Jana burst out laughing. 'You mustn't change back,' she said. 'You shall come back to the Grande Bretagne just as you are.'

Suddenly she turned her head; something had flickered in the corner of her eye. Something of the brightest azure. A figure, a person? She shrugged, thinking it must be a

114

trick of the moonlight. This sacred place must hold all sorts of magic.

They returned down the hillside to the Plaka, then back to Omonia Square and the sparkling chandeliers of the Grande Bretagne. Gravely, Stavros handed them their room keys without a flicker of surprise, and as they were served with their nightcaps, the blushing Chris, gazing adoringly at Sandra, received a discreet, '*Voilà, Madame*,' from the waiter. His smile became a beam of delight.

Cassie turned to Jana and said with a dry smile: 'This *is* Greece, after all, Mistress.'

The next morning Jana rose at 6.30, bathed long in the black and gold bathtub, reflecting that it would probably be some time before she could again enjoy such luxury, perfumed herself and applied talc and deodorant, then searched in her Gucci suitcase for something suitably maritime. The sea voyage to the Island of Maldona would take four hours from the port of Piraeus, and the sun would be hot. Smiling, she stroked with loving fingers her parfaite's harness. But this was not the time to wear it. She settled on a white cotton mini-skirt which showed a dangerous expanse of muscled bare thigh, sensible sandals whose sensibleness was offset by a golden slave bracelet round her left ankle to show that the Mistress of Maldona too was a slave, and a sea-blue silk blouse which she knotted up above her dimpled navel. Around her neck she wore a golden choker and then, impishly, she selected a long, thin golden chain which she wound four times around her bare waist, knotting it in front so that the ends dangled over her pubis, swaying when she walked. Thus adorned, she joined the others for breakfast. They were to depart at eight o'clock sharp.

Jana was the last to arrive, and joined the others in their coffee and croissants. Eyes sparkled with excitement: the prospect of a sea voyage, Jana thought, satisfies a primaeval craving, even if it is just crossing from Dover to Calais. Now, the mystery of their destination animated the group with desire, fear and curiosity.

Chris was once more splendid in blue blazer, white trousers and white shoes; every inch the captain.

Jana bit into a buttered croissant, and when she had swallowed, said innocently, 'I hope you and Thorsten got on all right last night, Captain Chris?'

Chris blushed and looked at Sandra, who smiled but did not blush.

'Chris and I got on very well,' said Thorsten gravely, as though to save face for Chris. He paused and added slyly, 'Because he was not there.'

The laughter that greeted this made Jana feel sorry, but not too sorry, for the wound to the sea captain's Greek dignity. She imagined Sandra and Chris slowly undressing each other – Sandra gently peeling off her flouncy orange dress, her tights, her knickers from his erect penis – then the two of them naked on the big bed, loving each other as the bright moon of Athene beamed through the window. Or perhaps on the balcony overlooking Omonia Square, where the skirted soldiers kept up their constant vigil. She found herself getting wet between her thighs and, fingers trembling, she dropped some jam, which came perilously close to her white skirt.

I should never sleep alone, she thought. It is wrong of me to sleep alone. Only slaves sleep alone.

She looked at Chris again and thought him unfairly handsome, then wondered if he would make a good slave. She imagined his tight buttocks bare and squirming under the caress of an olive branch, and had to take a deep breath and swallow to quell the onrush of desire which gripped her.

'Well now, it is time to move,' she ordered in as steady a voice as she could muster. She too was eager to reach the island although she dreaded it as well, for she knew it was the island of her recurring nightmare.

Baggage was fetched by porters, porters tipped, account paid and limousine delivered to the front steps of the hotel. Jana and Cassie embraced Gloria, who was to take a taxi to the airport for her flight to her archaeological dig, and Jana made sure she had the map coordinates to join them on Maldona as soon as she could. Jana already thought of the nameless island as 'Maldona'.

As Chris piloted the car into the chaotic traffic of Omonia Square, Jana glanced back and to her surprise saw the statuesque figure of a woman, wearing a dazzling azure dress and sunglasses, emerge from the lobby of the hotel, stare at their limousine as it passed her on the one-way system round the square, then stride purposefully in the opposite direction. Surely, Jana thought, there cannot be two such dresses in the world.

Long before they reached Piraeus, they smelled fish, diesel and the sea, even through the air-conditioning, and Jana's heart raced with an excitement she tried to conceal. Chris drove to a pier where his 80-foot craft lay proudly at anchor. On deck, two grizzled *matelots*, seeing their master arrive, hastily pretended to swab decks. Chris led them up the gangplank of the splendid ship, gleaming white under the beating of the sun, and installed them in a shady lounge, where a white-jacketed steward served coffee. Chris explained that he had to take his car to a secure lock-up only a few minutes away, and would return shortly.

They sipped coffee and examined their luxurious surroundings. The *Hesperides*, Jana understood, was Caspar's, and normally used as a cruise ship for private parties of those from Caspar and Netta's scene, who paid richly for the privilege of being able to indulge their fantasies at sea. The lounge was decorated with paintings and sculptures of delicate obscenity, much like those that adorned the walls of the house in Lennox Gardens, but all had a Greek flavour: satyrs proudly erect; bathing naiads combing their long hair in blue rivers and pools, while a salacious Eros, his penis monstrously hard, looked on, leering in undisguised lust; bearded Zeus pleasuring the goddesses Aphrodite and Demeter with mouth and cock, while the god Apollo attended to him between his buttocks . . .

Chris returned promptly and explained that they were free to rest in any of the six unlocked staterooms on board, or simply to sit on deck for the four hours of passage. He hurried off to the bridge, and soon Jana heard the sound of engines rumbling. The rest of the company excitedly went on deck to experience the elation of a departure, leaving Jana with Cassie in the lounge, finishing their coffee.

'Let's explore,' said Jana with a grin.

Cassie wore a simple, short white tunic with her hair swept back in a pony-tail, giving her a deliciously girlish look, and a fetching pair of large globe silver earrings, which Jana had not seen before. She looked closely at the curious indentations in the silver, and found that each globe was a tiny map of the world.

'*Where* did you get those?' she asked, trying to conceal her envy as they picked their way through narrow passageways.

'Portobello Road, where else?' laughed Cassie.

'I'm not sure it is permitted for a slave to wear such baubles,' said Jana thoughtfully. 'Perhaps I shall have to confiscate them and beat you for your presumption.'

'Perhaps you shall, Mistress Maldona,' said Cassie mockingly, 'but you must wrestle me for them first.'

'Insolence, too? Deserving of punishment. A grand beating, perhaps, or even a noble beating.'

'I know you are not joking, Mistress,' said Cassie quietly. 'And you know that I shall joyously accept whatever punishment you choose to inflict, and that my bare fesses shall always quiver with love for you.'

'Oh, Cassie,' sighed Jana, and embraced her slave and friend.

They opened doors and saw two of the comfortable staterooms, identically furnished with large beds, liquor cabinets, and the expected erotic paintings and bibelots. Each stateroom contained a flogging horse, a rack of whips, a rack of canes, and a rack of dildos prettily arranged in ascending order of size and complexity. There was one porthole, beside which on the bulkhead dangled handcuffs and chains.

In the third stateroom, Jana lingered to play her fingers over the racks of oiled, supple canes and whips. She found herself breathing heavily, and wondered if she should order

Chris to pack a selection into a chest, to add to the few instruments, including the four-thonged white whip of the Amir of Ubrique, that she already carried in her bag.

'Mistress!' cried Cassie. 'Look at this porthole! Isn't it curious?'

Jana looked, and found it indeed curious. The porthole was strangely at waist height, and she found that the glass slid smoothly back along oiled grooves to leave the window open. But it was no ordinary porthole: its rim was encircled by a steel belt backed with leather, which was connected by a screw to a bolt set into the bulkhead. Jana turned the bolt, and the belt moved. One end slid over the other, and as Jana turned, the belt, anchored to the bottom of the porthole, contracted to a circle the size of a quoit.

'Mistress, it is some kind of waist cincher!' said Cassie, her eyes bright.

'Yes,' said Jana quietly, 'I believe it is a punishment window. I believe something similar existed in the Castle of Maldona, when she was under the regime of the Amir of Ubrique. Errant wives had to lean out of the window as their croups were laced, so that the crowd could observe their misery. Much the same thing was inflicted on junior boys at our own Eton College.'

'You said I deserved punishment, Mistress –' said Cassie, already taking off her earrings. She handed them to Jana.

'They are yours, Mistress,' she said shyly. 'But please punish me for the imperfection of wearing them without permission.'

Jana thought for a moment, then smiled sternly. 'Very well, slave,' she whispered, her lips brushing Cassie's earlobe. 'I want you nude – I think you know how you should position yourself.'

Cassie stripped and gingerly put her head through the porthole.

'Oh!' she cried. 'There are handgrips here.'

Wriggling, she pushed herself through the porthole until all that Jana saw of her was the magnificent bare croup and the smooth long legs straining on tiptoe. She turned the bolt, and the steel and leather cincher began to contract around Cassie's waist, tighter and tighter until from outside she heard Cassie's muffled moan.

'Oh, Mistress,' gasped Cassie, her skin pinched into cruel creases by the tightening belt.

'Enough, slave?'

'Never enough, Mistress,' said Cassie faintly. Jana continued to tighten the belt until she thought Cassie must scarcely be able to breathe, then selected the longest, thickest rattan cane from the rack and stroked Cassie's bare buttocks with it.

'You know what this is, slave?' she said quietly.

'It ... it feels like a rattan, Mistress,' came Cassie's voice, as though far away.

'It is indeed, slave Cassandra,' said Jana in her sternest voice, 'and I propose to lace you on the bare with a nice tight six.'

There was a pause, and then Cassie said, 'Thank you, Mistress. But what a pity, here on this mirror sea, there is no one to watch my face of pain except myself, reflected in these blue waters.'

'Why, Cassie, there are the creatures of the deep, nymphs and sea gods, and all the timeless creatures of old who I am sure still watch over these sacred waters,' said Jana lightheartedly.

Without further ado, Jana silently lifted the cane high and brought it down on Cassie's clenched bare buttocks. The firm crack echoed through the metal walls of the stateroom, and Jana noted with pleasure the quivering of Cassie's fesses as a vivid crimson flush rapidly spread across the taut bare skin. A second followed almost immediately, right in the same place, causing Cassie to jump and her legs to tremble, and then a third, slightly lower, across the tops of her thighs. Cassie began to squirm uncontrollably, and Jana felt a delicious wetness seep from her fount.

'I think I'll take my time now, slave, and skin you nice and slowly,' she declared.

Cassie, though trembling, still made no sound.

Jana's free hand lifted the hem of her mini-skirt and quickly found her shaven pubis. She clasped herself with her palm and found her fount, and the soft insides of her top thighs, moist with her oily juice. Gasping, she slid four fingers slowly inside her flowing fount, while her thumb pressed on the swollen little pink of her nympha. She had to press her lips hard to stop herself crying out as the spasm of ecstasy made her shudder. Swallowing, she lifted the cane and lashed Cassie's buttocks as hard as she could, as though to punish the woman for bringing her such love, such pleasure.

'Two more to go, sweet Cassie, darling,' she sang out, her voice as cheerful as possible. Her breath was coming low and harsh now, as her thumb stroked her stiff nympha and her fingers moved softly in the wet secret cavern of her fount. She was near her plateau as she delivered the fifth cut, and as with shaking hands she lifted the cane for the sixth and last, she knew that she could no longer hold back. She brought the cane down savagely on the helpless bare nates, and just at the moment the cane cracked on bare skin, Jana was convulsed in an orgasm that made her cry out loud. Dimly, she was aware that Cassie had cried too – not cried so much as screamed, a yelp of pure fear.

When Jana had recovered her breath, she turned the bolt to release Cassie from the cincher, and the slave wriggled back into the cabin. Her olive face was pale.

'Come on, Cassie,' said Jana, her own face as flushed as Cassie's fesses, 'I know I can lay it on hard, but you've had a thousand times worse. Did I hurt you that much?'

'Oh, that,' said Cassie, her face creased in nervous apprehension. 'Oh, no, Mistress, it's not that. My beating was lovely, and I thank you for the just chastisement of my imperfection.'

'Then why all the yelling?'

'Mistress, I saw, or I thought I saw – in this blue haze, the light plays strange tricks –'

'What, then? A whale? A kraken? A giant sea-monster?'

'*Mistress, I saw a mermaid!*'

'Cassie, my sweet, the tears in your eyes as I laced you must have caused all sorts of strange visions.'

'Mistress, I am certain. The water is clear, I could see all of her. Long hair, perfect breasts, and below, a scaly tail like a dragon. But not the sweet mermaids you see in books of fairy tales. This one had fire and hatred in her eyes, and she looked at me as though she wanted to eat me, and flickered a red viper's tongue.'

Jana clasped Cassie to her breast. 'Sweet Cassie, you have been hallucinating,' she whispered gently. 'It is the sun, the excitement of our trip and the apprehension of what lies ahead. Your mermaid is a phantasm, a projection.'

'Mistress,' sobbed Cassie, 'I don't think it was an hallucination.'

'Even if it wasn't,' said Jana soothingly, 'what is the harm? You were not threatened, were you? So why so frightened?'

'Mistress,' whimpered Cassie, 'the mermaid had your breasts, your hair, your face. *The mermaid was you.*'

122

9

The Templar Castle

Flushed and excited, Jana and Cassie joined the others on the deck, where they sat under parasols sipping fresh iced lemonade and watching the Aegean glide past, wreathed in a blue heat haze almost as thick as clouds. Jana tried to hide her perturbation at Cassie's mermaid phantasm, and cautioned her to keep out of the sun.

Through the haze, the ghostly shapes of islands loomed like the backs of giant primaeval beasts, and Chris, on one of his fleeting visits from the bridge, took delight in explaining their history, the gods who dwelt on them, and their place in legend.

'And that one?' said Jana, pointing to a steeply rising hillock in the far distance. Chris turned pale.

'I do not know,' he said. 'Not all of these islands have names.'

'Nonsense,' said Sandra. 'All these islands have some sort of name. Now what is it – you cruise these waters, my boy, and must know.'

Her imperious tone made Chris blush and stammer, 'It is known as Circe's island. A witch lives there. No mariner dare approach it.'

'Such superstition!' scoffed Sandra. 'In this day and age!'

'That expression means nothing to the Greeks,' retorted Chris angrily. 'To us, there is only one age. The past lives with us always. We do not forget, because our gods are still with us.'

Jana looked at Kate, Melanie, and Sarah. Their faces were masks of blankness. She knew that it was on Circe's island they had been tattooed with the roses on their

123

fount-lips. She saw that the *matelots* had turned their backs on Circe's island, even though it meant looking straight into the sun, and were making feverish signs as though to ward off evil spirits.

'Circe's island is one of the few places in the Aegean where roses grow wild,' said Chris. 'The other, Mistress, is your island, the Island of Maldona.'

It was lunchtime, and a salad was served, but few had an appetite, such was the heat and the strength of their excitement. Ahead of them, through the mist, loomed the massive black peak that was the Island of Maldona.

'Another hour,' said Chris. 'We should be there by three o'clock. The sea haze has slowed us. But there will be light for another few hours. Night, remember, falls swiftly here; we do not have the long twilights of your northern lands. Here, it is either sunshine or starlight, with nothing in between.'

'How far is Circe's island from the Island of Maldona?' asked Jana abruptly.

'About six nautical miles,' said Chris, clearly irritated. 'But there is nothing there for you, Mistress.'

I could swim that, Jana thought. Better still, ride a turtle. Those minxes Sarah and the twins are not to be trusted, and I must see for myself. What if Maldona were to become not just an island, but an empire, like the dominions of the Templars of old? Drowsy in the sun, she dreamed of conquest. And then she realised that she was dreaming of the sweet tattoos on the founts of her new slaves, and trembled as she felt desire to be thus adorned herself.

As they approached Maldona, the talk was stilled. The giant black peak towered over them now, blotting out the sinking sun. There were muted gasps of awe, and Jana felt her own pulse race. For there, halfway up the mountainside, stood the broken, mouldering towers of the long-abandoned castle of the Templars. Apart from the towers, it was a low structure with crumbling battlements. The four towers, Jana surmised, were evidently the last redoubt of defence, if the low barbican were stormed by an enemy – by Saracens, by Barbary corsairs, by rapacious Christian knights.

The castle stood perhaps 70 metres above the landing beach which they now approached. It was a little cove surrounded by rocky outcrops of the same black rock which formed the island. The sand was volcanic grey powder: not, Jana reflected, for tourists, who demanded coarse but pretty white sand. But above the beach, the way up to the castle was a jungle of wild roses, thyme, lavender, bougainvillea and olives, all growing abundantly in the fertile volcanic soil. Jana was particularly taken with the wild roses.

There was no harbour on the island, Chris explained: they would have to go ashore and ferry their supplies by bumboat. The anchor was dropped, and the company was silent as they contemplated their new home. Supplies would last for six months, Jana explained, by which time the slaves of Maldona, goaded by the lash, would have grown enough to make the new islanders self-sufficient. How different from Spanish Maldona, where the castle was supplied in secret by trucks laden with produce from the farms and vineyards of Malaga! There, Jana had taken control of a structure which already existed; here, she would create her own.

She noticed that the *matelots*, while unloading sacks of flour, crates of wine, salt cod and pork, and – Jana had mischievously decided – boxes of Belgian chocolates, looked away from the island, and that whenever their gaze accidentally fell upon her, they shut their eyes before resuming their work.

'What is the matter with them?' she asked Chris, who was smoking a cigarette as he supervised. He took a deep breath.

'There are legends,' he said at last. 'The Templars ... that there is a treasure hidden somewhere on the island. In the diaspora of the Order, after its expulsion from the Holy Land – to Rhodes, Malta, Spain – the great treasures of the Order were divided amongst the different septs.'

'Then,' said Jana, watching the bumboats convey her supplies and her slaves to the beach, 'I would expect the place has been thoroughly looted.' She tried to hide her disappointment.

'No,' said Chris, finally. 'There is supposed to be a curse. The Templars were attacked by Barbary pirates in the fifteenth century, and the Templars were tortured most cruelly, flogged with thorned rose branches, to reveal its location. Finally they were burnt alive, and the castle sacked. But by that time, they themselves did not know where the treasure was hidden! Under the castle lies a labyrinth; many labyrinths, I have heard. I have been here before, Mistress, but only in passing. Never would I set foot on the infernal place, I confess. All the Templars of that time knew was that there was a map, giving the location of the treasure, which had been taken – stolen – by a witch from England who had enslaved them for a period, before sailing away.'

'What was the treasure?' asked Jana. 'Gold? Jewels? Holy relics?'

Chris shrugged. 'No one knows. And I think no one wants to know.'

'Was the witch named Maldona?' asked Jana quietly. 'Formerly Jana Ardenne, my ancestor?'

He hesitated. 'Yes, she was. And it is said she put a curse on whoever would seek to find her treasure – it is said that a freak storm sank the ship of the Barbary pirates just off Corfu – for one day *she would return to claim it.*'

Jana smiled now. 'And so she has,' she said softly.

Jana and Cassie were the last of the company to descend into a bumboat for the journey to the island. Before their descent, Jana removed all of her clothing except her chains and her sandals, and a light braided whip hanging in a loop from her waist-chain.

'Maldona must arrive naked on her island,' she said simply to Cassie. 'It is fitting.'

The ship lay a hundred metres from the shore, and the *matelots* rowed easily, gliding over the clear water in which Jana could see shoals of bright fish darting. Chris accompanied them, he and Cassie sitting with Jana at the prow; feeling the warm air caress her bare body as she breathed deeply of the sea.

'You will find,' said Chris, 'that there is plenty of food in the sea. The supplies are really to be stored, Mistress. Our sea abounds in fish of all sorts; lobsters, crayfish, mussels, oysters . . . you shall never go hungry. And the soil is fertile: you may pick fruit without end.'

'We shall grow corn to make bread,' said Maldona severely. 'Slaves are made to work and be punished.'

Jana stepped from the rowing boat on to the beach, and the company bowed to her. She was followed by Cassie, who took her place in the work party which Thorsten was even now organising in preparation for the ascent to the castle. The supplies were a mountain in themselves: Jana ordered that as much as possible should be taken up the serpentine, overgrown track which wound up the mountain, the rest left until morning. The *matelots* scuffed the water with their oars, impatient to be away from the place of the curse. But Chris lingered.

'I think I shall not set sail until dawn tomorrow,' he said, 'because it will be dark soon.' Then he barked in Greek to his *matelots*, who grumbled but assented.

'Why not stay with us here?' said Jana. 'We have straw, sleeping bags . . . it would be an adventure.'

Chris looked at Sandra, his face a mask of anguish. 'No, I cannot,' he mumbled. 'The curse –'

Suddenly Sandra stepped forward and embraced him with a kiss full on the lips, and to Jana's surprise lifted her light skirt and stepped out of her pink silk panties, which she handed to Chris. His face was as pink as the panties as she said, 'Farewell, my lovely girl.'

Jana watched the boat speed back to the waiting *Hesperides* and felt a yearning to be back in luxury. Then she looked up at the castle, and said out loud, 'Maldona must make her own luxury.'

The supplies had been packed so that each sack or box could be carried by one person, and with Thorsten taking the lead, hacking at the luxuriant foliage which wreathed the track as though in prayer, the group began the slow ascent to the castle. Cassie ruefully shouldered a sack of flour, while her mistress looked on, smiling.

'Never forget you are a slave, Cassandra,' she said, 'however much I love you.'

Thus laden, they took half an hour to reach the smashed portals of the castle. All were sweating heavily as they shed their burdens and stood aside for Jana to make her ceremonial entrance to the castle.

She stepped through the gap in the wood, preserved in its derelict state over the centuries by the dry heat, and entered the main courtyard of the castle, about a hundred metres on each side. The ground was a forest of flowers, creepers and small trees: there were olives, lemons and oranges, all mixed and entwined like lovers embracing in a house where the owners had gone away. In the middle of the courtyard, a stream of crystal clear water flowed jauntily, leaving the castle on the opposite side from the main gate. Jana surmised that the clear water emerged from an underground spring. Gingerly, she picked her way through the lush foliage and reached the nearest wall.

Three sides of the courtyard were studded with doors – Jana counted twenty on each side – and all in ruinous states of decay. Jana climbed over the debris of one door, and found herself in a cell, dimly lit by the narrowest of arrow-slit windows. Then she passed to the nearest of the four corner towers and looked up. The top was completely smashed, no doubt by the catapults and petards of the murdering Barbary pirates. She entered, and found a stone staircase, which she was able to climb as far as the second floor, at which point the staircase stopped and became nothing more than a heap of rubble, leaving her to gaze perilously into space through the shattered walls. The fourth side of the yard consisted not of cells but of a refectory or great hall, what must have been a kitchen, and a large vaulted chapel, now completely gutted and containing nothing but a smashed altar and some shards of broken stained glass. The refectory was surprisingly intact: the tables and benches were still there, hewn out of solid rock, and to Jana's surprise, in the adjoining kitchen there was an array of copper cauldrons, spoons and pots, covered in verdigris. She scraped at one with her fingernail and it came off easily, revealing a dull but clean copper body beneath. And there was a fireplace, with a chimney open to the sky, only half blocked by creepers.

Between the refectory and the chapel, a narrow passage led to another, smaller, courtyard with a floor of rock slabs through which weeds poked, and here Jana recognised the ruins of a bakery, a weaving shop and a shipwright's. She felt the melancholy of time.

Shivering a little in the heat as she contemplated the ghosts of those long-dead knights who might still watch over the decay of their workplaces, Jana returned to her companions, shivering again as she walked over the lush vegetation and realising that this growth had been fertilised by the charred bodies of brave knights.

'There is accommodation for us,' she announced, 'but there is much, much building to be done. Bring your burdens to the second yard, where there is a rock floor. I will show you.'

On Jana's orders, the supplies were laid out on the floor of the second yard, and Jana ordered Thorsten to lead a party down to the beach for a second load.

'Not you, Sarah,' she said. 'You will tidy and prepare a cell and bedding for me: a lamp, of course, and some rocks for a table.' Sarah bowed meekly, and Jana indicated a cell next to the chapel. 'There is much building to be done, but for the moment there are cells for us all, and a roof over our head. Henry, you shall cook for us. First you must fetch water and clean your pots and your cookhouse. Tonight we shall have a banquet with wine, my slaves.'

Thorsten led his party, consisting of Kate, Melanie and Sandra, back down the hill to the beach, while Jana instructed Cassie to unpack the food for the evening's dinner, then assist Henry in cleaning the kitchen. Now, Jana opened her case and donned a light linen chiton, the tunic of noble ladies of ancient Athens. As she supervised her slaves at their tasks, idly flicking her braided whip in the air, Jana was distracted by a strange flickering light out at sea. She hurried to the gateway and saw a burning ship. It was the *Hesperides*, and a boat was rowing fast towards the cove.

'Cassie! Henry!' cried Jana. 'Come quickly – look!'

'Oh my God,' said Cassie.

'What the hell –' Henry frowned as though the burning of the ship was a personal affront to him. 'Who is in the boat? It looks like only one person.'

Jana squinted into the distance. 'There are other boats, full of men,' she said finally, 'but they are not coming here. They are going towards that strange island – Circe's island.'

'But it is so far,' said Cassie, puzzled.

'Six nautical miles, it seems,' answered Jana. 'Not too far to swim, certainly not too far in a boat. The *matelots* are superstitious – they think our island accursed. Cassie, go to my cell and look in my large suitcase. You'll find binoculars. Bring them.'

Cassie fetched the heavy Zeiss binoculars, and Jana focused on the approaching boat.

'It is Chris,' she said. 'I wonder if he fired his own ship – Caspar's ship, in fact – as an excuse to be here, be with Sandra? Anyway, back to your tasks, my slaves. Burning ship or no burning ship, we must eat.'

She focused the binoculars again, this time on Thorsten's party who were trudging, laden, up the winding track. From their position on the other side of the hill they would be unable to see the burning ship, although the high petroleum flames and the swirling clouds of black smoke would be startlingly visible.

Jana watched, entranced, and feeling a strange sexual fascination and a seeping wetness between her legs. As she watched the ship hiss, belch flames, list and shake with the explosion of fuel tanks, she understood the perverted glee of the arsonist. Fire is sex, she thought – pure sex, bright and hot and as alive as pain.

The *Hesperides* keeled until she was standing vertically with only her stern poised out of the water, and then suddenly, with an explosive hissing of steam, she slipped beneath the surface with the frightening speed of an arrow. It was the swiftness of the destruction which terrified Jana; the whole sinking could not have taken more than twenty minutes. The sea swirled under the full moon which now loomed like a giant goddess over Maldona, and then was silent, as though the sleek ship had never been.

Thorsten's party returned, sweating from their labour, and Jana ordered them to bathe in the stream, after which a hot meal would be served. She curtly answered their questions about the smoke and fire they had seen, but reminded them that under the rules of Maldona, all questions were forbidden.

'What you need to know, slaves, Maldona will deign to tell you,' she said.

She left Henry and Cassie busy preparing their meal, and walked across the yard to her cell to inspect Sarah's preparations. She smiled as she saw how prettily Sarah had arranged her things – a wide straw palliasse, a table artfully constructed from rocks – and she reflected with approval that Maldona had certainly toughened Sarah's muscles. There were also candles and matches, and even a cracked vase of fresh flowers. She kissed the girl warmly and said, 'I am pleased, Sarah. Now, you know that soon I must award ranks, although we are as yet few in number. But others will come, I know, as word spreads of the rebirth of Maldona. I must have a hierarchy of adepts, prefects, corporals, parfaites . . .'

Sarah's eyes lit up. 'How I should love to be a parfaite, Mistress,' she said dreamily. 'To have the privilege of nudity, to carry a whip at my waist.'

Jana sighed. 'Sarah, you . . . you are somehow not ready. The rank of parfaite must be attained by challenge, by hard combat in Pankration wrestling. I do not think you are sufficiently trained.' Sarah's face fell. 'But for the moment I appoint you Mistress Almoner, with the *honorary* rank of corporal. That means that you may carry a short cane, not more than 40 centimetres, but you may not use it without my permission. Your task will be to oversee the cells, their tidiness and cleanliness, and report any offenders – now, to me, but later, to the appropriate prefect.'

Sarah knelt and kissed Jana's toes which peeped bare from her sandals. 'Thank you, Mistress,' she said. 'Adore Maldona!'

'There is one thing, Sarah,' said Jana. 'You know how lovely I think your tattoo, the beautiful rose that adorns your fount: she quite bewitches me. But you are a slave still, and must grow back your mink. Only adepts and parfaites may have the privilege of shaving, as you know very well.'

Sarah bit her lip. 'Yes, Mistress, I know,' she said ruefully.

'But in time, and with toughened muscles, you may reach the rank of parfaite: dream of it, sweet Sarah. And now, before we dine, you may begin your rounds of the cells to see that every slave has installed herself tidily.'

Sarah bowed low. 'Mistress, please instruct me.'

Jana was pleased she had learned to phrase her question so that it was not a question, as she herself had had to do so long ago.

'It's just . . . well, sanitary arrangements. If slaves have to . . . you know.'

'Oh. Yes,' said Jana. 'I'm afraid that until a bath house is built, we must use the stream, at the extremity of the castle, just before the water flows beneath the wall. So here, by the cells and refectory, we shall have clean water. Imperfect but necessary. You may instruct the slaves.'

Sarah bowed. 'I obey, Mistress,' she murmured.

Cassie and Henry had worked a miraculous transformation in the refectory as the company sat down to their dinner at the stone table. Candles lit the room, which, if not entirely spotless, was at least tolerably clean. Jana sat at the head of the table, with Cassie and Thorsten below her. From their supplies and fresh foods they had brought from Piraeus, Henry had prepared fish, salad, taramasalata and dolmades, and they drank harsh Greek wine from metal goblets.

'Look, Mistress,' said Henry, 'this is for you.' He showed her a battered brass goblet, burnished to radiance.

'A goblet,' said Jana, impatient for her food. 'Why, we all have goblets.'

Henry beamed. 'I found it, Mistress, here in the kitchen. Only one – look at the marking!'

132

Jana peered at the goblet, marvelling that she would drink her wine from a vessel so laden with history. It was engraved with the shield of the Templars, and underneath, in careful italic script, the message: '*Jana Perfecta Domina in Castello Maldona.*'

Jana gasped in delight and awe and felt a tingling of fear, as though she were in the grip of forces beyond her control. '*The Parfaite Jana Mistress in the Castle Maldona.*' She would drink from the cup that had belonged to her ancestor Jane Ardenne, the very first Maldona. Shaking slightly, she announced that grace was to be said. All rose, and Jana intoned, 'Adore Maldona!'

'Adore Maldona!' came the response from candle-lit mouths. Then they sat, and she nodded that the service of food should begin.

Fatigue had not dulled the excitement and conversation was lively. Jana sat and ate in silence, pensive. She thought of Cassie's mermaid, of the strange woman in the blue dress who, she was sure, was following her. Perhaps even here. Could she have anything to do with the sabotage of the *Hesperides*? Jana was sure that the burning was no coincidence.

As she ate, Jana cast her eye round the spacious refectory. There was an area in the far corner, away from the dining table, which Henry had not had time to clean. Cobwebs and flowering creepers covered the walls and floors, giving it the piquant aspect of a church abandoned to the pagan gods of nature. Jana focused on a strange stone structure enveloped in flowers. It was a large stone slab, like a vaulting horse, and to her surprise she could make out, underneath the foliage, pairs of cuffs and anklets. They were copper, shining with verdigris.

'Look, Cassie,' she said between sips of wine, 'what do you think that is?'

Cassie peered, then laughed. 'Why, Mistress, it is a flogging horse!' she cried in delight. 'How splendid! I have heard that the Templars would be entertained at dinner by the flogging of a wrong-doer. His cries would be their music.'

'How lovely,' Jana said with a dry smile. 'We must rein-state as many of the old customs as possible –'

Suddenly there was silence as a bedraggled, exhausted figure appeared at the doorway of the refectory. Sandra at once rose and embraced him.

'Chris!' she cried. 'Oh my sweet Chris, you've come!'

Jana rose. 'Chris!' she cried. 'What has happened? I watched as the ship went under. Who did this? What –' Henry, seat our captain and fetch a cup of wine.'

When Chris, perspiring, had regained his breath after the arduous climb, he looked at Jana with pleading eyes.

'Please, Mistress, may I stay, stay and be a slave of Maldona? My ship is gone: I must answer to Caspar. But I have no way of getting back to Athens now. Nor, in truth –' he touched Sandra '– do I really want to.'

'Did you fire your own ship?' asked Jana softly. 'So that you would be forced to stay?'

'No . . . I swear!' said Chris piteously. 'There was a fire in the engine room and it spread to the fuel tanks, and you know how much expensive wood panelling there was on the *Hesperides* – she was a tinder-box.'

'Was it an accident?' asked Jana.

Chris shrugged. 'Who knows? I . . . I cannot believe so. But who would do such a thing? Anyway, the crew all got off safely, but all our belongings had to be left.'

Noiselessly, Henry placed a plate in front of Chris and served him food.

'How deep is the sea there?' said Jana.

'Not more than 25 metres. Perhaps less.'

'Well,' said Jana, 'if it were no accident, more will certainly happen. We must simply wait and see. In the meantime we must at once start our work of rebuilding Maldona. The first task is to rebuild the four towers, the second to construct baths and a gymnasium. The third . . . well, we must complete those things first.'

Cassie cast a quizzical eye, as though guessing Jana's thoughts. 'There is something about these ancient waters, Mistress, that inspires the urge to conquer, is there not?' she said quietly. 'All these islands . . . places only inhabited by sea nymphs and mermaids and old, old spirits of water. Just think, Mistress, to rule an empire of the sea, to make the spirits of the waters submit to your whip.'

Jana allowed a thin smile to play on her lips. 'A little fanciful, my sweet slave. There are strange phantasms here. But reading Maldona's mind is, I am sure, an insolence worthy of punishment. I shall decide when to beat you, slave.'

Cassie bowed her head. 'I obey Maldona in all things,' she said, smiling.

Under the full moon and a starlit sky brighter than Jana had ever seen, she watched Sarah Pennington, the new Mistress Almoner, as she proudly ushered Jana's slaves to their quarters, making sure that candles were put out and bodies were on their palliasses. She had been quick to acquire a badge of rank – a short branch of dried wood, useless as a cane but potent as a symbol.

10

The Labyrinth

When all was quiet and the kitchen fires put out, Jana kissed Cassie goodnight and they each went to their adjoining cells. Jana sighed with pleasure as she stretched out nude on her palliasse in the sweltering night and lay watching the stars and the full moon which beamed bright through her narrow window-slit.

The nervous excitement which had filled her earlier was now gone, replaced by a serenity and joy, a feeling that she had at last reached home. She took a sip of water from the metal goblet which had come down to her through all the centuries from her ancestor, and thought of herself as part of a process; not Jana the individual anymore, but Maldona, who was eternal. Maldona is dead, long live Maldona.

Despite her fatigue, she could not sleep. She thought fleetingly that she was at last in the place of her dream, and hoped that by that she would be spared the dream. But she knew deep in herself that she would have to live it. Silently, she rose from her palliasse, donned her chiton and sandals, and went out into the moonlight. All was quiet except for the distant lapping of the sea. Jana knocked softly on the door of the adjoining cell.

'Cassie?' she whispered. 'Are you awake?'

'Yes, Mistress,' replied Cassie at once. 'I can't sleep. Please come in.'

Jana entered and sat beside Cassie on her palliasse. Cassie, nude, sat up and Jana smiled at the glinting moonlight on her taut bare breasts. She took Cassie's hand, and Cassie rewarded her with a smile.

'Is it that you don't want to sleep alone, Mistress?'

'You are reading my mind again, slave,' said Jana.

'Oh! Another punishment, I suppose?' said Cassie, grinning.

'Naturally, you darling. But first, let us take a walk in the moonlight. I am curious about the sinking of Caspar's ship, and I am sure it was no accident. Let's go down there and look. The walk will be cool in the moonlight.'

Cassie put on her own chiton and hand in hand the two women left the castle and strolled down the winding track to the cove, and the sea which had swallowed *Hesperides*.

'I am sure Caspar is covered by insurance,' said Jana, 'but that hardly matters. It is the here and now that concerns us. She can't be deep. We can dive, and the water is so clear we can see everything. Perhaps a clue. We don't yet know if we can trust Chris – maybe he was the arsonist.'

'We could salvage some things,' said Cassie, practically. 'You know, pots and pans and maybe some money left lying around.'

Jana laughed. 'Cassie, we are on Maldona! What use have we for money?'

They came to the cove and climbed into the beached bumboat. Once floating, they rowed vigorously to the spot where Jana thought she had last seen the ship. The sea was a mirror, flat and calm, and they felt safe in leaving the boat unanchored.

'I'll dive first,' said Jana, stripping off her chiton and sandals. 'I reckon I can hold my breath for about two minutes, and I'll see how deep she lies.'

She eased herself into the water and swam straight down, into a turquoise half-lit world where shoals of silver and golden fish brushed her naked body. She smiled at their icy, ticklish caress as she felt her hair stream behind her like sea flowers. She could see the sandy bottom quite clearly, but there was no sign of the shipwreck. After swimming for a minute and a half, she decided to return to the boat, and emerged from the sea, gasping for breath.

'The good news is that the water is scarcely fifteen

metres deep,' she said. 'The bad news is that we're in the wrong place. No sign of the ship.'

'Let's try over there,' said Cassie, pointing. 'I'll go down this time.'

They rowed a hundred metres, and this time Cassie stripped and dived, Jana watching with admiration as her slave's slim body slid into the water like a flashing brown eel.

After two minutes, Cassie reemerged, panting and looking glum.

'Nothing, *nada*, *nichts*,' she said with a moue of disappointment. 'Lots of pretty fish, though. We certainly shan't go hungry.'

'No mermaids?' said Jana mockingly.

'Oh, Mistress, you are cruel, a cruel beast!'

'It comes with the territory, Cassie, my sweet. Come on, let's go again. The night, as they say, is young.'

Jana lost track of time as they took turns to dive, moving their boat after each try. Finally, as the first light of dawn was washing the stars away, Jana said that she would make the last dive and then they would go home. They were far out from shore now, and the castle was only a dim shape against the mountainside. Jana splashed overboard and swam down through the crystal water. Her vision was obscured by a shoal of brightly striped fish and when it had passed, she found herself bobbing on the sandy bottom. She could see the shape of the boat overhead, and when she looked around her, she almost gulped water in her astonishment.

Before her stood two white pillars, festooned with weeds and eroded by seawater. Jana had read legends of Greek cities sunk under a tidal wave, but these pillars with their remains of strange hieroglyphic carvings were none of the familiar styles – Ionian, Corinthian, Doric – of temple architecture. This could be no Greek temple. Around them stretched crumbling walls, six or seven metres high in places; in others, where the sea had done its work, little more than foundations. She swam in through the portal and her eyes opened wide. At first she thought she had found a sunken temple, which was exciting enough – she knew of the legends, or true accounts, of earthquakes and floods and volcanic eruptions which had caused the Aegean Greeks to ascribe such mighty and thunderous powers to their gods – but as she continued, lungs bursting, she saw that the pillars, walls and colonnades stretched far out to sea, further than she could discern even in the clear moon-lit water. Quickly, she surfaced again, and swam back to the boat.

'Mistress, you look frightened!' cried Cassie. 'Let us go home.'

'No, no,' said Jana. 'Cassie, we shall dive together. Yes, I'm frightened. What I've found –'

'The ship?'

'Cassie, a whole ruined city under the water. Bigger than you can see.'

The two women dived and as far as their lungs would permit, explored the periphery of the city. While Cassie swam up eerily deserted streets, now populated only by bright fish, shiny black lobster and banks of gnarled oysters, Jana lingered in the vast temple – for so it must have been – through which visitors to the city evidently had to pass. She examined the strange altars, blocks of stone and intricately carved artefacts, some of which were crumbled, some in good repair, but all mysterious.

She knew that this place had something to do with her, with her destiny, and suddenly felt the overpowering presence of her ancestor, the witch Jana Ardenne, the first Maldona. Jana Ardenne, speaking to her across the centuries, had sent her the wine goblet, and now had brought her here. For the first time in her life, Jana felt truly afraid.

She paused by a raised block of white stone which occupied pride of place in the centre of the temple. On it were carved faces twisted in agony, so that they looked scarcely human; bodies contorted in impossible positions; creatures with human faces, but with webbed hands and feet, being flogged by grinning mermaids.

And in the centre of this panoply of torment was carved, in beautiful, intricate detail, the whorled petals of a rose.

139

At each corner of the block were pairs of cuffs made of what seemed to be bronze. Suddenly, Jana realised that it was the same as the stone block which stood in the corner of the Templars' refectory. The most sacred shrine in this underwater city was a whipping block.

She waved to Cassie that they should return to the surface, and was turning to swim up, when something caught her eye. It was a glint of amber metal under the dais of the whipping block. She reached to pick it up and found a large bronze key, encrusted with shells of small crustacea, but with its tines still sharp. She surfaced swiftly, just having time to conceal the key in the folds of her chiton before Cassie also surfaced.

They lay in the boat, exhausted, recovering their breath. Jana looked at Cassie and saw that she too had been struck by fear.

'Whatever happened here, and whenever, Mistress, it can happen again,' she said.

Jana was silent, and in silence they rowed back to the cove.

As they climbed back to the castle, Jana said, 'Slave, you must swear to tell no one of this.'

'I swear, Mistress.'

'We shall return, discreetly, at night, and organise for a proper search of the underwater city. Although I dread to think what we might find. *But no one else must know.*' And she told Cassie of the whipping block in the temple. She did not mention the bronze key.

They entered the castle yard, and found it silent. Dawn was not yet fully on them, although there was a glimmering in the sky as one by one the stars went out.

'Go to your cell, Cassie,' said Jana. 'I'll be ... that is, may I join you there? Please?'

Cassie smiled with joy in the pale light. 'Oh, Mistress, I should whip you for insolence ... of course! Oh, please join me.'

'In a minute, then.'

When Cassie had gone to her cell, Jana hurried to a fig

tree which grew outside the chapel, and with a sharp rock, dug a hole where she buried the bronze key.

Minutes later, Jana was lying in her slave's arms, the two bare women overcome with fatigue, wonder and nameless fear, holding each other tightly, breast against breast, thigh against thigh; two frightened animals cuddling for comfort in their lair.

If there was a treasure of the Templars, Jana thought, where better to hide it than an underwater city, not easily found, and once inside, a maze where only an adept can lead the way. Did my ancestor find the treasure and take it away to Spain? Or did she have no use for it – perhaps she too believed in the curse – and left the key for me, *knowing I would find it 600 years later, and that I alone would be strong enough to overcome it.*

Her lips nuzzling her friend's soft black hair, her arms clasped tight, Jana drifted into an exhausted sleep as she heard the first birds shrill their cries of pride. The birds, she thought, the spirits of the tormented, the spirits of the whipped, ascending to freedom from the prison of the flesh.

They slept a deep sleep for only a few hours, and were awakened by Sarah Pennington, bearing a tray of coffee and bread.

'Forgive me, Mistress, but I thought I might find you here,' she said coyly.

'Thank you, Sarah,' said Jana, sitting up and brushing her tousled hair back from her forehead. 'You are certainly taking your duties as almoner very seriously. I am pleased.'

'Thorsten has organised a work party, Mistress, and the slave Aelfric has fed the company in the refectory. All have washed in the stream, and now we await your instructions. May I say, Mistress, that I am so glad you cut my hair, because I'd forgotten how hot it is here. Only my mink is beginning to grow back, and she itches terribly.'

'Itching,' said Jana coolly, 'is the smallest torment to concern a slave.'

Sarah smiled slyly, bowed, and withdrew.

'My plan,' said Jana, 'is to rebuild the four towers. Only when we have degrees of physical elevation can we have the necessary degrees of social rank. After that . . . Cassie, today, you and I shall explore the labyrinths which apparently honeycomb the ground beneath us. Exploring the underwater city must wait till nightfall. You were right to think that I have conquest in mind: there are so many deserted islands in this part of the Aegean. But I must have something first. I must have a dungeon.'

'The treasure of the Templars, Mistress,' said Cassie, swallowing the muddy Greek coffee. 'Perhaps the labyrinth contains the treasure?'

'Perhaps,' said Jana, without conviction, her eyes glinting at the thought of the underwater city.

The two women, nude, made their way to the stream at its point of exit, and, in full view of the company who were sitting on the grass awaiting Jana's instructions (she noticed to her amusement that Chris was wearing Sandra's chiton, and that she had shaved his legs and rouged him), squatted in the waist-high, surprisingly cold water. Then they moved upstream and dived under the surface for a minute, to emerge dripping and pink from the cold, rapid stream. They returned to their cells to dress. Cassie wore the simple chiton: Jana, her parfaite's harness, feathers up, and carrying a four-thonged whip at her waist.

Jana gave her instructions. When a rhythm of life had been established in Maldona, she explained, ranks would be fought for and awarded. In the meantime, honorary ranks were: Sarah, the mistress almoner; Aelfric, as she now thought of Henry Gordon Playste, was manciple, in charge of the kitchen and refectory; Thorsten was master mason, in charge of all construction work. These were honorary, temporary ranks, necessary for the reconstruction of the castle: in due course the proper hierarchy of Maldona would evolve. The orders of these temporary adepts were to be obeyed by all, including the other adepts, within their sphere of authority, on pain of beating, and they were permitted to carry short canes as symbols of authority; but any beatings had to be referred to Jana herself. This done, she ordered Thorsten, Henry and Sarah to go about their business: Chris and Sandra obediently followed Thorsten to the tower in the north-east corner, to begin surveying the work to be done. On the beach were piled sacks of cement and bricks which Jana had prudently sent ahead, although she wanted her towers built as much as possible from the rocks of her island.

Kate and Melanie were detailed to take scythes and clear the courtyard of its jungle of weeds, creepers and thorns.

'Mistress,' said Melanie, frowning as she scratched herself where her mink was beginning to grow, 'who shall be prefects? And parfaites?'

Jana laughed. 'A question? You are imperfect, Melanie, and have earned a lady's beating for your insolent forgetfulness. But I shall answer. We are as yet few in number,' she said. 'I, Maldona, am both prefect and parfaite.'

'Well, how about an honorary rank, Mistress?' said Sandra, turning round. 'After all, if this . . . this *girl* –' she pointed scornfully at Sarah '– is to be an honorary adept, then why shouldn't there be parfaites too? Then, when we have our ranks, newcomers can be welcomed into an established order.'

'Very well,' said Jana quietly. 'A parfaite there shall be. But you know that the rank must be fought for. By the rules of Pankration wrestling, meaning almost no rules at all – gouging, arm-twisting, and the most vicious, intimate kicks, are all permitted. Do you still want to be parfaites, you three slaves? Even if only honorary parfaites?' All three nodded vigorously.

'Very well, then. This evening you shall wrestle according to the rules of Pankration, and –' Jana permitted herself a sly grin '– it shall be a three-cornered contest. You shall all fight each other at the same time. Almoner Sarah, you will please ensure that an open space is cleared in this undergrowth suitable for a wrestling arena.' The lips of the three contestants, opened in surprise and fright, now pursed in grim determination as they bowed in obedience. Leaving the slaves to their tasks, with Thorsten already bellowing like an overseer, Jana led Cassie to the chapel.

'It is a day for exploring,' said Jana. 'In particular, I wish to find the entrance to the labyrinth.'

'I shouldn't know where to start, Mistress,' said Cassie.

The door creaked as they entered the musty old church. Some of the stained glass windows, though cracked, were still intact, and they depicted not the lives of haloed saints, but the bloody deeds of warriors. White-robed Templars sliced heads and arms from wailing Saracens, their horses steaming and flaring with heavenly fury. Other windows depicted flogged men and women, their bared backs or fesses streaked crimson under four-thonged whips wielded by armour-clad women. Except for the largest, central window, which had miraculously survived almost unscathed. In it, a knight, strapped to the flogging block, received a beating on his bared nates from a blonde woman wearing the parfaite's harness, fan feathers proudly erect as she flogged the defenceless naked male. Jana's eyes opened wide. The blonde woman was a mermaid, standing erect on a tail of golden scales. Cassie shivered.

'Mistress, it is you. She has your eyes, your hair, your lips, your fine high cheekbones. Your ... your lovely breasts. Oh, it is cold in here. Mistress, I wonder if I would like to be a parfaite. After all, I *was* Maldona herself, until you wrestled me to submission to claim your rightful throne.'

'*I* do not want you to be a parfaite, Cassie, for I have better things in mind for you,' said Jana thoughtfully. 'And I have learnt that parfaites must not be allowed too much power. It is important to make them worry about little privileges, like the right to go nude, to carry whips, to shave their minks, so that they have no time to plot and intrigue. That is what Louis XIV did in France: to quell his rebellious barons, he summoned them to court and made them consume their energy squabbling over who should have the right to bring him his shirt or his stockings each morning. Now, we are in the chapel because here there will be a vault full of sarcophagi. And how better to reach a labyrinth than from a vault which is already underground?'

The two women paused to inspect the chapel. Instead of

an altar, raised high on a dais, was a flogging block exactly the same as the one Jana had seen in the underwater temple. No seaweed, but grime and cobwebs covered this, although still clear in her centre was the carved rose.

'There must be a vault,' said Jana, 'and hence a way to it.' The two women searched for doors, windows or moveable traps, but after half an hour's perspiring search, found nothing. Jana sat down glumly on the dais beneath the flogging block.

'What marvellous acts of worship they must have had,' she mused, caressing the petals of the stone rose. Then she paused. 'Cassie! Come here! This rose . . . she is loose. Not part of the block.' She took the rose in both hands and twisted it, and to her delighted surprise, it turned a full circle on creaking hinges. At that, the entire flogging block swung round at 90 degrees, revealing an opening and a flight of stone steps leading down into the bowels of the castle.

'We've found it!'

Gleefully, Jana ordered Cassie to fetch oil lamps and a ball of twine, and then the two women made their cautious way down the mud-caked stone steps. The flight was only ten steps deep, and they found themselves in an enormous vault, crammed with stone tombs, each with the escutcheon of the fallen warrior carved on its lid.

'This is fascinating, but it's no labyrinth,' said Jana. 'Ah, that door –'

She opened a door with rotted hinges in the far corner, and saw a passage leading into darkness.

'Aha!' she cried. 'I think we have our labyrinth. Now, tie one end of the twine to that curlicue there, and hold the ball, unravelling it as we walk.' Cassie looked puzzled. 'Don't worry, it's a rather old trick, to lead us back safely. Never heard of Theseus and the Minotaur?' Cassie shook her head. 'Well,' laughed Jana, 'you shall have a beating for your ignorance, my sweet. Come.'

They gingerly took their first steps into the dank passageway, smelling of fungus, decay and must. The corridor was just wide enough for two people to pass through, on a floor of hard baked clay. They rounded a corner, and came to a fork in the passage – two corridors bifurcated to either side. Jana smiled.

'Yes, a proper maze,' she whispered. 'We'll take left. Always left.'

Jana noticed that the path led them steadily downwards, and that it was becoming hotter.

They went on for twenty minutes, coming to divisions of their path, of two, three, sometimes four, corridors, and always went to the left.

'Cassie,' said Jana, 'do you realise? We are always turning left – we are going the long way round, on the periphery, but closing towards the centre. Cassie, I think that if we could look down on this labyrinth, we should find it is in the shape of whorled rose petals.'

At last, Cassie said that her ball of twine was nearly exhausted, and just then they emerged into a large, gracefully furnished chamber with a high ceiling painted black like the walls and floor. Jana gasped in delight. She ran her fingers over the equipment and furniture which thronged the chamber. There were racks, complicated devices with pulleys and chains, flogging blocks and frames, braziers and branding irons, and a whole wall of metal rods, whips and lissome canes.

In ornate deal wardrobes, carved with the symbol of the rose, hung an array of leather corselages, straps, hoods and face masks, and long leather lace-up boots with curly pointed toes in the Arab style. There were also what Jana took to be mediaeval waist cinchers, impossibly tight little corsets to thrust out breasts and buttocks into plump tight melons and cause maximum discomfort to the flogged victim, whether male or female.

The dust of six centuries was everywhere, but at a touch of Jana's finger, the surfaces beneath were revealed as good as new.

'The dust and the dry air have preserved this wondrous place,' said Jana happily. 'Well! I feel quite at home.'

Cassie's eyes glittered as she stroked the array of whips. 'Mistress,' she said, 'on several occasions you promised me a beating. Don't you think this is the ideal occasion?'

Jana's face grew stern. 'Cassandra, you are a slave, and must be beaten in public, before your peers. *I*, on the other hand – well, you promised *me* a beating, and I, Maldona, can do as I please.'

Jana's eyes shone as in the eerie glow of the oil lamps, she made Cassie lace her in the boots which came almost up to her fount-petals, then strap her in a black leather waist cincher, the leather dry and cracked but still strong and so impossibly tight that Cassie expressed her concern.

'Don't,' said Jana, flushed and breathing heavily. 'Now the mask, Cassie sweet, and the gag – yes, that's it . . . mmmmm.'

Jana walked, or hobbled, to a woven cane flogging frame and waited impatiently as Cassie cuffed her wrists and ankles. Then, in silence, the slave selected the hardest and longest four-thonged whip from the rack as Jana, head twisted, smiled, pleased that her slave needed no further instruction.

Jana's body shook in surprise as the first stroke landed, not on her croup as she had expected, but on her bared shoulders, and her body shook at the impact. Cassie's arm was raised high to deliver her blows, and Jana saw a wicked sparkle of white teeth as she punished her mistress. At the fourth stroke, Jana moaned long and loud, and thereafter was silent, the only sound being the rustling of the cane frame as her trussed bare body slammed against it at the force of Cassie's expert flogging.

After seven strokes, Jana's back was well crimson, and Cassie now applied her whip to Jana's naked buttocks, forced outwards to a ripe, vulnerable swelling by the pressure of the antique waist cincher. Seven lashes on the trembling bared croup reduced the Mistress of Maldona to a shuddering glow of beauty and pain, and Jana felt the oily wetness seep from her fount, moistening the soft insides of her thighs. She flowed with love as she was beaten by her friend, her lover, her slave. If only, she thought, Cassie knew. She was at the plateau of orgasm, and after the seventh stroke to the fesses, Cassie suddenly threw down the whip and knelt before her mistress.

Jana felt the delicious tingling of a firm tongue on her cunt-lips, as Cassie licked and swallowed the sacred moisture that came from her beloved mistress's fount. And then her tongue was on Jana's nympha, the tip darting and licking and pressing until Jana moaned again, moaned louder, and her moan became a howl, echoing through the dusty chamber, as fire invaded her belly and melted her in the sweetest of honeyed orgasms. Panting, she looked down, and saw that Cassie too was trembling, moist of eye and shiny of lip, as she masturbated and, respectfully waiting for Jana's spasm to subside into serene contentment, whimpered and squealed as her agile fingers brought herself to climax.

Standing to remove Jana's gag, she pressed her wet finger against her mistress's lips, and Jana kissed it, sucking her slave's gentle oils. Her eyes swam with loving tears.

'Thank you, my slave,' she whispered.

When Jana had been released, she instructed Cassie to lead the way, feeling their path from the twine laid on the passage floor. As she put her accoutrements back in their closet, something caught her eye. On the side of the waist cincher was embossed: '*Jana Ardenna Domina in Castello Maldona.*'

Looking back at the scene of her chastisement, Jana murmured, 'At least Thorsten won't have to build us a dungeon, for my ancestor has already bequeathed me one. And I feel I've been here before.'

11

The Rules of Maldona

Jana ordered that the three-cornered wrestling match of Sandra and the twins Kate and Melanie would take place at midnight, when the air was cooler, by torchlight. Sarah had seen to it that an arena had been cleared amid the thorns, wild roses, poisonous oleander and olive, fig and orange trees. Henry, the slave Aelfric, served an early supper, and the slaves were allowed a couple of hours thereafter to rest. Jana was pleased to see that Thorsten had already made considerable progress in clearing the debris from the tower, and he assured her that building work could begin almost at once.

'All slaves, whatever their rank, shall assist,' said Jana. 'And you, Thorsten, have total authority as overseer – except that all punishments must be referred to me.'

Thorsten nodded and bowed.

At supper, Jana addressed her slaves. 'Those of you who are new to the rules of Maldona must by now have some inkling of what is in store for you. Nevertheless I shall outline the regime to which you must submit, now and for ever.' The company hushed nervously. 'Yes,' said Jana, 'for ever. You may be sent out into the world, but there is no escape from Maldona, and nor, when your bodies smart from the lash and ache from never-ceasing toil, will you wish to. Maldona is submission; submission to the rules, submission to beauty, submission to life herself. For only in true submission is there true freedom. Under the lash, my slaves, the body and all contingent reality dissolves in a sea of pain; you become a single point of light, a pure spirit, and it is only through total submission, total obedience, total acceptance of punishment, that the spirit can fly like a bird from her bodily prison and be truly free.

'But to practicality. The rules are the cornerstone of Maldona, and they must be obeyed without question. These rules have been laid down by Maldona in her manifestations over six centuries, and I am her latest manifestation. The rules *are* Maldona, a mirror image of the unseen rules which bind the ignorant in the outside world: ignorant, because they cover up reality in all the petty meannesses and sadnesses of what they call real life. But Maldona is real life, stripped of the inessential, and reduced to its shining truth: that everything is rank, power and obedience, and only when you have accepted this truth can you achieve true beauty. There is no meanness, no sadness in Maldona, only the fire of submission to beauty, and the kiss of the whip. Maldona *is* beauty, sweet slaves.'

'Adore Maldona,' murmured Cassie, and the smiling company loudly repeated her words.

'When our numbers are greater, we shall organise our society according to the rules. Below me shall be my superior, my deputy superior, then the council of adepts: manciple, almoner, armourer, hospitaller and so on. Maldona is divided into *auberges*, or houses: the *Auberge de France*, the *Auberge d'Angleterre*, the *Auberge d'Espagne*, the *Auberge d'Allemagne*. England, France, Spain, Germany: a remnant of our Templar heritage. Each *auberge* is divided into septs – seven females in each, and will have an adept as housemistress. Under her will serve prefects, and under them, with a lesser authority to award punishment, the corporals. The parfaites answer directly to me, and occupy their own quarters. *They* may inflict punishment as and when they please, except within the confines of an *auberge*, where the housemistress's authority is paramount.

'There are no clocks in Maldona, for the four bells daily are the only time you need to know. There are no maps, for Maldona is the only world you need to know. And there are no locks on any door, for there is no falsehood in Maldona. Female slaves – virgins – are forbidden to shave their minks, or to be nude except when bathing, and must submit to a short haircut befitting their abject status. Virgins must be nude under their chitons, however: neither panties nor the strophium – you would call it a brassière – are permitted, except on special days.

'Male slaves, however, being lower than females, must wear their hair long, like a girl's, and if ordered to adorn themselves with paint and powder and perfume by a female superior in rank, must obey. All, however, will be issued with a golden neckchain, which they must never remove on pain of thrashing and more. Disputes are resolved by combat in the arena, or, if I decide, by the ordeal of the lash, in which the two disputants are whipped side by side, and the first to beg for mercy is the loser.

'Some virgins get the regrettable habit of wagering their chains on wrestling contests and the like, but a virgin who loses her chain thus must expect to be reduced to a status lowlier even than that of a male. Generally, they join the melancholy underclass of whipping girls; that is, virgins who take punishment in another's place, in the hope of reward. Virgins will also be issued with a gag and a restrainer, which must be kept brightly polished, in the event that lesser punishment than beating is awarded.'

There were puzzled looks. A restrainer?

At a nod from Jana, Cassie slipped from the refectory and came back bearing canvas kitbags, which she handed to each of the company. Eagerly they opened them and took out their neckchains, all fastening them with smiles of pride. Sandra removed a curious device of gleaming steel and looked at it, frowning.

'That is your restrainer, Sandra,' Jana explained. The device was a tight waistband with a steel flap to cover buttocks and pubis, into which was built a cylinder of solid steel, the size and shape of a well-endowed man's cock, and placed directly opposite the anus. Sandra looked in wonder, then inspected her shiny gag, a steel band fitted with a large steel ball to fill the mouth. She looked at Jana with a rueful smile.

'Your gag and restrainer, Sandra,' said Jana softly. 'Be sure and keep them polished, for you never know when I shall order you to wear them.'

Jana knew that as the company of Maldona grew, so too would the intrigues, the outbursts of passion, spite and resentment which are part of any closed community. She decided to keep an eye on the tough, mannish Sandra, feeling that she could become a force for rebellion and must be tamed as soon as possible. Sarah, to whom a restrainer was nothing new, was purring with delight over her two pairs of blue silk ceremonial panties, as were Kate and Melanie. Apart from that, the kitbags contained washthings, footwear, changes of clothing, combs and brushes.

'Are the rules written down, Mistress?' asked Sandra. 'May we see them?'

'Yes, they are written down, slave Sandra,' replied Jana with a thin smile, 'and no, you may not see them. One of them is that all questions are forbidden, because questions imply ignorance, and ignorance is imperfection.'

'Oh,' said Sandra uncertainly.

'Maldona is self-knowledge. A slave must come to know herself and *feel* the rules instinctively. Imperfection is punished, even if the slave was not aware of the imperfection, because ignorance and false consciousness *are themselves imperfection.*

'Henceforth, the female slaves, even those with honorary rank, shall be known by their correct title of virgin –' Sarah Pennington made a moue '– and the males shall be simply slaves. A male who is lucky enough to gain the favour of a parfaite may become her knight, become her property, accept her robing him as a woman, and serve her in all things.'

Jana noticed that Thorsten, already flushed with wine and exertion, blushed a deeper red.

'You seem troubled, Thorsten,' said Jana impishly. 'Do explain.'

'Oh, it's nothing.'

'It's something!' rapped Jana. 'There are no secrets from Maldona! Explain, slave, or be whipped.'

'Well,' stammered Thorsten, 'it's just that . . . when I had just started in business for myself, doing household repairs, plumbing, and so on – I was about eighteen at the time –

one day I had to do some plastering in an old house in the Flensburger Strasse. I was let in by the lady of the house; very attractive, dark haired and about forty years old. She showed me the room to be plastered; it was only one wall of the marital bedroom, and space had already been cleared for me. Then she said she was going to the stables for her riding instruction, and left me there alone.'

'Very trusting,' said Sandra acidly.

'We Germans are honest!' exclaimed Thorsten. 'I began my work, and it was summer, very hot, so I took off my shirt, then stripped to my shorts, and finally, being unseen, I was quite naked. I was distracted by the scent of that bedroom: the lady's perfume hung over it like a veil of gauze, light and tempting, and . . . I became hard. At last I could stand it no longer. A strange yearning came over me: I wanted to know that woman, I wanted to *be* her. I had never felt such a thing before. I finished my work, too quickly perhaps, and then began to open her drawers. I found stockings, panties, garter belts, slips. I tried them on. Oh! I was in ecstasy! I did not know what I was doing. I was in a frenzy, swapping underthings, and the bed was strewn with them. I had quite forgotten myself. Suddenly the front door opened, and I awoke from my dream. I froze in panic as I heard her come up the stairs! She stood in the doorway and looked at me. She was wearing a silvery grey business suit, which, with her short bobbed hair, gave her a curiously masculine look.

' "Well," she said, with a sly smile, "it seems that you have been amusing yourself." I could say nothing: I was wearing her pink tights and red panties, and a white corset far too small for me, and over that a white satin blouse. She laughed.

' "I can see you need some lessons in how to be a woman," she said, "and some lessons in how to be a plasterer. What a sloppy job! But I shall attend to that later. First –"

'With that, she stripped off my blouse and laced up my corset until I felt I should burst. She pulled down the pink tights and made me sit while she painted my toenails bright

153

red, and my fingernails too! When the varnish was dry, she put red silken stockings on me, to match the panties, with a lacy red garter belt, which she fastened to the tops of the stockings. Then from her closet she took a most magnificent black ball-gown with the thinnest shoulder straps and a very deep cleavage. She touched my chest and stroked my nipples under the cloth, then put her hand inside and stroked my bare skin.

'"You have lovely breasts, like a woman's," she said, "but they are all muscle. How lovely." And suddenly her hand lifted my dress right up and went to my balls, which she squeezed quite distressingly. Oddly, this caused my erection to become firmer and I begged her not to stop. I was being seduced by a woman – turned into a woman – and began to realise what a woman must feel like when she is melting and giddy and confused as a man makes love to her. Despite my proud penis, I was her plaything, helpless and wanting to be helpless. She was not finished: she fetched rouge and kohl, and painted my lips and eyelashes, then swept back my long hair and pinned it with a jewelled slide. She adorned me with a glittering necklace, gold bracelets, and diamond earrings and put perfume behind my ears and on my breasts. Then she made me look in the mirror. I scarcely recognised myself! Here was this wondrous creature, dressed as a woman, yet more of a man for it. I can't explain. I *understood* for the first time a tiny part of the mystery of woman. Now she took a riding crop and said that I was to be punished for being a bad girl and doing an inferior job. I was so dazed, I did not resist when she put me over her knee and lifted my dress to my shoulders, then pulled down my red panties. She began to beat my bare buttocks. How I wriggled and squirmed and fought back the tears and the lump in my throat as the pain burned my naked fesses! I thought I could not stand it, but after a dozen or so lashes, and she showed no sign of stopping, I reached a state where the pain was not pain anymore, but a state of white-hot sensation; bliss almost. Under that riding crop, Mistress, I felt I was truly alive, that I could *feel*. And then I knew that my life could achieve fulfilment.'

'And afterwards?'

Thorsten grinned 'Nature took her course,' he said simply.

'Now,' Jana continued, 'the order of beatings is as follows, depending on the seriousness of the imperfection. First, know that all punishments are delivered on the bare, normally on the naked fesses but in serious cases on the bare back as well. There are no exceptions to this rule. A corporal may administer punishment of up to six strokes on a virgin's bare buttocks without reference to house-mistress, prefect or adept.

'A lady's beating is the lowest of the formal punishments. It is received in private, either from a prefect or from a corporal under the supervision of a prefect. The virgin must lift her chiton well above her waist, and bend over with her bare buttocks up and well thrust. When delivered by a corporal, the maximum number of strokes is seven; by a prefect, fourteen, or, with special permission from house-mistress or myself, as many as twenty-one.' There were gasps of thrilled astonishment, and Jana smiled within herself. 'A grand beating,' she continued, 'is more serious. She takes place indoors, but is witnessed by at least six other virgins, and the virgin to whom punishment has been granted must strip completely naked to take the cane, whip, or tawse on the buttocks *and* the shoulders. This is only administered by a prefect, who of course carries a longer and harder cane than a corporal. The number of permitted strokes is the same as for a lady's beating, except that the punishment is applied double, to both back and buttocks. Finally, there is the noble beating, a very rare thing indeed. It takes place before the whole assembly of the *auberge*, and the recipient of chastisement is naked, gagged and hooded, and bound to a flogging block by wrists and ankles in full view of her peers. At my discretion, she may also be chained.'

Jana swallowed wine and took a deep breath as she felt her fount moistening at the delicious music of her words. Eyes bright, she licked her lips.

'The noble beating is administered with the flagrum, or

many-thonged scourge of pickled olive branches, and is given on back, buttocks and the backs of the thighs. The first stroke is delivered by housemistress or adept, or perhaps myself. As for the number of strokes, there is no maximum. Each stroke is administered by a prefect in turn, so that the lashes of a noble beating follow very, very rapidly.

'Of course,' said Jana mildly, 'at any point during a beating, the slave who has been graced with punishment need only cry "I go down!" and the beating will cease. Then the slave is free to leave, and be cast out of Maldona for ever. But such an imperfection is almost unheard of: any virgin foolish enough to go down soon finds that the world outside is a very lonely and stupid place, far from the certainties of Maldona.

'That is all for the moment,' she said, 'but, Sandra, there is the little matter of your imperfection in asking a question.'

'Mistress, I didn't realise —'

'Ignorance! That makes two imperfections. I award you a lady's beating, Sandra, and you will please position yourself on the flogging block in the corner — Henry has made it nice and shiny for you — and lift your chiton well above your waist.'

Trembling, Sandra obeyed. Once she was spread-eagled on the block, with her bared buttocks thrust high in the air, Jana unfastened her four-thonged whip and approached her.

'Such a lovely firm croup,' she whispered, stroking the tight globes. 'Well, Sandra, your punishment should put you in a righteous rage for tonight's contest, so you must thank me. It'll be six, I think. Three for asking a question, three for professing ignorance. You do agree?' Hesitantly, Sandra nodded, yes. 'There's one other thing —'

Swiftly, Jana took Sandra's restrainer and, parting the cheeks of her croup, positioned the steel shaft on her anus bud and with one motion, thrust it deep inside Sandra's anus, then fastened the steel belt tightly around her waist.

'Oooo . . .' Sandra murmured, squirming. 'Oh, Mistress.'

Jana made the beating as swift and harsh as possible, scarcely pausing for an instant between each stroke. Her whipping arm rose and fell like a piston, and the six strokes were delivered in as many seconds, leaving Sandra shuddering in a dance of crimson pain.

Jana knelt and embraced the flogged woman.

'Mistress, I'm so sorry. I promise it won't happen again.'

Jana kissed her lips and stroked her hair. 'And I promise you it will,' she said softly.

A large arena was cleared in the centre of the yard's jungle of foliage, and at a minute to midnight Maldona made her appearance, followed by Cassie, carrying a kitbag. The company was assembled, faces flickering in torchlight, eager for the contest, and Jana saw that there was already evidence of bets being exchanged. She sighed, hoping that she would not be obliged to inflict too much punishment too quickly. She brushed against the scented blossoms and the tender leaves of the orange trees, and murmured to Cassie that it would be a pity to cut such ripeness.

'Everything grows again, Mistress,' said Cassie. 'Eternally.' Then she stopped, and knelt. 'Look!' she cried. 'How strange!' She plucked a stalk blooming with pretty red flowers in a star-shape.

'A nice flower,' said Jana. 'But why strange?'

'It is a hippeastrum. The horseman and star. See how the petals seem to ride each other? Mistress, the hippeastrum is only found in South America! Truly we are making Maldona in a strange place.'

The contestants were already nude and oiled by their attendants. Chris rubbed Sandra's body lovingly with olive oil, while Thorsten attended Kate and Melanie. All three breathed hard and had hatred in their eyes. Jana told Cassie to open the kitbag.

'While the contest is according to the rules of Pankration,' said Jana, 'I do not want to have any serious injuries just now. We have no hospital, and no surgeon mistress. Therefore I ordain that you shall fight gagged and wearing your restrainers, to slow you and prevent biting or injury to the front.'

The attendants quickly filled the anuses of their charges, to their groans of mingled pain and pleasure, and fastened the steel gags tightly around their chins. Jana signalled that the contest should begin.

Despite the discomfort of restrainer and gag, there were no holds barred right from the first second. Sandra flew at the smaller Melanie and Kate and banged their heads together, so that they stumbled in surprise and fell. Then Sandra pinioned them both with her large, muscled frame, kicking Melanie's breasts and face while twisting Kate's arms behind her and viciously butting her face. Suddenly Melanie managed to free herself and pulled Sandra's hair, so that she gave a muffled shriek, then, after delivering a savage kick to her sister's head, had her on the ground and sat on her belly, pummelling her breasts and face with tight fists. Now it was Kate's turn to rise, and, wrenching Melanie's head round, threw her down and returned the kicking while with her fists she pummelled Sandra's belly, breasts and face. The contest continued in this way for, Jana estimated, a good twenty minutes, with no sign of the raging contestants tiring.

'Look at our company's faces,' said Jana. 'See the blood lust, and see how the fighters hate each other. Kate and Melanie, sisters, seem to reserve the harshest punishment for each other! These are the instincts of humankind, and that is why Maldona must always keep her sacred flame burning, to tame them.'

At length, after about an hour, it seemed that the fighters were too exhausted to continue. The end position was that Kate had spread-eagled herself over her sister and Sandra, with both their arms twisted hideously behind their backs, and was feebly kicking and pummelling their prone bodies. Jana stepped forward and declared Kate the winner. She knelt and removed gags and restrainers from all three women.

'Henceforth, Kate, you shall be honorary parfaite,' she announced. 'My congratulations. I hope you can be friends with your sister after this excellent but vicious contest. And I hope there are no bones broken, for we do not yet possess a surgeon mistress.'

'Mistress,' said Kate, rising, 'that is not fair. Melanie and I are twins –' she lifted Melanie and embraced her, leaving Sandra, groaning, to be helped up by her bejewelled and rouged Chris '– and we do everything together. So it would be imperfect for me to have a higher rank than Melanie. Let Sandra be parfaite.'

At this, Sandra spoke. 'No, Mistress,' she said, breathless but sly. 'I was beaten fairly. But there is a position I covet, of greater power than a mere parfaite.' She looked disdainfully at the twins. 'You know that a flight attendant must have a basic knowledge of first-aid procedures. Mistress, I did not tell you that before joining the airline I spent three years as a nurse at the Radcliffe Hospital in Oxford. So –'

Jana raised her hand. 'Enough,' she said. 'I have decided, then. Kate and Melanie shall both be honorary parfaites, but with no power to whip without my permission.' The twins smiled and hugged each other. 'You, Sandra, shall be surgeon mistress.'

Sandra beamed and embraced Chris. 'Thank you, Mistress, she said softly.

Now, Sarah Pennington began to shoo her charges back to their cells for the night, and as Sandra left with her slave Chris (for, as Jana saw, slave and mistress alliances were forming naturally, without her inspiration or command) Jana heard her whisper to Chris, 'Those two think they have power now. But as surgeon mistress, sweet Chris, I have the greater power, the power over life and death.'

Over the next two months, the Castle of the Templars was speedily and, Jana thought, perhaps miraculously transformed into the Castle of Maldona. Thorsten kept his work gang at constant toil, while Jana, with the help of Cassie the Superior, pored over plans for the extension of the castle on to the slopes facing the sea.

There would be a gymnasium, bath house and sauna, a hospital, and, in the fullness of time, a swimming pool, all built as far as possible from the abundant local stone, as well as separate buildings for the four *auberges*.

The question of the sunken *Hesperides* and the lure of the underwater garden was put off and put off again, for Jana found herself overwhelmed with work. And she was, deep in her heart, frightened of what secrets she would find. The question of her swim to Circe's island was also put off, for she feared that there she would find the clue to a mystery of whose nature she was only dimly aware. Any questions she put obliquely to Sarah or the twins were with equal obliqueness fended off. Jana knew that a cabal had formed among the three tattooed women, and knew too that the time would have to come when she must break it or absorb it to herself.

She mentioned the wreck of the *Hesperides* to Chris, who seemed curiously unconcerned.

'I cannot swim,' he said, 'therefore neither can I dive. Seamen do not learn to swim, Mistress: it takes longer to drown. And anyway, it is impious and unlucky to take from the sea god what he has claimed as his.'

Jana let the matter rest because already there had begun a steady trickle of newcomers, mostly young women, but with a sprinkling of males, who arrived by rowing boat, by swimming from passing ferries, from all the corners of the world. Some mentioned Caspar and Netta; others had simply heard by word of mouth in the subtle network of the scene. It became a priority to build *auberges* as lodgings for the newcomers and Jana and Cassie had their work cut out inducting the new virgins and slaves, introducing them to the rules of Maldona, assigning them to *auberges* and accustoming them to hard work. For the meantime they lodged in cells around the yard: when these were full, new buildings outside the castle walls must be ready.

Jana found that the simplest if most basic way to induct the bedraggled but eager newcomers was to feed them while saying as little as possible, then order them to strip, and, wordlessly, beat them on the bare with a rattan cane. This, she found, had more of an effect in taming them than her painstaking explanation of the rules. Always she received their tearful thanks.

One advantage of the newcomers was that Maldona now possessed quite a flotilla of beach rowing boats.

'We shall soon have a navy,' said Jana jokingly to Cassie. And there was a faraway gleam in her eye.

Meanwhile, Thorsten found frequent occasions to send his workers to Jana for a whipping.

'Laziness is the worst imperfection,' he would growl as Jana raised her whip yet again to redden the bare buttocks of slave, adept and parfaite alike. She knew that those of rank resented this demeaning treatment – *they* should be the ones wielding the whip! – but Jana explained that their rank was only honorary and that the work had to be done. She permitted the slaves to work naked if they desired, because of the heat, and loved to watch the bare bodies gleaming with sweat as they laboured – laboured for her, Jana.

At the end of a month, the renovation of the corner tower was complete, and Jana's apartments were ready for her on the top floor. Below her, the Superior Cassie had her own rooms, both apartments reached by a winding stone staircase and, Jana made sure, secured behind a heavy wooden door. There was no lock, of course, but Jana felt safer with a pile of heavy rocks ready to block unwanted incursions, from whatever quarter.

Work then started on the stone buildings of the *auberges*, and, with the increase in numbers, on the bath house and gymnasium, all stone structures outside the walls facing the sea. Kate and Melanie were each put in charge of separate work gangs beside Thorsten's, and Jana now accorded them the privilege of delivering punishment without recourse to her. High in her tower, now, she heard throughout the day the resonant crack of whip on naked flesh as Kate and Melanie pursued their metier as parfaites with exemplary gusto.

161

12

Aphrodite

It was rare that a whipping was given on the back, but once, Sarah Pennington earned such a harsh and humiliating punishment. Sarah, the sly, elfin submissive, relished a caning on the bare, and time after time would approach the limit of insolence in her attitude towards the parfaites, who knew to their fury that she would like nothing better than to receive a sound thrashing on the naked croup. Jana had to advise them discreetly that the worst punishment for Sarah was to refuse her the privilege of punishment, leaving her to attend, unsatisfactorily, to her own needs with a branch or bare hand, whose crack on her own buttocks would echo eerily through the castle yard as she writhed on her palliasse.

But one day, she showed imperfection to Jana herself. She petulantly threw aside the heavy rock she was carrying, and exclaimed that she thought herself ill-used, that their work was all a waste of time, and that she wanted to go home.

'This is your home, Sarah,' said Jana with chilling simplicity. She swished her whip lightly in the air, scattering gnats and butterflies in the hot eddy of dust. On that sweltering day, she wore nothing but sandals, a crown of flowers, and her parfaite's harness, enjoying the tickle in her filled sex and anus as she sauntered through her new demesne, and the delicious seeping of wetness which made her thighs glisten. Her constant state of sexual arousal made all her senses keener, making her heart glow at the beauty of her creation, and heightened the loveliness of the sky and sea, the naked rock and the bright flowers blooming in its crevices like young, budding women's lips, and the tan bodies that laboured for her. She felt a rush of anger at Sarah's insolence, and with a swift pressure of her sphincter muscle, raised her fans of plumage to full height so that they seemed to quiver with her rage. Jana pointed to the whipping post.

'You have earned yourself a noble beating for your insolence, miss,' she said, and Sarah's mischievous eyes sparkled. She no longer looked tired but, rather, made vital by the prospect of being trussed for a thrashing on her naked body. She bowed her head meekly.

'Twenty-one, Mistress? And on the bare bum? How harsh you are, but how just. In my moment of foolish imperfection, I am sure I have earned a noble beating.'

'No, miss, I'm not giving you that satisfaction. I know only too well how your little bum loves to squirm. I'll whip you on your bare back, like some wretched *matelot* at the mainmast.'

Sarah's eyes moistened a little with disappointment, but she placidly allowed herself to be strapped to the whipping post, her arms high above her head and wrists knotted tightly by Melanie and Kate.

'See how well I take it, you soft creatures,' she whispered, but loudly enough for Jana to hear. Sarah threw her head back, rippling the strong shoulder muscles, and as her mane of hair glistened in the sunlight, Jana felt a flutter of desire in her belly. In a strange way, she loved Sarah, as one never forgets one's first lover, and Sarah, by submitting to Jana's hesitant cane, had been the first woman to awaken Jana to her true nature, her true beauty. Melanie and Kate, glowering at Sarah's insult, tightened her bonds until she mewed in distress, and Jana suddenly felt a rush of moisture bathe her inner thighs as her heart leapt with the desire to flog the helpless woman's smooth bare body. She ordered the two parfaites to stand aside, and raised her whip.

Her eyes blurred with sweat and she raised a hand to wipe her brow. Through the moisture, Sarah's body shimmered golden like a trembling flower in the midst of the

163

island's arid beauty, and Jana longed to pluck her. She wanted to make her quiver and shake in the pain of the whip's caress until her petals cascaded one by one and Jana could gather them up. She wanted to press them to her breasts and the petals of her own sex, and breathe the sweet girl-scent as she took Sarah inside the intimate openings of her body and rubbed the soft petals of her against her tingling nympha, before melting into the lushness of orgasm as Sarah's perfume filled her.

Jana shook her head to clear her fantasy, and found she was breathing harshly in excitement. She put out her hand and stroked Sarah's back gently, and with little cooing noises she touched the taut flesh that her whip would caress. Sarah too breathed deeply, but said nothing, until Jana's hand crept down her spine, the fingers lightly walking down to the cleft of her buttocks. When Jana had reached the spine's base and stroked her there, in the centre of her vital energy, Sarah gave a little moan and parted her thighs slightly, revealing her pink anus bud and open sex. The petals of her sex were red and swollen with unmistakable desire, and, as the silent company nervously watched, Jana's hand, trembling, slid between the cheeks of Sarah's buttocks to caress her anus before moving to the protruding red sex-petals, where she found the nympha distended and hard. She rubbed her with a feather's touch. Sarah cried out softly.

'Oh, Mistress,' she said, 'you know you are tormenting me. Is that part of my punishment?'

'You know it is, Sarah,' said Jana hoarsely as, flowing with wetness in her own slit, she probed Sarah's quim with quivering fingers. The young woman began to writhe in a sinuous motion of her buttocks and pelvis, pressing her clit on Jana's hand and mewling with little cries of faint ecstasy. Jana could feel the hardening of her own nympha as her juices bathed the soft thigh-skin beneath her swollen lips, and she knew she must stop before her desire for Sarah's young body made her forget her task as mistress.

As she withdrew her glistening wet hand from Sarah's soaking quim, she kissed her lightly on the shoulder, and whispered, 'You are so lovely, Sarah. Your cunt is so sweet and wet for me. But I must do my duty. I must whip you with all my strength, for your imperfection.'

'With all your strength and more, sweet Mistress,' said Sarah. 'Please, do it to me. I long for your whip to mark me in love.' Abruptly, she bent her head forward, and her back and legs stiffened in anticipation of her beating.

Jana suddenly brought her whip whistling down to crack across Sarah's shoulders, with such force that Sarah jerked in her bonds and sighed with a long, low moan that was both pain and desire. Thereafter, as Jana mercilessly applied the four-thonged whip to every inch of her naked shoulders and upper back, she jumped at every stroke but uttered no sound save for the increasing harshness of her gulping breath. As she watched her victim's skin redden under her lash, Jana herself felt the moisture flow unchecked from her sex, and the tingling of her swollen clit became almost unbearable. She longed to take Sarah by the head and press her mouth there, in the hot oily wetness of her gushing cunt, and let the young woman's tongue flicker against the stiff nympha until Jana could cry out in the blessed relief of orgasm.

Sarah took 21 strokes without a murmur, although at each one her body twitched violently, and when the cruelly grinning parfaites loosened her bonds, her face was as red as her livid back. Jana felt her sex swimming with loving warmth at the sight of the flogged girl bending stiffly, her pert breasts bobbing and her nipples hard, to bow low before her mistress.

'Sarah Pennington,' said Jana, her voice quivering, 'you are brave, as brave as a woman can be, and have taken your punishment like a true slave of Maldona. You have thus, I deem, earned ennoblement, and I raise you to the rank of Parfaite of Maldona. Melanie, you shall fetch Sarah her flagrum of olive branches, and when she grasps it, you and Kate shall embrace your new sister.'

'Mistress,' said Sarah, wide-eyed, 'the honour I have dreamed of . . . I don't know what to say.'

'Then say nothing, Parfaite. Now that you are three, it

is time for my parfaites to take names befitting their rank. You shall no longer be Kate, Melanie and Sarah, but shall bear the timeless names of your nobility. I shall inform you of my choice. For the moment, Sarah, you must know in your heart that to submit to the rules of Maldona, mere submission, the unquestioned baring of your naked body to her chastisement, is not enough. A woman who is a parfaite of Maldona, must also learn to rule.'

At the end of the third month Maldona was if not complete – Jana knew that Maldona could never be complete, for how could the world be complete? – at least fully formed. There were four sturdy stone structures to serve as *auberges*, a far cry from the sumptuous palaces of Jana's castle in Spain, but she had artfully designed them so that they were easily capable of extension, either upward or outward.

There was, however, a sumptuous bath house, complete with two fountains, or toilets, one for slaves and one for adepts, equipped with a circle of stone commodes, on which Jana liked to squat for lengthy, intimate chats with Cassie or Sarah, of whom, an exemplary parfaite, she was growing more and more fond. One day, she and Sarah were squatting, Sarah with her skirt up, and Jana nude except for her golden waist chains.

'Your mink is growing back nicely, Sarah,' said Jana. 'Does she itch?'

'No longer, Mistress,' said Sarah.

'I see you have kept your hair short although, as a parfaite, you are not obliged to.'

Sarah blushed. 'It is more comfortable, Mistress,' she said, 'and I am not sure I am used to being a parfaite just yet. But please, Mistress, let me warn you of something. It is just a whisper in the air, a breeze. The twins Melanie and Kate – I am close to them, as you know, but not as close as they are to each other. Watch them.'

'Is it to do with the rose tattoos? With the island of Circe?'

'Yes, Mistress. Circe is a witch. It was she who did the

tattoos. With Caspar's encouragement. And the tattoo can go either way; that is, it can give great power or subject you to great power, the power of Circe. I suspect that the twins are somehow under Circe's power.'

'And you?'

Sarah smiled, and gently, surprisingly, touched Jana's naked quim. 'You know that your power over me is stronger, Mistress.'

Jana smiled. 'Tonight, I shall make Henry prepare a banquet, to celebrate the completion of the first stage of the Castle of Maldona.'

'The first stage, Mistress?'

'Sarah, there will be no end to the building of Maldona, to the empire of Maldona. Already I have plans and secrets, which you will have the good sense not to ask about. Anyway, the banquet shall be only for us first members of the castle.'

She rose from the commode and wiped herself, then smiled goodbye to Sarah.

The banquet that evening was a proud affair. All had taken the liberty of adorning themselves garishly, like wood sprites, naiads and satyrs. Sandra wore a revealing swimsuit, and even Thorsten had a wreath of olive leaves and branches for his hair, giving him the sultry aspect of some Nordic god. Jana knew that soon she must oblige them to cast aside these fancies for the stern uniform of virgins and slaves of Maldona.

The table was bright with flowers and shining crystal as all toasted their mistress and her enterprise; their enterprise, for every human being takes pride in building. Chris, in make-up and still tethered by his ball-chain, which snaked under his leafy cache-sexe, and made his cock rings jangle as he walked, served dishes of fried fish and steaming pink crustaceans. As the conversation became animated by wine, Jana, silent in her high place, crunched lobster shell and surveyed her slaves. Already they took their labour not as duty but as pride, and the air hummed with speculation about the second storey of the castle, and

167

the third – perhaps a fourth, a fifth! Maldona knew no limit. She would look out, impregnable, over the blue Aegean as the Templars had in the old times. Jana spoke.

'There shall be seven storeys to the Castle of Maldona,' she said drily. 'It is the perfect number.'

'Higher than Maldona herself, in Spain?' asked Cassie in wonder.

'Higher,' said Jana.

There was an uneasy pause before Henry raised his glass and cried, 'Adore Maldona!'

And at that, there was an uproar of joy, as the entire company followed him, chanting the words as they drank to their mistress. Jana's heart swelled, and she felt herself smiling and blushing as she shared her slaves' joy. Then she wiped a small tear from her eye, for she knew that Maldona was love.

Suddenly, Sarah Pennington's voice cried softly, 'Look Mistress! There is a ship. All glittering with lights, a big, rich ship, and so pretty.'

Jana rose to look. 'You were not thinking of leaving us, Sarah?' she said acidly. 'Some rich man come to whisk you away?' She flicked her whip against Sarah's breasts, making her wince.

'Never, Mistress,' said Sarah. 'You know that. I was just curious.'

Jana looked round the faces of her slaves, who craned to see the ship from their seats. 'A ship,' she said. 'How exciting for us all. We can be rescued. Does anyone wish to take the boat and travel out to that ship, and plead for a passage to what you call home? Away from a life of slavery, punishment, and backbreaking toil? For make no mistake, there shall be no easy life in Maldona, for any of you. Just when you think your pain is at an end, and you have earned a life of ease and comfort, why then the pain will double, and double again. I shall not say "until you cannot bear anymore", for you shall always be able to bear more. Pain and love without end, my slaves, that is Maldona's rule. And now anyone is free to leave my table and make their way down to that friendly ship.'

No one moved, and Jana smiled a thin smile, though her heart was pounding. She nodded in appreciation.

'Good,' she whispered, 'for I can see our ship is already turning to leave –'

'Mistress,' said Chris, 'I know that ship. I served on her once. She belongs to Adamo Lines, of Athens. She's owned by Alexander Damoglou.'

'I know of him,' said Jana carefully, scanning the moonlit water. 'He is very rich indeed. And I believe he has a daughter.'

'Aphrodite Damoglou is a prize beyond measure,' said Chris reverently, 'but she is a law to herself. There are all kinds of strange stories about the fates of her lovers, mysterious fates all . . .' And he shivered deliciously.

'I think stories can wait until later, slave,' said Jana sharply. 'Someone is coming; I hear footsteps, quiet and sure and with little good in them.'

The footsteps were clearly heard in the hush, above the sound of cicadas and the distant hooting of night owls. The steps were slow and measured, slapping in sombre rhythm on the stone flags of the castle's entry, like some golem or spirit come to haunt the living. Though flushed with wine and gaiety, the company sat in nervous silence. The footsteps were soft, like silken sandals, and of only one person, yet all shivered at the arrival of the stranger.

The refectory door opened and a young woman entered. She was tall, taller even than Cassie, and almost naked. Black, lustrous air cascaded over her smoothly muscled shoulders and ripe brown breasts. Her body shone with droplets of sweat mingled with streaks of salt water, and the perfume of the sea hung on her like the breath of a goddess. Strands of gleaming seaweed wreathed her belly and sex, and she wore nothing else save for necklaces of seashells which criss-crossed the swelling pride of her breasts, leaving the tall crimson hillocks of her nipples bare. A thong of woven gold scarcely covered the rich smooth mound of her shaven pubis.

Slowly, as the company of Maldona watched with still breath, she unwound her golden girdle, revealing it to be one long, fine chain wrapped around her sweetly jutting sex and fesses. And when she was nude, her nether garment now a glittering pile of gold in the palm of her hand, she went to Jana and knelt, silently offering the gold to her. Jana gravely accepted the golden offering, still warm and damp from the woman's vulva and anus, and scrutinised the nude female in obeisance at her feet. Her body was the body of a goddess; slim and firm with full, strong breasts, the nipples as round and swollen as little crimson cups, and the croup a lush swell of ripe peaches. Dark brown eyes gazed up at Jana, beseeching her.

'Who are you, woman?' said Jana, fingering the shining strands of gold, feeling their salty wetness and scenting the perfume of the woman's sex.

'My name is Aphrodite,' said the woman, bowing her head, 'and I come to bare my body and my soul to the kiss of Maldona.'

13

A Goddess Whipped

All were mesmerised by the insolent yet fragile beauty of the woman who had come to them from the sea.

'Be seated, Aphrodite,' said Jana softly, her eyes wide with wonder and foreboding. She gestured to Chris that he should make a place at the high end for the sea-wet goddess, for to Jana's eyes, a goddess she seemed. Aphrodite took her seat beside Jana, while the eyes of every other woman sparkled with jealous curiosity. Jana clenched her eyes shut for one brief moment as she remembered her dream, and when she opened her eyes again she knew Aphrodite had observed her flash of fearful remembrance. The flickering candlelight illuminated the soft crevices of Aphrodite's perfectly muscled body, lithe as an eel, her flat belly and firm, almost conical, breasts. It threw into shadow the twin soft cupolas of her nipples which, Jana noticed, were standing quite stiff, as though her nudity aroused her.

'You are welcome, Aphrodite,' said Jana in a loud, slightly trembling voice. 'It is strange and happy that you should know of our presence here.'

Aphrodite gave a shrug, and creased her lips in a soft pout. Her wide, sulky lips looked as though a smile rarely graced them.

'News travels,' she said in the silky English accent only ever obtained by foreigners.

'You will take wine?', said Jana.

'I shall take water. Aphrodite does not take wine, for Aphrodite is wine.'

A pitcher of water was brought and she drank it, then

crooked her little finger for another. When she received it she said nothing, but poured the water over her breasts in a swift movement so that it trickled over her bare belly and on to the impossibly full swelling of her naked mons, then between her fleshy sex-petals, where a stiff nympha peeped in hard pink loveliness. As Aphrodite slowly rubbed the salt and dust from her skin, sighing at her cleansing, Jana breathed sharply, realising that Aphrodite's exposure of her body had excited her already to a state of tingling hardness, of both nipples and nympha. She touched Aphrodite's upper thigh with fleeting, friendly fingers, to find the soft skin oily with her juice.

'You are excited to be in the company of Maldona, Aphrodite,' whispered Jana, her lips pressing the woman's ear. It was a statement, not a question.

It was then that a slow, beautiful smile creased Aphrodite's lips, and in her smile Jana saw the sea and the stars shining.

'You are indeed perceptive, Mistress,' she said, 'for why else would I present myself thus to your gaze? I wish to join you – I have brought tribute.'

'Your body is tribute enough, sweet Aphrodite,' said Jana. 'You will share our food now. We are comfortable, we have nuts and fruit and olives and the riches of the sea.' She realised, faced with the glistening beauty of the goddess, herself seaborne, how trite her phrase sounded.

When Aphrodite had nodded to indicate that she should be served, the company resumed their lively talking.

Aphrodite was brought plates of fruit, shellfish, nuts and salads. She ate sparingly and disdainfully, and spat stones and shells and skins on the floor in the manner of one used to servants. As she watched the woman eat, so arrogantly yet so gracefully, Jana sipped wine, trying to hide the nervous trembling of her lips as she suddenly felt herself quiver with a desire to reach out and embrace her.

Jana could not fail to notice Cassie's moue: the two women beside her were so alike in their sultry Mediterranean beauty. The droplets of sweat and seawater had dried from Aphrodite's burnished skin, and if she was indeed

Aphrodite Damoglou – there seemed to be no other explanation, if Chris was to be believed – then she was every
inch the spoiled, beautiful heiress. Yet there was nothing
spoilt about her superb body. There was not an ounce of
fat on her graceful muscles, betokening a devotion to gymnasium and tennis court and, Jana thought, intrigued,
perhaps more. She allowed her fingers to touch Aphrodite's taut biceps, and the woman did not flinch but
smiled another serene smile. She then touched the hard
fullness of the thighs, which Aphrodite gently parted, looking up, so as to allow Jana's fingers to stray dangerously
near the crimson, parted petals of her sex, from which her
stiffened clit stood so boldly. Aphrodite suddenly yawned
and stretched herself.

'It is fitting that Aphrodite should arrive amongst you
from the sea, the fount of life and love, is it not?' she purred. 'But the skin dries so in the salt water. I had to swim
from my yacht – well, I am obliged to do nothing, but I
chose to.' And, without warning, she stood and picked up
the amphora of olive oil which had dressed her food, and
poured the whole of it, about half a litre, over her bare
body.

Jana smiled at the haughty impertinence and felt herself
thrill as Aphrodite slowly and deliberately rubbed the oil
into her skin, lingering on her taut breasts and erect
nipples, her eyes smouldering mischievously, clearly aware
of what she did and the effect it had. She was superb, a
goddess indeed, as she caressed herself, rubbing the limpid
oil along her smooth legs and the ripples of her back, then
into the crevice of her sex beneath the gorgeously swelling
mons, shining so tenderly in her shaven nudity.

When she was covered in oil and glistening like star-
shine, Aphrodite graced the company with an open yet
slightly mocking smile, and with an impish flicker of her
eyelashes, opened the petals of her sex to show a clitoris of
sweetly extravagant size, stiff and pink like a tight crab in
her shell. Jana's eyes widened as she thought, alarmed, She
is bigger than I.

'Isn't this what you want to see?' said Aphrodite defiantly,

173

her lips addressing the company but her eyes on Jana's. 'The thing that gives me the arrogance to come here uninvited, to Maldona?' She yawned again, but Jana saw it was only a pretence. 'I know of Maldona, of course, the Maldona of old Spain. And I have decided to become part of her. I shall enter as a virgin, of course, but when I have fought and defeated you all according to the rules of Pankration, our ancient Greek wrestling, I shall be Superior.'

'Pankration wrestling is very hard, Aphrodite,' said Jana quietly.

Aphrodite turned to smile broadly at her. 'And I am very hard, Mistress,' she said. 'It is my nature. I am born to rule, but also, deep in me, I know I am born to serve and obey also, to submit with grace to . . . to the rules. In my life out there –' she waved imperiously towards the sea and the distant Greek shore '– I make my own rules. Here, I shall learn to obey the rules of Maldona, for Maldona is the one place where to command and obey are one and the same thing. Do you approve of my body, Mistress? My hard muscles, my swelling nympha under my bare mons? These things I have received from self-discipline; now I crave the perfect discipline of Maldona. For I have received other discipline too, less than perfect.'

Aphrodite turned abruptly and displayed the spread cheeks of her naked fesses, and there were gasps of awe and delight as she revealed herself to bear deep crimson.

'So you are no stranger to the whip,' said Jana.

'I think I wear good enough credentials,' said Aphrodite with a strange, passionate seriousness in her eyes, almost a pleading. 'I have taken many, many strokes on the bare, Mistress, and long to take many more and sweeter.' Jana blushed, feeling her sex wet with desire for the body and the smile, the soul herself, of the young woman. She saw that Henry's eyes were also narrowed, fastened on her gleaming ripe body.

'I shall have a cell here,' declared Aphrodite.

'Yes, of course. It shall be made ready. But tell me, Aphrodite – the marks of chastisement your body bears – how . . ?'

174

Aphrodite smiled again and sat, but still kept her fingers idly on the petals of her sex, caressing herself there and obviously knowing that she tantalised Jana.

'I see Chris here,' she said. 'He is a good sailor, but talks much. You know that my father Alexander owns ships, and has money, although the yacht I came on is my own, his gift. I am my own mistress – now. But I long for Maldona to be my mistress.' She paused, frowned, and picked up the tips of Jana's whip, rubbing them gently against her breasts so that the thongs shone with the oil from her body. 'You wear a parfaite's flogging harness, Mistress,' she said. 'One day, I shall too. You are so beautiful, like a winged bird.' Her eyes darted to the glistening of love-oil which had seeped from Jana's sex over her soft inner thighs, and she smiled distantly. Then her fingertips delicately touched Jana there and stroked her. When her fingers gleamed with Jana's liquid, she brought her fingers to her lips and sucked them, her eyes on Jana's. Jana felt herself blush.

'You taste of the sea, Mistress, of the waves and the life beneath them. It is good.' She fingered her necklace of seashells, and began to rub Jana's liquid into the thongs of her whip. 'May I?' she added suddenly, detaching the whip from Jana's belt.

Jana, mesmerised, nodded yes, her sex flowing now in the melting intensity of her desire. Aphrodite placed her fingers on Jana's sex-lips and moistened them with the pool of liquid which Jana was powerless to stem. She licked her fingers again, smiling slyly, and rubbed more of the oil into the whip's leather thongs.

'It makes the whip more supple, more painful,' she said thoughtfully, rubbing the thongs against her. 'I love the caress of a whip on my breasts, Mistress.'

'I am not yet your mistress,' said Jana faintly, but knowing that nothing could stop her from making Aphrodite her slave. Cassie and Henry, from their eyes, knew it too. How long can I keep this woman as my slave, Jana wondered, before she wants to – she could not bring herself to think, take my place. 'You are to tell your story,' she said.

175

Her fingers unconsciously strayed to Aphrodite's necklace of seashells and stroked it, her eyes misty with desire. The shells were small and smooth and shaped like little snail-shells.

Aphrodite smiled at her curiosity. 'It is a kind of clam, particular to our Aegean Sea,' she murmured, 'and said to possess magical properties. One must dive very deep for them, and according to our custom must cut the shell open there on the sea bed and eat the creature alive, and only then is it permitted to adorn one's body with the shell. I myself fetched all these shells from the sea bed, near an island which was my father's. I must tell you that Alexander Damoglou is not . . . my father.'

'So, you are adopted?' asked Jana.

'Not exactly adopted,' said Aphrodite. Her smile faded and her eyes lowered. 'I was a foundling, an orphan, I suppose. I was abandoned . . . I was found amongst rocks, by the lapping waves, on one of these islands. Alexander Damoglou's yacht hove to, by a chance, lucky or not, and he took me for his own.'

'So, Aphrodite is born of the sea,' said Jana in wonder. 'An infant, in a crib of shells and bright fishes, the swirling weeds your coverlet.'

Aphrodite smiled, and Jana saw that the woman's hand began to caress her clit again, a frown of concentration on her brow.

'I only knew when my father Damoglou, or my guardian if you will, took me back to the place on my eighteenth birthday. He said it was time I should know where I came from. Who put me there, or how, I do not know. How often, since then, have I thought of my real mother and father, who they were and why they left me to die, on the island Damoglou owned. He had no plans for the island, no ugly building; he simply liked to own it, as a toy, almost, the way he liked to own me.

'During that voyage, I made friends with a young crewman. He was very beautiful, with curly silken hair, and a smile that . . . well, it was he who taught me to dive for the shells, and . . . taught me to love. Together we would dive, and embrace under the water, as the fish and weeds caressed our bare bodies. I learned to hold my breath like a true diver, for minutes, and we would love each other, quickly, and in secret, under the concealing waters. One night, when Damoglou and his wife slept – I could not think of them as father and mother now – we swam to the island and made love on the beach, again and again, until it was dawn. I remember the full moon and the scent of the lapping waves as my naked young man took me, in . . . in all my places, Mistress, and all the time he would touch me there, as I touch myself now, remembering him. As I felt him wash me with his love, and the stars and moon shone down on us, I thought myself in heaven. But we stayed too long, and saw the sun rise before we swam back to the ship. Our clothes were wet, it was obvious what we had done, and my guardian threatened to leave us marooned on his barren island unless we agreed to take punishment for our insolence. We had to agree: what choice was there?'

Aphrodite was now rubbing her stiff nympha quite vigorously, and her eyes were narrow, her breath hard.

'Your punishment, then?' whispered Jana. 'Or is the memory too painful?'

Aphrodite casually rubbed some more oil from her shining breasts into the thongs of Jana's whip, then sopped up the juice from the love-pool under Jana's engorged sex-petals and applied that too.

'Mmm,' she said, smelling the shiny leather, 'they smell so lovely and salty now, Mistress, like you.' Jana felt her face redden, as Aphrodite went on. 'Damoglou, my guardian, made me swim again to the island, quite naked, for my humiliation, and fetch a switch of olive branches and carry them between my teeth back to the ship. Then I was obliged to watch as my lover was trussed to the rail to take twelve strokes of the switch on his naked buttocks. As I watched, to my shame, I found myself wet in my sex at the sight of my beautiful naked man tied to be flogged, and I saw my stepmother's face redden, and knew that as she watched, she was as excited as I was. But then, Mistress, my cruellest of guardians told me I was to administer his

177

flogging! I wept, but had to obey, and to my horror I found that as I lashed my lover's naked buttocks, my sex moistened and there was sweetness in my belly. I was angry at him for making no sound, and lashed him as hard as I could! Then it was my turn, and I too took twelve on my bare fesses, my hands and ankles tied to the ship's rail, delivered by my own lover. As I faced our island, each stroke sent fire through my body and my cheeks were wet with salt tears. I looked at the island and longed to be there. It hurt abominably, the more so as my skin was wet. But strangely, as my beating progressed, I felt a flutter in my belly and wetness in my sex, and the searing pain of the olive quirt began to seem like the caress of a lover on my tenderest parts. I turned to look at his body, and saw that his penis stood as he beat me!

'Damoglou was consumed in his vengeful fury, and did not even notice my excitement, my ecstasy . . . Each stroke came, lacing my buttocks with fire, and I felt a surge of power and pleasure in me, knowing that I had taken the pain without protest. At the twelfth stroke, I felt my sex flow wet, and my belly heaved, and then I gave a little cry, because I was coming. I cried out not from pain, but from the beauty of the pain and the excitement of being watched as I was beaten naked, and the warmth of the orgasm which made me shudder.

'It was then that I discovered the pride in bearing pain, in being exposed naked and helpless to the cruel gaze of others as I triumph over them by enduring my chastisement. Is it not thrilling to expose our women's bodies to the eyes of others, Mistress? To feel abject, humiliated, a slave who in her very submission is all-powerful? As I am now, Mistress, showing you myself so blatantly, and doing . . . this . . .' Aphrodite was now panting, and her face was flushed as she rubbed her swollen, almost obscenely stiff nympha, mesmerising Jana. 'Since then, sweet Mistress, I have needed a beating, or needed to dwell on my sweet memories of chastisements past, before, oh, before I can . . . come!'

And as Jana and the entire company watched,

Aphrodite moaned loud and high as she shuddered in the intensity of the orgasm to which her flickering fingers had brought her.

When her climax had passed and her moans had died to a soft sighing purr in her throat, she looked shyly at Jana.

'You must think me rude, Mistress.'

'No, Aphrodite, I think you beautiful and truthful, which are the same. But I am not yet your mistress.'

'I have behaved badly, arriving uninvited and then making a mess for my servants to clean up. Except that I am bereft of servants here. Aren't you going to order me to clean my own mess?'

Jana smiled at this coy game. 'Yes, Aphrodite. Down on your knees, you pig, and clean. And keep your bum well in the air, my lady, for you must pick up your mess in your mouth. No hands.'

Aphrodite handed the whip to Jana and slid from her chair, crouching on the floor with her buttocks stretched wide and high to Jana's intent gaze. She looked at the two tan globes, smooth and naked, and knew they begged to be caressed with a rod of punishment. She said nothing, but picked up her whip as Aphrodite snuffled around the floor, picking up nutshells and morsels of flesh with her lips and teeth. In truth, she had not left much mess at all. Jana raised her whip.

'Oh!' cried Aphrodite softly, and her bottom shivered as the four shining leather thongs cracked across her bare skin. 'Oh, Mistress –'

'I shall count to twelve, Aphrodite,' said Jana, lifting her flogging arm once again.

'Thank you, Mistress,' murmured Aphrodite, 'but wait.' She took off her necklace of shells and, spreading her buttocks very wide so that the pink bud of her anus was exposed, laid the necklace in the cleft of her cheeks. 'There are twelve shells,' she whispered. 'Please, Mistress, don't you know how I must be punished?'

Jana took the necklace and held Aphrodite's cheeks apart as she brushed the bud of her anus with the end of the necklace. Swiftly, she bent and put her lips to the woman's tender pink anus, and Aphrodite shivered in pleasure. Then she put her finger between her own thighs, smearing it generously with her love-oil, and applied it to Aphrodite's bumhole as a lubricant. Her finger tickled the bud, then crept inside the tight passage, making Aphrodite squeal softly with delight. The necklace slid easily into her channel until only a dangling shred of string was visible. Aphrodite's cheeks clenched and squirmed as she moved the shells with her sphincter, moaning with the pleasure of her filled nether hole. Then Jana began to count the strokes of her whip, and at each stroke, she pulled the string of the necklace, one shell at a time, out of Aphrodite's tight anus. At each cut of the four thongs on her naked arse, and at each tug of her necklace, the goddess groaned and her buttocks squirmed in her strange dance of ecstasy.

After the twelfth stroke, when her buttocks were twin glowing orbs of crimson skin, Aphrodite sighed as the final shell popped from her anus and to Jana's surprise rolled herself on to her back and opened her thighs to the eyes of the assembly. With a trembling hand, she touched her distended clitoris, just once, and cried out loud as she quivered in orgasm.

Jana looked with envy on the woman's writhing body, both of her exuberant self-abasement and her ability to achieve ecstasy with the sweetest and most bizarre of torments.

'Aphrodite,' said Cassie in a tart voice, 'now that our mistress has, I suppose, inducted you into Maldona –' she looked at Jana, who nodded in agreement '– do you mind telling us what is this tribute you bring?'

'Why, I had my crew unload a cargo at night, thinking it would help in the building of Maldona,' said Aphrodite, still crouching, as Jana rubbed oil into her bruised bottom. 'It is a whole shipload of German brick and Carrara marble. Oh, and tons of cement.'

'I give you Aphrodite, new virgin of Maldona!' cried Jana, helping Aphrodite to her feet and embracing her. Both women glowed with love; Henry and Cassie watched stone-faced.

'One thing puzzles me, Aphrodite,' said Jana. 'This island your guardian owns –'

'Owned,' interrupted Aphrodite. 'It was a toy, and he tires of toys. He even tired of me ... well, he sold the island. To whom, and for what intended purpose, I do not know. And I'm not sure it matters now.'

'Where was it, though? The island where you were born, where the sea gave you up to our dry world?'

'Why, Mistress,' said Aphrodite, unsmiling, but inclining her body in a curtsey of obeisance, 'it was this one.'

14

The Secret Garden

That night, Jana dreamt of neither treasure nor sunken city nor monster; just a radiant palace with a golden throne whose steps she ascended, above the clouds, one by one, until she had almost reached the shining place, and then she would wake. She had still not reached that throne, and began to feel that dreams were no happiness; Maldona must certainly be built on earth. At midnight, she pulled tight on the golden chain which hung beside her bed and heard a muffled squeal from Henry. She grinned, knowing that the chain suddenly squeezing his balls would summon him.

'Come, Henry,' she cooed, knowing he could hear through the thin wall, 'come, sweet, naked to me, and in obeisance.'

And Henry Gordon Playste, her slave, appeared at her door on all fours, nude and unable to disguise the reaction of his penis which, to Jana's delight, was throbbing stiff for his mistress. His body was shivering and goose-fleshed from the draughty corridor, and an eerie candlelight penetrated Jana's chamber as Henry pushed the door open with his head.

'You want me, Mistress?' he said, with shy happiness.

'Not you, but the virgin Aphrodite,' said Jana tersely. 'I wish to speak with her. Go and wake her and bring her to me. You may rise,' she added.

Henry looked crestfallen. As he left on his errand he did his best to conceal his massive, erect cock, but at the sight of the powerful engine gleaming in the candlelight and the sadness of the moue on his little boy's face, Jana felt suddenly kind to him, although she knew her kindness was well tinged with lustful curiosity.

'Bring Aphrodite, and . . . and you may attend us as we talk,' she said quietly. Henry beamed like a sun.

When Aphrodite arrived, walking before Henry, she was rubbing her sleepy eyes and clutching a sheet around her body. Jana threw back her own coverlet and ordered the new virgin to attend her in her bed. Aphrodite eyed Jana's nude body.

'What can my mistress want with me?' she asked mockingly, her eyes wide open now.

'The rules of Maldona forbid questions,' said Jana severely. 'Questions reveal inadequacy, which is imperfection. I can – I shall – have you punished.'

Aphrodite smiled and said nothing; her sparkling eyes said everything for her. The two women embraced, nude under the coverlet which Henry tenderly replaced over their entwined bodies. Their lips met for a long kiss, and Jana felt Aphrodite's strong wet tongue penetrate her mouth like an attacker as her own hands stroked the taut globes of her slave's bare croup.

'You are very lovely, Mistress,' whispered Aphrodite softly, breaking away from her tonguing. 'Are we to talk, or is it more you wanted?'

'Oh, don't tease,' moaned Jana, despite herself, as Aphrodite slid down the bed to place her lips softly on Jana's cunt-petals. 'Oh, you are lovely too, my slave.'

'Mmm . . . thank you, Mistress,' murmured Aphrodite, as her tongue found Jana's stiffening clit and began to flick at the hard little damsel.

'Don't stop,' sighed Jana, arching her back as the spasm of pleasure tingled in her spine.

'Why should I stop what gives me pleasure, Mistress? Your body is so lovely, hard and strong. I wish that you would . . . that you'd squeeze me between those strong thighs of yours.'

Jana laughed. 'Of course, slave, I must make you know your place,' she gasped, and pinioned Aphrodite's head hard between her naked thighs, over which droplets of her flowing love-oil were beginning to trickle. The new virgin's dark head bobbed between the grip of Jana's thighs, as her tongue licked the nympha to blossom into stiffness. Jana stroked Aphrodite's flowing dark locks as the woman tenderly made love to her mistress with agile lips and tongue. Henry looked on, blushing, his penis stiff as an oak, and once Jana saw him touch the swollen crimson bulb as though to pleasure himself, but at a warning nod from her he desisted.

'That treasure is for me alone, my man,' she said, 'but Aphrodite, my tongue is lonely here.'

She swung on her haunches until her own mouth found Aphrodite's swollen clit, thrusting from the naked cunt-petals like a smooth red ruby, and Henry watched, longingly, as the two women, mouths on cunts, tenderly gamahuched each other, clasping each other with palms pressing hard on their wriggling bare buttocks, as eagerly as two schoolgirls sucking sweetmeats. Jana slid her tongue from stiff nympha to wet slit, back and forth, as she felt Aphrodite's nose and lips buried in her own luxuriant mink, her mouth chewing the engorged lips of Jana's cunt. Jana saw Henry watch as their bodies writhed in the flickering candlelight, his face a mask of longing, and being naked and observed intensified her joy at Aphrodite's expert caress.

Then, Jana gasped as she felt sharp fingernails suddenly penetrate her tender anus bud, and a ruthless finger – no, please no, two! – pushing deep inside her tender place, and she moaned and squirmed with maddened pain and pleasure as Aphrodite finger-fucked her anus. She responded quickly to this caress, and her own fingers found Aphrodite's bumhole, where she plunged with sharp, probing fingers into the silky opening, until both women were locked in the sweetest embrace, licking each other's wet founts and exploring the soft elastic nether passages. Jana found herself crushed by the full weight of Aphrodite's gently writhing body, and had her index and forefinger thrust to the very root of Aphrodite's anus, tickling and thrusting in the tight little hole, when suddenly, Aphrodite squeezed her powerful sphincter and Jana found her loving fingers expelled abruptly from their tender home.

Aphrodite rose, and swiftly, before Jana had time to protest, she squatted full on Jana's glistening face, crushing her with her arse-cheeks and naked, swollen sex-lips. A flood of hot liquid bathed Jana's mouth, and she opened her lips wide to drink of Aphrodite's love as her tongue probed the oily petals of the cunt that so mercilessly pinioned her face.

'How does that please you, Mistress?' whispered Aphrodite. 'My naked quim-lips on your sweet face. Isn't it lovely, and can't you see why I am bare-shaven? You can feel my flesh, my naked cunt, without anything to come between your lips and mine.'

Jana moaned with pleasure, for although disappointed at the removal of Aphrodite's tongue from her throbbing clit, and her own finger from the beauty of the goddess's arse, she had the sweet sensation of the woman's full weight, cunt and anus pressed against her helpless face. She could not speak, as though gagged by her oppressor's wet sex, which trembled with her helpless moans of joy. Locked under the woman's flowing cunt, she inhaled at every breath the freshness of the sea and the rich earthy tang of Aphrodite's anus. I am in heaven, she thought, trapped between the sweet land and the rich ocean.

'Oh,' moaned Jana, her voice a muffled hum as she felt Aphrodite take her stiff clit between her bare toes and gently rub her with strong, insistent strokes until Jana could not help squealing in her throat as the spasms of pleasure shook her squirming body, bringing her closer to what she knew would be a shattering orgasm. Nothing else in the world existed except the woman's moist bottom pressing on her, annihilating her in the dark universe of total surrender and total joy.

Her tongue probed for Aphrodite's own nympha and found her hard and swelling, so distended that Jana was able to take her full between her lips, sucking her as she would a man's stiff bulb, and at that, Aphrodite began to moan herself, writhing and pressing her swollen clit against Jana's kiss, with her anus bud sweetly on Jana's nose and wriggling as she felt the tickling there.

Aphrodite, giving little squeals of pleasure, had the toe of one foot thrust deep into Jana's anus while the toes of her other foot – Jana could not count, but it felt like all five! – were inside her wet cunt, artfully massaging lips and nympha. The two women's bodies rocked together like one creature possessed.

Suddenly, a male voice cried, hoarse with desire.

'Mistress, oh sweet Mistress, forgive me, but I cannot stand it any more!' said Henry in longing anguish. 'Punish me later if you will, yes, please punish my insolence, but now, I must . . . must . . .'

Jana, her face blanketed by the soft nether flesh of her queen, her goddess, suddenly felt Aphrodite's feet pushed away from her cunt, and Henry's stiff cock thrust vigorously into her soaking slit. Her heart pounded as she abandoned her quivering body to the moment, to the power of her implacable lovers: fucked by Henry and queened by her new slave, she squirmed, slippery with sweat and love-oil, as her own body was made a mere plaything to be used, fucked and tantalised as the mingled scents of male and female lust washed over her in a sea of gratified pleasure.

It only needed sweet Cassie, she thought, and would have called to her if the pressure of Aphrodite's body on her face had permitted her to speak. But she heard the door slide open and, as if summoned magically, Cassie slipped into the room.

'Mistress, I heard, and could not stay absent from you,' she whispered. And then Jana felt Cassie's head placed between Henry's belly and her own, and her tongue stab at her throbbing nympha, making her buck as her cunt melted with honeyed joy. She felt Henry's stiff cock thrust harder and harder inside her, and Cassie's tongue was on her clit, while Aphrodite had her nose, lips and eyes trapped under her squirming cunt and arse, as though Jana were breathing the scents of a whole world of goddesses. She could resist no longer, and abandoned herself into an orgasm that made her buck and writhe and squeal in a spasm of triumphant happiness. At that moment, Cassie raised her head, and Jana heard her lips smack against Aphrodite's until the two women, and Henry too, moaned in their spasms of pleasure, and as Jana licked the trembling clit of her bare goddess she cried out again in astonishment, as Henry's hot spunk bathing the neck of her womb made her belly shudder in another, sweeter orgasm.

'My friends, my slaves,' whispered Jana. Four bodies lay entwined on her bed, their skin gleaming: four friends now. Jana stroked Aphrodite's hair and nuzzled Cassie to her.

'Our mistress,' murmured Cassie. 'We adore Maldona! If only Gloria were here to share our joy.'

'Soon, my sweet slave,' said Jana. 'Perhaps she will find some fabulous treasure, and bring it to us for the glory of Maldona.'

'There is much treasure here in our islands,' said Aphrodite dreamily. 'Think of our Greek history, and all the histories before that, stretching back into unrecorded time. Who knows how many lost civilisations have sailed these waters and loved on these islands? How old is man? A million, two millions years? Isn't it possible that in all that time, our own paltry six thousand years of history have flowered and died and disappeared in the dust and the sea, many times over?'

'You make me shiver,' said Cassie, placing her head on Jana's breast.

Jana opened her eyes and thought. 'Tell me, Aphrodite,' she said slyly, 'what is the real reason your guardian bought this island years ago? Did he expect to find treasures?'

Aphrodite laughed. 'You are quick, Mistress. Yes, Damoglou thought there was some treasure hidden here, in a secret vault in the centre of a labyrinth far beneath the ground. You know how we Greeks love our myths, and take them seriously as facts. Something to do with an order of knights, who had been obliged to flee the Holy Land at the end of the Crusades, with all their treasures.'

'The Templars, perhaps,' said Jana drily.

187

'I think so, yes. How did you know?'

'There are many things about Maldona you have still to learn, virgin Aphrodite,' said Jana, kissing her.

'Damoglou said, when he would let anything slip, that the knights were dispersed to various islands: Rhodes, Malta, and, he reckoned, to smaller, secret places – like this! – where they cached the bulk of their treasure.'

'Yes,' said Jana slowly. 'After the Templars were annihilated with torture and death in the fourteenth century, by a pope and a king of France intent on robbing them, not one of them revealed the true location of their old, unimaginable treasures, even as the flames licked their tortured bodies. They were suppressed, and their lands stolen – everywhere but in Spain – but the treasures remain hidden, if treasures there be. I myself think it is mythology.'

'My guardian had the idea there was a key of some kind, lost from a sunken ship by the shoreline here, and that if he found the key, he could enter the labyrinth and open the vault. The key, he thought, would be a clue to the location of the vault, as well as the means of opening it. But he's an obsessive, consumed with passion for his interest of the moment, and forgetting it utterly a week later. That's why he sold the island. And that's why he punished me and my lover so harshly that day; he would have killed us, I think, but afterwards he was sorry, and a loving guardian again. Except that –' She paused and sighed.

'Except that you discovered that you wanted to be chastised, Aphrodite,' said Jana quietly. 'Isn't that it? That you craved submission to the whip on your naked body?'

'Yes, Mistress,' said Aphrodite.

'And you've had many men?'

'Of course.' She laughed gaily. 'I am a rich girl, a rich bitch, as you say, with wealth and hence power. What would people think if I failed to abuse a succession of young men? Luckily, Damoglou is powerful and brutal enough to keep me out of the women's scandal magazines. Where he is concerned, insolent photographers are lucky to lose only their cameras. Word got round, after one of

188

them had to abandon his marriage plans – any marriage plans.'

Jana shivered in horrified admiration at the brutal egotism of a man prepared to go to such lengths to defend a woman's honour, and found herself wanting to meet this strong, obsessive man. And suddenly, in fantasy, she saw naked giants, fighting with no holds barred under the Aegean sun for the body and honour of her, Jana Ardenne. Helplessly thrilled, prepared to offer herself totally to the brutal male who had killed and maimed for her, she watched as with knife and claw, the victor pitilessly mutilated his screaming vanquished rival, and kneeling before his lady, presented her with her hideous trophies, the proof of his lust and his dominion over her.

At her vivid, momentary fantasy, her pulse quickened and she felt a moist stirring in her sex. How little it takes, she thought, for a woman to turn to the old primitive truths, to give herself to man the conqueror, the strongest and most ruthless. And how close we are, here on our island, to stripping away all veneer of civilisation and reverting to the cruelty that is all life. Only the rules of Maldona stand between us and savagery.

Jana sighed, opened her eyes, and began to stroke Aphrodite's soft breasts.

'The breasts of woman,' she murmured, 'the breasts of life and sweetness, yet covering a heart as savage as any male's. I think we should sleep now, and dream together. And, Aphrodite, do not dream of treasures, for I think that such things are made of dreams alone.'

As she stroked Aphrodite's silken hair, she drifted into sleep, thinking of the crusted bronze key she had taken from the sea and buried under the fig tree.

Before sunrise, when the moonlit castle was still glimmering in the dark, Maldona rose from her bed and went to the fig tree. Swiftly she unearthed the bronze key and took it back to her cell, where she joined the gently snoring Aphrodite. Jana smiled. So, she thought, even goddesses snore.

But Aphrodite's words intrigued her: Damoglou, when

master of the island, had been unable to find the entrance to the labyrinth. Jana, by the simplest of deductions, had found it: but the bare walls of the labyrinth seemed to be nothing more than an elaborate rose leading to the holy of holies, the dungeon.

She had found the key underwater, in the sunken city. What, then, if the treasure were concealed there? The more Jana thought, the more likely it seemed. She resolved that in the day, she and Cassie should comb the labyrinth for secret doors, but that at night, she would dive alone to the sunken city.

In the morning, Aphrodite was issued with her kit, which she accepted with pride and pleasure, gravely stroking her burnished steel gag and restrainer, and accepting without demur the humiliation of wearing a simple chiton and having her locks cut boyishly short by a lithe Englishwoman named Rose, whom Jana had appointed as fulltime mistress almoner, or matron, because she reminded her so much of the Matron of Maldona who had first inducted her into Maldona, the castle in Spain.

After breakfast at dawn, Aphrodite gladly went to work with the other gangs, for Jana had no intention of stopping the construction of the new Maldona. When all the towers were completed, as quarters for adepts and parfaites, she was sincere in her desire to build up to the seventh storey: to build a new Maldona higher than the old.

When all were at labour and the crack of the lash echoed smartly around the castle – Jana smiled, relishing the enthusiasm of Kate, Melanie and Sarah, her parfaites – she and Cassie entered the chapel and opened the entrance to the underground labyrinth. Again, Cassie was charged with the ball of twine to stop them getting lost in the maze. 'I dub thee Mistress of the Sacred String,' said Jana, po-faced, and they both laughed. Jana was nude, save for sandals and belted whip, according to her rank, and Cassie too had permission to go unadorned because of the heat deep underground. The two naked women lost track of time as they prowled every inch of the maze, Jana searching for any opening, any door, that might conceal a keyhole. But there was nothing. Time and time again they were led back to the fearsome, beautiful dungeon.

'Mistress,' said Cassie, sweating, 'what is it you are looking for?'

'We are not looking for anything,' replied Jana irritably. 'We are exploring.'

'I think you are looking for the hiding place of the Templars' treasure,' said Cassie, slyly. They were once more in the dungeon, resting, but Jana suddenly exploded in anger.

'You are a slave, nothing more!' she cried. 'I have made you superior, but you are still slave of Maldona – my slave!'

'Oh, Jana, sweet, my lovely Mistress,' cooed Cassie, stroking Jana's sweating brow. 'You know I love you and would never hurt you or betray you. If I have offended you, then you know what I deserve.'

Jana smiled. 'You are as bad as Sarah,' she said.

'I suppose I am,' replied Cassie, her eyes twinkling. 'What's it to be, then?'

'Oh, Mistress,' murmured Cassie, feigning doubt. 'Perhaps you should conserve your strength ... not a long session, but something short and sharp.'

She went to the wall-rack and selected quite the heaviest rattan cane, a full four feet long and half an inch thick. Jana gasped in awe.

'Have you forgotten Maldona in Spain, Mistress?' said Cassie evenly. 'The chastisements with which both you and I were blessed?'

Jana smiled and nodded.

She took the heavy cane and flexed her, swishing the air with a whistling sound. Slowly, the lithe, naked Cassie bent over and touched her toes.

'Like an English schoolboy,' she said dreamily. 'Seven of the best. Seven is the sacred number. And afterwards, Mistress, you are supposed to say, "This hurts me more than it hurts you." '

Jana laughed. 'You've been reading too many schoolboy yarns,' she exclaimed. 'And I won't say that, because it's not true, and I should be guilty of imperfection, and then

I should deserve punishment in my turn. With this beautiful instrument, I shall play such sweet music on your naked croup that she will wriggle like an eel and turn as crimson as the dawn. Oh yes, this cane, she is really, really hard.'

She stroked Cassie's stretched bare buttocks, then knelt to kiss her there, allowing her tongue to stray across and into the tight bud of Cassie's bumhole. As she licked and kissed her naked slave's anus bud, she felt the moisture begin to flow within her fount, and her heart beat with sudden desire, and anger that the sight of her slave's smooth bottom so eagerly submitting to her could imprison her in that desire, making her helpless before such cowed beauty. As if in revenge, she raised the cane high and cracked Cassie's buttocks, leaving vivid crimson.

'Ouch!' said Cassie mockingly. 'That stings! You certainly know how to lay it on, don't you, sir?'

'It's no more than you deserve, you inky wretch,' said Jana, grinning now. 'You are a disgrace to the lower sixth. Kissing town girls and smoking behind the cricket pavilion, indeed!' She delivered a second savage cut, and Cassie mewed softly. Her firm fesses were unable to stay still, but quivered as she clenched them to absorb the smarting. 'No cry-baby stuff, you worm!' cried Jana. 'Look, your bum's quivering like a jelly! Is that the way of a Maldona boy? How can you serve the Empire if you don't keep a stiff upper lip?' And the third stroke lashed Cassie's defenceless bare nates.

'I'm trying, sir, but you cane so tightly . . . Oh, it's almost unbearable.'

'But not quite, eh?' drawled Jana as she laced her friend with the fourth lash.

Cassie gasped and began to breathe hoarsely, her whole body trembling now.

'Sir,' she said faintly, 'have you noticed something strange about our new arrival? Aphrodite?'

'Don't sneak, you toad!' cried Jana, and stroked her bare reddened bottom a fifth time. The sixth and seventh lashes followed with cruel swiftness, and when Cassie stood up her face was flushed and she trembled, fighting back her tears. Jana threw down the cane and tenderly embraced her. Jana's own juices were now trickling down her inside thighs, and she held Cassie tightly to her, fount on fount, in loving frottage.

'Truly, that did hurt me more than it hurt you,' she whispered as she kissed Cassie's ear, then her lips, her eyes, even, playfully, her nose.

Cassie giggled. 'Imperfection, sir? Caught in a fib? I think you know that you deserve what for.'

'Yes,' said Jana, stretching herself over the flogging block, 'I do . . .'

They made their way back through the maze, uncertain of the time. When they emerged from the chapel, the sun told Jana it was already late afternoon. She ordered Henry to prepare salads, and as they ate, Jana explained that she thought the treasure lay elsewhere.

'But where?' asked Cassie, innocently.

'I have no idea,' lied Jana.

As the sun went down and the company of Maldona were at supper in the refectory, a lone figure slipped through the castle gates and made her way down to the darkening cove. She dressed in a simple purple chiton, belted at the waist with a gold chain. She had taken special care of her maquillage; Maldona must look imperial, even in an underwater city. Thus attired, she made her way down to the cove, where she took one of the beached boats and rowed slowly out towards the sunken city. She thought of Cassie's words about Aphrodite. Yes, there was something strangely familiar about her.

After anchoring the boat, she stripped, dived and swam, spiralling down to the ghostly white shapes of the sunken city. She found herself treading water just before the temple door and passed quickly through, timing herself for when, lungs bursting, she would have to return to the surface for air. Remembering Caspar's film, she suddenly wondered how it was that Kate, Melanie and Sarah could manage to stay under for so long. And fear gripped her as she swam rapidly through the temple, her bare body caressed by glittering fishes. Was it something to do with the tattoos on their founts; something to do with the island of Circe? She told herself not to be paranoid, but here in this half-light, surrounded by ruins older than Maldona, older than Greece herself, all kinds of phantasms invaded her brain. The legend of Atlantis, recorded by Plato, and dismissed as invention. But maybe it was not invention – there were notable cases of Greek islands, Santorini for one, disappearing beneath the waves in a volcanic cataclysm. What if she, Jana, had found Atlantis?

Beyond the temple, a long straight avenue stretched about a kilometre in length, and she swam towards its end, where another large, indistinct structure loomed. On either side, streets led off the boulevard in an orderly grid pattern. Jana felt that there was a clue to the mystery in the distant building. A palace? Another temple? Three times she had to surface for air before she reached its open portals.

She swam inside and almost swallowed water in her astonishment. It was indeed another temple – vast, about a hundred square metres – but bereft of altars, tombs and carvings.

This temple was a garden. Jana's body was kissed by strange fronds and creepers as she swam slowly through a jungle of pale blossoms and algae that caressed her as though wishing to devour her flesh. The weak sunlight could produce no bright colours down here so that the garden was a delicate collage of pastel shades, like the clothing of an elegant matriarch. The plants soared so that they reached the high walls of the garden, and some snaked greedily over it as though in search of prey. Jana surfaced for air once more, gliding through the waving fronds, who seemed to help rather than hinder her passage. She even imagined she felt a friendly pat on the fesses to speed her along, and smiled at her silliness.

Returning to the garden after gulping air, she swam on, and suddenly there was a clearing, as though no plants dared invade a sacred place. In the clearing she saw a replica of the temple at the gate in miniature, the size of a small hut but built of the same white stone. In its wall stood a bronze door and in that door was a keyhole. Jana tried the door, and found it locked, as she knew she would. And when she looked at the keyhole, she knew also that her bronze key was made for it, and that it was here that she would find the treasure of the Templars, or such as her ancestor had bequeathed to her.

Rapidly, she made her way back to the surface and swam back to her tethered boat. The stars were bright, and she lay back, panting from the day's exertions, wondering what the sky had looked like when her ancestor Jane Ardenne had looked up, or when the old Greeks had named Orion, Cassiopaeia, Andromeda ... the stars were gods and goddesses. How could they not be worshipped? Worship, the oldest instinct of man, the highest worship the worship of a goddess, of woman.

Then, taking her oars, she wondered what the sky had looked like when the people had built the sunken city with its strange, eternal garden. And, with the friendly lights of her castle beckoning her, she almost dropped her oars as the thought struck her like a bolt: what if the city were not buried by the dark volcano? There was no sign of burning or ash or any blackening. *What if the city had been built underwater?*

Troubled by this thought, she marched briskly back to her castle, her slaves, her refectory, her high apartments and all things familiar and away from the cool and darkening waters. It was only when she entered the castle gates and saw a group of slaves chattering and laughing, with Aphrodite regally the centre of attention, that another thought disturbed her. Remembering Cassie's words, she looked at Aphrodite and imagined her in blue: and then she knew that Aphrodite was the mysterious woman who had been shadowing her since her arrival in Greece.

15

The Noble Beating

The work of building the Castle of Maldona continued throughout the winter months which, to Jana, scarcely seemed like winter at all. The sun became less oppressive, but still bathed them in heat and light and spirit. Maldona, truly, seemed an island without seasons: without time, except for the bell, brought from Athens, that tolled four times a day, summoning the slaves to rise, to eat and to retire. Maldona was a world out of time, where past, present and future merged and blurred in the shimmering heat; where each individual slave was alone with the pain and self-knowledge of chastisement.

Daily, Jana watched her tower take shape until a seventh storey was finally added above her apartments. She promptly moved higher, to an apartment which occupied the whole seventh floor, and moved Cassie up with her. But she decided that the other towers should remain as they were, since none should be as high as Maldona. By this time the company of Maldona numbered 263 slaves, including six parfaites alongside Melanie, Kate and Sarah, twelve prefects and twenty-four corporals. Prefects and corporals occupied cells in their *auberges*: the parfaites' tower was the one diagonally opposite the tower of Maldona herself.

The ranks Jana had bestowed as honorary were made permanent: Sandra was the surgeon mistress, pleased with her new, if primitive, clinic and her privilege as an adept of shaving her mink, growing her hair and wearing a white coat. Chris, Jana observed, was well enslaved to her, in all but name, although only parfaites were permitted to have knights. Sarah Pennington formally took as her knight Agostino, a pretty Italian boy whose black curly hair contrasted piquantly with her own straight blonde locks, now grown again, as was her privilege as parfaite.

Nude, she strutted proudly, her mink bare-shaven, showing her glowing tattoo; and her cane swinging at her golden belt, with Agostino following meekly behind her, pretty in his woman's attire, as she patrolled the castle, looking for imperfection. Jana wondered how Sarah could devise such a variety of costumes for her willing slave: one day, a flouncy lace nightie, the next a flowing peasant skirt or a sober grey business suit of shantung silk, with padded jacket and narrow skirt over ivory tights and impossibly high stiletto heels. The shoes made the poor young man teeter alarmingly on the uneven ground, and gave him the humiliation he craved. Jana never saw him happier than when he was obliged to leave his cell wearing nothing but a white satin basque, much too tight, garter belt and stockings, over red panties, which Sarah nonchalantly lashed from time to time as she walked along, smiling as she bit into a peach.

Thorsten seemed to have formed a similar alliance with both Kate and Melanie, although neither had asked Jana for permission to make him their slave. He was in all but name. The twins liked to adorn him with flowers and rouge, and make him wear their clothes and panties. Jana knew that they beat him: passing the parfaites' tower at night, she could hear the crack of whips from the apartment shared by the inseparable twins.

Maldona had baths, a small swimming pool and a gymnasium, and occasionally Jana and Cassie would take their steambath or sauna knowing that slaves would be there, gossiping. Jana had the idea that since the new Maldona was smaller than the old, a policy of seclusion would not do. If not democratic, she wanted to be friendly. But she began to notice that as she sat in the dry heat of the sauna, lathered in sweat and feeling the sting of the birch rods as Cassie beat her bare back, the conversation would still in her presence, and the slaves drift away, bowing to her as they left. She also noticed that little alliances were forming; groups of slaves clustered in the corners of the courtyard, who would smile blankly as she passed.

Many of the slaves were now employed on the land, the fertile slope which stretched in front of the castle down to the sea and which was the charge of a new arrival, a woman in her late twenties named Sabine, who came from a farming community in the region of Marseille: her familiarity with vines, tomatoes, olives and all things Mediterranean made her a natural choice to assume the role of Demeter, guardian of crops, although Jana quite liked the name Sabine.

Each new arrival was given a new name, like Jana herself, formerly Jane, on her induction to Maldona. She favoured names from the Greek, names of Muses, naiads, satyrs, heroes, famous *hetairai*, the respected courtesans of ancient Athens. A virgin who entered Maldona was truly a virgin, no matter what her past.

But it worried Jana that the 'old guard', the first company of Maldona, conspicuously addressed each other by their former names. Thorsten was Decius now, and Henry, Aelfric; Kate and Melanie were Castor and Pollux, and Sarah Pennington, Sappho. Yet to each other, they remained Thorsten, Kate, Melanie, Sarah. And when Jana was near they would raise their voices deliberately so that she could hear.

Sabine – Demeter – took Jana's fancy as soon as she saw her. She arrived bedraggled and cursing, for her boat had overturned due to the clumsiness of her rowing and she had had to swim ashore. She had come from a tourist island 40 or so kilometres away, where she had been on some package tour with her husband – '*un brute!*' as she put it succinctly. Overhearing gossip in a *matelots'* bar, she had learned of the existence of Maldona and on impulse made the decision to throw herself on her mercy.

She was small, with very large breasts and croup, and a tiny waist. Surprisingly, she was blonde, but a true Provençale in manner, her mouth never resting from a stream of invective, indignation and complaints about weather,

Greeks, sea, Frenchmen, the world – all delivered with eye-balls rolling to heaven and a magnificent Gallic shrug. Walking insolently through the gates, she walked straight up to Jana and demanded to know if she was in charge. Jana, taken aback, said that she was Maldona.

'*Alors, c'est ici que les jeunes filles se font fouetter?*' asked Sabine, looking disdainfully around. '*Mon dieu! Quel bordel!*'

Jana replied that yes, indeed, this was where women endured the lash. Sabine's eyes lit up.

'*Vous avez un dongeon, alors? Avec tous les instruments de supplice?*'

'Yes,' said Jana, in French, 'we have a dungeon, for the punishment of imperfection.'

'*C'est parfait!*' cried Sabine. '*Je suis très, très méchante, moi, et ce qui me manque dans cette vie, c'est d'être bien cravachée autant qu'il vous plaira, chère Maîtresse. Mon imbécile de mari ne veut rien me fournir selon mes goûts particuliers.*'

'I am sure you are naughty, and need to be beaten,' said Jana carefully, repressing a smile, 'and many of our virgins say the same – that their menfolk have no sympathy with their particular tastes, their need to submit to the pain and beauty of the lash. I shall induct you, Sabine, and where better to do it than the dungeon on which you have your heart set?'

Jana suddenly realised that she wished to keep the existence of the dungeon a secret, or at least its location. Suspicions began to invade her mind; suspicions of the knots of slaves who seemed far too intimate, both with each other, with prefects and even parfaites. But something in her warmed to Sabine, the effervescent Frenchwoman. Jana felt she could be a useful ally if –

She did not wish to think about any ifs.

She permitted Sabine to ascend to Cassie's apartments, where she selected a hood and mask from Cassie's generous stock. Then, briskly, she marched the hooded and unseeing Sabine across the yard and into the second yard, where they entered the sacristy of the chapel by a back door. There, Jana opened the entrance to the labyrinth and gently led Sabine down into its depths, following the twine path until they reached the dungeon door.

'The dungeon is one of the most precious secrets of all Maldona,' she said. 'Only I know of its location. All who come to be awarded chastisement must take their strokes unseeing and unknowing.' She did not add that Sabine was to be her first slave to submit to the dungeon's kindnesses.

She saw that Sabine was trembling as she opened the door to admit them to the chamber.

'Well, Sabine, what shall we do with you?' she mused. 'Such lovely ripe fesses, I think, deserve to be stretched over my flogging horse.' Sabine purred with pleasure. 'You must be fully naked, of course. It is the way of Maldona. All chastisements are given on the bare. As she kisses, the whip must taste naked flesh.'

'Of course,' said Sabine, her lips joyful. 'What other way is there? And now, my beating, if you please, Mistress,' she said, and began to peel off her light sundress with the grace and avidity of a hungry cat. 'I love to be beaten, to feel the glow of a *fessée* from a strong hand, or the crack of a whip on my bare bottom. My husband, he would not. He is very *brimé*, very repressed. He does not know what a special woman, perhaps every woman, craves. I used to go to a special house in Marseille, just behind the Gare St Pierre; there were strong young men . . .'

Nude, Sabine stood, her hooded head bowed in submission before Jana, who felt her desire moistening her: Sabine's body seemed a ripe, swelling fruit, ready to be plucked and give her juices to Jana's hungry lips. She placed her fingertips on Sabine's lips, then let them stray to her breasts, whose brown plum nipples were already hard, each with a wide aureola of delicious tiny gooseflesh. Her hand rubbed Sabine's flat, downy belly, then slipped into her lush black mink. Sabine did not resist, closing her eyes when Jana found her stiff, oily nympha and stroked her there. Sabine sighed and her hips shuddered.

'Oh, Mistress,' whispered Sabine, 'I have never had another woman caress me there, and though it makes me hot and wet and yet shivery, it does not displease me. You are so gentle. In the house in Marseille, the canes of those young men would make my fesses flame so sweetly!'

'Maldona,' said Jana, brushing Sabine's lips with her own, 'will make your whole body flame, and your spirit too. Now position yourself. You are no stranger to the flogging block, I think.' She took Sabine's hand and led her to the squat, ominous block of punishment.

'Mmm,' sighed Sabine, deep in her throat, as Jana deftly cuffed her wrists and ankles and fastened a tight steel belt around her midriff, pinching the soft flesh. 'Mmm,' breathed Sabine once more, wriggling in helpless pleasure as the cold metal bit her. Her thighs were widely splayed, allowing Jana a full view of her open fount, the lips swollen, wet and red in the intensity of the woman's desire to submit. And Jana recognised the familiar effects on herself: the quickening of her heart, the unchecked flowing of warm oil in her own tingling quim, and the pulse of excitement in her engorged clit.

'You are naughty indeed, Madame,' she said hoarsely, 'for the sight of your naked fount, and your thighs and fesses spread in submission to me, have made me as excited as you are.'

'Then hurry and chastise me, Mistress, I beg. How lovely it is that a woman who wins prizes for the lushness of the fruits she grows should wish to feel her own ripe fruits bruised by the whip! How strange we women are! Hurry and chastise me, Mistress, I beg.'

'I'm not yet your mistress,' said Jana, 'but this punishment will serve as your induction, and when you have been beaten, you shall be a virgin of Maldona.'

'I, a virgin –' began Sabine, and her words choked in her throat as Jana viciously brought the four thongs of her quirt down on to the taut, swelling rump-skin of her naked captive. Sabine cried out and jumped convulsively.

'Too hard?' said Jana mockingly.

'Oh, Mistress, no!' she moaned through clenched teeth, her bottom crimsoned and quivering to Jana's smiling eyes. 'Oh, to be flogged by a woman! Oh, *quelle volupté*! What a bizarre joy! *Encore, encore,* and harder, I beseech you, sweet tormentor! But please – do not reveal to me how many strokes I am to take. The uncertainty makes my punishment all the more delicious: I tremble at the blows of your whip, and in fear of what is to come, and my sex flows so wet, knowing that I am helpless, knowing that my bare fesses are shamefully exposed to your gaze. Oh, Mistress, make me feel that I am truly your slave.'

'So,' said Jana, rubbing her whip handle, 'you are something of a gardener?'

'Why, an agricultural specialist, Mistress! My fields of courgettes and melons, my groves of olives and oranges, my tomatoes, beans and peas, are second to none in all of Provence; in France herself!'

'Very interesting,' said Jana thoughtfully. 'Well, it is time to leave matters agricultural and attend to the cultivation of blossoms on your noble bottom, Madame.'

As Jana continued Sabine's beating, she wondered how long it would be before her pleas became pleas for mercy. But Sabine did not plead for mercy. She took her flogging like no other virgin, not in tight-lipped silence, but with great whoops and exclamations of '*O là là!*' and '*Plus fort, plus fort!*'

'Why,' panted Jana, 'I am lacing you as hard as I can! I have even lost count of the strokes!'

'It is thirty-seven, Mistress. I have a croup of steel, you know?'

Jana was sweating now, and her belly fluttered with desire as she watched the wet spread quim of her victim writhing in a sensuous rhythm beneath the lash. Jana's own sex felt as though she would never exhaust the loving juices that her body contained; that this ripe woman's body would drain her of all her strength and love.

As she counted 50, she could stand it no longer, and, throwing away her whip, she knelt between Sabine's spread thighs and began to lick the lips of her fount, taking the sweet salty juices into her mouth, then flicking the hard distended nympha with her tongue. With one hand, Jana stroked her new virgin's crimson buttocks. With her other, moaning, she caressed her own quim and clitoris, faster and faster in time with her frottage of the trussed virgin. Sabine shuddered and writhed while emitting loud mews of tormented joy, and as her voice climbed to a high squeal and her body shuddered, Jana felt herself arrive at her own plateau. She buried her lips and nose full in Sabine's soaking quim and the two women dissolved in cries of painful pleasure as their spasms shook their bodies.

When it was over, and they had regained their breath, Jana released Sabine and the two women embraced silently, each with tears of joy glistening on flushed cheeks.

'Thank you, Mistress,' murmured Sabine, as Jana helped her dress, kissing the light scented cloth as she did so.

'Yes,' said Jana, as she led the still-masked slave from the dungeon, 'you may now call me Mistress, Sabine, and I shall name you Demeter, the goddess of fruits and plants. You are inducted into Maldona, sweet Demeter, and I appoint you as of this moment to the honorary rank of adept: you shall be Mistress Fructifier, charged with making our island blossom with crops, flowers and fruits.'

Jana smiled at Demeter's profuse thanks, and when they emerged from the chapel into the bright sunlight she took the new virgin – though honorary adept – to Sarah Pennington, who, she knew, would not answer to the name Sappho, and charged her, as mistress almoner, with installing Demeter in a cell and issuing her with kit. She saw that Aphrodite was lolling in Sarah's quarters, and that she was nude, although as a mere virgin she had no right to be. Aphrodite smirked crookedly at her, spreading her bare thighs, and Jana saw that her fount was shaved and adorned with the bright red tattoo of the rose.

Once back in her own quarters, Jana found herself trembling. She lit a cigarette, something she had not done in a long time, and sat brooding. Suddenly she felt very alone in this place. Aphrodite had gone, without permission, to the island of Circe, and had flaunted her tattoo. Were these slaves forming a cabal within Maldona herself? A sisterhood of the tattoo? And in that parfaite's chamber, she had not dared to reprimand Aphrodite or decree punishment – cowed, perhaps, by the memory of her own awe, a nervous virgin, before the beauty of the parfaite Leandra, now regent of Maldona in Spain, in Jana's place. She suddenly found herself longing to be back amidst the cruel, loving certainties of that gaunt castle. She hoped that the nightmare would not return; the monster with her own face taunting her for cowardice.

And then Cassie's mermaid, the mermaid with her face. Everywhere she seemed to be looking in a mirror, pursued by her own likeness. Jana felt afraid. She knew that to prove herself to herself, she would have to climb the mountain, alone; she would have to discover the Templar treasure, alone; she would have to –

Suddenly there was a knock at the door, and it was Cassie. Without a word, Jana rose, and, sobbing, embraced her friend tightly and desperately.

'Oh, Cassie,' she cried, 'I must go to Circe's island. I must. And I must go alone.'

Throughout the rest of the day, Jana brooded in her chamber. She smoked and thought of Aphrodite, her insolence in shaving her mink, in going nude, in leaving Maldona to have the accursed tattoo done, undoubtedly by the sorceress Circe. Then she laughed and checked herself. How could a thing of beauty be accursed? And sorceresses – they were a figment of demented imagination. Aphrodite was simply a spoiled rich bitch who needed a good hiding as punishment for her insolence.

That evening, Jana dressed in her parfaite's harness, feathers up, and adorned herself with maquillage: she put on her reddest lipstick and painted her face white, then her entire body; she circled her eyes with the blackest kohl, so that her appearance was that of an avenging white angel, with the black eyes of a demon. As well as her four-thonged whip, she carried her hardest, longest rattan cane, swinging from the golden belt at her waist.

When she made her late entrance to the refectory, the supper was already served, but no one was permitted to eat before Maldona had taken her place. There was a gasp of astonishment at her forbidding aspect, and when she went to her place at the head of the table, she did not sit down. In a stentorian voice, she announced, 'A grave imperfection has been committed by a slave, a virgin of Maldona.' Her eyes fixed on Aphrodite, whose face was stone. 'Virgin Aphrodite, you will stand and remove your chiton.'

Aphrodite looked around uncertainly, at Sarah, Kate and Melanie, but to Jana's relief they turned their heads nervously under the power of Jana's burning eyes. Good, she thought, I'll break this little cabal.

Aphrodite rose, and stood naked.

'Come out, virgin Aphrodite, where we can see you fully,' rapped Jana, and hesitantly Aphrodite obeyed, her face a mask of cunning and a sly smile curling her lips. Jana took her cane and flexed her, swishing the air and cracking the body of the flogging horse.

Magnificently nude, and clearly aware of her beauty, Aphrodite stood, hands behind her back and head bowed in what Jana knew was only mock submission. Suddenly furious, she cracked her cane full against Aphrodite's bare bottom, and she started in surprise but made no sound, yet her eyes smouldered.

Jana placed the palm of her hand on Aphrodite's swelling, tattooed mons. She marvelled at the brightness and clarity of the intricate red tattoo, so different from the muddy conconctions of cheap sailors' parlours.

'Aphrodite,' she said, 'you have been imperfect in many ways. You have shaved your mink, not permitted to a mere virgin; you have been tattooed, without permission; and to do so you have left Maldona, again unpermitted. You have visited the island of Circe, the tattooist. Taking one of Maldona's boats unlawfully! And you have showed yourself naked, when you know that according to the rules, slaves must be clothed, except when bathing.'

'Mistress,' Aphrodite said coolly, with a hint of sarcasm, 'you saw me naked in a parfaite's quarters. A parfaite has the authority to allow me the privilege of nudity.'

'Slave, do not tell me the rules of Maldona,' hissed Jana.

'Insolence upon insolence, imperfection upon imperfection. You shall be well punished. Place yourself on the flogging block, so that your cries may entertain us while we eat.' Aphrodite did not move.

'Well?' Jana barked. 'You said you longed to bare your body to the lash of Maldona, you wretched slave, and now is your chance. On to the flogging block!'

Aphrodite looked round at her allies, but Jana's gaze was there first, and as she faced her parfaites – her rebellious parfaites? – they turned away, cowed by the Mistress of Maldona in her inhuman fierceness.

'I – I thought I was committing no imperfection,' stammered Aphrodite.

'A lie! A further imperfection! You knew very well, you insolent slut! Now bend over the block, or I shall throw you from Maldona with my own arms!'

'No . . . no . . .' murmured Aphrodite, clearly perturbed now, and slowly stretched herself on the block. Jana nodded to Henry, who swiftly cuffed her to the legs of the block, then strapped the metal waist cincher around her midriff, tightening it until it would tighten no more. Aphrodite gasped, her belly squeezed to half her normal girth.

'I thought you had earned a grand beating, Aphrodite,' said Jana calmly, stroking the cleft of the woman's tightly stretched buttocks with the tip of her cane, 'but now I think you deserve a noble beating. You are fully naked and well trussed, and the whole company is here to witness, as required. It remains to gag and hood you. Let the slave's equipment be fetched from her cell.'

She gestured to Cassie, who left the hall and rapidly returned bearing gag, black rubber hood, and shining steel restrainer. Aphrodite looked round, her eyes now wide in alarm. Jana smiled coldly.

'You like to take punishment when you, feigning submission, are really dominant, not so, Aphrodite? You like the thrill of the shells caressing your intimate place as you climax, but now the real Maldona claims you as her miserable slave, to be chastised and *restrained*.' Jana relished the roll of that awful word.

Aphrodite's eyes widened as she saw the steel belt in Cassie's hands, its tight steel thong supporting a massive steel penis.

'Not . . . not the restrainer. Mistress, flog me, but –'

'Well, said Jana in cruel triumph,' it takes time to accustom oneself to the proper restraint.' She squeezed her sphincter muscle, feeling the delicious fullness of her anus and quim. Her fan feathers fluttered.

She ordered Henry and Thorsten to present themselves, and lift their flowing robes, the woman's *himation*, to reveal their naked penises. Both men, she noted with delight, were already fully erect at the spectacle of the helpless Aphrodite, and needed neither command nor encouragement to straddle her, one after the other. Thorsten was first, his massive cock tickling Aphrodite's spread anus bud for a moment before plunging to the hilt into her tender opening. He grasped her by the shoulders, pressing on her with his full weight, and as he fucked her with merciless thrusts deep in her anus, Aphrodite began to squirm and moan.

'What, Aphrodite, can't take it?' mocked Jana. 'Wait for Henry, he is a little smaller than our German bear.' She saw a look in Henry's eyes that was puzzlement or anger, and regretted her words. 'But just as beautiful,' she added hastily, hoping no damage had been done. She watched Thorsten's muscled croup moving in a tender, savage rhythm as he bucked on the helpless body of the woman, his growls, truly ursine, and desire quickened in her. She would have Thorsten, Sandra or no Sandra.

'Remember, Aphrodite, you are not yet gagged, and have only to say the words "I go down" and your torment will cease. All slaves of Maldona are slaves of their own free will.'

Cassie smiled fleetingly. 'Mistress, that can be taken in two ways,' she said.

At that moment, Thorsten cried out in his climax, his voice drowning the moans of the buggered woman. Then it was Henry's turn. Aphrodite's moans increased in intensity as Henry strove, by the force of his ramming thrusts to her anus, to outdo Thorsten in ruthlessness.

And when he too climaxed, Aphrodite was mewing with little sobbing sounds.

Swiftly, she was gagged and hooded, and then Jana herself took the restrainer, moistening her with olive oil, and thrust her into Aphrodite's now stretched anus. The device slid in smoothly, right to the base of the shaft, and then Cassie fastened the metal belt around her waist, below the block's cincher, and even more tightly, so that Aphrodite groaned again.

'It will be a full twenty-one, Aphrodite, dear slave,' she said quietly, lifting her cane and stroking the woman's bare, taut buttocks with her fingertips. 'How red your olive skin will be! But just remember, gagged though you are, just shake your head to say no, I go down, and you will be released and set free from slavery.'

With that, she began the beating. The cane whistled before cracking on Aphrodite's bare nates with an impact that made Jana's sex moisten and her breath quicken. Aphrodite moaned loud and long in her throat at the first stroke, but thereafter kept silent, her distress evident only from the frantic squirming of her tethered body and the maddened clenching and twisting of her naked buttocks. Jana laid the strokes on her very rapidly, and, feeling at her most cruel, in the same place, which soon spread an island of darkest crimson on the smooth brown skin of Aphrodite's tormented fesses.

'Eat, my slaves,' she ordered the entranced company. 'This is the first noble beating you witness, and it shall not be the last. Eat, for slaves must be fed as well as entertained.'

And, despite their excitement, the slaves of Maldona attacked their food, laughing and cheering as stroke followed stroke on Aphrodite's bare flesh, and her writhing shudders became more and more desperate. Yet still she made no sound.

When it was over, Jana nodded to Cassie to release her from her bonds, her gag and restrainer. Sobbing slightly, Aphrodite stood up stiffly, and bowed to Jana.

'Thank you for my righteous chastisement, Mistress,'

she said. Only Jana could see the cold fire of hatred in her eyes. 'But,' added Aphrodite, contemptuous now and her voice loud for all to hear, 'there was a mistake in your punishment. I did not take a boat unlawfully to go to Circe's island. I *swam* there all the way.'

That night, Jana, all energy, could not sleep. Aphrodite's taunting words rang in her ears. Around midnight she reached for the bell that summoned Cassie.

'Mistress?' said Cassie, rubbing her eyes. 'Your slave awaits your bidding.'

Jana stood before her, the bright moonlight glinting on her nude body. She gestured to an amphora on her dressing-table.

'Oil my body, Cassie,' she said simply. 'Very thick.'

'You are not wrestling at this hour, Mistress?' asked Cassie, obediently rubbing the heavy scented oil into the crevices and hillocks of her mistress's muscled body.

'No,' Jana replied, her skin tingling at the sweet massage, 'I am going swimming. To the Island of Circe.'

16

Circe

The stars were bright in the velvet sky as Cassie tearfully kissed Jana farewell. Save for her golden waist chain, Jana was naked for her swim, her oiled body gleaming in the starlight as she approached the soft blue waters. They stood by a line of beached boats and, beyond, hulking piles of stores were silhouetted like dark monstrous creatures. Jana carried a backpack with clothing, food, biscuits, binoculars and flotation bags.

'You are regent in my place, Cassie,' she said. 'If I don't come back ... well, as superior, you become Maldona. There may be some fighting, but you are good at that.'

'I wish you weren't going, Mistress,' murmured Cassie. 'I feel so alone now. Something strange is happening. I don't trust Aphrodite, nor her influence over our parfaites. Kate, Melanie and Sarah have changed somehow. If only Gloria were here! It has been so long, and no word from her. She is a true friend.'

'Yes,' said Jana, 'I wonder. It has been so many months, and I have been so busy. Perhaps her dig is overrunning its time. Perhaps she has lost her guide, and is not even sure where to find us. At any rate, Cassie, keep your eye on Aphrodite and her little cabal, if that is what it is. Do not spare your whip on her bare bum, and at the slightest provocation, divest her of her necklace, making her a common whipping girl. I think these tattoos, as well as beauty, are a way to power. But whose power? I think the answer is in the Island of Circe.'

'Do be careful,' whispered Cassie.

Jana grinned. 'I'm not unequipped: I carry a knife – and a whip.'

She slipped into the warm water and swam easily out until she was far from the dark outline of Maldona. Only then did she look back, and waved goodbye to the tiny figure of Cassie, standing on the beach.

As she swam out into the dark blue waters, Jana suddenly felt a surge of exhilaration. It was the old joy of travelling, the excitement of being on the move to an unknown destiny: and the thrill of an impending conflict. She soon fell into an easy rhythm, as though the water was pushing her along, and found her thoughts had the clarity of the pure sea that bathed her and nurtured her. Exulting in the strength and grace of her physical self as she glided through the still water, she mused about all that had happened to her and all she had learnt, since she first entered Maldona in Spain. I had to leave London, she thought, to find Cassie, to become Maldona by intrigue, by combat. But that was not enough; I had to go back to London and be Maldona outside, spreading the word and power of Maldona. Then I had to come here and build the new Maldona, and almost at once I am thinking of conquest, of spreading the rule of Maldona, whether in territory or in spirit, like the Templars of old.

Judging that an hour had passed, she paused, and floated on her back for ten minutes, counting the stars. Perhaps, she thought, I am born to wander, and only in moving can I find myself. I cloak myself as Maldona, but inside, I am Jana Ardenne. I am my ancestor, the witch. Am I a witch? And is that why I must find this Circe, to confront her, nullify her power, for in her I shall see a portion of myself? Buoyed by the warm water, Jana flipped over and began to swim again. Ahead of her, in the far distance, she could see the forbidding crag that was the Island of Circe.

Hour succeeded hour; at each rest pause, Jana inspected the stars, imagining that as she crossed the sea, they shifted slightly. They are my slaves, she thought, they move as I move. She was not alone in the sea: shoals of fish brushed her, nuzzling and caressing the crevices and hillocks of her bare body, and their sensuous stroking made her passage

211

a delight of tingling skin. In the pale glimmer of the coming dawn, she could see the hues of their sparkling scales, the golds, reds, blues, and their mouths, like parodies of human lips, gulping comically for unseen algae. Keeping their distance, swordfish circled her, and sometimes a band of flying fish swooped upwards from the water, to reimmerse themselves with a crash of spray.

The Island of Circe loomed ever closer. Jana felt she could rest for longer periods, having made good time, but realised she was tired and hungry. She opened her pack and took a sip of water and nibbled a biscuit. Then suddenly, a small flying fish landed on her with a smack, right between her breasts. She was so startled she dropped the biscuit – it was that which the fish sought – and it wriggled, mouth flapping, to escape her clutch. But she held it tightly between her breasts, and gradually its struggles ceased as it drowned in the air.

Jana took her knife and cut the fish, then ate the tough flesh. How strange, she thought, that I am a fish of the land; I am Artemis the huntress, fallen to earth from the starry night sky; I am Maldona, hence all things, yet here I am eating a fish of the sea, and being of earth, I cannot breathe in its home. Then she frowned: what if the people who built the underwater city were at home in two worlds of land and sea? She shivered at the possibility and the challenge.

When she had finished eating, she threw the fish carcass far into the water, and it was at once engulfed by a mound of its struggling, snapping fellows, who were in their turn dispersed by a smoothly gliding swordfish who gobbled Jana's fish in one gulp. But who, she asked, resuming her swim, will eat the swordfish?

That made her think of Aphrodite, or, more gloomily, the problem of Aphrodite. Why was the woman following her in Athens? Jana was sure that it was Aphrodite who had been responsible for the destruction of the *Hesperides*. To maroon them on Maldona? But they were already marooned, by choice. The treasure of the Templars: it must be that Aphrodite was shadowing her, expecting her to lead her to the key which Jana had safely hidden. At any rate, Aphrodite spelled danger, both to Jana and the safe fabric of Maldona. Too readily – Jana frowned at not seeing it earlier – Aphrodite had taken to the role of the most abject slave, uninterested in rank, knowing that total submission can become total power.

Dawn was breaking as Jana neared the Island of Circe, and she took out her binoculars. The island was more forbidding close up than the dark crooked shape glimpsed from afar: a mountain of bare rock, not more than two kilometres in diameter, almost denuded of plants save for a few stunted bushes. There was a small rocky beach, on either side of which the slope plunged directly into the sea. Not quite a cliff – it was climbable – but so steep that a fall seawards would kill. Jana felt a stab of fear: surely someone who could live in such a barren place must indeed have magical powers.

The top of the island was not a point; rather the hellish slope seemed to twist abruptly into a plateau, the extent of which Jana could not see. There, then, would be the obvious place for Circe's dwelling.

Jana suddenly realised that she was very tired and needed rest. A couple of hours stretched on the little beach would do, but suddenly fear struck her as she realised that her limbs were rapidly growing numb and that the sea here was icy cold. She floated, shivering and afraid, her limbs feeling as heavy as lead. The lightening sky, orange with the first peep of the sun, swirled before her eyes, and she felt giddy. She could not move, and her fear turned to panic. That fish! Poisonous, perhaps.

Jana realised too late that she was ignorant of fish, at least the uncooked, unsauced kind. But she had heard of strange fish, with poison fangs. Would she be paralysed and die a lingering death before sinking under the water, her dreams, her beauty, rotted by cruel mischance? She looked at the waxing sun and thought it might be her last view of him, when she became aware of a rippling pleasure on her body, like the wake of a ship. She swivelled her eyes and saw, paddling serenely towards her, a huge turtle, its wrinkled face creased in a benign, almost foolish, smile. The giant turtle nudged Jana's supine body, rocking her, and nuzzled its head against her breast, still wearing its dopy smile. Numb, Jana was unable to move. Did turtles eat people? Surely not. But then, with surprising swiftness, the turtle moved its head and spat into her mouth. Jana felt disgust, but could not prevent the sour liquid from entering her throat. The turtle withdrew and watched her placidly, and gradually Jana felt pins and needles in her limbs, felt warmth in her belly. And found she could move her lips and turn her head. And she could smile.

She smiled at the turtle, who seemed to smile back, and then with a rush of water, the turtle disappeared. Jana lay feeling life come back to her, and felt tears of gratitude welling, when suddenly she was lifted up into the air, and, clawing for balance, found herself astride the turtle's back. Well, well, she thought, knowing that this must be – that this *was* – the same turtle on whose back Kate and Melanie had sported in Caspar's film.

And the turtle calmly began to paddle towards the Island of Circe.

Jana had straddled the giant turtle, legs splayed wide and feet hooked under the edges of its shell, making two frothing wakes as they trailed in the icy water. The sun was up now, and warmed Jana's body. She looked at Circe's island as they approached the tiny shingle beach, and it seemed to her that despite the golden sunrise, the island was still in shadow.

In a short while the turtle, still grinning, waddled on to the shingle and shook itself, making Jana slither off on to the sharp shingle. And as smoothly as it had arrived, the turtle slid into the sea and paddled away.

Jana sat on the beach, letting the hot sun dry the last droplets of moisture from her oiled body, though most of the oil had gone in the seawater. She felt full of energy, not needing to rest as she had expected. She thought of the acrid liquid the turtle spat into her, and flexed her muscles, wondering how many turtles there were in the Sea of Maldona. She smiled at the conceit. Yes, this was the Sea of Maldona. She shifted her legs and felt a sharp sting; permitting herself an 'Ouch!' she looked down and saw that the shingle was not rock but the massed shells of small crustaceans. In wonder, she sifted through them, finding whorled conches, mussels, oysters, ribbed limpets, all in myriad shades of pink, blue, black and grey. There were shells in fantastic shapes that Jana was sure appeared in no known book. So much debris, she thought, so many lives washed up by the unimaginable past.

She ate the rest of her biscuits and drank some water, then began to search for a path up the sheer slope. It was unpromising, but she selected a route where scrubby bushes seemed to afford plentiful handholds. The hill was more a mountain, much higher than she had thought, and she estimated it as about 200 metres at least. She remained naked for her climb, not wishing to sully her *himation*, and set off.

By the time she had reached halfway up the precipitous slope, she found a small ledge and stopped, panting. Sweat poured from her and her bare skin was scuffed with the thorns and branches of the tough little thickets she traversed – almost as if they are whipping me onwards, she thought wryly. She looked down at the sheer slope, and no alpinist, marvelled that she had managed to climb so far and so steep. In the distance, across the shimmering mirror that was the Sea of Maldona, she saw her island, a black silhouette against the sun.

Rested, she climbed on, and at last, bathed in sweat, reached the top, where the slope abruptly levelled out. She got both hands on the rim of the plateau and to her surprise felt grass, moist and ripe. With a heave she hoisted herself on to a green blanket of lush waving grass and tumbled on to its softness. She lay on her back for a while, eyes closed, to recover her strength, and became aware that the sun had gone away. She was in shadow.

'Welcome to my island, Mistress of Maldona,' said a cool, fluting woman's voice.

Jana started and opened her eyes, to find that she was

lying in the shadow of a woman who stood over her, looking down with a thin, sardonic smile that was not quite a smile.

Jana scrambled to her feet.

'Circe,' she said.

'The same. You chose the noble way to approach my domain, to make yourself a creature of the sea before you once again became a land-woman. It is good.'

Jana looked around and gasped in astonishment. Here, on the top of this arid rock, was a vast garden, almost a jungle, blossoming with fruit trees and flowers, among which prowled boars, peacocks, deer and even leopard cubs. And in the centre stood one pearl-white building beside which a bubbling spring nourished a pool, from which a stream meandered to the far side of the plateau.

The house was wreathed in climbing roses, and beside it stood a shady apple grove.

The house was a replica of the temple in the underwater city.

Circe took Jana by the hand, and Jana felt the coolness of her flesh as it pressed hers.

'Come,' said Circe, and led her across the grass towards the temple. Circe seemed a woman of about 30 but Jana felt a chill as she looked into her dark green eyes, because those eyes seemed as old as time itself. Circe was slightly shorter than Jana, but her body well-rounded under a flowing purple robe, the fesses ripe and swaying against the flimsy material, the breasts swelling like lush hard fruits. To Jana's surprise, her hair was honey-blonde, only slightly darker than Jana's own. Her graceful frame jangled with a kaleidoscope of golden necklaces and bracelets, set with ruby, amethyst, pearl and diamond. Circe is a walking Asprey's, Jana thought irreverently. But another flash of those dark eyes quickened her mind, and her expression assumed a guarded friendliness which concealed her stone suspicion. If Circe had somehow expected her – seen her, swimming through the darkness? – then she must have some idea of Jana's unfriendly intentions.

'It is a great honour to receive Maldona herself,' said

Circe cosily as they entered the temple. Inside, the living space was bright, sparsely but comfortably furnished with rugs and cushions, the walls white and hung with tapestries, paintings, carvings and an array of bright bronze swords and axes. One whole wall was an intricate mosaic of seashells dyed crimson, and the mosaic was a rose.

'Thank you,' said Jana non-committally as Circe showed her to a large striped floor-cushion, into which she gratefully sank.

'You will take some wine?' said Circe, leaving the room through a curtain that was strings of seashells. It was not a question, but Jana nodded, relishing the cool of the temple's interior. There was a faint perfume of the sea, a fresh lively odour that invigorated her.

Circe returned with a bronze tray carrying an amphora of wine and two bronze goblets, and a bronze platter of dried fish, tomatoes, onions and flat cakes of unleavened bread.

'It is an honour to be so received,' said Jana cautiously as she sipped the dark red wine.

'You have come for the sacred tattoo,' said Circe.

'I come, Circe, to pay my respects,' said Jana carefully, 'as one sovereign to another.'

'Ah yes,' said Circe, fixing Jana with eyes like blades. 'We are indeed both sovereigns, perhaps holding in common what we adore as sacred. Why, you know that three of your slaves – and, lately, a fourth – bear the sacred rose tattoo. It should do me honour to so adorn their mistress.'

Jana smiled. 'The art of the tattoo is a mystery which has long fascinated me,' she said.

Now Circe smiled, a warm, radiant smile, and Jana knew it for the smile of one in whom the cold white worm dwells that feeds on suffering and gnaws at men's dreams.

'There are mysteries which may not be explained,' she said, 'but the tattooist's art is no mystery. In a short while, I shall show you, but please say that you will stay with me awhile and accept my humble hospitality.'

'You live alone here, Mistress Circe?' asked Jana.

'Not exactly.' Jana digested this information as Circe

poured more wine. 'Perhaps you would like to rest?' said Circe. 'After your long swim –'

'Oddly, Mistress Circe, I don't feel tired.'

'Ah yes, you had an encounter with one of my servants.'

'The turtle. Yours?'

'Owing allegiance to me,' said Circe airily. 'I know what happened: the sea can yield fruit or poison, so I sent him to you. As it happens, the flying fish, rare in these waters, eat certain algae containing domoic acid, which acts as a poison in the human nervous system. The turtle's juices absorb and neutralise the domoic acid.'

'That is truly wondrous, and I must thank you,' said Jana warily, and took wine. 'Mistress Circe, it is said, no doubt by idle tongues, that you are a sorceress.'

'Of course, dear Mistress Maldona,' laughed Circe. 'As are you, and as is every woman.' Jana laughed too. 'What is the role of woman,' continued Circe, 'if not to rule the creatures of the land and the sea – especially the *male* creatures. You, Maldona, bring the grace and wisdom of servitude with the cane and whip, and I must admit that such delicacies form a discreet part of my own repertoire. But there are other means.'

'Like the tattoo?' asked Jana.

'Perhaps,' replied Circe, unsmiling, 'but the rose is the woman's *cunt*, Mistress Jana, the fount of life that leads to the sea we women carry within us. The rose is to be adored, the symbol of the sea; the great woman who has rooted herself in land, to conquer men, as bringers of seed to our thirsty wombs.' Circe rose, and offered Jana her hand. 'Perhaps you should see my chamber,' she said.

The halls through which Jana was led were, as in the underwater temple, decorated with gargoyles and carvings of sea creatures, some familiar to Jana, some startling in their strangeness, and she asked their provenance.

'Why, many of these creatures lived in these waters many eons ago,' said Circe in a faraway voice. 'Before the dawn of time, thousands, perhaps hundreds of thousands of our years ago. Before the Achaeans, the Minoans, Greeks came. These beasts are extinct. Life continues, but her manifestations change, except for those few adepts who are beyond life.' She turned abruptly and stared at Jana with her mesmerising eyes. 'Are you such an adept, Mistress of Maldona?' she asked. 'Are you one of the Immortals?'

Jana felt she was in the presence of either a deranged woman or a true sorceress. Yet the temple was here and the mountain plateau blossomed like Eden. She thought of her affinity, the bond she felt ever more strongly, with her ancestor, the witch Jane Ardenne. Could it be that there was reincarnation; that adepts of whatever magical art Circe practised could hand on a portion of their spirit, their noumenon, to their descendants? That in this way, there was no death? The idea frightened and thrilled her.

'Who, then, made the sculptures on your walls, Mistress Circe? The builders of your house – they must have lived at the same time as these fabulous creatures.'

'You ask much for one so young, Mistress Maldona. But of course you are an adept, a mistress. You wonder about reincarnation, the transmission of the *atman*, as the Buddhists have it, from one generation to another. I can tell you that it happens, but not to the common multitude, only to those whose spirits have been honed to a bright, shining blade of wisdom. And obviously the builders of my house observed these creatures of the deep, for the world of humankind is far older than you think, Jana. All religions and creeds are vague stumblings in the dark to rediscover the true light of the dawn, when the ocean –'

Abruptly she stopped. Jana was wise enough not to press her.

Circe smiled again. 'This house is very old,' she said simply. 'It is a copy of the Temple of Poseidon in the sunken city which lies beneath these waters.' Suddenly her face turned to a hideous frown of frustration and rage, as though she had become one of her own gargoyles. 'But the city's location is unknown, as is its true name. I cannot find it, try though I have over all these – these years,' she corrected herself hastily. 'The city's name was not Poseidon – it was the Greeks, thinking it a mere legend, who called it that. Its name is far older, and unknown. It is said that who finds the city and knows her name will rule the sea and thus all things: but that the city has the power to dissolve, to reform herself in different places, waiting for the one who can know her name and open her secrets.'

'That is incredible,' said Jana, deliberately ambiguous.

'Perhaps. But the city is there, I know it.'

'Wise Mistress Circe,' said Jana, as the woman opened a shining bronze door, 'how can you be so sure?'

'Because before the city had a name,' said Circe fiercely, '*I watched her being built*.'

The door swung open, and Jana was admitted to Circe's lair.

17

The Dungeon Again

Where the rest of the house was bathed in light and sea air,
Circe's 'chamber' was warm and dark and imbued with a
curious scent of must and incense, and other stranger perfumes which Jana could not identify, but thought rather
like the pot-pourri smell of a theatre or cinema lobby, the
mingling of different odours forming a cloying, exotic fra-
grance. Her *himation* robe, which she had donned after
finishing her wine, began to feel hot and sticky. She had to
adjust her eyes to the dim candlelight, and when the room
took shape she saw that it was low-ceilinged but very long,
almost as large as the refectory of Maldona.

'What pretty candles!' she said vaguely. 'I am a candle-
maker by trade, you know.'

'I do know,' said Circe, behind her. 'And your candles
were most delicate: modelled from the erect phalli of your
lovers. A pretty conceit.'

Jana started. 'How –' she began, and felt Circe's arms
encircling her, a finger to her lips.

'Hush! I know many things.'

In contrast to the sparse receiving room, the chamber
was an organised clutter of statues, instruments of wood
and bronze, paints, candles and jars of coloured liquids.
Most of the chamber was devoted to the tattooist's art,
with arrays of needles, couches and basins for water and
inks.

The walls had once been white, but now were entirely
covered by intricate blood-red or marine-blue frescos of
distorted faces and bodies – human, animal and piscine –
linked by a series of symbols and diagrams which to Jana

meant nothing, although on the uncarpeted stone floor she recognised a witch's pentagram. The paintings depicted centaurs and satyrs, half-man, half-beast, and all with fantastically enlarged stiff penises; tentacled monsters of the deep, grinning with human faces and pointed teeth; mermaids, full-breasted and lusciously inviting the spectator to take them with their eyes and stroke their fleshy tails which sparkled with a thousand golden scales. At the end of the chamber was another bronze door, bolted, and before it a series of wardrobes.

'The little alcove need not concern us for the moment,' said Circe sharply, following Jana's gaze to the locked door, 'but I shall show you my clothes. Then, perhaps, some display of my art!' She said this with a surprisingly girlish giggle, and the smile that wreathed her lean face was quite genuine.

'I'm a little girl, really, Mistress Jana,' she said as she opened her closets to reveal the most glittering array of robes Jana had seen. Silvers, golds, purples and yellows; every hue imaginable was there in utmost vividness. No pastels for a sorceress, she reflected. And in the last closet Circe opened, with an impish grin, Jana saw things warm and familiar to her, and her heart beat a little faster. There were articles of leather, strange harnesses and corsets, wigs, straps, chains, gags and hoods, and on the wall of the closet, neatly rolled, hung half a dozen thick leather whips. Automatically, she reached to caress one, the strong leather lovingly oiled. Her fingers came away smelling fishy.

'Our interests as mistresses coincide somewhat,' said Circe. 'You see, when I said I lived alone – well, sometimes a slave comes to me, begging to be adorned, or properly chastised.' She smiled her cold smile. 'I am sure I am but a novice, and you could give me lessons, Mistress.'

Jana smiled politely in demurral, remembering Circe's words – that she had *seen* the underwater city being built – and wanting fervently to dismiss the woman as a crazed solitary. But she could not: Circe seemed so icily sure of herself, and there was the matter of the parfaites' tattoos, and the pristine Eden that was Circe's garden. Circe suddenly interrupted her thoughts.

'Not Eden,' she said. 'I have nothing to do with the false myths of the Nazarene. No, my garden is the Garden of the Hesperides, who guard my golden apples, albeit from afar. And now I have added a fourth! Thanks to you, Mistress. Soon, I hope, a fifth.'

And she reached out to stroke Jana's face, then allowed her finger to stray over her breasts and down to the fesses, rippling against the thin silk of Jana's *himation*. Jana took the touch of the sorceress with a tingling excitement that she knew, despite herself, to be intense desire. Circe's eyes fixed on her as her hand moved between Jana's thighs, pushing the silk tightly against her fount.

'You are wet, Mistress,' she said with cruel softness.

Jana swallowed nervously, unable to speak or break the spell as Circe artfully stroked her cunt-lips through her wet dress, but not wanting her to stop. Suddenly Circe broke away.

'Let us play at painting and costuming ourselves!' she cried. 'It is my favourite, favourite pastime!'

With that, she began to rummage in her closets, throwing clothes in a heap. She smiled radiantly at Jana as she threw off her own clothing, and stood golden and nude, as though for inspection. Jana looked with awe at the woman's perfect body; the rippling undulations of thigh and breast, the flat belly and lush mink beneath, a forest of golden curls that came up almost to her deep dimpled navel. The hairs were so long that Circe had braided them into five spiky points, in each of which was knotted a tiny red rosebud. Circe's breasts were so round, creamy and firm that in different circumstances Jana would have suspected an implant, and she saw that the nipples were curiously inverted. Evidently, she too was invited to remove her clothing, and stepped out of her *himation*, grateful for her nudity.

Circe sat at a vanity table laden with jars and brushes and with her back turned to Jana, began to paint herself. Jana noticed that there was no mirror; in fact, there was not a mirror anywhere in this house. But the woman's absorption in her face-painting gave Jana time to think. The Garden of the Hesperides ... the three sisters who guarded the golden apples! Kate, Melanie and Sarah ... and now a fourth, Aphrodite.

She had no doubt now that Circe, whether sorceress or just touched by the sun and isolation, was a threat to Maldona; that in tattooing, she exerted influence, and had Jana's women in some way under her destructive, mesmeric power; that her aim, despite her honeyed words, was to remove Maldona from 'her' domain.

'You do not shave your mink, Circe?' she asked diffidently. 'I understand, though, she is wonderfully ripe and full. And such a lovely adornment of roses.'

'No,' said Circe, 'I am but a virgin, Mistress Jana, no adept, and have not the right to shave. How I envy you! I must content myself with painting and robing.'

Now Jana knew that she spoke a mocking lie. It was clear that Circe, whoever she was, made her own rights.

'And you wear no tattoos yourself,' she added. 'Your skin is smooth as milk, dear Mistress Circe, so I see you do not wish to conceal her from adoring eyes.'

'Why, thank you,' purred Circe, and Jana thought that vanity was perhaps this woman's weak spot.

Now Circe stood and began to apply paints to her whole naked body. She was in shadow, and Jana could not see her clearly, but despite herself, felt an urge to join in the game. She went to the costumes heaped on the floor and began to sift through them, thinking to surprise Circe when she presented her maquillage. She tried on flowing robes of gossamer silk, hats wide-brimmed or conical, hung with oyster shells, ancient coins, amethysts and rubies, but at last could not resist a wasp corset; a strange design that she knew must be many centuries old. It was purple, and the metal stays, perhaps bronze, pinched abominably: Jana gasped as she clipped the fastenings tightly around her, and longed for a mirror to inspect her upthrust breasts. She felt an irrational instinct to please Circe.

She took stockings of silk, patterned with red and yellow

roses, and a pair of yellow satin open-toed slippers with very high pointed heels on which walking became a balancing act. She was flushed with pleasure now; a little girl's pleasure in dressing in another's clothing. She swept her blonde mane under a black wig whose tresses reached down to her fount, though not covering her. Then, jewels: necklace upon necklace, bracelet upon bracelet. Lost in her delving, she was suddenly startled by a loud laugh from Circe, who had crept up behind her.

'You look divinely pretty, Mistress Jana,' she drawled. 'You can see how excited I am by your beauty.'

Circe wore a wig like a horse's mane, and her nude body was painted so that her feet were hooves, her legs muscularly equine, and her torso and breasts were a rainbow of colour: whorls, starbursts, fish and flowers. But what fascinated and frightened Jana was Circe's midriff: from the luxurious forest of her mink stood an impossibly thick and strong penis, a monstrous shining pole standing flush with her belly, right to her ribs, that was tipped by an obscenely swollen crimson bulb whose peehole was a single, staring eye; from the pupil of the eye spurted a powerful jet of creamy white seed that became a fountain splashing her breasts and lips.

It was so lifelike – almost three-dimensional in the shadowy candlelight – that Jana thought she could reach out and grasp that magnificent painted cock.

'Well!' cried Circe, 'How do you like the Great God Pan? Half-man, half-beast.' Jana was speechless, and smiled, miming applause. 'You see, that is the beauty of maquillage,' continued Circe. 'A woman can become anything she pleases: a god, a fish, a beast, a mermaid, even another woman.' She fixed Jana with a pointed stare, making her shiver. 'I can be Medusa with snakes for hair, I can be Perseus with his winged horse, who slew her! I can be Hera, the wife of Zeus, or I can be Zeus himself!'

Circe's trance-like excitement was infectious, and Jana began to feel that she was in the presence of a great and powerful mystery, which could easily suck her into its power. Still, the small voice of her reason told her that she

225

was here to destroy that power and enslave Circe, not to be captured by her.

Suddenly Circe calmed herself, and flashed her brilliant white teeth.

'But now,' she said, 'I am a horse-god, a male rampant with seed in my balls, and only Mistress Jana knows what brute horses require.'

Abruptly she knelt, and with an unnerving whinny began to lick Jana's bare toes. Jana smiled as Circe patted her naked painted horse's rump, and stroked the woman's head. She went to the closet and selected a short but springy braided whip with splayed tip, which looked fit for a horse's, or a god's, flanks. She turned to find Circe crouching on all fours, head in her hands. And her naked rump stretched high.

Jana lifted her horsewhip and cracked her savagely across her bare fesses, making her quiver and cry out.

'Yes!' shouted Circe. 'Yes! I need that. I have needed it for so many ages! To be properly worshipped by the supreme mistress!'

Jana was unsettled by the extravagant praise that Circe cried at each whiplash, but beat the prone woman with all the strength of her muscled arm. So tight was her corset that she was panting hard by the fifth stroke, and vivid crimson was showing on Circe's croup even through the paint. At each harsh stroke she wriggled and shrieked in ecstasy, her body a symphony of shuddering pain. Jana lost count of the number of times she lashed the woman – the sorceress – and knew that the sight of that cowering naked body truly bewitched her. As the beating continued, she knew that Circe spoke the truth; that she had been waiting long for her thrashing from a mistress. But how long?

Jana began, now, to flog Circe's bare back, laying vicious strikes from her quirt square across the woman's shoulders. This made Circe's ecstasy even greater, and she cried out as one demented by joy. The idea brushed Jana that perhaps Circe's game was to use her powers, such as they might be, to establish dominion over Maldona; to tap

226

the vital energy of punishment, submission and love which her solitude here denied her. Circe longed to be chastised, to be whipped for whatever imperfections she had committed; except that here, in her perfect, solitary world, there was no one to witness or judge her imperfection, and no one to punish her for it.

At last, when Circe's painted flesh was a mass of crimson, Jana threw aside her whip.

'It is over, Mistress Circe,' she gasped. 'Such prowess under the lash! You must have taken a good hundred.'

Circe rolled over on her back and stretched her legs and arms in the air, wide apart so that under the painted penis Jana could see the glistening lips of her fount, red and swollen and oily with her juices of excitement. Jana's own fount began to seep with her love-oil, and she realised that though she feared and perhaps hated Circe, she desired her intensely. The invitation could not be ignored, and slowly she sank to her knees, then entered Circe's embrace, the cunts of the two women rubbing together in fierce gamahuching as their lips met.

Circe's lips were cold, as was her cunt. It was the cold of the ocean. But Jana bucked and kissed the cold sorceress, breasts and erect nipples pressing, and when the nymphae of the two women touched, they both shuddered in orgasm, Jana moaning, Circe silent. We fuck what we fear, thought Jana. Fucking is a weapon like any other.

'It was a hundred and eighty-nine strokes, Mistress,' whispered Circe. 'I was counting.'

Suddenly Circe broke away from Jana's embrace and, still nude, darted to a candle-lit recess near the locked bronze door, and prostrated herself briefly, intoning words in a language which Jana did not recognise, but which sounded unearthly. A word like 'B'homit' was repeated often. She followed, and as Circe rose, she saw that the object of her adoration was a painting perched on a column carved as a giant phallus. The figure depicted was quasi-human in form, but frightening: it had a human body but a goat's head, with a flaming torch between its horns, and was seated against a starry background, sitting on a large red cube, its bare human feet resting on a blue globe. The naked penis was grotesquely large and erect. The creature had a woman's breasts, blue in colour, and the belly was green and scaly like a fish.

One hand pointed upward to the sun and crescent moon, the other held a four-thonged whip and pointed down to the bare roots of a tree, whose lush foliage, entwined with climbing roses, framed the creature, the winding branches and leaves curled into the shape of a woman's naked body. The roots bathed in a lake where fish swam in the tree's tendrils. Above the creature's head, a white dove flew up towards the moon.

Circe smiled gleefully.

'Baphomet,' she said with reverence. 'The god of the Templars. You know, of course, Mistress.'

'Of course,' said Jana, not knowing.

'I painted this from old memory,' said Circe in a faraway voice. 'The Templars in the East gathered much of the wisdom and truth of the Eastern way. That was partly why the wicked exterminated them as heretics, and in envy of their vast, and suspicious, wealth. It is thought that Baphomet is a corruption of Muhammad and . . . *Baal*.

'Baal,' said Jana. 'The god of evil, Lord of Flies.'

'There are many Baals,' said Circe, 'just as there are many goods and many evils. It is evil to cause pain, some say, but the surface evil contains a deeper good, because pain is truth. As when you flog your virgins of Maldona, and flogged me, Mistress Jana. Baal was a god of the Midianites; Baal-Peor, the god of fertility and manly strength, as in his stiff penis; Baal-Samin, god of the heavens; Baal-Shemesh, the sun god; you are thinking of Baal Zeboub, or Beelzebub. *He* is Lord of Flies. Baphomet is the Absolute, Jana. It is hermaphrodite, symbolising the unity of male and female, and of all things. It sits on a cube, the symbol of four, which is the square and foundation of all things, and sometimes is depicted at a crossroads, the sacred place where four roads meet; and its feet rest on the world herself. It is wreathed by the Tree of

228

Life, whose roots, like Yggdrasil, the world tree of the Norse, are in water, our primordial home, which in this last age, the degenerate, evil Age of Iron, the fish have inherited. Yes, Jana, we are in the last of the four ages: Gold, Silver, Bronze and Iron, each, after the perfection of the Golden Age, more dismal than the last. This is what the Hindus call the Age of Kaliyuga, when Kali, the goddess of destruction and pain, reigns supreme. And only by the work of adepts in teaching the necessity and the beauty of overwhelming pain and submission can the wheel turn full circle and the Golden Age return. Some of us must wait as guardians, ready for our chance to teach and lead. Others, adepts like you, Maldona, must be the vanguard.'

Now I know she's touched, thought Jana, suddenly missing the playful certainties of Caspar's strange but pleasantly exotic parties in Lennox Gardens.

'Just when is this age supposed to end?' she asked.

'The Age of Iron, or Kaliyuga, according to the Hindus, whose teaching the Templars undoubtedly absorbed, is to last four hundred and thirty-two thousand sidereal years,' said Circe calmly. 'Only a very few years are left.' She chuckled, a cold, rasping sound in her throat. 'And now, Mistress Jana, I should like to show you the art of the tattoo.'

'Mistress Circe, I must say that I am not ready to be tattooed,' said Jana uncertainly.

Circe took a key from her table and unlocked the bronze door, which swung open without a sound. Jana saw only blackness.

'You will see. Please enter,' said Circe.

'It is very dark,' said Jana nervously.

'Of course, *you* will need a candle,' answered Circe, and fetched one in the shape of a rampant snake, the flame its tongue.

'I'll follow you,' said Jana, concealing her wariness.

'Of course,' said Circe, and entered, with Jana following.

Before Jana could adjust her vision to the darkness, the door suddenly crashed shut behind her and there was a click and a hiss from the unseen ceiling. Jana felt a sharp blow to her head, and then a cold slithering across her naked body. She cried out but Circe was not to be seen. Jana was enveloped in a sheath of chainmail, finely woven but inhumanly heavy, so that she was forced to sink to the stone floor under its weight.

Furious and terrified, she screamed, and at least Circe reappeared, smiling as always.

'It is for your own good, Mistress Jana,' she said. Jana knew that to protest would be useless. Suddenly, the fatigue of her long swim, her poisoning by the fish flesh and the wine she had drunk hit her like the body-blow of the imprisoning mesh. She felt utterly drained of strength, unable to move a muscle and scarcely able to talk.

'What do you want?' she mumbled feebly, but Circe ignored her question.

'You are to meet a long-lost friend,' she murmured.

Her eyes accustomed to the gloom, Jana saw she was in a large dungeon crammed with implements of the tattooist, just as outside, but in addition the dungeon contained what Jana recognised as mediaeval or ancient engines of torture. She shivered violently, and despite herself, felt her bowels loosen. This, she knew, was a *real* dungeon, and bitter self-doubt came to her that perhaps she, Jana, had been play-acting no less than Caspar's posing followers. Circe grinned in mock sympathy and shook her head.

'Dear, dear,' she said mildly, and, scooping the metal folds of the mesh, dragged Jana into the centre of the dungeon. There, Circe pulled her on to a metal frame, or rack, and swiftly lifted the bottom of the shroud to clamp Jana's ankles in tight metal cuffs. She rolled the mesh off Jana's body, then fastened her waist, breasts and neck in metal cinchers before she could rise; finally her arms were stretched above her and Jana felt cold cuffs clamp her wrists.

'There,' said Circe. 'Now I must fetch my inks and needles.'

'Don't tattoo me! You witch! I won't bear your evil mark!' screamed Jana.

Circe laughed cruelly. 'Given your present circumstances, Mistress, that is rather academic,' she said. 'But the tattoo is not for you – yet. Not until you accept her necessity; not until you *beg* for it, Mistress.'

She lifted the candle, and there, stretched beside her on a rack like her own, was Gloria. Jana shuddered in horror. Gloria's naked body was covered in garish tattoos; designs of lurid colour so bizarre that in a painting they would be hailed as the work of genius. On the bare body of her friend, Jana found them obscene. The designs radiated out from the rose that adorned her naked pubis: there were seagods, monsters, dragons, birds and stars, all possessing an eerie beauty if their canvas had not been the living tormented flesh of a woman. Jana thought Gloria was unconscious but she was not, her terrified eyes meeting Jana in a plea of sympathy and despair. Jana saw that the system of chains and levers attached to Gloria's rack were stretched tight: that Gloria was already suffering under the threat of the agonising stretching torture, and dared not speak for fear of Circe's cold anger.

'Gloria has proved a most responsive slave,' said Circe. 'She is not yet of Maldona, so I have been able to imbue her with much more of my power than my Hesperides that are already amongst you, Mistress Jana. I have Gloria groomed for greater things: that is, unless you accept the tattoo, and her wondrous powers. Not,' she added thoughtfully, 'that you will have much choice. And now I must leave you for a moment. I am sure Gloria will tell you of the glorious future that awaits you both . . . the magnificence of Maldona enriched by your newfound power . . . as my vassals.'

'Oh, Gloria . . . how? How?' said Jana. Then she saw that Gloria's expression was not of pain, as she had thought, but of a kind of stony serenity, even of grandeur.

'It is necessary, Mistress,' she whispered. 'The pain of the tattoo, I mean. To achieve beauty and truth.'

'Gloria! Only Maldona's way is the way of truth. Circe's way is perversion and darkness.'

'No, Mistress, look at my bright tattoos. Circe has shown me light. And when my adornment is finished, and you have been likewise adorned, we shall return to Maldona: you to rule, and I to serve, for ever.'

Jana groaned, not from pain but at despair that Gloria had been twisted thus.

'How did you get here?' she asked numbly.

'A storm, Mistress, a freak of nature that blew my ship off course: we ran aground on this island, and Circe cared for us. She tattooed the crewmen, on their male organs, which delighted them, then let them go, but she kept me. At first I resisted as you do, but then, as my tattoos grew, I saw wisdom.'

'What will happen to you – to us?' said Jana, seeing no way of escaping from this horror.

'Why, we will learn the secrets of the deep,' said Gloria. 'To breathe under the water, to be as fishes. There is a city, a key to the treasure of the Templars. I have found a document and a map during my excavations on Poros, the island where we dug: but they tell only half the story. Circe believes that only you, reincarnated noumenon, of the first Maldona, have the power to –'

'To lead *her* to the treasure,' said Jana drily. 'And then, whatever this treasure is, we must serve her, imprisoned by these tattoos. She may be crazy, Gloria, but I know she has powers, sorceress or not.' And she related the episode of the fish and the turtle. 'Although,' she concluded, 'it could easily have been concidence. Witches and snake-oil healers always take credit for coincidence.'

Circe re-entered the dungeon, and she was no longer the god Pan. Her maquillage and costume were even more fearsome: the pseudo-god Baphomet, blue-breasted and goat-horned, with a fish-scaled belly and the addition of curling, writhing hair that was a tangle of living snakes, their tongues darting in hatred.

'I told you that I can be anything,' said Circe. 'Here, the great god Baphomet, but the Medusa too, whose hair was living snakes, and turned men to stone. Man and woman in one: but do not worry, the sight of my hair shall not turn you to stone. I am a fake Medusa, a make-believe. For such is my pleasure and destiny.'

At that, Jana felt a sudden surge of hope. Yes, Circe was

a fake; a vain, primping charlatan. She looked at Gloria, and saw doubt in her eyes: she had been visited by the same thought. Jana smiled weakly in encouragement.

'Now,' said Circe, 'the tattooing of my luscious Gloria must go on.'

She moved to Jana, and took hold of her head, which she twisted sideways and clamped in another collar, round her forehead, so that she would be forced to observe the operation on her friend.

'You must watch, Jana,' said Circe, 'and it will not be pretty. Tattooing the ancient way is painful, and Gloria will scream. To stop her torment, you only have to accept the tattoo yourself, and I promise you it shall be done without pain.'

'What if I don't accept?' hissed Jana.

'Then, when Gloria's adornment is complete, I shall start on you, in any case, and not painlessly. But before that, you shall suffer the cleansing beauty of pain more than you have ever dreamt of.'

She spun a wheel at the side of Jana's rack, and the rack moved. Jana gasped as she felt her spine, her whole body, stretched; not enough to cause pain, but enough to herald pain. Circe continued in a matter-of-fact tone.

'That is nothing, Jana. Think what it must feel like when your spine, your arms and legs, are stretched so that your bones threaten to burst from their sockets. You shall be masked and gagged, of course, and as the rack grinds I shall administer the sweetest of floggings on your bare breasts, your belly, between your legs – yes, on the very lips of your fount. Imagine the four-thonged whip, *there*!'

'I am no stranger to floggings,' said Jana hoarsely.

'Or,' said Circe airily, 'when I have stretched and flogged you, I might stand you up and collar you, to attend your naked fesses and shoulders with a good cane.'

She gestured to a bronze ring suspended by a chain from the ceiling, which was lined with sharp spikes inside. Circe laughed cruelly.

'Wearing the spiked collar, you must take your flogging perfectly still, and standing straight, for if you move as the cane bites you, my spikes will do their work on your smooth sweet neck-flesh. Now, I have two more areas to cover on Gloria's body; her right breast, and her lips, inside and outside: both very painful. But when it is finished, she will be utterly under my dominion, and yet happy, as you will be, Jana, *for you will not know it*.' She picked up her needle and tray of ink pots, and squatted beside Gloria. 'Well, Jana?' she taunted.

'No, Mistress,' cried Gloria suddenly. 'I have been bewitched; I must live or die with this tattooed body.'

Suddenly, Jana yawned. Despite her confinement, fatigue invaded her body, which demanded the bliss of sleep.

Circe lifted the needle and paused. 'Perhaps I shall postpone the operation until you are in full command of your faculties, Mistress Jana. It grows late. I shall return when it is past midnight and you may listen to the hoots of the owl between Gloria's cries of pain.'

She picked up a pitcher of water and splashed some on Gloria's and Jana's bodies, then allowed them to drink. When the pitcher was empty, she placed it, humiliatingly, under Jana's spread buttocks.

'There are certain things which even Maldona cannot control,' she sneered, and left them in the candlelight.

For a while there was no sound except Gloria's hoarse breathing, interspersed with sobs, and Jana felt herself drift into a light doze. It lasted not long, for once again she was woken in a cold sweat by the terrible nightmare of fighting the monster on the mountain top; the monster with her own face.

Half asleep, she muttered, 'What are we women? How can we treat each other so? We spend our lives looking in mirrors, and when we see ourselves truly, we see a monster. So much disguise, so many artifices! Clothes and perfumes and wigs and jewels. But the mirror reveals all in time.'

'Mistress!' cried Gloria. 'You are awake?'

'Yes,' whispered Jana. 'Gloria, I'll take the tattoo. I have no choice, and I cannot bear to see you suffer.'

And Jana proceeded to tell Gloria all that had happened in Maldona: the intrusive power of Circe and the unsettling arrival of the treacherous Aphrodite. For her part, Gloria

234

recounted the hard toil of digging and the artefacts they had discovered – humdrum except for a fragment of manuscript in Latin, purporting to be the journal of one Aelfric, slave of Jane Ardenne, known as Maldona, together with an incomplete map with some gnomic verses about the location of a treasure in the Island of the Templars. In her excitement, Gloria had realised the significance: Poros, it seemed, had been either visited or even settled by the wandering Templars over 600 years ago. So she had hidden the papers in oilskin and tucked them between the planks of her boat's hull.

'The boat is here?' asked Maldona urgently.

'Beached, but intact, and unsearched.'

Jana pondered. 'Then we have some chance,' she said. 'When Circe comes back, I'll agree to take the tattoo and feign submission – who knows, I might even like it. Yours, Gloria is really quite beautiful. If only I didn't know its provenance!'

In the guttering light of the failing candles, she saw Gloria smile, and knew she loved her. She felt tears as she realised that she loved all women, and all men – the sweet, confused, submissive creatures. But then, her heart chilled. Am I the only woman I do *not* love, she asked. Is it only the hateful mirror that I love?

The door of the dungeon opened, and once more Circe approached Gloria, without greeting, and took up her tattooist's instruments.

'Mistress Circe,' cried Jana, 'I will gladly accept your art. I was confused and foolish to refuse. Make me part of your domain. I shall be yours. Maldona shall submit.'

Circe smiled a thin smile. 'Your change of heart does you credit, Mistress Jana, but you have displeased me with your hesitation. So there will be a lesson of pain, after all, for you both.'

She lifted the dripping needle, and poised it over Gloria's breast.

'No!' howled Jana. 'Do what you want with me, Circe, or Baphomet, or whoever you are, but spare Gloria the pain! I shall take it, all of it!'

235

Circe tightened the rack another notch, and Jana groaned, this time in real distress. Bitter tears filled her eyes at her indignity. Circe smiled cruelly and held the needle over Gloria's nipple.

Gloria screamed.

At that moment the door burst open and a figure clad in a black rubber mask and catsuit, glistening with water droplets, burst into the dungeon. The figure carried a long bullwhip, which Jana, twisting her head, recognised as Circe's. For a split second, the scene was frozen, Circe gaping in anger and alarm, and then suddenly the bullwhip lashed out, caught her and snaked round her neck in a whirling embrace that had her helpless. With a tug she was on the floor, and the stranger pinioned her to fasten her wrists with the whip, then completed her trussing with tight chains. Circe screamed abuse and her eyes rolled as she squirmed on the floor, helpless as a wingless insect. The stranger took off her mask.

'Cassie!' cried Jana. 'Oh, Cassie!'

'So Gloria is *here*!' exclaimed Cassie as she released the two women from their bonds. 'I have her to thank for my prowess at the lasso!'

The two captives stretched, and, too dazed to ask questions, helped Cassie carry the wriggling body of Circe to the living quarters, where they dumped her roughly on the floor while Gloria went in search of food and wine. Sweating, Cassie stripped naked in the sultry heat, and Jana gasped in dismay as she saw her bare back.

'Oh, Cassie!' she cried. 'My love! How . . . who did it?'

'Aphrodite,' said Cassie. 'There is little time, Mistress, but I'll tell you the terrible events.

'When Jana's departure was noticed, Aphrodite, helped by the treacherous Sarah, Kate and Melanie, chose her moment. Aphrodite declared that Maldona, the woman known as Jana, was dead, drowned at sea, and that she, Aphrodite, was the new Maldona.'

'And they accepted?' asked Jana bitterly. 'The new virgins, I could understand, but our old companions –'

'Mistress, Aphrodite has the evil eye. All, mesmerised, they took frightful noble beatings and submitted.' She

236

shuddered. 'I refused to look at her, and I took *three* noble beatings. Oh God, Mistress, you must return, you must rescue Maldona from her enthralment by this witch!' She indicated the snakes writhing on Circe's livid face. 'I escaped, and swam here. You have a boat?'

'Yes,' said Gloria. 'My boat is seaworthy. But when is the best time to surprise Aphrodite and her gang?'

Jana sipped her wine and thoughtfully chewed bread. 'Now,' she said.

18

False Maldona

There were two pairs of oars on the small boat which had carried Gloria to the island, so the three women took turns at rowing, two on the oars while the third watched the trussed figure of Circe, although secured as she was, a helpless gagged bundle of hatred, she seemed to present no threat. They were halfway to Maldona when the glow of dawn began, and Jana looked up to see moon, stars and nascent sun all gleaming in the turquoise sky together. Suddenly, her heart was full of joy.

'Look!' she breathed. 'How strange our situation, yet in this eeriness, how much beauty!' The others looked.

There was a violent rocking of the boat, and they looked round from their celestial distraction to see Circe, furiously wriggling so that her bound body was halfway over the side of the boat. Jana made a frantic lunge to stop her from falling but she was too late. With a final wriggle and a malevolent rictus of triumph, Circe fell loudly into the water and plummeted down into the clear depths.

'She has killed herself!' cried Cassie. 'The crazy woman! Did she think we were going to hurt her?'

'Weren't we?' said Jana drily. 'Anyway, deranged though she was, that is one problem out of the way.'

'I wouldn't be too sure,' said Gloria nervously. 'I'll dive for her.'

'And I,' said Jana. 'Perhaps she is more useful alive.'

'No, Mistress. I alone. I . . . I can last longer underwater than you.' And without further explanation, Gloria stripped bare, and her magnificently tattooed body splashed backward into the sea.

238

Jana and Cassie sat in silence for what seemed an age, and were exchanging anxious glances when suddenly Gloria reappeared at the gunwale, pale and gasping for breath. She hoisted herself into the boat and lay panting: all around them the water rippled as fish darted to the surface to snap the insects of the dawn, as though the women were part of the living fabric of the sea.

Gloria said that she had found Circe, lying trussed on the sea floor, alive and squirming, bubbles spurting from her throat and her eyes still burning with hatred. Before Gloria could make any move to untie her and take her back to the boat, she felt a blow to her back, sending her spinning some distance away. Righting herself, she saw a giant turtle calmly biting loose the ropes which bound Circe, and to Gloria's amazement the beast flipped Circe on to its back and carried her upward, in the direction of her island. Cassie was astounded, Jana less so. She looked back towards the distant island, and through her binoculars saw that a speck in the sea was the sorceress herself, carried on the back of the turtle.

'So Circe is still a threat,' frowned Jana, 'but we have a more pressing matter to deal with: Aphrodite, the false Maldona. I'll take my turn at your oars, Gloria, and if we hurry –' she grinned slyly '– we should be in time for breakfast.'

The sun was already a golden orb above the horizon as they beached the boat on Maldona's island, and once more Jana found herself in the shadow of the black mountain. She was glad that not all their copious stores had been transported to the castle, and from the hulking chests piled on the sand they were able to put together a makeshift meal of dates, dried fish and biscuits, washed down with bottled mineral water.

'Not exactly the Hotel Grande Bretagne,' said Jana, 'but we need the energy. Just as important, we need these –' Breaking open another crate, she distributed a belt, kukri knife, ropes, chains, a cane and a whip to each of her companions. Then Jana and Gloria discarded their robes and donned black rubber catsuits like Cassie's, with full-face pixie hoods.

'The disguise may serve for a short time, until we can cross the yard and reach the refectory,' said Jana. 'They will think we are slaves who have been placed on punishment for some imperfection. Gloria, this is what you Americans call playing hardball, but tell me, how was it you were able to stay underwater for so long without surfacing for air?'

Gloria suddenly looked frightened. 'Circe must have told you about the tattoos,' she said timidly. 'The special inks from her plants, from the spit of turtles, from powdered seashells, mean that the bearer of the tattoo has the power to stay underwater without breathing for a long time, and – oh, but she's crazy! – to *breathe* underwater! It's nonsense, of course, but –'

'Gloria,' interrupted Jana firmly, 'there is such a thing as mind over matter. Control of the body, self-control, the ability of Maldona's slaves to endure punishment, the caress of the fiercest lash – *because they have learned to know themselves*! Look at the followers of yoga, the "yoke" of discipline and self-knowledge: the levitation, the holding of breath, the yogic flying; you have been well brainwashed, Gloria, and the ability you have gained is psychosomatic, the tattoos merely an emblem.'

'I guess so,' said Gloria, looking reassured.

'And now,' said Jana, 'we go up. They should be in the refectory, and –'

'What's your plan, Mistress?' asked Cassie. 'I'll brave anything to have Aphrodite squirming under *my* lash.'

Jana suddenly realised that she had no plan, and squatted to ponder. Then she rose, and with grim lips, told Cassie and Gloria that brief though her imprisonment by Circe had been, she had nevertheless learned things.

'Circe has the evil eye,' she said simply. 'A way of mesmerising by a stare, to bend the will of others. The Ancients knew this, and feared it. I am sure Aphrodite has it, and as I lay on that rack of pain, my bowels loosened and trembling with terror, the small thought comforted me that I too have it, as did my ancestor, Jane Ardenne. That is how she bewitched her followers, and it is how I . . . inspire mine.'

240

'A duel between you and Aphrodite,' murmured Cassie.

'Physical combat will be necessary,' said Jana sombrely, 'according to the rules. Even Aphrodite cannot deny the rules if she fancies herself the new Maldona.'

Keeping in the shade of the trees, they made their way up the winding path towards the lush pastures and groves which Sabine lovingly nurtured. Jana explained that, on bursting into the refectory, they would not pause but make straight for the high table, where the old companions would be sitting. The newer virgins and slaves would, she reckoned, be too confused, with luck even unwilling, to rally to Aphrodite. As they neared the castle walls they moved from the track and dived into the olive and orange groves for cover. Jana suspected that Aphrodite would have sentries on duty in case of her reappearance, though she was probably over-confident of Circe's prowess as jailer and torturer.

'The castle gates will undoubtedly be closed, although locks are against the rules of Maldona,' said Jana. 'So the way in is underwater, via the river that flows under the walls. No problem for you, Gloria,' she said, smiling.

Still concealed by the trees, they were not far from the castle walls when they were stopped in their tracks by the sight of a woman's body strapped to a tree, standing alone in a clearing, in full view of any watcher from the castle. Jana looked through her binoculars and saw to her horror that it was Sabine, known as Demeter, the mistress fructifier. She was naked and bare-headed in the now burning sun, and gagged, her inert body slumped in bonds of heavy ropes and her back and buttocks a mass of cruel crimson. She had evidently endured the most terrible of bare floggings. Cassie moved forward to hurry to Sabine's aid, but Jana stayed her.

'It is a trap and a warning,' she said grimly. 'Poor Sabine! Aphrodite shall suffer for this. They want to draw any intruders – us – into the open.'

Thinking rapidly, Jana ordered Cassie and Gloria to proceed under cover to the castle wall, then swim through the river tunnel. Their wet rubber suits should swiftly dry in the sun, after which they were to make their way to the refectory, where Jana would join them in minutes.

The two women set off cautiously, and Jana ran towards the tree to which Sabine was tied. The woman's face was streaked with pain and tears, and swiftly Jana ungagged her then slashed her bonds with her kukri knife. Sabine collapsed, sobbing, into her arms, and Jana carried her back to the concealing shade of the grove.

She bathed Sabine's raw back and fesses with water from her canteen, and the tortured woman blurted her story. She had been tending her beloved fruits and flowers when Aphrodite mounted her *coup*. Returning to the castle, she could not believe it, and refused to submit to Aphrodite, believing that Jana her protector could not be far away. Thus, as a lesson and a warning to invaders, she had been bound naked to the tree and thrice flogged with the flagrum, the ferocious many-thonged scourge bound in steel wire.

'From you, Mistress,' she said, calmer now, 'I should have taken my punishment in love and gratitude, but Aphrodite's strokes had only darkness and hatred.'

Once she was rested in shade, the tough Sabine was not as hurt as Jana had feared.

'You are Demeter, remember,' she said, embracing her, 'and goddesses cannot be subdued by an upstart slave.'

'I shall have my revenge, Mistress,' said Sabine quietly. Jana resisted the temptation to tell her there might be a long queue, but helped her to her feet and ordered her to follow to the river under the wall.

Once at the river, the two women dived and swam under the rushing water for half a minute before surfacing right inside the castle yard. The yard was not deserted as Jana had hoped: a flogging was taking place before breakfast. That meant it was for a serious imperfection.

Jana and Sabine took cover behind a walnut tree and watched as the dread punishment proceeded. Jana felt her throat tighten in outrage. The victim of punishment was Sandra, her proud body stretched nude on a tall flogging frame in the centre of the yard. But what chilled Jana was the nature of the frame.

'That is against the rules!' she hissed in fury.

The frame was that of a noble beating: Sandra's naked body was strapped, stretched and cuffed, in the shape of a St Andrew's Cross, to an upright wooden lattice, not aslant as was normal. As a result, she was obliged to support herself on tiptoe, a treatment which made the flogging more agonising because the helpless woman would be unable to twist and squirm to dissipate the pain. But in a hideous refinement of cruelty, her feet rested not on the ground but on a narrow bar a head's breadth off the ground and her arms were stretched not straight above her but up behind her back, so that if she lost her footing she would fall from the bar and be left dangling, her arms agonisingly wrenched behind her. Sandra was gagged and hooded – this procedure was within the rules – but tiptoe was a refinement of cruelty no mistress of Maldona could condone. It seemed that Sandra was to be flogged with the flagrum by Aphrodite, Kate, Melanie and Sarah in turn, and this too was in the rules. But each carried *two* flagra, and Jana felt her gorge tighten as Aphrodite delivered the first strokes, hitting Sandra's trembling body with sledgehammer force, and making her struggle to maintain her precarious foothold.

'She is putting her to the *strappado*,' said Jana bitterly. 'Such an inhuman punishment is a terrible imperfection, a punishment of men by men, born of brute self-hatred. Oh, Sandra, be brave. Aphrodite shall pay for this.'

They watched, horrified, as Sandra took a full 30 with the doubled flagra, her pain-wracked body teetering at each stroke, which followed in quickfire succession, but never quite losing her quivering foothold. When the punishment was over, she was cut down, and toppled from the bar to lie shuddering on the ground. Aphrodite contemptuously stepped over her writhing body and strode off towards the refectory, her minions and the whole company following in utter docility, none daring to stop and comfort the flogged woman.

Jana saw Thorsten, his face a mask of misery, and as he tried to break rank and go to his friend, Chris pulled his arm and held him back, with a whisper. Thorsten nodded, and grimly followed the others in to the refectory.

'That was imperfect,' said Jana, 'and Aphrodite knows it. If she is ready to break one rule, she is ready to break all, and the being of Maldona is destroyed. I know now that it is Circe's malign influence, for at first I saw in Aphrodite a sincere and loving woman, joyful in submission. But now –'

'Mistress,' said Sabine anxiously, 'are you sure it is not a case of *l'amour trompé*, of love thwarted? That you desire Aphrodite for your own?'

'Never!' spat Jana. 'I have many loyal, loving slaves.'

'Perhaps, Mistress, you desire Aphrodite as an image of yourself. A slave who is neither loyal nor loving ...'

The yard deserted, Jana and her companions unzipped their hoods and went to Sandra's side.

'Sandra!' cried Cassie, cradling the beaten woman, 'oh, Sandra, what have they done?'

Sandra smiled weakly, her breath laboured and her face a lake of tears so bright that Jana could see her own blurred reflection in it. 'I'll be OK,' she panted. 'I've taken worse. From worse than that ... that bitch Aphrodite. Mistress! It's you! Oh, thank heaven!'

'Quickly,' said Jana, 'to the refectory.'

Cassie and Sabine helped Sandra to her feet, and after stretching, Sandra found she could walk unsteadily but unaided.

'What was your imperfection?' asked Jana.

'I was found with a mirror,' said Sandra bitterly. 'Just a small one, as if that makes any difference. I didn't even know I had it! None but Aphrodite may look in the glass, that is what she said. I argued that mirrors are everywhere, in a pool of rain, in a scallop shell, in the sea herself, but –'

'True, it is an imperfection,' said Jana, 'but scarcely meriting more than a perfunctory lady's beating, a good seven on the bare bum and a long cold shower. A noble beating! Quite imperfect, out of proportion.'

'What are you going to do, Mistress?' asked Sandra. 'Whatever it is, I'll help.'

Briefly, Jana explained the events on Circe's island; that Aphrodite was a usurper, guilty of the lowest imperfection, and must have the evil thrashed from her, for only the most severe chastisement, the harshest pain, could redeem her spirit and body in loving submission.

'Well!' exclaimed Sandra. 'What happened here was so fast, it was a *fait accompli* before any of us knew what was happening. Aphrodite appeared in the refectory, flanked by those parfaite friends of hers, and told us you had been drowned. Then Sarah announced that the parfaites had secret instructions from you designating her as the new Maldona! She even said a prayer for you, in – well, I thought it might be Greek, but I'm sure it wasn't. It sounded eerie.' She shivered. 'Anybody who objected got hauled from their seat, strapped and caned with the rattan, bare bum of course. After that, we were all searched, and our cells turned over; anything imperfect was confiscated, and the owners beaten. That is where I got caught; my punishment was the last, because Aphrodite thought my imperfection the most heinous. A simple little pocket mirror! But it was odd: they seemed to be looking for something specific. I heard Aphrodite and Sarah muttering something about a key –'

Jana nodded as she digested this news. 'Well,' she said 'this is where we put things right.'

Cassie and Sabine, at a nod from Jana, thrust open the door, which banged loudly, causing a surprised hush as the virgins and slaves looked up from their tables. At the high table, Sarah, Kate and Melanie looked startled, Kate and Melanie even dropping their spoons: twins in everything, thought Jana, each a reflection of the other.

Only Aphrodite seemed undisturbed. Then, thought Jana, she is the only one who knows I am not dead.

'Aphrodite,' she cried. 'Remove yourself from the high table and take your just place, on the flogging block. For your insolence and treachery, abetted by the sorceress Circe, you have merited thrice a noble beating.'

Aphrodite curled her lip and spat.

'Who are you?' she sneered. 'I recognise your companions,

imperfect virgins all, but not you, young lady. Do you wish to be inducted into the sacred ranks of Maldona? This is not the proper procedure, and it is you who merit just chastisement. Take hold of her, Kate and Melanie, and lash her to the block.'

But Sarah and the twins hesitated. They were pale as they grasped the enormity of their imperfection.

'You were drowned, Mistress,' stammered Sarah, and Jana knew that her addressing her thus signalled her victory. Aphrodite knew it too, and her face darkened.

'Drowned? Apparently not,' said Jana easily. She marched into the centre of the hall, between the long tables, and flicked her whip. 'What do you think, Chris? You, Thorsten?'

'Mistress!' cried Thorsten and Chris together, Thorsten's eyes smiling at Sandra. But Jana saw that the ranks of newer virgins were undecided, looking to Aphrodite for guidance. She realised that most of them had not seen her close up, and would not recognise her.

'Seize the imperfect one!' shouted Aphrodite among the growing hubbub of confusion. Some of the virgins began hesitantly to rise from their seats.

'It is not you talking, Aphrodite,' countered Jana, 'it is the wicked tattoo, implanted by the sorceress. I know you for a loving, loyal slave of Maldona, sweet Aphrodite. Submit, and take your just punishment, and be loved once more.'

'I do not want to be loved!' shrieked Aphrodite, her eyes rolling. 'I am Maldona! I shall be feared! Take this impostor, this lying bitch, that I may justly punish her!'

'In your places!' cried Jana to the assembly. 'You shall be forgiven your mistaken following of the false Maldona, but not for wilful imperfection!'

With that, she struck a savage blow with her whip to the bare shoulders of a willowy blonde virgin seated nearest her: the woman yelped and cringed. Then Jana passed along the table, dealing whipstrokes to all sides. Cassie and Sabine did likewise, until the hall was a mass of moaning slaves, all clutching their bruised shoulders, backs or breasts, such was the ferocity of Jana's indiscriminate flogging. Every table was served thus, until the entire assembly, frightened and confused, was cowed to submission. The parfaites seemed uncertain.

Suddenly, Chris shouted to Sarah, 'Mistress! Take hold of the false Maldona, the tattooed witch! The tattoo is not invincible! It is in *your* mind alone!'

Sarah rose, grim-faced, and turned on Aphrodite with whip raised. But before she could act, Sandra had leapt to the high table and, taking a glancing blow from Aphrodite's own whip, got her forearm around her neck in a crushing hold of Pankration wrestling.

'One whipstroke is nothing compared to what you've just made me endure, you whore,' she snarled, and, weaponless herself, forced Aphrodite to the floor of the dais, pinioning her in a knee-hold to the neck, and began to savagely beat her with her fists, sparing no part of the squirming Aphrodite and oblivious to her shrieks of defiance and pain.

'Bind her!' cried Jana, throwing her coiled rope on to the dais where Aphrodite was pinioned. 'Sandra, let her be! You shall have your opportunity for just chastisement! Well, Sarah, Kate, Melanie, is your love stronger than your tattoo? Rope this slave of Circe, and strip her of her unlawful adornment.'

Sarah took the lead and, with Sandra still holding the subdued Aphrodite, swiftly stripped her, tearing her golden chains from her waist and neck, and the feathered parfaite's harness of Maldona from her anus and fount. Then she roped her until she could barely squirm.

'Virgins of *Allemagne*, of *France*, of *Espagne* and *Angleterre*,' Aphrodite shrieked, 'come to the aid of your lawful Mistress Maldona!'

But no one moved.

Jana mounted the dais, and explained that Aphrodite was under the malign influence of the sorceress Circe; that the reason for her own absence had been to confront Circe, in defence of Maldona, of all of them; that she had defeated Circe and destroyed her magic, which was no magic, but lust for domination, the power of suggestion, and her strange hypnotic gaze, which could inspire the most bizarre phantasms. There was no magic, only autosuggestion and abandonment of the senses to delusion.

Jana's voice trembled a little at these words, for she suspected darkly that they were a wishful truth. She turned to Kate and Melanie.

'Do you submit, parfaites?' she said loudly.

The twins looked at one another, then in one movement, both knelt and kissed Maldona's feet. Sarah joined them in obeisance, and then Chris and Thorsten marched to the dais, knelt, and did the same. Gradually, they were followed by the others, until a column of virgins, prefects, adepts and slaves formed, meekly giving their loyalty to Jana, the true Maldona, while the naked, trussed Aphrodite squirmed in powerless rage, her belly clamped by Jana's raised foot.

'No! No! You fools!' she cried. '*Allemagne*, do not desert me! Circe lives!'

Jana noticed that the virgins of the *Auberge d'Allemagne* were the last to rise and troop to kneel in submission, and when they did so, their faces were not wet with the righteous tears of atonement, but dry and stony, their kissing perfunctory.

When all were again seated, Jana ordered that Aphrodite be helped to her feet and held upright. Her ankles were unbound, and Jana announced her decision: that Aphrodite would receive a cleansing punishment, a chastisement so severe that all evil would be driven from her and she would be once more welcomed into the loving sisterhood of Maldona. So severely was she to be punished that the refectory flogging bench lacked sufficient majesty: instead, Aphrodite would be taken at once to a secret place, her chastisement to be witnessed only by those of prefectorial rank and above. The virgins and slaves would remain in their cells until second bell, when the punishment would be complete, and then Aphrodite would appear to make a confession of her imperfection.

The company obediently trooped back to their cells; a

248

slight nervousness was in the air. They had already been forced to witness Sandra's flogging, and now, alone, they could only imagine in fearful phantasms what Aphrodite was undergoing.

'Am I too harsh? Perhaps imperfect?' said Jana quietly.

'Mistress, it is impossible for Maldona to be too harsh,' said Cassie, with Sandra's eyes gleaming exultantly at the prospect of Aphrodite's agony, 'for Maldona is perfection.'

Jana sighed, and suddenly caught a glimpse of her own face in a shiny nacreous scallop shell, whose contents Aphrodite had just eaten. There she saw a distorted face, frowning and severe, with fire in the eyes that frightened her, for it was not the fire of love, but the fire of resentment, jealousy and vengeance. She took a deep breath, wondering what she had become. And then she led the way to the chapel, the secret entrance to the labyrinth, and the dungeon.

249

19

Duel Underwater

Unlike the accompanying witnesses – the housemistresses, prefects and adepts – Aphrodite seemed in no way surprised at the entrance which led down to the labyrinth, nor did she pay any attention to the twine which guided the nervous party to the centre. Her lips wore a faint grin, which caused Jana to frown, as though Aphrodite had some secret: as though she had been here before. The closer they came to the dungeon, the surer Jana was that Aphrodite knew every step she was taking. She whispered to Sabine, Cassie and Sandra that Aphrodite was to be held and tightly bound hand and foot the moment they entered the chamber, to thwart any trick.

So, no sooner had the strangely incurious Aphrodite entered the dungeon than they seized her and carried her to the upright flogging frame, where she was swiftly cuffed at her ankles and wrists. Immobile and helpless, she looked back at her captors in silent scorn, her eyes no longer dancing with hatred but with mockery. Jana signalled to Cassie that Aphrodite was to be fully bound for her punishment, and as Cassie and the others set to work, Jana addressed the group of witnesses as they looked round with wide eyes at the marvels of pain's refinement which adorned the Templars' secret chamber.

'It has been a shameful day for Maldona,' she said darkly, 'when a misguided virgin has tried to unsurp my lawful authority. Her punishment shall be accordingly severe. She shall receive thrice a noble beating, nevertheless delivered with love and pity, to free her from her enslavement to the sorceress of the tattoo. There will be an hour's interval between each beating, but after you have witnessed the first, those of you with business to attend are free to go. You may now kneel in obeisance to the power of Maldona.'

Promptly, the assembly genuflected; Jana noticed that the housemistress of *Allemagne*, a tall, strongly built Swiss woman named Lydia, was the last to kneel, and allowed her knee to touch the floor only briefly, wearing a blank expression that was almost sullen.

A full binding meant that Aphrodite was gagged and hooded in rubber, her waist strapped to the frame by a leather cincher with gleaming steel buckles that Jana made sure were fastened tightly enough to crease her soft waist-flesh; then her long legs were wrapped in strong leather cuffs, pinning her to the frame, each with a tight buckle, the column of straps ascending almost to the cleft of her buttocks so that she seemed to be wearing shiny black skin-tight boots. Jana felt safe now, knowing there was no way Aphrodite could escape, whether she knew the dungeon or not. She was fully bound and helpless; only her back, shoulders and croup left bare to receive the kiss of both whip and cane.

Jana took her four-thonged whip, Cassie selected a stout rattan cane, as did Sandra, and Sabine took a long braided bullwhip with a wickedly splayed tip.

The four women positioned themselves for the beating of the woman's naked flesh.

'How many strokes shall the usurper receive, Mistress?' growled the housemistress of *Allemagne*.

'The noble beating is without limit, as you well know, Lydia,' said Jana. 'It shall end when I say so. Sandra here took thirty with a double flagrum, so I cannot think it shall be less than that. She is entitled to revenge.'

'I quite agree,' said Lydia with some enthusiasm. 'No punishment is too much for a false Maldona. I am looking forward to hearing her screams, although I admit I have taken bets that she will take thirty strokes before screaming. I shall possess many necklaces of my sisters before your work is done.'

There was a veiled insolence in her tone which caused

251

Jana a tremor of apprehension, but she raised her arm and delivered the first stroke of her whip to Aphrodite's bare buttocks, which clenched as the leather thongs kissed her skin. This stroke was followed by a second, passionate and even harder, from Sandra, who lashed the woman's buttocks with her heavy cane exactly in the same place. Two more strokes followed, from Sabine and finally Cassie, all landing precisely at the already crimson centre of Aphrodite's squirming croup. But Aphrodite made no sound, except, to Jana's annoyance, a faint purring in her throat which could have been pleasure.

She redoubled the force of her lashes, and felt the sweat bathe her as she panted with her effort. The other chastisers were exerting themselves just as strongly, yet nothing could wrest a scream from the tethered captive. The only sound was the infuriating purr of satisfaction as her naked flesh was reddened by whistling cane and whip.

The thirtieth stroke was delivered, and still Aphrodite took her punishment in silent shuddering, causing Lydia to grin mightily as she collected the gold she had won. Jana shifted her strokes to Aphrodite's bared back, marking her well until her whole body was a pretty mass of glowing crimson, and yet still Aphrodite did not cry out.

At the 49th stroke, Jana signalled that this noble beating was at an end. She unfastened Aphrodite's gag and gave her a cup of water to drink, then asked her if she was ready for her two further beatings.

'An academic question, Aphrodite, since you are going to get them whether you like it or not,' she murmured.

'*That* was a noble beating?' sneered Aphrodite. 'Why, two more or twenty more, it makes no difference. One butterfly's kiss is the same as another.'

There was muted laughter from the prefects and adepts.

Furious at Aphrodite's continued insolence, Jana commanded in a steely voice that she be cut down from her bonds. The cinchers and leg straps were removed and she was uncuffed from the flogging frame, the metal cuffs being at once refastened to chain her wrists behind her back and her ankles together.

Jana smiled. She had a new idea.

'Well, Aphrodite,' she said slowly, 'I think what will break you is not a noble beating, but . . . a perfect beating.' There was a shocked silence. A perfect beating: something the company had hoped never to witness.

'Every Maldona must endure a perfect beating, as I myself had to,' said Jana smoothly. 'So if you think yourself Maldona, sweet lady . . . The perfect beating is more terrible than anything your poor red fesses can imagine, because it is the unknown, the endless. Of course, like any virgin, you have only to shake your head and you will be sent down, cast from Maldona for ever. Shake your head, Aphrodite.'

Aphrodite's head was resolutely still. Jana smiled, and indicated that the assembly must remain to witness Aphrodite's perfect beating.

'A perfect beating, Aphrodite, is not only more painful than you can possibly imagine, it is humiliating. The dignity and honour of nobly bearing the lash will be stripped from you until you howl for mercy. Still silent?' Aphrodite curled her lip, saying nothing. 'Leave her ungagged,' rapped Jana, and then, to the amazed stares of the assembly, she took hold of Aphrodite's tethered body and carried her to a footstool, where she sat and forced Aphrodite to bend over her knee. Sandra and Cassie knelt to pinion Aphrodite's head and ankles, and now the woman began to moan in indignant protest.

'Yes, Aphrodite,' said Jana, 'you shall be denied the honour of submitting to the lash again. It is not worth it to dignify you. *Your* perfect beating shall be exactly what you are worth: a simple, old-fashioned, bare-bum spanking, just like when you were a little girl.'

Now the laughter was on Jana's side, directed against Aphrodite, and with a grin Jana raised her bare hand and brought it down with a resounding slap on Aphrodite's glowing red bottom. That elicited a muffled squawk of protest. Jana gleefully kept up the spanking, relishing the new flushing of Aphrodite's squirming croup and the laughter of the witnesses as they watched the ungainly wriggling of their would-be mistress. Jana was pleased that the loudest laughter came from Sarah, Kate and Melanie.

She spanked harder and harder, joyful now as her breath rasped and sweat bathed her, and feeling exultant at this simple subduing of her enemy, her friend. As she watched the full ripe buttocks quivering helplessly beneath her, she felt a sudden spasm in her belly and knew that the liquid between her thighs and the tingling lips of her fount was not sweat. Giddy with her power and strength, she imagined suddenly, like a flash, that the buttocks desperately squirming at her every slap were somehow her own, and the thought both thrilled and frightened her. In an effort to drive the thought away, she began to spank with both hands at once, her face a mask of rage, but the harder her blows fell, the more it seemed that the lush naked flesh she spanked so mercilessly was her own. My friend, my enemy, she thought: *I am punishing myself.*

'Spank me, humiliate me, Jana,' hissed Aphrodite, 'but I know you have the key.'

'And – you – have – not – *found* it, Aphrodite,' panted Jana, each word accompanying a savage slap to her victim's bared nates.

'But I know where the treasure is. *My* treasure! And I shall destroy it, destroy the whole sunken city, rather than let you have her. She belongs to me; she has always belonged to me!'

And it was then that deep in her throat, Aphrodite screamed in her humiliation and pain.

At once, Lydia, her neck glistening with the golden chains she had won, leapt forward, knocking Jana from her stool and swinging Aphrodite's tethered body over her shoulder. Frozen for a split second by her astonishment, Jana saw Lydia pinion Aphrodite against the upright flogging frame, as though trying to smother her, and then Lydia's arm snaked to the top of the frame and reached behind it. Her hand emerged holding the end of an oiled lever, which she pulled gently, and that split second was enough for the frame suddenly to swivel round as a section of the stone floor slid smoothly open, revealing a steep stone chute that led down into darkness.

Aphrodite looked back, taunting. 'A curse on you, Jana,' she cried. Jana and her companions were on their feet, but it was too late. The flogging frame, positioned directly over the chasm, neatly deposited its occupants into the depths, and the two women, Lydia grinning fiercely, plummeted out of sight into the dark earth. There was uproar, but Jana quelled it with a wave of her hand, and told the adepts and prefects to return to their duties.

Sandra, Sabine, the parfaites and Cassie were left.

'Cassie, you are once more regent,' she said grimly. 'I must follow Aphrodite.'

'We shall all go,' said Sarah. 'I want to give that beast a hiding, Mistress, for the way she tricked us.'

'She was a smiling villain,' said Kate.

'Not Aphrodite,' said Jana fiercely, 'but Circe, the sorceress. And I know where they have gone. Until my return, be wary, all of you, of the *Auberge d'Allemagne*. Aphrodite has obviously made other alliances than yourselves. She needs Lydia to release her from her bonds, down there.'

Seeing the moue of resentment on Sarah's face, she told her softly that she must also be wary of jealous emotion, for that too was imperfection.

'Down where?' asked Sandra, puzzled.

'I shall fully explain later, when all is done,' said Jana tersely. 'The chute can only go to one place, a place Cassie and I have visited.' She whispered to Cassie, who left the chamber at a fast pace. Then, as she stripped for her immersion in the sea, she told them of the sunken city.

'Such places are common in the Greek waters,' she said. 'The great lighthouse of Pharos, one of the seven wonders of the world, toppled into the sea at the harbour of Alexandria, after the earthquake of the year 1100 in our era, carrying a whole city with it: temples, houses, statues, huge blocks of marble a hundred tonnes or more. It is said that Atlantis was an island city which sank under the waves after a volcanic eruption. We have such a city here. But . . . I do not know if it is a true sunken city, or if it was built under the water, vast eons ago.'

'Maybe it is Atlantis,' said Melanie excitedly.

'It doesn't matter: there is a treasure – I know the legends to be true – and it lies there. The treasure of the Templars is the rightful property of Maldona, and I must stop the possessed Aphrodite from destroying it, whatever means she has of doing that. She knows it is in the city, but she has no key to its hiding place.'

Cassie returned, panting, carrying the bronze key wrapped in wax paper, which Jana took and fastened to her belt, beside her whip and knife. Then she added a hard rattan cane.

'For comfort,' she said, smiling.

Cassie and the others pleaded to go with her.

'No! I must go alone,' declared Jana firmly. 'I am Maldona. And no argument.'

Slaves of Maldona, they knew better than to argue, as their mistress plunged into the dark underground.

Fear gripped Jana as she slid down the smooth, almost sheer slope of the chute. She was in darkness, trapped in this falling tunnel, to end perhaps in a plunge into deep water, far from the city, far from Maldona, far from anywhere. The descent seemed to go on forever, and she wished now that Cassie was with her. The tunnel was narrow, scarcely high enough to sit, and Jana had to hunch over to avoid scraping her head. As she fell, the tunnel twisted in dizzying loops and spirals, so that she no longer knew which way was up or down. Her skin burnt with the friction of the rock and she breathed in hard gasps, tears of pain in her eyes as her skin was scorched. She was panicking now, but told herself that Aphrodite and Lydia had passed this way so the passage must be safe. But what if they knew of a side turning, an escape from the tunnel that the devious Templars had dug to lure unwary pursuers to their death?

Her gorge tight with fear, she wondered whether she was being punished somehow; for my arrogance, for my will to power? No; I am being punished because as I was beating Aphrodite, I did so with rage, not love, in my heart. I am guilty of imperfection. My reflection in the scallop shell: a woman possessed by hatred. How just it is that no mirrors are in Maldona! A mirror is a tool of vanity, which is imperfect, but also a reflection of ugliness, which is a worse imperfection.

Suddenly she noticed that the slope was levelling out and that her descent had slowed. She was deep underground now and the heat was intense, so that, nude as she was, she was covered with perspiration. Her weapons hissed on the smooth marble as she slid along, slowing all the time until the tunnel was almost horizontal, at an angle of no more than twenty degrees.

Now she was obliged to crawl along, and noticed that the air was becoming fresher. She crawled as fast as she could, her anguish now replaced by an urgency that she must reach the underwater garden and the locked temple before Aphrodite could destroy the unknown treasure. Phantasm took her once more and she imagined Aphrodite in possession of an array of devices – underwater explosives, battering engines, hammers. There was nothing that the sorceress Circe could not bestow on her acolytes, the sisters of the Hesperides.

Her nascent terror was stilled as she rounded a bend in the tunnel and found herself knee-deep in water. Now there was light: the iridescence of a thousand glowing fishes, shoals of them in luminous turquoise water into which the tunnel dived. And beyond, below her, the pale white shapes of walls and houses. Jana knew she had reached the sea, and the sunken city.

The tunnel widened now and she was able to stand. She waded through the glittering water, brushed by the myriad fish, deeper and deeper, until the sea came up to her breasts. Then she was immersed, and suddenly she felt at home. She dived rapidly and timed herself at 25 seconds until she reached the temple gate of the city, the sky now fainter and far above. So, she thought, 25 seconds to reach air. But what chance have I against Aphrodite, with her tattoo? She swam on, through the fronds and ruins of the city streets, their marble arcades deserted but for the shoals and weeds which seemed to caress her, embracing her in loving encouragement as she passed. Tattoo? she thought, heartened by her welcome in these depths. I am mistress here, I can hold my breath. Mind over matter ... I am a diver of pearls and oysters and gold; the sea is Maldona's domain.

She counted 90 seconds until she came to the underwater garden, and cautiously picked her way through the pale aqueous flowers, fish flitting among their petals like bees. And at last she reached the locked door of the small temple where she knew the treasure lay, her hunch, or ancestral memory, reinforced by the fragment of map Gloria had brought from Poros. Aphrodite and Lydia were nowhere to be seen.

Feverishly, Jana unwrapped her bronze key, watching the wax paper float away to be nibbled by hungry fish. She counted that at least three minutes had elapsed underwater, felt the hammering pressure in her lungs, and knew she must soon resurface for air. She looked up at the dim sky above, and calculated that a direct ascent would be quicker than a return to the chute, where she might find her enemies lying in wait. She pushed the key into the lock and twisted it, pushing on the door. The key turned, but the door refused to open.

Swiftly, she kicked her way to the surface and lay on her back for a minute, recharging her body with oxygen.

Three minutes, she told herself: next time I shall make it four. Breathing to the full, she plunged down again.

Three times she dived, and at each attempt, the door failed to open. She searched for secret levers or cut panels of rock but found none. Knowing the Templars' fondness for such secretive tricks, she was sure such a device must exist, but where? Perhaps on the sea floor, perhaps even concealed in the greater temple that was the city gate. Despair took hold of her: she surfaced again, and then dived for a fourth and, she accepted bitterly, final time. Perhaps Aphrodite and Lydia had given up on their idle threat, knowing that the garden temple was inaccessible for ever. Perhaps they had simply lured her here to finish her. Desperately, she wrestled with the lock, but still the door remained obstinately closed. And then she saw two pale shapes in the blue water: the nude bodies of Lydia and Aphrodite swam towards her, wriggling like fish, and Lydia carrying a large block of glowing material under her arm.

Clipping her key to her belt, Jana tried to retreat, but the two women moved so fast that she was trapped: Lydia at her back and Aphrodite facing her. Lydia put down her load on the sea floor and Jana recognised it for phosphorus. Phosphorus caught fire in oxygen and she guessed that a compacted block that size, exposed to the air, could become a bomb and explode with enough force to destroy the temple, the garden, the treasure, and, of course, anyone in the way. Smiling, Aphrodite put her hand out, gesturing at Jana's key.

She could not escape. Glancing at the malevolently grinning Lydia, half-hidden by fronds and stems, she saw that she also wore the rose tattoo on the ripe mound of her shaven sex. Jana put aside the sudden, deadly desire to kneel in obeisance and kiss the woman's lush quim-petals. Bubbles curled insolently from Lydia's lips, as though in mockery.

Suddenly, Jana lunged at Aphrodite and hit her in the belly (quite according to the rules of Pankration, she thought briefly), her thrust in ungainly slow motion taking the woman by surprise. Aphrodite toppled on to the sea floor where Jana sat astride her, and with slow fists pummelled her breasts and face until her body waved in pain like the petals of the pale flowers. Jana forced her knee between the woman's thighs and began to thrust at her open sex, causing Aphrodite to grimace in a fierce rictus of pain.

Overcome by fury and desire for revenge, Jana forgot about the grinning presence of Lydia behind her until she felt the pressure of a forearm around her waist, squeezing her belly in a bear hug. In agony, she abandoned the writhing Aphrodite and kicked beneath her, overturning Lydia in a somersault so that they both floated to fall on Aphrodite, Jana's back pressed against Lydia's breasts. She felt teeth clamp savagely on her shoulder and waves of pain filled her as Lydia clawed with sharp fingers at her tender breasts, her nails squeezing Jana's nipples like pincers as her teeth gouged the soft flesh of her neck and shoulders in an obscene parody of a loving bite. Lips pressed white to keep her mouth from opening in a scream, Jana cracked the back of her head hard against Lydia's forehead, and felt the teeth and the clawing nails loosen as Lydia recoiled. The Swiss woman slithered clumsily backwards into the midst of a shoal of blue and golden fish, who seemed to hover like spectators at a prize-fight. Jana watched in amazement as Lydia was swallowed up into the body of the shoal, which, like one giant living creature, gently enveloped her and carried her away, helpless in their wriggling embrace.

The phosphorus bomb, held by steel wires, glowed softly on the sea floor, and suddenly it too was engulfed by darting fish, who began to nibble at it as though some strange new food. As they tasted, they spat out the crumbs of phosphorus and swam away, but their place was taken by others, and rapidly the brick of phosphorus was loosened from its wire cage and disintegrated, the tiny glowing sparks floating in a cloud up to the surface. Lydia's bomb was now useless.

Aphrodite was stirring, so Jana swiftly jumped and kicked her between her thighs with both feet. Aphrodite's face crumpled in a grimace of pain and she floated back to collide with the temple door, right above the lock. As the two naked women grappled, slithering like eels, Jana felt a throbbing that seemed to emanate from the temple, as though the very structure was vibrating. Above them, the sea was suddenly filled with a dazzling white light as the granules of phosphorus flared and died harmlessly on their exposure to the air on the surface.

Taking advantage of Aphrodite's surprise, Jana finally took her in a pinion hold, forced her on to her back on the sea floor and held her neck between her thighs. She knew that this was the moment that she must force a submission. She focused her stare into Aphrodite's burning eyes, whose pupils seemed a mirror of her own: nothing but her eyes, she

260

thought. Stare her out, mesmerise her, with my evil eye. Her lungs gasped for air but she knew she could hold for a minute more. She stared for what seemed an age, and gradually Aphrodite's eyes glazed and softened. Jana's lips made 'Submit'.

To her surprise, Aphrodite did not struggle or shake her head in defiance. Instead, she returned Jana's gaze; not as one trying to outstare her but as a frightened beast caught in a searchlight. Jana did not relax her stare; she felt power burn in her eyes, transfixing and subduing her captive. Again, she mouthed 'Submit', and now, with a piteous expression, Aphrodite opened her eyes very wide, looking nowhere but at Jana, and as she did so her frown turned to the most beautiful smile Jana had ever seen. She mouthed the words, 'Yes, I submit, I submit, Mistress.'

Jana knew she had won. She climbed from Aphrodite's pinioned body, helping her to her feet. The throbbing was more intense now and Jana wondered if the impact of Aphrodite's body had triggered some ancient mechanism. A prehistoric burglar alarm? she thought in foolish delight at Aphrodite's submission.

Then Aphrodite knelt and kissed Jana's bare feet in obeisance, taking her toes in her mouth. When she rose again, Jana kissed her and took her cane from her belt, then delicately pressed it across Aphrodite's bare buttocks, holding it for a moment before releasing the pressure. Aphrodite smiled and the two women embraced tightly. Aphrodite was once more a virgin of Maldona.

Jana pointed upward, and, still embracing, the two women kicked their way up to the surface, accompanied by nibbling shoals of fish, like a brightly coloured bridal train.

When they broke the surface and gulped air, Aphrodite said simply, 'The spell is broken, Mistress, and my foolish arrogance with it. You are the greater, the more powerful. You are Maldona, and I beg forgiveness for my sin. Water is the mother of life and beauty, but is also the mother of sin. And my sin could only be washed away in water, by my defeat at your hands. By you ... Oh, Mistress, by *me* ...' Her face was blank with awe.

Jana put a finger to her slave's lips. 'It is against our

rules to say you are sorry for anything, Aphrodite,' she replied sternly, 'for that is to admit that you knowingly did wrong, which is imperfect. You were beguiled, a victim, and I have freed you from your beguilement by vanquishing you in love.'

'Mistress, you have the key?' asked Aphrodite. Jana nodded yes. 'Then dive now. It will open the door. The old mechanism has been started by the commotion of our wrestling. Probably we fell in a sequence of places which would free the lock for the key. I know much of this place, Mistress, but not all. I knew I needed *you* to guide me.' She laughed. 'How furious I was not to find it! And how petty and vainglorious and imperfect!'

'We shall both dive,' Jana said.

Aphrodite frowned. 'No, Mistress, you must go alone. The treasure is yours, is Maldona's, and you are Maldona. I am a mere slave, guilty of the worst treachery, and deserving of the harshest punishment. Besides, I do not know where Lydia has gone: perhaps back to the castle, to collect her *auberge* behind her. But if she returns here, I must be waiting to tell her some story. Go, Mistress, now.'

'But I do forgive you!' cried Jana. 'There was no imperfection, merely . . . sorcery.'

'Mistress,' answered Aphrodite with a moue of mock displeasure, 'if I were only a victim of Circe's spells, then I should not be worthy of punishment. But for my grievous imperfection . . .' she smiled slyly.

'Aphrodite, my sweet slave, I promise that you will be punished *most* severely,' she said. 'Wait for me.'

Pressing her friend's hand, Jana took hold of the bronze key, kissed it for luck, and dived.

20

The Black Mountain

The water caressed Jana's body with the strange, insistent vibration from the garden temple, and as she approached it became more and more insistent. She saw that the shoals of fish were stationary, and that the tendrils and flowers no longer waved in their lazy dance: it was as though the denizens of the underwater garden were waiting, drinking in and absorbing a message they, or their distant forbears, had not heard for eons.

Jana approached the door and touched it. The vibrations were very strong; a rhythmic pulse that made her whole body tremble.

Nervously, she put the key in the lock, and it turned as smoothly as before – but this time it turned twice. She hesitated, imagining what the treasure would be. Gold? Jewels? Priceless artefacts and antiquities? And the thought struck her that if this sunken city had indeed been built long before the Greeks, long before what was called the dawn of time, by some unimaginable civilisation, then her discovery would bring, at the very least, unwelcome attention to Maldona. It would destroy her proud isolation.

What I find here could change the world, she thought. If the treasure is plundered gold of the Templars, well and good. Gold, after all, is gold. But if it comes from a civilisation of sea-builders, perhaps truly an aquatic race of men, then it had best be left in concealment.

A race of men! She laughed inwardly. Why not a race of women? Women are the sea, are life. What if all those eons ago, the males had foraged on the harsh dry land while females built a culture in their true home?

Jana found that she could now control the pressure in her lungs much more easily, but still she realised that her reverie must end. She must open the door. Tremulous, she pushed it, and it swung open on easy hinges. She looked into a small chamber like an ante-room, beyond which, a metre away, stood another door. And the room was full of air. The vibrations stopped and there was a moment of utter calm.

For a split second she took a deep breath, then suddenly a wall of water rushed at her, knocking her over and pushing her into the chamber. The floor was not even but striated with vents, or drains, and as the water rose rapidly around her, she realised that the chamber was an airlock, the vibrations coming from a subterranean pumping system. It was impossible to close the door against the water's weight. Breathing deeply, she waited until the sea had come up to her neck and the flow had diminished, but still she could not shut the outer door. She waited until she was completely immersed, terrified now, and then pushed the door shut. Suddenly she felt utterly alone, in a coffin of water, tricked by Aphrodite, by Circe, by Sarah and the twins, by everyone.

The vibrations started again and gradually she saw the water level start to go down. At the same time the outer vents began to pump oxygen into the chamber, little spirals of bubbles rushing up into the space left by the draining water. The process seemed agonisingly slow, and minutes elapsed before, lungs bursting, she could stretch her head above the now-clear water and gulp precious air. The air tasted musty and had a curious marine perfume that to Jana's whirling brain smelled of past ages, past deeds, past love, but as the water went down, she collected her thoughts and tried her key in the lock of the second door. It turned, but as she expected, the door did not open.

It was only when the airlock had been completely drained that her key made its second turn, and the inner door of the airlock swung open into a small chamber sweet with oxygen and glowing with the fluorescent crystal which formed its walls. Jana closed the door behind her, and in awe and wonder and joy looked at her treasure.

* * *

'Mistress?' said Aphrodite, as Jana surfaced once more. 'You have found the treasure?' Jana nodded, not smiling, and Aphrodite's excited expression turned grave. 'There is bad news?' she asked. 'The treasure has been spoiled, looted? Oh, to think I was such a fool as to wish her destruction! Even if only a few shards remain, she is priceless.'

'The treasure is intact,' said Jana, her face sombre but glowing with a royal serenity, 'and she is indeed priceless. But she is only a treasure if she is left untouched in her hiding place. The treasure cannot be moved; must wait for other Mistresses of Maldona, my successors, to find her. My ancestor, Jane Ardenne, the first Maldona, knew that all those centuries ago. Ask no further questions, Aphrodite, for I must remind you, virgin, that asking questions is against the rules. I think we shall now swim back to the castle, unless you want to clamber up that uncomfortable tunnel.'

'As you say, Mistress,' said Aphrodite, and they set off at a brisk crawl stroke under the hot sun.

Fish were all around, and Jana smiled in sadness and joy. 'I feel that this is the last time I shall ever make this swim,' she said, 'and the last time I shall ever climb the hill to the Castle of Maldona.'

'Mistress!' cried Aphrodite. 'What –'

'No questions, virgin.'

They swam in silence, their powerful strokes bringing them steadily near the shore. Jana's eyes blurred with sweat, despite the cooling water. She looked up at the towering black mountain and felt that she was, always had been, in the grip of forces stronger than herself; that the spirit of her ancestor lived within her and had brought her to this place, and that there was one more thing for her to do. She had to climb the mountain, as her dream had foretold.

She murmured, 'The treasure, Aphrodite, has taught me . . . destiny.'

Suddenly, through eyes dazzled by the sparkling water and the bright fish that seemed to leap for joy at her passage, she saw a new, brighter light, a sheen of gold in the water. She peered and saw that it was a figure, swimming far in front, and towards Maldona. Jana swam as fast as she could, leaving Aphrodite a short distance behind, and got closer to look at the fleeing figure. It was a woman, with long blonde hair, naked to the waist, and under her belly was –

Jana could not believe her eyes. The woman had a thick tail of gold. As she watched, the woman made the beach and waded ashore, then, in a curious but rapid crablike motion, walked on her magnificent fish's tail up to the track that led to the castle. The gold of her tail shimmered, dazzling under the sun, and Jana felt she had witnessed beauty. She had seen a mermaid.

She paused to let Aphrodite catch her up, and resumed her strokes.

'Did you see, virgin?'

'See, Mistress? I see the ocean, the islands, the fish, the castle, the paradise that is Maldona's empire. Which unaccountably you seem desirous of leaving!'

'No,' said Jana, 'a mermaid!'

Aphrodite was silent, pondering this. 'I saw no mermaid,' she replied slowly, 'although I do not disbelieve all the old stories in these isles. But the sun has dazzled you, Mistress. It is a trick of the light.'

They were approaching the beach, and Jana cried, 'She came to the beach, and went up the track to the castle! Look, virgin!' She looked herself, seeking a tell-tale glint of gold on the hillside.

'I see nothing, Mistress,' said Aphrodite. 'You are excited by the treasure. There is no mermaid.'

As they waded the last few metres on to the beach, Jana said sombrely, 'I am not excited by the treasure, Aphrodite. I feel wisdom, joy and serenity for having found her. But excitement is not the right word. However, I am excited now, and we must get back to the castle at once, because there *was* a mermaid.'

They made their way up the track, Jana thinking to herself that this would be the last time she would make the ascent, for a long time at least. The two women did their best to shade their nudity from the hot sun, and kept to the trees, pausing for a brief rest when they found a cooling arbour. The afternoon sun was fierce but Jana had no desire to rest: adrenalin flowed in her. She could not believe how much had happened in such a short time, and already the events in the underwater city – her battle with Aphrodite and her discovery of the treasure – seemed to belong to a distant past.

'The sun annihilates time, Aphrodite,' she said suddenly.

The woman took this philosophically, and added, 'As does the ocean, Mistress.'

'That is what I like about the Greeks, the Spanish ... even the French,' said Jana, merry now that they were approaching the castle gates. 'You are not put off by mystical propositions. How different from my rainy, common sense England!' She pushed open the portal.

'But you are not obliged to go back there, Mistress,' said Aphrodite, smiling at Jana's brightening mood.

'Maybe I am,' said Jana, grinning. 'I am Maldona, and Maldona is everywhere.'

They entered the yard and found it deserted, save for a small group around the flogging scaffold, to which a blonde, heavily built woman was trussed, gagged and hooded. It was Lydia. Cassie was in front of the group, wielding a flagrum. Jana recognised Thorsten, Chris and the women she had left in the dungeon. Each was armed with a whip or cane, and Lydia was in the process of receiving what was evidently a noble beating. Jana and Aphrodite hurried towards the scaffold and Cassie lowered her whip after dealing a heavy blow to Lydia's bare buttocks, then went to Jana. Alarm was in her face.

'Mistress, thank heaven!' she cried. 'Such turmoil! I had to order the slaves to their cells –'

'Calm yourself, Cassandra,' said Jana sternly.

'A mermaid!' cried Cassie. 'The same mermaid as I saw from the ship! I *told* you, Mistress!'

Then she blurted the whole story, her words punctuated by the crack of leather and wood on the helpless Lydia's

267

bared fesses and back. The Swiss woman wriggles nicely, Jana thought. What a pity she will have to go down: unless she gives full obeisance.

Cassie explained that Lydia had returned to announce that Jana had submitted to Aphrodite, and Aphrodite, as true Maldona, would shortly arrive bringing her captive to take chastisement and submit. She appealed to the virgins of the *Auberge d'Allemagne* to support her, but they were confused, and demanded time. Lydia flew into a rage – a severe imperfection in itself – and said there was no time; that the Mistress of Maldona must shortly show obeisance to a higher mistress, an adept, the centre of whose timeless wisdom lay across the sea.

At that point the portals had opened and the mermaid entered, glittering with her golden tail. Lydia promptly knelt in obeisance and urged her virgins to do the same. But Cassie had cried no, and struck the mermaid with her whip. The mermaid only glowered cruelly, sneering that whipstrokes of Maldona were like the kiss of a gnat's wings. It was then that Thorsten pushed forward from the ranks of the slaves and seized Cassie's whip. He also seized the mermaid by the neck and furiously began to lash her bare back. The mermaid only stood stiffly, and spat.

Thorsten had then turned his attention to her bottom, whipping her so hard that the golden scales of her tail jangled as they danced with her unconcealed squirming. Now the mermaid, under the force of Thorsten's hard flogging, lost some of her composure. Lydia cried to the slaves to kneel, but seeing this bringer of timeless wisdom dancing under Thorsten's lash, they hesitated, then with murmurs of indignation cried, 'Adore Maldona!'

Lydia had then been seized for her treachery and the mass of slaves advanced in one body on the now abased mermaid. Thorsten cried that there were no mermaids, that this was another part of Aphrodite's wicked and imperfect usurpation, and that the mermaid must be duly chastised, along with her accomplice. At that, the mermaid broke and fled. Unable to break the wall of bodies that blocked the portal, the chapel and the refectory, she fled in the only direction open to her. Lydia was seized and chastisement ordered threefold. The entire assembly had witnessed the first strokes, and then Cassie had sent them to their cells, fearing an abrupt change of heart. After all, the mermaid was still at large somewhere.

Jana looked up towards the forbidding volcanic crag.

Yes,' said Cassie quietly. 'There. No one, none of us, dared to go after her. All the legends – your dream, in London – all came back to me, and I could see the slaves sensed this too, their faces full of foreboding, so I ordered them to keep in their cells while we continued Lydia's chastisement.'

'You did right,' said Jana, and told her something, but not all, of what had happened under the sea.

'Aphrodite is released from her spell and has made obeisance,' she said tersely. 'She is once more a virgin of Maldona: but on this occasion, I think she may be allowed to take part in the chastisement of Lydia, her false friend, who was also enslaved by Circe's tattoo. Meanwhile –' she peered up at the mountainside '– I have a final task, which I must accomplish alone. Aphrodite, when you rifled the cells of the slaves, looking for the key, what did you do with the confiscated items?'

'In your apartment, Mistress.'

'Accompany me, slave.'

Jana and Aphrodite ascended to her top-floor apartment, and when they emerged back into the yard, Jana wore once again the resplendent plumed parfaite's harness. In her hand was the white, four-thonged whip of the Amir of Ubrique, the most sacred possession of Maldona. She turned and headed towards the mountainside.

'Mistress,' cried Cassie, 'let me accompany you.'

'No,' said Jana with a dismissive wave. 'Continue Lydia's chastisement, Superior Cassandra. This I must do alone, for you see, Maldona is always alone.'

The climb up the barren mountainside was agony. Jagged rocks scraped Jana's stout sandals, and the few bushes were all thorns, seeming to reach out and tear at her flesh.

She thought of the welcome caress of the fish and flowers under the water, and this, the real earth, seemed a hostile place, far from Sabine's lush fruit groves. It grew colder and colder, and she came to a region of mist, so that she could only see a few metres ahead of her.

Panting, suddenly she stumbled and lost her footing. She felt herself fall and slide, and realised she had found the top of the mountain, a huge crater that had once been the spout of the volcano. She lay on the concave black crater, rivulets of black ash being carried down her body by her perspiration. And once more she felt afraid.

She lifted herself to her feet, and when she turned round, she jumped in terror. The mermaid was standing in front of her, the golden tail shining dimly in the mist. Jana stared, frozen. The mermaid had her own face: she was staring at herself.

'So Jana, Maldona once more, you have come to pay obeisance to your rightful mistress,' said the mermaid.

'Wrong, Circe,' answered Jana, uncoiling her whip, 'I have come to subdue you and make your power my own. I have never stopped being Maldona, nor, in generations to come, will I.'

Circe stepped closer and Jana saw how artful was her maquillage: a perfect facsimile of Jana's own face. The golden fish-tail she recognised as a tight skirt of delicate golden scales, in foil as light as gossamer. She brandished her whip.

'Submit, Circe,' she said quietly, with a firmness she did not feel. 'Your powers are of no use here.'

'On the contrary, you poor fool. This mountain top, high above my sea and my islands, is the centre of the earth energies which complement my sea power, and give me strength that is yours a hundredfold.'

She stepped closer, grinning, and Jana lashed her across the breasts – her own breasts! – with the white whip. Circe continued to advance.

'No use, little Jana,' she sneered. 'You have flogged me before, and you know what I can take. Consider: here are two Maldonas, two Janas. One Maldona will come down the mountainside, carrying the other, who will be attired as a mermaid with a tail of golden scales. The burden shall be you, Jana, but you will be unable to tell of your defeat because you will be unable to speak. Yet you shall live a fruitful life under my domain: the tongueless in these ancient waters are regarded as holy, as prophetesses and seers. Before that, you shall tell me of the treasure.'

Again Jana lashed at Circe; this time she spread the thongs so that the woman's face, breasts and belly were cruelly reddened, but Circe did not falter. And as Jana raised her whip for the next stroke, she lunged, catching Jana around the throat and toppling her to the black ash of the ground.

'Submit, and you shall live!' she cried.

Jana, struggling for breath, tried to get a hold on Circe's slippery body, but could not. The pressure on her throat tightened and she felt a weary black faintness, as if all the fatigue of the last hours suddenly burdened her. Desperately, she fumbled at her belt. Circe was on top of her now, her full cold weight crushing Jana's body. She withdrew the weapon she had taken from Aphrodite's confiscated articles, and with a wrench, freed her hand and pushed it against Circe's face.

Circe screamed. Then she jumped back and lay in the black dust, holding her face in her hands and wailing in a loud, unearthly sob. She was broken.

Wearily, Jana got to her feet and gave Circe her hand. Then she put her arm round the sorceress, now a sad figure in her defeat, and said softly, 'Do you submit now, Circe? Have you learned?'

Sobbing, Circe nodded. 'I submit, Mistress. Your powers are greater, you have the power of Hermes the trickster. I thought I had such power, but you have deeper.' She smiled through her tears. 'All these years . . . you guessed my Achilles' heel! I can only do you homage now. My days and dreams of power are at an end.'

Jana took hold of Circe and hoisted her over her shoulder to begin the treacherous descent down the mountainside.

'No Circe,' she said gently, 'your days of power are not over: rather, you shall return to your island and use them for the good of Maldona. You shall rule the first satrapy of Maldona's seaborne empire . . .'

The weapon she had used to defeat Circe fell to the floor of the crater; Jana did not stoop to pick it up. Sandra's pocket mirror would lie there untouched for eons, its work done. Circe had been subdued. She had been forced to look at herself.

21

Anthesteria

Lydia, after her noble beating, begged to be permitted to remain in Maldona, and Jana agreed, on the condition that she be stripped of all rank, even of her necklace. Lydia, from her status as adept, became a whipping girl, to take punishment for the imperfections of others. As a mere virgin, she, like Aphrodite, was also obliged to grow her mink, hiding her tattoo. Her place as housemistress of the *Auberge d'Allemagne* was given to Gloria, whose tattooed body now seemed to Jana a creation of beauty rather than repugnant dominion.

Jana did not oblige Sarah or the twins to do the same: they were, after all, parfaites, and had the right to shave their bodies. One day, however, Sarah approached Jana at the high table, and whispered to her.

'It is not necessary,' said Jana. 'You cannot be held responsible for the delirium of a moment, and neither can Aphrodite. The spell of Circe is broken now, and she is on her island, healed and a loyal slave of Maldona.'

'You whipped her well, Mistress, before sending her away. It was odd, though, that she refused a boat and chose to swim.'

'She begged to be whipped, Sarah, and I obliged her,' answered Jana. 'As for swimming, I don't think she swam very long. I followed her with my binoculars. She was carried regally to her island –'

'The turtle!' exclaimed Sarah. 'How wonderful!'

'Exactly. Now, what is it *you* want?'

Sarah blushed. 'What I always crave, Mistress. You know that, and that I speak for the twins, and Aphrodite too. To purge our imperfection, we ask for chastisement.'

'Sarah ... you are a parfaite. I cannot beat you now without a very just cause,' said Jana.

Sarah's face creased in a moue of discontent. 'Then it would be better, perhaps, if we were not parfaites at all,' she said. 'Mistress, Circe is gone and her spell with her –'

'Her spell is not gone,' Jana interrupted. 'Rather, she shall use it for good. The tattoo is beautiful, when used to serve beauty. Those who come to Circe to be thus adorned will be henceforth in the domain of Maldona, serving her outside, or, if Circe deems fit, despatched to this castle to join us.'

'Mistress,' Sarah continued, 'you say we can be forgiven our imperfections in betraying you because we were under her spell: but when we were first tattooed – you saw Caspar's film – we imperfectly accepted her dominion, and placed ourselves knowingly under her spell. The same goes for Aphrodite.'

Jana sighed. 'But why, Sarah?' she asked.

'I don't know, Mistress,' said Sarah, her head bowed in shame. 'The lure of the unknown, the wickedness that is the mark of our rebellious years? At any rate, the wickedness must be beaten from us; we must come to terms with ourselves under your lash, Mistress, must let the pain of our flogged backs and fesses bring us to knowledge of ourselves.'

'A very pretty speech, Sarah,' said Jana, sighing again. 'But if I beat you, I should beat everyone. What about sweet Henry, my slave Aelfric? And Thorsten? Chris?'

'Oh, they are mere males,' said Sarah scornfully. 'They have scarcely a brain between them, and will follow a strong woman like the lambs they are. *We* were the ringleaders, Mistress; it is our croups that must dance.'

'It is noted, Sarah,' said Jana, 'and now you must attend to your duties as parfaite. Don't forget you are here to administer punishment rather than to take it, and I am sure the log will be full of chastisements before the day is out.'

Sarah smiled conspiratorially. 'You can be sure of that, Mistress. Would I ever let you down?'

Jana laughed too, thinking of Circe's spell. 'I know you

274

wouldn't, Sarah,' replied Jana. 'I promise I shall think about your request. Perhaps you are right, that there has been some chastisement earned – and not just by you four.'

'You are right, of course, Mistress, and you know we are right,' said Sarah as, bowing, she turned to go.

Jana said nothing, but in her heart she said yes. She would have to beat the four women, harder and with more fierce love than they had ever experienced. And in the meantime, she began to make plans for her own departure.

At night, Jana shared her bed. She did not wish to sleep alone, and chose one or more of her slaves as her companion. It amused her to tease Cassie, Gloria, Henry and Aphrodite as they vied for her favours. But when they made love, naked on her soft bed with the stars their canopy, all were surprised by the intensity and the desperation of her love-making. Cassie, one night, said that she knew the reason.

'How you exhaust me so sweetly, Mistress! I don't think my fount has ever been so wet, nor my fesses so bright from your spanking. But I've noticed: you don't whip my bottom, or cane her, it is always a bare-bum spanking, with your bare hand.'

'So?' said Jana, panting, for she had Cassie over her knee, holding her with four fingers of one hand sunk deep in her flowing quim-oil, while with the other she delivered the fiftieth, or perhaps sixtieth, spank to Cassie's beautifully squirming red croup.

'Mmmm,' murmured Cassie, 'how lovely to feel your bare hand on me, Mistress! Naked flesh on naked bum – and that is how I know you shall leave us soon, and it makes me sad. Oh, don't stop, yes – Oooo! – so good when you frot my nympha, yes!' Cassie wriggled with pleasure as her bare buttocks and her writhing hips danced in love of her mistress. 'You are trying,' she gasped, 'to achieve the greatest intimacy with those you love. So, not the impersonal distance of cane or whip, but flesh to flesh, a sign that you are frightened of departing from us. It is the desperation to cling for as long as possible to flesh that one may never know again. A very normal thing.'

'Oh, Cassie,' cried Jana, 'you know me better than I know myself. And yet, now, having seen the treasure, I *do* know myself. And my knowledge is that I must go.'

She ceased the spanking and there was a minute's silence as the two women embraced fiercely and sorrowfully; but sorrow soon gave way to ecstasy as Jana felt Cassie's erect nipples gently flicking against hers, and her hand rubbing the stiff bud of her damsel, tingling within wet cunt-lips.

The silence was broken by the sighs of the two women as tender fingers brought each other to quivering orgasm.

'Mistress,' said Cassie after a while, as they lay in each other's arms. 'I am not so foolish as to try and dissuade you, but the stars and the fruits of Sabine's garden tell me it is nearly spring, and time for the festival of Anthesteria. I have made plans for everything, so please do not go before that. It would be a fitting farewell.'

'The Anthesteria?' repeated Jana. 'When the souls of the dead come from the underworld and walk the earth? Fitting indeed, my slave.'

'But, Mistress, the Anthesteria is to honour the living, the rebirth of the earth and her fruits: the spirits of the departed come to pay homage. The three days of feasting, the merriment; all is in honour of Dionysos, the god of wine and joy.'

'Very well, I shall stay until the Anthesteria is over,' said Jana. 'I am not so happy about the spirits of the dead, though.'

'Why, it is only a fiction, Mistress,' said Cassie mischievously. 'The main business is . . . orgiastic. And anyway, the good spirits pay their loving homage and depart serenely.'

'You suggest there are bad spirits,' said Jana drily.

'Well, the unhappy ones tend to linger, but at the end of the festival, the cry goes up: "Out of the house, out of doors, ghosts! The Anthesteria is over and done!" – and they just melt away.'

Jana laughed. 'You've sold me,' she said.

'Mistress,' said Cassie after a time, 'I know I shouldn't ask questions, but where will you go?'

'You are right, you shouldn't,' Jana replied. 'And I shouldn't answer them, but the answer is, I don't know.'

'This isn't a question, Mistress,' murmured Cassie. 'Please take me with you, wherever you go.'

The day of Anthesteria dawned not long after, and from her tower, Jana watched the orgiasts at their celebrations. All distinction of rank or power had been abandoned for the three days of wine and unbridled sensuality: many wore masks, virgins took advantage to shave their bodies or disguise themselves as men, troops of them prowling to seize the not unwilling male slaves, give them a stern whipping on the bare, then force them to attend each and every fount presented. From time to time, Jana descended, to take wine and receive the obeisance of her ecstatic slaves, but mostly she kept to her apartment, attended by Cassie and occasionally the grinning Henry, who tended to be flushed, dusty and red of both cock and buttocks from his orgiastic pleasures.

Jana kept to herself the plan she had made for the culmination of Anthesteria.

On the morning of the third day, she saw from her tower that a ship was approaching from the horizon. She scanned with her binoculars and saw her to be a seventy-foot cabin cruiser. On the bridge stood Caspar and Netta, also with binoculars, and beside them a tall black man at the wheel. Jane started, recognising him: he had fucked Netta in Caspar's film, on the beach.

She adorned herself with white body paint and black circles around her eyes, put on her parfaite's harness, and with her white whip at her belt, awaited their arrival. The body paint made her feel somehow purified, before the ordeal that was to come.

'Well, Mistress, I am pleased!' cried Caspar. 'I thought that Anthesteria would be the best time to pay you homage. And, of course, to do some filming.' He looked down hungrily at the naked, writhing bodies, wine-slopped and laughing, on the yard below. Jana smiled.

'Aphrodite has settled in well?' asked Netta, who. despite

the heat, wore her customary black rubber: a light filmy skirt and corset of black latex, which left bare her generous, nipple-ringed breasts. She crossed and uncrossed her legs, showing bare thigh and bare fount where Jana saw, to her secret amusement, that each lip bore a ring as well, causing a musical tinkling when Netta walked. Caspar wore his customary Grecian tunic, in bright crimson, while their smiling black companion was simply attired in gleaming white T-shirt and pressed designer jeans: a concession to his role as sea-captain.

'Aphrodite!' said Jana, surprised. 'Yes, she is a loyal virgin.'

'Excellent,' said Caspar. 'Pity about the ship: I was rather fond of the *Hesperides*. But still, the insurance has more than covered the loss. And Chris has decided to stay, has he? Thought he would. Circe was probably a bit of a nuisance, but I expect you have given her the proper treatment and made her submit. She *needs* to submit.'

Jana was dumbfounded. 'You seem to know everything, Caspar,' she said as acidly as she could.

Caspar grinned, and sipped wine. 'A good bouquet: should be laid down, I think, to drink in a few years,' he said. 'Well, I do know some things, Mistress. You have found the sunken city, of course, and the treasure . . . No! Say nothing!' Caspar put his hands up, his face stern. 'Tell me neither where the treasure is, nor what it is, Mistress. It is a secret for Maldona alone – for you, Mistress *Jana*.'

'Very well. I suppose you also know that I must shortly leave here,' said Jana gravely.

'I had guessed as much,' said Caspar. 'The treasure found, a new empire of Maldona built and consolidated by your knowledge of the treasure, and the threat of Circe turned into an advantage – your work here is, for the time being, at an end. I do not dare ask you where you intend to go.'

'And I do not dare tell you,' said Jana, 'for I do not know. But I shall depart after the end of Anthesteria, which is today.'

Caspar rose and bowed. 'Then I must start filming immediately,' he said. 'I have many potential ... customers for your women, Mistress; those of them who are true slaves. I trust you have not forgotten the finishing school, the beatitude of those women who are truly submissive, and can achieve for themselves a lifetime of pleasure and satisfaction with a loving master?'

'I have not forgotten,' said Jana, thinking of the men – buyers – who had thronged the arena of Maldona in Spain at the special day, a huge auction for the bodies and spirits of willing female slaves. Men whose need to dominate, she knew, masked a secret desire, hidden in their powerful hearts, to be the slave of the woman they outwardly dominated. And that is the purpose of Maldona, she thought. To teach us to dominate and be dominated, to take and give punishment. The most abject slave the most powerful dominatrix ...

'You will, of course, be transported aboard my humble ship, Mistress,' added Caspar. 'She is small but powerful, and wherever you wish to go, there she will take you. The Azores, the Canaries, the Indies East or West, the Americas, Africa: you will instruct me when it is fitting.'

Jana nodded. 'You came for me, didn't you, Caspar?' she said softly, dismissing her guests with a nod.

'Yes, Mistress,' replied Caspar, bowing. 'It is time.'

A fourfold flogging frame was set up in the centre of the yard. It was late in the afternoon when Sarah, the twins, and Aphrodite were led, their naked bodies chained, trussed and hooded, to take their places and be strapped with tight thongs for their merited chastisement. The orgiastic assembly hushed and stood still to witness the four noble beatings.

Jana, white whip in hand and her body shining in white paint, explained that the four miscreants had demanded punishment to cleanse their bodies and spirits of evil spells which had led them to imperfection, and that she would deliver the beatings herself, as was fitting. Beside her, Cassie stood holding a bundle of long canes.

Jana lashed Sarah's bare buttocks first, then applied her

whip to Kate, then Melanie, and finally Aphrodite. Then she walked back along the tethered bare bodies, delivering the next stroke, and proceeded in this turnabout fashion. After half an hour of constant beating on their reddened fesses, the four women were quivering, and their bodies seemed to Jana to wave like the flowers in the underwater garden. She applied her whip to their bare backs for another half-hour; then to the croups, then to the shoulders. After two hours, the four women hung limply in their bonds, yet none had uttered a sound, and, gasping from her exertions, Jana indicated that the beating was over and that they should be cut down. The four women, released, knelt and kissed Jana's feet.

'That is the end of Anthesteria, then? A splendid climax,' said Caspar, camera whirring.

'Not quite,' said Jana quietly. 'The sun is still in the sky, and there is one more task to accomplish before the spirits of the departed may be put to rest.'

So saying, she nodded to Cassie, and mounted the flogging block, positioning herself to be bound as Cassie handed tough, springy canes to the four flogged women.

'When imperfection is to be punished,' cried Jana, 'the highest must be punished most of all, since their crime is the greatest imperfection. My imperfection was that when I chastised Aphrodite, I did so in rage, not in love. And that is the most heinous crime against the rules of Maldona. I shall take the cane, not the whip, for I deserve the greater humiliation.'

For an hour, Jana felt herself shudder and dance as the supple canes bit her naked flesh. Tears and sweat blinded her under her hood: tightly gagged, she could not cry out. Her body and her senses seemed to disappear: her whole existence was a bright point of white burning light, the searing pain that engulfed her, washed her, set her spirit free. At last she felt kind hands release her, and, blinking in the dusky twilight, she stood up and then bowed in obeisance to the whole company of Maldona: her slaves, her mistresses.

'Out of the house, out of doors, ghosts!' she cried joyfully. 'The Anthesteria is over and done!'

* * *

Jana stood at the guard rail of Caspar's ship, the engines throbbing comfortingly below and a light breeze in her hair. She watched the lights of Maldona, bonfires lit in honour of her departure, twinkling in the distance. She calculated that it was very near dawn, but did not want to sleep. The smarting of her crimson back and fesses, which caused her to be nude for the small comfort, would prevent her getting much sleep, she thought ruefully. There was a noise behind her, and a glass was pressed into her palm. She sipped the rich, fruity wine, and it seemed to contain all the sights and smells of the blue Aegean that she was leaving. Not for ever, she told herself. Surely not . . .

'Feeling sad, Mistress?' said a small voice.

'A little, Cassie,' she replied. 'Departures are always sad, even if they are only temporary.'

'Departures are never temporary, Mistress,' said Cassie. 'Something is always lost, that never returns.'

Jana smiled. 'Still, I have you, Cassie. You knew very well I couldn't leave you. You sly, conniving, beautiful creature.'

'Thank you, Mistress, I shall take all those as compliments.'

There was the sound of bare feet padding on the deck and Caspar appeared, carrying his own glass of wine.

'May I join you?' he asked. 'What a splendid night. We shall be passing Circe's island soon; no doubt you will wish to wave her goodbye.'

'I can leave Circe to my regent,' said Jana. 'Aphrodite will know how to handle her. And Henry will be useful. I expect we shall see him again soon, when he has the urge to take up his high finance for a while. Gloria, as superior, will be very useful. She never wants to go down, go back to her archaeology; she knows she has found her true home. Sandra too: after being a flight attendant, a servant, she relishes her rank as housemistress. I suppose the virgins of *Allemagne* are no more unruly than the average planeload of holidaymakers.'

They all laughed. Draining his wine, Caspar excused himself, but Jana halted him.

'Caspar,' she said. 'The sunken city. There is much you haven't told me. These legends: that she was built by a race of beings long before the Greeks, lost thousands of eons ago, in an unknown past when there were races of women who possessed the secret of living under the sea. Tell me what you know, I order you.'

Caspar smiled. 'The sun gives rise to strange fictions and phantasms, Mistress,' he replied. 'The truth is often a disappointment. Would you believe that I built her years ago? As a film set, for one of my more surreal efforts?'

'Oh, Caspar!' cried Jana. 'It is no disappointment! How comic! How wonderful!'

When Caspar had gone, Cassie said, 'But the treasure was there, Mistress. It *was*!'

'Certainly,' said Jana, then, turning to face Cassie, she said, 'The treasure! I have told no one of it, but I shall tell you. And the secret stays with you.'

Cassie nodded, and Jana told her of the glowing inside of the treasure chamber, and the treasure she had found, framed in a glittering garland of pearls in their oyster shells.

'*It was a mirror*, Cassie,' she said, with awe in her voice, 'nothing but a bright, clear, full-length mirror. And I saw myself truly for the first time. That is the only treasure, Cassie. My ancestor knew it, and that is why she guided me here and led me to it. To know myself, for the first time. Oh, Cassie, that is the greatest, the only, treasure.' And the two women kissed.

'Look, Mistress,' said Cassie. 'We are passing Circe's island!'

Jana looked and was dazzled: a hundred mirrors saluted their passage, making Circe's island a beacon of light and radiant beauty.

'Well, Mistress, you have your empire, sunken city or no sunken city. There is just one thing that puzzles me.'

'Yes?'

'I've never seen Caspar barefoot before, Mistress. Did you notice his toes?'

'No, Cassie, I didn't. You did, though,' said Jana sarcastically.

'It's just that he has six of them – six toes, I mean. And little webs, like a frog's, between them.'

'The sunken city . . .' mused Jana. 'I decree it to be a film set, Cassie. Just a film set.'

In the distance, a hundred mirrors bathed the two women, and their sea, in starlight.

NEW BOOKS

Coming up from Nexus and Black Lace

Faith in The Stables by Elizabeth Bruce
March 1996   Price £4.99   ISBN: 0 352 33062 7
In this, the sequel to *The Teaching of Faith*, Alex sends Faith, now ordained as one of the Chosen, to complete her education in The Stables, a training centre in Sussex dedicated to the instillation of total discipline. Complete obedience is mandatory, no matter how outrageous the command, and even Faith's liberated imagination is stretched to its limits.

A Chalice Of Delights by Katrina Young
March 1996   Price £4.99   ISBN: 0 352 33061 9
Times are hard and fun-loving Gaelicia becomes the kept woman of a lascivious nobleman, in return for a wide variety of sexual favours. When she tires of this arrangement, she finds that the earl is not prepared to let her off so easily; the terms of her contract are physically as well as legally binding.

Christina Wished by Gene Craven
April 1996   Price £4.99   ISBN: 0 352 33066 X
Three flatmates – unrestrained, raven-haired Christina, meek Susan and Cathy, mysterious and immersed in a world of rubber and leather – embark on a voyage of sexual discovery. Each must face tests and undreamt-of pleasures, and push her sexuality to its limits, before she can release the wanton inside her and revel in the power of discipline.

Pleasing Them by William Doughty
April 1996   Price £4.99   ISBN: 0 352 33065 1
Into Dreadnought Manor, home to Robert Shawnecross and his young and beautiful wife, come the puritanical Mr Blanking and the wicked Sir Horace. They seek satisfaction through control and cruelty and their hosts, along with the servants who have been carefully selected and trained to cater to even the most bizarre desires, must stretch their skills to find suitably extreme pleasures.

Ace Of Hearts by Lisette Allen
March 1996   Price £4.99   ISBN: 0 352 33059 7
Marisa Brooke, a swordswoman and card-sharper with a taste for fleshly pleasures, lives by her wits amongst the wealthy, hedonistic elite of Regency England. Gambling dominates every gathering and, with love and fortune being lost more easily than they are won, Marisa has to use all her skill and cunning in order to hold on to her winnings and the young men she seduces.

Dreamers In Time by Sarah Copeland
March 1996   Price £4.99   ISBN: 0 352 33064 3
In a hostile world, four millennia from now, two thousand people remain suspended in endless slumber, while others toil for the means to wake them. Carnal desires have long been forgotten until Ehlana, a time-traveller and historian, finds the key to her own sexuality and, in so doing, unlocks the door to everyone's primal memories.

Gothic Blue by Portia Da Costa
April 1996   Price £4.99   ISBN: 0 352 33075 9
Set in a remote and mysterious priory in the present day, this dark, Gothic-erotic novel centres on Belinda, a sensual and restless heroine who is intrigued by the supernatural unknown. Written by one of Black Lace's most popular authors, it explores the themes of sexual alchemy and experimentation, the paranormal and obsession.

The House Of Gabriel by Rafaella
April 1996   Price £4.99   ISBN: 0 352 33063 5
Researching a feature on lost treasures of erotic art, journalist Jessica Martyn finds herself drawn into a world of strange, sexual power games and role-play, in the elegant, Jacobean mansion of the handsome, enigmatic Gabriel Martineaux. She also finds trouble, in the shape of her arch-rival, Araminta Harvey.

NEXUS BACKLIST

All books are priced £4.99 unless another price is given. If a date is supplied, the book in question will not be available until that month in 1995.

CONTEMPORARY EROTICA

THE ACADEMY	Arabella Knight	
CONDUCT UNBECOMING	Arabella Knight	Jul
CONTOURS OF DARKNESS	Marco Vassi	
THE DEVIL'S ADVOCATE	Anonymous	
DIFFERENT STROKES	Sarah Veitch	Aug
THE DOMINO TATTOO	Cyrian Amberlake	
THE DOMINO ENIGMA	Cyrian Amberlake	
THE DOMINO QUEEN	Cyrian Amberlake	
ELAINE	Stephen Ferris	
EMMA'S SECRET WORLD	Hilary James	
EMMA ENSLAVED	Hilary James	
EMMA'S SECRET DIARIES	Hilary James	
FALLEN ANGELS	Kendal Grahame	
THE FANTASIES OF JOSEPHINE SCOTT	Josephine Scott	
THE GENTLE DEGENERATES	Marco Vassi	
HEART OF DESIRE	Maria del Rey	
HELEN – A MODERN ODALISQUE	Larry Stern	
HIS MISTRESS'S VOICE	G. C. Scott	
HOUSE OF ANGELS	Yvonne Strickland	May
THE HOUSE OF MALDONA	Yolanda Celbridge	-
THE IMAGE	Jean de Berg	Jul
THE INSTITUTE	Maria del Rey	
SISTERHOOD OF THE INSTITUTE	Maria del Rey	

JENNIFER'S INSTRUCTION	Cyrian Amberlake	
LETTERS TO CHLOE	Stefan Gerrard	Aug
LINGERING LESSONS	Sarah Veitch	Apr
A MATTER OF POSSESSION	G. C. Scott	Sep
MELINDA AND THE MASTER	Susanna Hughes	
MELINDA AND ESMERALDA	Susanna Hughes	
MELINDA AND THE COUNTESS	Susanna Hughes	
MELINDA AND THE ROMAN	Susanna Hughes	
MIND BLOWER	Marco Vassi	
MS DEEDES ON PARADISE ISLAND	Carole Andrews	
THE NEW STORY OF O	Anonymous	
OBSESSION	Maria del Rey	
ONE WEEK IN THE PRIVATE HOUSE	Esme Ombreux	Jun
THE PALACE OF SWEETHEARTS	Delver Maddingley	
THE PALACE OF FANTASIES	Delver Maddingley	
THE PALACE OF HONEYMOONS	Delver Maddingley	
THE PALACE OF EROS	Delver Maddingley	
PARADISE BAY	Maria del Rey	
THE PASSIVE VOICE	G. C. Scott	
THE SALINE SOLUTION	Marco Vassi	
SHERRIE	Evelyn Culber	May
STEPHANIE	Susanna Hughes	
STEPHANIE'S CASTLE	Susanna Hughes	
STEPHANIE'S REVENGE	Susanna Hughes	
STEPHANIE'S DOMAIN	Susanna Hughes	
STEPHANIE'S TRIAL	Susanna Hughes	
STEPHANIE'S PLEASURE	Susanna Hughes	
THE TEACHING OF FAITH	Elizabeth Bruce	
THE TRAINING GROUNDS	Sarah Veitch	
UNDERWORLD	Maria del Rey	

EROTIC SCIENCE FICTION

ADVENTURES IN THE PLEASUREZONE	Delaney Silver	
RETURN TO THE PLEASUREZONE	Delaney Silver	

FANTASYWORLD	Larry Stern	
WANTON	Andrea Arven	

ANCIENT & FANTASY SETTINGS

CHAMPIONS OF LOVE	Anonymous	
CHAMPIONS OF PLEASURE	Anonymous	
CHAMPIONS OF DESIRE	Anonymous	
THE CLOAK OF APHRODITE	Kendal Grahame	
THE HANDMAIDENS	Aran Ashe	
THE SLAVE OF LIDIR	Aran Ashe	
THE DUNGEONS OF LIDIR	Aran Ashe	
THE FOREST OF BONDAGE	Aran Ashe	
PLEASURE ISLAND	Aran Ashe	
WITCH QUEEN OF VIXANIA	Morgana Baron	

EDWARDIAN, VICTORIAN & OLDER EROTICA

ANNIE	Evelyn Culber	
ANNIE AND THE SOCIETY	Evelyn Culber	
THE AWAKENING OF LYDIA	Philippa Masters	Apr
BEATRICE	Anonymous	
CHOOSING LOVERS FOR JUSTINE	Aran Ashe	
GARDENS OF DESIRE	Roger Rougiere	
THE LASCIVIOUS MONK	Anonymous	
LURE OF THE MANOR	Barbra Baron	
RETURN TO THE MANOR	Barbra Baron	Jun
MAN WITH A MAID 1	Anonymous	
MAN WITH A MAID 2	Anonymous	
MAN WITH A MAID 3	Anonymous	
MEMOIRS OF A CORNISH GOVERNESS	Yolanda Celbridge	
THE GOVERNESS AT ST AGATHA'S	Yolanda Celbridge	
TIME OF HER LIFE	Josephine Scott	
VIOLETTE	Anonymous	

THE JAZZ AGE

BLUE ANGEL NIGHTS	Margarete von Falkensee	
BLUE ANGEL DAYS	Margarete von Falkensee	

BLUE ANGEL SECRETS	Margarete von Falkensee	
CONFESSIONS OF AN ENGLISH MAID	Anonymous	
PLAISIR D'AMOUR	Anne-Marie Villefranche	
FOLIES D'AMOUR	Anne-Marie Villefranche	
JOIE D'AMOUR	Anne-Marie Villefranche	
MYSTERE D'AMOUR	Anne-Marie Villefranche	
SECRETS D'AMOUR	Anne-Marie Villefranche	
SOUVENIR D'AMOUR	Anne-Marie Villefranche	

SAMPLERS & COLLECTIONS

EROTICON 1	ed. J-P Spencer	
EROTICON 2	ed. J-P Spencer	
EROTICON 3	ed. J-P Spencer	
EROTICON 4	ed. J-P Spencer	
NEW EROTICA 1	ed. Esme Ombreux	
NEW EROTICA 2	ed. Esme Ombreux	
THE FIESTA LETTERS	ed. Chris Lloyd	£4.50

NON-FICTION

HOW TO DRIVE YOUR MAN WILD IN BED	Graham Masterton	
HOW TO DRIVE YOUR WOMAN WILD IN BED	Graham Masterton	
LETTERS TO LINZI	Linzi Drew	
LINZI DREW'S PLEASURE GUIDE	Linzi Drew	

- - - - - - - - - - - - - - - - - - - -

Please send me the books I have ticked above.

Name ....

Address ....

....

....

.......................Post code ....

Send to: **Cash Sales, Nexus Books, 332 Ladbroke Grove, London W10 5AH.**

Please enclose a cheque or postal order, made payable to **Nexus Books**, to the value of the books you have ordered plus postage and packing costs as follows:

UK and BFPO – £1.00 for the first book, 50p for each subsequent book.

Overseas (including Republic of Ireland) – £2.00 for the first book, £1.00 for the second book, and 50p for each subsequent book.

If you would prefer to pay by VISA or ACCESS/MASTER-CARD, please write your card number and expiry date here:

....

Please allow up to 28 days for delivery.

Signature ....

- - - - - - - - - - - - - - - - - - - -

Please send me the books I have ticked at one

Name

Address

Postage

Send to Cash Sales, Arrow Books, 17 ... Ladbroke Grove, London W10 6SP.

Please enclose a cheque or postal order made payable to Arrow Books Ltd ... the cost of the books you have ordered plus postage and packing charges as follows:

UK and BFPO - £1.00 for the first book, 50p for each additional book.

Overseas including Republic of Ireland ... £2.00 for the second book, and 30p for each subsequent book.

If you would prefer to pay by VISA or ACCESS/MASTERCARD, please quote your card number and expiry date here.

Please allow up to 28 days for delivery.

Signature

THE 1996 NEXUS CALENDAR

The 1996 Nexus calendar contains photographs of thirteen of the most delectable models who have graced the covers of Nexus books. And we've been able to select pictures that are just a bit more exciting than those we're allowed to use on book covers.

With its restrained design and beautifully reproduced duo-tone photographs, the Nexus calendar will appeal to lovers of sophisticated erotica.

And the Nexus calendar costs only £5.50 including postage and packing (in the traditional plain brown envelope!). Stocks are limited, so be sure of your copy by ordering today. The order form is overleaf.

Send your order to: Cash Sales Department
Nexus Books
332 Ladbroke Grove
London
W10 5AH

Please allow 28 days for delivery.

Please send me _____ copies of the 1996 Nexus calendar @ £5.50 (US$9.00) each including postage and packing.

Name: _____

Address: _____

_____

_____

_____

☐   I enclose a cheque or postal order made out to Nexus Books

☐   Please debit my Visa/Access/Mastercard account (delete as applicable)

My credit card number is:

____ ____ ____ ____

Expiry date: _____

FILL OUT YOUR ORDER AND SEND IT TODAY!